WAGES OF SIN

Also by Penelope Williamson

Mortal Sins
The Outsider
The Passions of Emma

WAGES OF SIN

PENELOPE
WILLIAMSON

WARNER BOOKS

An AOL Time Warner Company

This book is a work of historical fiction. In order to give a sense of the times, some names of real people or places have been included in the book. However, the events depicted in this book are imaginary, and the names of nonhistorical persons or events are the product of the author's imagination or are used fictitiously. Any resemblance of such nonhistorical persons or events to actual ones is purely coincidental.

Warner Books, Inc., 1271 Avenue of the Americas, New York, NY 10020

Visit our Web site at www.twbookmark.com.

An AOL Time Warner Company

Printed in the United States of America

First Printing: March 2003
10 9 8 7 6 5 4 3 2

Library of Congress Cataloging-in-Publication Data
Williamson, Penelope.
Wages of sin / Penelope Williamson.
p. cm.
ISBN 0-446-52841-2
1. Police—Louisiana—New Orleans—Fiction. 2. Clergy—Crimes against—Fiction. 3. Passing (identity)—Fiction. 4. New Orleans (La.)—Fiction. I Title.

PS3573.I456288 W34 2003
813'.54—dc21 2002033111

For Samantha and Danielle, with love . . .

Wages of Sin

Chapter One

New Orleans, 1927

Tonight, he would write to her with his own blood.

He'd been planning the letter for some time now, ever since this one movie that he'd seen: a spectacle film where a Russian peasant girl lay dying and they brought in the doctor to bleed her. The director had shot a decent close-up of the lancing blade piercing flesh, opening up a vein into a bowl, and then the optical effects guy had doused the camera lens with blood. They'd probably used pig's blood, but on the par speed film it had looked like ink and that was when the idea first came to him. About how he could warn her by writing to her with his blood.

Not that he had bothered with giving much of a warning to the others, hadn't really given them a chance to save themselves. Fuck 'em. They wouldn't have listened anyway. Always, when a new one was first chosen, he'd feel some hope that this time it would be different. But after he had watched them for a while, after he'd looked into their hearts and seen the real *them,* he always came around to accepting the inevitable: that even death couldn't redeem the hopelessly lost.

And yeah, okay, okay, sometimes he did go ahead and fuck them anyway before he killed them. It was only sex, after all, and he was never selfish about it. He always tried to make it good for them, too. To give them a few moments of sweet pleasure, however fleeting, before that big postcoital sleep.

Anyway, the others . . . call them small sacrifices of appeasement, if you will, because ultimately she was the only one truly worthy of salvation. She wasn't a chosen one, she was *the* chosen one, but she was also his one. She was his love, his destiny, the only reason he had for drawing breath. So it followed, *ipso* frigging *facto,* that if killing her was the only way to save her, then he'd have to kill himself as well. They'd have to die together, just like Juliet and her Romeo.

"Romeo," he said aloud and tried to laugh, but the noise he made sounded too much like a sob. "Yeah, that's what I am to you, baby. I'm your fuckin' Romeo, so don't you make me do it. What do you say, huh? Don't you make me do it . . ."

Christ, but he hated sad endings. He was always the poor sap sitting way in the back, in the dark, holding out hope until the bitter end that Juliet would wake up before Romeo swallowed the poison and died.

When the idea had first come to Romeo—to sacrifice a little of his own blood in the pursuit of his true love's salvation—he had tried pricking himself with a pocketknife and writing to her with his bleeding fingertip. The letters came out all smudgy and smeared, though, and he'd snatched up the paper, crumpling it in his fist, and thrown it against the wall.

The walls were plastered with her face: glossy publicity stills and pages torn from fan magazines. Grainy tabloid shots and candid ones he'd taken himself. He'd surrounded himself with her image because she was beautiful and she was his, but the special keepsake, the one that mattered, he'd put into a silver frame next to their bed. In it her head is tilted back and her wide, scornful mouth is laughing, and she is pushing her fingers through her dark, shingled hair. The whole world had seen her do that a thousand times, but only he knew what it meant.

"Hey, never mind, baby," he had said to her that day, kissing her, and the glass that covered her face was cool against his lips. "We don't want to rush into this anyway, 'cause when we do it, we want it to be right."

What he needed, he had told her, was a set of bleeding knives.

You couldn't just walk on down to the drugstore, though, and ask the guy behind the counter for such a thing, and maybe the truth was he hadn't even been looking so hard. Then this morning he'd been strolling along Rampart Street and not even thinking about her for a change, when his eye had been caught by something in the window of a curiosity shop. It had a thick tortoiseshell handle and its three knives were spread out in a fan for display, and he recognized it instantly as the instrument that the doctor had used on the Russian peasant girl.

The shop owner was wrinkled like a dried seed pod and had eyeglasses the size of thumbprints perched on the end of his nose. He peered at Romeo through those funny little glasses as if he knew all and he approved. "These are lovely knives," he said, as he polished the blades with an oily rag. "Lovely, lovely. In our modern day we think of bloodletting as barbaric, but in truth it often did more good than harm. Lowering the patient's temperature and inducing a calm state of mind. And in some ancient societies bloodletting was a rite of purification."

"No kidding?" Romeo smiled. He didn't give a shit about ancient societies, but the love he felt for her was so rare and beautiful and *pure* that surely it deserved its own ritual.

He walked home slowly with the knives in his pocket. He relished their weight, anticipating what he would do with them. He rounded the corner onto Canal Street and walked into the back of a crowd that had gathered to watch a couple of paper hangers glue sheets to an enormous billboard on the roof of the new Saenger Theatre. He stopped to watch the men at work, as first her eyes appeared and her mouth and then her neck. Eventually all of her was spread out on the board, and he saw that she was lying crossways on a bed like a spent lover—her head hanging down over the side, her arms flung out wide—to advertise her latest flick, *Lost Souls.* It was a wildly innovative and truly scary movie about a dead woman whose haunted, restless soul leaves her grave at night and takes the form of a vampire bat to suck the blood out of the living, and only a star like her could ever have pulled it off.

Romeo laughed out loud so that a few in the crowd left off staring at her to stare at him. He didn't care; they were fools, especially the women. They'd all be wearing bloodred lips and bat-wing capes by the end of the week. They tried so hard to look like her: bobbing their hair like hers, trying to paint her exotic face on top of their own, even trying to copy that smooth and languorous way she had of moving. Believing that their flattery and worship gave them ownership over her, when she would never belong to anyone but him.

He'd shot enough junk into himself to know how to apply a tourniquet and pump up a vein, but the oddity of the bleeding knives had him nervous. Each of the set's three knives had two blades, a long one on the bottom that ended in a hooked point and a smaller, triangular-shaped blade on top. He had no idea which to use and that worried him. He didn't want to butcher himself and end up bleeding to death. Christ, he thought, but wouldn't that be just too fucking much, if he ended up leaving this vale of tears without her.

He tested the edge of one of the hooked blades and he smiled. Sharp enough to cut through skin and flesh and bleeding veins.

He hummed to himself as he brought his shooter's kit from out of its hiding place and took a soup bowl from out of the kitchen cupboard. He was flying high, but it was a pure high, coming from the moment. He wrapped a length of thin rubber tubing around his arm and tied it tight with one hand and his teeth. He made a fist. The veins in the crook of his elbow bulged blue against his skin.

He stared at the knife and his high trembled a little as it slid toward the edge of fear, then he thought, Fuck it, and he picked up the knife and pressed the point of the top blade into the pulsing vein.

He let out a little yelp of pain, and dropped the knife as blood spurted bright red jets into the air. His blood. The thought frightened and exhilarated him, and he stared at it, red and thick and pulsating out of his flesh in an arc, until he remembered to hold his arm over the bowl.

The blood was so beautiful. He almost left it until too late to release the tourniquet.

He pressed the heel of his hand into the cut he'd made. He blinked, swaying on his feet. His head felt thick, his body heavy, as if he was just coming down off a nod. He looked around, bemused, at the splatters of blood on the primrose yellow wallpaper, the pools of it on the brown linoleum floor, but his imagination was already leaping ahead to the moment when she would read his words and understand how she had to wise up and save herself, had to save *them* before it was too late. No more other men, no more other loves. Just Juliet and her Romeo.

He wouldn't make the mistake of sending the letter through the mail. She got twenty thousand letters a week from her fans, each one carefully answered by studio secretaries who typed out the same reply over and over and rubber-stamped her signature. He wanted her, and only her, to see these words, written in his blood, and so he would have to deliver it himself to a place where only she would find it.

He picked up the fountain pen that he'd bought for just this moment—an automatic shading pen used, the young woman in the stationery store had told him, for fancy lettering and show card writing. He'd already spent hours planning what he would write: the single, perfect sentence that would make her understand how desperate the situation was, how she had to change things before it was too late.

He filled the pen's pearl barrel with his blood. He held the fat gold nib poised for a moment over the pristine sheet of paper, and then he wrote.

Are you scared yet, Remy?

CHAPTER TWO

Carlos Kelly stood at the pier's end, with the muzzle of a big ol' revolver pressing into the bone behind his left ear. River water, black and oily, slopped against the wooden pilings beneath his feet, and the wind stank of dead fish, sour mud, and fermenting boiled potatoes from the stills in the gin mills along the wharf. It was still a sweet, sweet world, though, and he didn't want to die.

"Aw, Jesus," he said. "Don't do this."

The goon with the hog's leg only laughed and ground the bore deeper into Carlos Kelly's head.

Carlos Kelly drew in a sobbing breath and closed his eyes. "Just give me a day, okay? One day, and I'll make things square with Tony."

"Yeah, sure you will." The goon had a laugh raspy as a dull saw ripping through green wood. "Man, you've had all the days you're gonna get."

"Please. I got a mother, a sister." He was crying now, his face slimed with tears, snot dripping out his nose. "Aw, Jesus, aw, Jesus, you can't do this. You can't."

Carlos Kelly was only seventeen and up until this moment he'd held the conviction that he would live forever. He still couldn't get his mind around the idea of dying, but he sure enough had a firm grasp that he was now in the worst trouble of his life.

It was all the fault of the cards, but a guy couldn't play without paying and who would've ever thought a losing streak could last a fucking month. So he'd borrowed a little off the bag money he'd been carrying for Tony the Rat, and somehow the man had found out and now he was playing hardball. Only Tony the Rat didn't mess with brass knuckles or blackjacks, breaking jaws and kneecaps being too subtle for a guy like him. When he sent his goon to see you, you ended up waltzing through eternity with the catfish.

The wind died. Carlos Kelly heard the click of a hammer cocking.

Aw, Jesus.

The crack of a gunshot smacked off the water and Carlos Kelly fell to his hands and knees. His palms burned and his nostrils filled with the acrid odor of urine and in the next instant he realized that if he was pissing all over himself, then he wasn't dead.

The goon realized it, too. He had whirled at the firing of a gun and the screaming going on behind them, but already he was spinning back around and pointing the big-bore revolver at Carlos Kelly's face.

The boy rolled and lashed out with his legs just as the goon pulled the trigger, and for the first time in his young life Carlos Kelly got lucky. His heavy brogan clipped the goon in the back of the knee, knocking his right leg out from under him. The goon's arm had flailed as he fired, and the bullet went wide. Carlos Kelly kicked again.

The goon staggered, catching his heel on a gap in the warped boards. He teetered a moment, then pancaked backward off the pier and into the river.

Carlos Kelly didn't even hear the splash. He had already scrambled to his feet and was off and running, away from the open waterfront and toward the crosshatch of narrow, broken-down streets that was the Quarter.

* * *

Even at past two o'clock in the morning the Quarter wasn't asleep, but all the action was happening behind the bolted doors and boarded-up windows of the speakeasies. Those working girls and boozers who still walked the streets were past helping anyone.

Carlos Kelly ducked into the shadows of the wide arched stone portico to an abandoned macaroni factory. He strained his ears for the patter of following footsteps, but his breath sawed too loudly in his throat and his heart beat too hard for him to hear anything but his own fear. His legs trembled so badly he could barely hold himself up.

The brick wall he sagged against was papered with peeling posters advertising a long ago boxing match. The broken glass panes in the fan light above his head rattled and moaned in the wind. The double barnlike doors of the factory were padlocked together, but he saw where the hasp had busted loose. The weathered wood had been scrawled with hobo graffiti: two parallel wavy lines slashed through with five hash marks. He didn't know what it meant and he didn't care. All he wanted was a place to hide.

The wind gusted around the corner, and Carlos Kelly shuddered with the sudden chill of it on his damp skin. Jesus, he had been sweating scared. He was still scared but he was beginning to feel some shame now in the way he'd behaved, the begging noises and the tears. He stank of his own piss; his trousers were wet with it.

A trash can clattered nearby, followed by glass smashing on cobblestone and a snarled curse, and Carlos Kelly nearly pissed himself again.

His feet twitched, wanting to take off running, but the street was empty and harshly exposed in the white light of the incandescent lamps. He pressed deeper beneath the arched portico, his hands feeling the door behind him for the broken hasp.

He pried it free of the rotting wood and then eased the door open carefully, praying that the hinges wouldn't squeak.

It was dark inside, with the barest of light coming in through the cracks in the boarded-up windows. He heard a rustling noise and he looked up through the grated catwalk above his head, and nearly jumped out of his skin as he caught the flapping of dark wings out of the corner of his eye. A high-pitched squeal echoed in the rafters of the deep, pitched ceiling.

Aw, Jesus, bats.

His blood pounded in his ears and a scream clawed at his throat, but he wouldn't let it out. He hated bats, really hated them, but at the moment their company was preferable to another do-si-do on a river pier with Tony the Rat's goon.

He stood unmoving for a long while, hardly daring to breathe as his eyes got used to the darkness. Slowly, he craned his head back and peered up through the latticed metal of the catwalk again. The bats, thank God, were gone.

Where he was, on the floor of the macaroni factory, strange machinery cast hulking shadows on the walls: cement vats and long wooden troughs and huge wheels and pulleys connected together by thick fan belts, like giant slingshots. Then he saw, deep in the farthest corner, the flicker of a fire.

Tramps, he thought, but unlike the bats they didn't scare him. Their company would be a good thing right now, and maybe he could join them in the morning when they hopped a train. What Carlos Kelly really needed to do was get his sorry ass out of town.

Hobos who rode the rails didn't travel unarmed, though, and so he made some deliberate noise as he walked down the length of the cavernous factory. "Hey, there," he called out, nice and friendly. He could smell meat cooking, but as he got closer he realized that it wasn't a fire he had seen. It was a cluster of burning votive candles, and above the burning candles something was hanging from the crossbeam of a large drying rack.

Something that whimpered and then made a horrible noise as he came up to it. It was a noise he'd heard only once before, but once was enough for him never to have forgotten it—the wet, popping gargle of a man strangling on his own blood.

Then he got close enough to see it all, and for the second time that night Carlos Kelly fell to his knees, sobbing.

"Aw, Jesus."

Chapter Three

They'd run out of the labeled stuff an hour ago and the champagne that homicide detective Daman Rourke now drank tasted like sugarcoated paint thinner. It was melting his teeth and making his lips go numb.

Like almost everyone else in the crowded front parlor of the elegant plantation house, he was watching Remy Lelourie *be* Remy Lelourie. Beneath the blaze of the crystal chandeliers, her bare arms and legs were the same pale gold as her silky slip of a dress, and the dress was all that she was wearing. No headband or jewelry, no stockings, not even any shoes. Just the silky dress and that incredible, breath-stopping face.

The tabloids called her the most beautiful woman in the world. It might have been the truth.

It was deep into that cool October Friday night and in the old French colonial house overlooking the Bayou St. John, Remy Lelourie was throwing what the newspapers were calling the Party of the Century, even though the century was only twenty-eight years old. New Orleans had always been a city that relished its balls and parades, but this was something special, for Remy Lelourie was one of the world's brightest stars and yet she was theirs. A hometown girl.

It was all happening at the film idol's ancestral home of Sans Souci, a bygone confection of white colonnettes and broad galleries that had been part of a sugar plantation a century ago, and the scene of a scandalous and brutal murder only last summer. Bright Lights Studios didn't care about that, though. Publicity, whether good or bad, was still publicity and publicity was good for business.

Most of the guests at the party were in some way connected with the studio. For three weeks they had been shooting on location in the swampland east of New Orleans—a swashbuckling boudoir intrigue called *Cutlass* about a Southern belle turned swamp pirate who sailed the Caribbean searching for her lost love. Tonight they were celebrating life and love with all the extravagance and flamboyance of the movies they made.

Chandeliers blazed in the front parlor, where a five-piece jazz band was playing "Three O'Clock in the Morning" even though it was only half past two. Negro waiters in white tuxedos served bootlegged champagne in glasses bigger than finger bowls, and the air had the crackle of a live wire, as if everyone was still waiting for the party to turn wild. So far the most exciting thing to happen had been around midnight, when a budding starlet had thrown off her clothes and danced naked on top of the grand piano before passing out underneath it.

Daman Rourke leaned against the wall near the French doors that opened onto the upstairs gallery. He watched Remy Lelourie flirt with a skinny guy who was supposed to be some kind of writer for the studio. A scenario writer. He had patent leather hair and a little black mole on the right side of his upper lip that looked inked on with a fountain pen, and maybe was. The trousers he had on were wide enough to fit an elephant's legs. What the college kids nowadays were calling Oxford bags.

Remy Lelourie had a reputation that was mostly sin and trouble, but this time she was playing it soft and sweet. Still, after only two minutes of her company, the writer in the Oxford bags already had *the look:* like he'd been smacked in the face with a ball peen hammer. Even when she wasn't trying all that hard, even when she didn't care, Remy Lelourie could do anything with any man she wanted to.

As Rourke watched, she laughed at something the writer said, letting her head fall back so that the light of the chandelier fell full on her exposed throat. She bit her lower lip to stop another laugh and pushed her fingers through her hair, and Rourke felt a pang of pure lust laced with a little jealousy.

"Do I look like I got a sex complex?" said a young female voice close to his ear.

He turned, and the girl who had spoken raised a cigarette in a long silver holder up to her lips for him to light. She held his gaze a moment after he had obliged her, then averted her face, pursed her lips, and blew out smoke.

Her mouth looked like the bow on a candy box, and her eyelids had been greased to make them shiny. The dress she wore seemed to be mostly swaying fringe with nothing underneath it. The effect was mesmerizing.

"You look fine to me," Rourke said.

She blew more smoke out in one long sigh and then sucked down a long drink from the gin rickey she had in her other hand, striking just the right pose between boredom and amusement. The epitome of razz-ma-tazz.

"Freddy told me I got a sex complex," she said. Her voice had a bit of a pout in it that was as intriguing as her fringed dress. "But he's only sore because I wouldn't go to bed with him. I told him a girl wants a fella's full attention on her. Know what I mean?"

From the direction of her yearning look, Rourke figured the Freddy with the wandering eye must be Alfredo Ramon, the silver screen's latest Latin lover sensation. At the moment Freddy was having something of an argument with *Cutlass*'s director, although most of his attention was on his own reflection in the gilt mirror above the yellow Italian marble fireplace.

"She's the biggest box office draw the studio has," the director was saying. He wore a monocle in his left eye and had a reckless taste in old-fashioned spats. His beard, clipped to a dagger's point, jabbed the air, punctuating his words. "Without me you wouldn't even be in this picture, so quit giving me grief."

For an answer, Freddy pushed out his sensuous lower lip and flared his nostrils in a Rudolph Valentino moue. His hair, hard and shiny with brilliantine, glistened like lacquer in the refracted light of the mirror.

"Freddy thinks he wants Remy," the girl was saying. "But then everybody thinks he wants Remy."

The big bangles on her arms jangled as she took another long pull on her gin rickey. Ice clicked in her now empty glass. She turned and searched Rourke's face with drooping, glazed eyes. "Are you somebody famous?" she said.

Suddenly the razz-ma-tazz was gone, and Rourke saw that she was even younger than he'd thought. Young and hard and naive and hungry, and he felt sorry for her. "No, I'm just a cop," he said.

Her gaze moved up and down the length of him, from his black suede-topped shoes back to his mouth, and stopped. "You look like you ought to be famous."

Rourke laughed and shook his head. "I think Freddy just glanced your way."

It was only after she had walked away from him without another word that he realized he'd never learned her name.

The musicians had been passing reefers back and forth among themselves all night, and their horns were now hitting some wild and ragged notes that burst through the open door in shards of sound.

She stood alone on the upstairs gallery, with her back partly to him and her hands resting on the balustrade, looking out at the vanishing night where a wafer of a moon seemed to be jittering over the bayou and the black sky was popping with stars. He could just make out the line of her jaw curving out from beneath her ear, limned by the light spilling out of the house. Her short-cropped hair exposed the white nape of her neck and that delicate protrusion of bone that always made a woman seem so vulnerable, and Daman Rourke thought, *Jesus, I've got it bad.*

"Do you want something, Detective?" Speaking into the night, she'd kept her back to him.

"Uh huh." He'd brought a fresh glass of champagne out with him and he swallowed down a big swig of it. "I've been thinking about your behavior earlier this evenin', before the party, and I'm afraid I'm going to have to arrest you for soliciting sex from a cop." He took a couple of steps, coming up behind her, close enough to touch her now, although he didn't. "Drag you downtown," he said, "and give you the third degree."

She turned around and leaned back, resting her elbows on the balustrade while she looked him over. A smile touched her mouth, and she did something with her eyes. Made them go hot and droopy. She wasn't sweet Remy anymore, but the red-lipped, black-souled vamp who picked up men, bled them dry, and threw them away.

She did a little shiver. "Oooh. The big, tough cop. Should I be scared?"

"Very scared."

"Tell me again what you're arresting me for, Detective," she said in a whisper. "I just love to hear you say the words. They make me shiver."

"What words?"

She made him wait for two beats and then she said it, low and sultry, "Soliciting sex."

"Lord, if you aren't at it again. You're a one-woman crime wave."

He'd gestured with his hand to make his point, and the champagne sloshed over the rim of the glass. She took his hand and licked the drops off his fingers. "You shouldn't waste it like that," she said.

"It's awful stuff. It deserves to be wasted."

She laughed, and he felt the warmth of her breath on the wet skin of his hand. "You're swacked on it, though."

"No, I'm not," he said, although maybe he was. A little.

She let go of his hand and reached up, wrapping her arms around his neck to pull his mouth down to hers. "I do love you, Day Rourke," she said, and she kissed him.

"Let's get out of here," he said a bit later, when she let him.

She shook her head, her lips brushing back and forth across his. "Can't. It may not look like it, but I'm working."

She kissed him again, though, and she seemed to be swooning, to be singing into his mouth, and he let himself go with it, even though with Remy Lelourie the fall was always so long and so hard.

A camera's flash lamp exploded in their faces, and they jerked apart, blinking in the sudden intense wash of light.

"Hey, you two lovebirds," the reporter said, raising his camera again as he sidled back toward the gallery's outside stairs, from where he'd come. He popped another bulb into the lamp, slid a new plate into the box, and put his finger on the shutter. "Smile for *The Movies.*"

"Wait," Rourke said. He smiled like the guy had asked, and the smile was easy. "How about a scoop to go along with that shot?"

The reporter stopped, lowering his camera. "Really?" He was coming back now. He was a scrawny fellow with a big nose and ears, and front teeth square and yellow like kernels of corn. He had a deep hitch in his stride, as if one leg was shorter than the other. "Say, did you two kids just get engaged?"

Rourke was still smiling when he grabbed the camera out of the man's hands and swung around, smashing it against the hard cypress wall of the house. The bellows tore and the wooden box shattered open. Rourke smacked it against the house one more time for good measure, and the flash lamp attachment bent like a pretzel.

He handed the mess back to the reporter. He was still smiling. "Next time you'll leave wearing it around your neck. Now, get lost."

"Aw, jeez," came a rough voice from behind him. "I swear I can't leave you alone for a minute."

A big, lumbering man in a rumpled pongee suit stood filling the doorway from the front parlor. Fiorello Prankowski, Rourke's partner in homicide detection. They were catching tonight, which meant that if Fio was here then somebody somewhere in New Orleans had been murdered.

Fio raised his eyebrows at Rourke, but he didn't say anything more. His face had its perpetually tired look, deep creases lining it like the rings of a seasoned tree.

He lifted his hat to Remy. "Miss Lelourie," he said, but his voice was flat, his eyes hard and flat as well. Fio remained convinced that the most beautiful woman in the world had slashed her husband to death with a cane knife last summer and had gotten away with it.

The reporter was still hovering at the top of the stairs. Rourke gave him his mean cop look. "Aren't you lost yet?"

"Say, Day, can I see you for a while?" Fio said, stepping between Rourke and the reporter, serious now, and Rourke sensed the tension in him. Whatever had happened, it must be bad, if Fio didn't want anyone else to hear about it.

Rourke turned to Remy. He touched her cheek with his fingertips. "I got to go, darlin'."

"I know. You're working, too," she said, and she seemed all right with it. Her eyes might have looked haunted a little, but then they always did. It was what the camera caught and was part of her appeal. Her seduction.

He and Fio left the gallery by the outside stairs. The wind was tossing the moss-laden branches of the huge live oaks and rattling the fronds of the tall palms. Rourke looked back up at the house, where the party went on in flashes of jazz and light. Remy Lelourie still stood where he'd left her, and he was thinking now that there had been something in her kiss, something that would worry him if he poked at it hard enough, and so he probably ought to just let it lie.

For one sweet summer eleven years ago they had been lovers, until she'd left both him and New Orleans and gone off to make herself rich and famous. Four months ago they'd gotten back together and ever since then he'd been waiting for the day when she would leave him again, looking for signs of it in everything she did and said, and if he wasn't careful, if he didn't stop, he would only end up bringing on the thing that he most feared and he'd be sorry then, uh-huh. Like picking up a stick and poking it at a cottonmouth.

Still, that kiss . . . there'd been something. Not goodbye yet, but something.

"Let's take the 'Cat," Rourke said.

"Let me get the crime scene stuff from the squad car then," Fio said, veering off down the shell drive that wrapped in a half circle around the front grounds of the house.

Rourke waited for Fio by his own car, a canary yellow Stutz Bearcat roadster. A group of men stood on the lawn within the black pools of shadow cast by the oaks. They were talking loudly, laughing and passing around a bottle in a brown bag. Most of them had cameras, and Rourke saw that the reporter whose camera he had wrecked had found another somewhere. The guy from *The Movies.* Rourke thought he'd seen him hanging around before this. Since the murder of her husband, the gentlemen of the press had been making Remy Lelourie's life a misery.

Rourke helped Fio dump the forensics gear into the Bearcat's trunk and then they slid into the plush, buffed Spanish leather seats. The six-cylinder, air-cooled Franklin engine caught with a low growl.

Rourke stood on the gas pedal, and the roadster leapt forward, its tires spitting out loose shells behind them. He spun the wheel, aiming the Bearcat's silver hood ornament at the knot of reporters beneath the oaks. Light from his headlamps caught them frozen in a tableau of astonishment, before they scattered, screaming and bellowing as they dove and rolled to get out of the way. Rourke smiled.

The Bearcat bounded toward a gap in the big oaks, its engine roaring, its tires clawing grooves in the soft grass, but the space between the tree trunks suddenly looked too narrow and beyond the gap another tree loomed square in their path.

Rourke began to hum beneath his breath.

He gripped the steering wheel hard as the Bearcat surged between the trees, missing the trunks on both sides by less than an inch. The oak in front of them seemed wide as the mouth of a tunnel, impossible to miss. Rourke flipped the wheel hard over and the Bearcat slewed, fishtailing violently. Moss slapped at the windshield, the tires screeched, and Rourke laughed.

He barely missed hitting two more trees before he pulled out of the skid, and then they were careening across the lawn, back onto the drive, and by the time they passed through the wrought iron gate, he had the Bearcat's roaring engine back down to a purr.

He turned up Esplanade Avenue, and they rolled along in silence a couple of ticks before he stole a look at his partner.

Fio had hair sparse and stiff as salt grass and at the moment it seemed to be sticking straight up. "Don't ever do that again," he said.

"Okay."

" 'Cause if you do it again, I'm going to have to seriously hurt you."

Rourke began to sing. "Let a smile be your umbrella . . ."

Fio gave him another wild-eyed look. "I'm stuck in a car with a fucking maniac."

"Yeah, yeah." Rourke's blood was strumming a high note now, as he felt the first razor-edged rush of the hunt. "So where are we going, and who's dead?"

Fio let his breath out slowly and let go of his white-knuckled grip on the dash. "Someone came upon a dead priest in an abandoned macaroni factory down on Ursulines and Chartres." He lifted his big shoulders in a shrug. "The desk sergeant said . . . I don't know, I must have heard it wrong. He said the guy had been crucified."

Chapter Four

The macaroni factory was in a bad block, between a hookshop and a flophouse, where you could rent a cot for two bits a night. Across the street, sagging, rusting chicken wire fenced off a hot car farm that had been raided and shut down only last week as part of the mayor's latest crusade to cut down on crime in the City That Care Forgot.

Rourke got out of the Bearcat and paused to look around. His face felt cold and his chest hurt as if someone had just beaten on him with a baseball bat. He was scared of what he would find inside this place. He told himself that there were two hundred and seventy-five priests in New Orleans, and so the victim didn't have to be his brother, Paulie.

He'd be somebody's brother, though.

A uniform cop sagged against the factory's brick wall, staring down at the puddle of vomit between his feet. As Rourke came up, he lifted his head and peered at Rourke's detective shield with bleary eyes.

"You the one called it on the signal box?" Rourke asked.

The young cop swallowed and wiped his mouth with the back of his hand. "My partner did. He's inside. We were ordered to stay by the body until you detectives arrived, but I couldn't . . ." The bile rose up again in his throat and he gagged. "Oh, God."

"Breathe through your mouth," Rourke said.

The cop nodded and gulped down a big gobful of air.

Rourke waved his hand at Fio, who was getting the cameras, fingerprinting kit, and an electric torch out of the trunk. "Maybe if you can give my partner a hand?" he said, thinking it would give the kid something to do besides dwell on what he'd seen.

The young cop nodded again and gulped at more air. Some of the green was starting to leave his face.

Rourke looked around the entrance to the factory. The wind had blown scraps of newspapers, dead leaves, and tamale wrappings into a pile in one corner of the arched portico. Glass from the broken fan light in the transom littered the stoop. The hasp on the door's lock was broken.

"Did y'all do that to the lock?" he asked.

The boy shook his head. "No, sir. It was like that when we got here. The kid who found the body . . . We were in a speak around the corner, uh, taking a leak, when this kid came running in, yelling about a crucified priest. Maybe he was the one busted it."

"Yeah, okay." Rourke covered his hand with his handkerchief before he pulled the door open, even though the beat cops and God knew who else had already left their fingerprints all over it.

The factory wasn't so abandoned that the electricity had been cut off. Lights in wire baskets hung by chains from the ceiling rafters. At least half still had their bulbs and were burning. Rourke turned back to ask if the lights had been on when they got here, but the patrolman had already gone out to the curb to help Fio.

The factory was long and narrow and still filled with all the machinery for mixing, rolling, cutting, and drying the macaroni. Another uniform cop stood at the far end of the building, next to something that promised to be bad.

The buttons and shield on the cop's blouse gleamed in the yellow electric light. He was pulling a cigarette out of a box, but he kept his gaze on Rourke as he licked the seam and lit the end. He flicked the spent match onto the floor, and then he began to swing his nightstick in his hand.

The heels of Rourke's shoes clicked on the stone floor as he walked. His breath was coming hard and hurting now. As he got closer he smelled the blood, and something he hadn't expected—burnt flesh.

Closer now, and Rourke could see that the something hanging was indeed a priest. Or at least someone dressed like a priest in black cassock and white bands.

Rourke pushed his hands into his pockets to hide their trembling. He'd always been a betting man. He'd bought the Bearcat with gambling winnings; he'd been known to drop a C-note at the track and not feel the pain. A betting man would go with the odds. Two hundred and seventy-five to one.

It wasn't his brother.

The size of the body was all wrong—too short by at least three inches and too lean. The dead man's mother would have been hard pressed to recognize him by looking at his face, though. Both cheekbones were broken, his nose was smashed, and you couldn't see either one of his eyes. His mouth was pulpy and ringed with blood.

He hung from the crossbeam of one of the drying racks, nailed to it through the wrists. His feet were bare and bound together with rope, and burned to bloody raw blisters on the soles. The dead man had been hung so that his feet dangled just an inch or so above a cluster of votive candles.

Rourke squatted on his haunches. He took a fountain pen out of his breast pocket and pressed the tip of it into one of the candles, next to the wick. The wax was still soft.

Rourke stared at the feet. They were slender and well formed, and pale where they hadn't been burned. There was something, he thought, so vulnerably human about the sight of bare feet. He'd always hated this part of the job—looking at the dead bodies. The murdered ones.

Rourke's gaze lifted to the beat cop. The man was in his early thirties, around Rourke's own age, with ruddy good looks and Irish red hair. That deep, loamy auburn color. His blue uniform blouse strained over his deep chest and a belly that was already showing a tendency to swell with fat. He seemed to be finding Rourke's presence at the crime scene something to smirk about.

"Were these candles burning when you got here?" Rourke asked.

The cop took his time drawing on his cigarette before he answered. "Naw. The stiff was so fresh, though, you could still smell the death fart."

Rourke looked back down, breathed. He could feel blood shooting through his hands. He wanted to hit something.

The killer, he saw, had carefully removed his victim's shoes and socks, rolled up the socks and put them inside the shoes, and then neatly set them aside. Near the shoes lay a bloody cloth that looked like a piece of ripped-up sheet. Its ends were twisted, as if they had once been tied into a knot.

"Was there a gag in his mouth?" Rourke asked.

"Jesus, we didn't touch nothin', all right? 'Cause we knew we'd get our asses chewed by you jumped-up, jackass dicks if we did."

Rourke pushed himself to his feet, twisting half around, so that when he came up he was right in the other cop's face. When your daddy was a drunk and you have those demons inside of you as well, you know the signs of a man with a load on. The bloodshot, baggy eyes. The grip on the nightstick to hide the booze tremors. The smell of the cheap rye sweating out the pores of your skin.

"I don't believe I caught your name," Rourke said, letting a little mean show in his smile.

The other cop answered with a sneer of his own. "Jack Murphy."

"Well, keep up the good work, Patrolman Jack Murphy," Rourke said, tapping the cop's shiny badge with his finger. "Keep smiling and kissing ass like you're doing, and maybe someday you, too, can be a jumped-up, jackass dick."

Fio made a harsh grunting noise when he saw the dead priest. "God almighty."

Rourke stepped up to the body and slipped his hand inside the cassock's side pocket. He found a rosary, some loose change, a key ring with two keys, and a library card. "Father Patrick Walsh," he read aloud.

Fio groaned. "Aw, man, don't tell me that. Why are we always the ones to catch the political hot potatoes?"

There were two hundred and seventy-five priests in New Orleans, but only one had the celebrity of Father Patrick Walsh. He'd had a book of his homilies published, which had become a best-seller, and worshippers came from as far away as Texas and Mississippi to hear him celebrate the Mass at his church, Our Lady of the Holy Rosary. He had a preaching style that was more evangelical than Catholic, with his talk of being baptized in the spirit of Jesus, and with the gospel singing, and the speaking in tongues. His flamboyance and unorthodoxy had gotten him into trouble with the Church hierarchy more than once, but he was known affectionately as "our Father Pat" to his flock and his fans. They adored him.

Or so the *Times-Picayune* had said in a story the newspaper had done on him not long ago. The article, Rourke remembered, had said Father Patrick Walsh was an orphan who knew nothing about his origins beyond a foundling home in Paris, Louisiana, a little sugarcane town sixty miles northwest on the Bayou Lafourche. This priest hadn't been anybody's brother after all.

"Are we sure it's him?" Fio said. He was setting up the grid camera on a high tripod. "A library card don't mean much. Maybe it's not him."

"It's him."

In life, Father Patrick Walsh had possessed the flat green eyes, wide mouth, and heavy bones of north Louisiana hill people. Rourke could make out the remnants of those features now, in spite of the beating that had been laid on him.

Fio took a shot of the body, the camera's flash lamp strobing harsh white light onto the bloodied face, the bare, burnt feet, the nails piercing vulnerable flesh.

"Where's the hammer?" Rourke said. "What did he use to drive in the nails?"

Fio studied the area around the drying rack, "A shoe, maybe."

"Not heavy enough."

"Yeah, you're probably right." Fio took a slow look up and down the length of the building. "It's going to take a frigging army to canvass this scene. I'll dust for latents, but in a factory like this—there's going to be a million of 'em."

"Concentrate on the candles and around where he drove in the nails. Who knows, we might get lucky."

The beat cop had been swinging his stick and smirking as he watched them work, but now he snorted aloud.

"That's Jack Murphy," Rourke said to Fio. "He doesn't like us—thinks we're jackass dicks, or something like that. Or maybe he's just in a sour mood because this time the corpse turned out to be a priest, so there wasn't any diamond stick pin or money roll for him to lift before calling it in on the signal box."

Murphy gave Rourke a don't-fuck-with-me look but he said nothing, and Rourke thought his jab had probably not been too far off the mark. In the tradition of veteran beat cops on the pad everywhere, Jack Murphy had probably rifled through the dead priest's clothing looking for something he could steal while his rookie partner was outside puking his guts out.

Rourke stared at Jack Murphy until a tiny tremor began to jitter below the patrolman's right eye and he looked away. "So what about this kid who found the body?" Rourke said.

Murphy took his time answering, not looking at Rourke, taking another drag on his cigarette before he gestured with his nightstick at the far corner of the factory where most of the lights had gone out.

Rourke could just make out the shadows of a boy sitting on an upended oil drum, one hand cuffed to a water pipe on the wall.

"Kid goes by the name of Carlos Kelly," Murphy said. "He probably didn't do it, but you can always make him for it, being as how you homicide dee-tectives are always wanting to close the case quick to get on the good side of the brass. And a lowlife like him with a dago wop for a mother ain't gonna be no loss to society."

He fished the cuff key out of his pocket and tossed it toward Rourke. "Unless you'd rather pin it on some wharf nigger. I got a couple names I could give you."

Rourke snatched the key out of the air, then looked at Fio and heaved a put-upon sigh. "And here you were telling me what a tough case this was gonna be."

Even scared and filthy, Carlos Kelly had a face that belonged on a holy card, with his full mouth, cap of dark curls, and cerulean blue eyes. The handcuffs seemed almost an assault on such beauty.

Rourke took them off before he pulled up an oil drum and sat down. He let the silence build. Over here you couldn't smell the blood and burnt flesh, just dust and rust and the oil that had been ground over the years into the floor.

The boy, who had been staring down at his wrist, rubbing it, looked up. His gaze sheared off Rourke, went to the body, then slid away.

Rourke took his hip flask out of his tuxedo pocket and held it out in a wordless offering. Carlos Kelly's hands trembled as he drank, his teeth knocking against the flask's silver lip.

He handed the flask back to Rourke and tried on a smile.

"You are sure in some kind of jam, Carlos," Rourke said, putting an edge on it. "Man, killing a priest. The law's going to figure using our new-fangled electric chair would be going too easy on a guy who did that."

The boy's head jerked as if he'd just been slapped. "Hey, wait a minute. What are you . . . ? Aw, Jesus. I didn't do it. Why would I do it and then run for help, huh?"

Rourke said nothing. The boy moaned and leaned over, bracing his elbows on his knees and burying his face in his hands.

"Sometimes," Rourke said, gentle now, "a man can wade into trouble that ends up being way over his head."

The boy pressed his face into his hands hard, then he took a deep, groaning breath and slowly raised his head. "Do you know that sidewalk banker, Tony the Rat?"

"Yeah," Rourke said with a smile. "He and I go way back." Tony Benato was a loan shark who sometimes dealt a little cocaine on the side to support his own habit, and who'd gotten the moniker Tony the Rat not because he'd ever squealed on anybody, but for the hole he had in his pointed nose, damaged by years of packing anything up there that would give him a high.

"Well, my mama got sick and she needed an operation or she was gonna die, and so I borrowed a couple of Gs from Tony to pay for it, only the vig was a whole fifty percent, and I couldn't even keep up with the juice payments, let alone make a dent in the original two thou. Not even working two shifts on the docks."

"Yeah, that's tough. And so he sent his hatchet man to make an example out of you," Rourke said, feeding into the kid's tall, sad tale in the hope that at least some of his lies were being coated with a gloss of the truth.

Carlos Kelly's head was bobbing eagerly. "Tony's goon, he made me go with him to the Esplanade Wharf, and he had his heater, a big ol' hog's leg, pressed right up to the back of my head when this other gun went off and somebody screamed. The goon got distracted and I got away."

Rourke didn't bother to ask if the kid knew the name of the guy with the hog's leg. Tony the Rat was a two-bit shark and weekend dealer who only had the one enforcer. Ironically, the enforcer's moniker was also the Rat. Guido the Rat. Guido had gotten his nickname as a kid, when for ten cents he would bite the head off a rat for your entertainment.

"After you got away from Tony's goon," Rourke said, "why come here?"

The boy shrugged. "I wasn't thinking. Just running."

Fio had found another oil drum to stand on and was dusting the crossbeam with mercury and chalk powders. Carlos Kelly watched a moment, his throat moving as he swallowed. "All I wanted was a place to lay low for a while, you know?" He shuddered, hard. "I should've vamoosed soon as I saw the fuckin' bats."

Rourke looked up. Moths and palmetto bugs rattled around the lights, but no small furry bodies hung from the rafters. "Bats?"

Carlos Kelly waved his hand at the catwalk that rimmed the factory two-thirds of the way up the wall. "They were roosting, or whatever they do, up there. I saw their wings flapping and I heard 'em squealing. Then I noticed the fire—leastways, I thought it was a fire. That some tramps were camping out in here, boozing and cooking up a meal. But when I got closer I saw . . . him. Hanging there. His breath was coming out of him hard. In bloody bubbles. He said, 'Mercy,' like he was calling on God to forgive him, or to help him, I guess." The boy drew in a sudden, gasping breath. "Oh, Jesus. I thought it was meat cooking, but it was his feet."

"And so you put out the candles."

The boy nodded, and the light glinted off the tears on his cheeks. He'd been crying for a while now. "He was alive when I ran for help, I'd swear to it. He was alive . . ."

"Yeah, okay," Rourke said.

Carlos Kelly was probably nothing more than a mutt, a bagman for a penny-ante loan shark who had then turned around and stolen from his employer and nearly paid the expected price. It had taken some courage, though, for the kid to leave his bolt hole, knowing that Tony Benato's goon was out there searching for him.

Rourke looked from the boy's bent head to the body of the tortured priest, thinking. Fio had finished dusting the beam and was now shooting a close-up photo of the nail-pierced wrists. The New Orleans parish coroner had just arrived.

"What I can do," Rourke said, "is have you taken all the way out to Mid-City Precinct and held incognito as a material witness for a while."

Carlos Kelly let out a long slow breath. "How long?"

"You got family, friends? Then long enough," Rourke went on as the boy nodded, "for them to try to make things square with Tony Benato on your behalf." He patted the boy's shoulder as he stood up. "Only stay out of that running pinochle game those cops've got going out there. Those guys, they would cheat their own mothers."

Carlos Kelly snorted a laugh, but it came out as more of a sob. He brushed his face then looked at his hand, as if surprised to find that it was wet. He made the sign of the cross, then flushed when he realized that Rourke had seen him do it.

"When I first came in here," he said, "it was so dark and with the machinery and the bats and the flames—it made me think of hell. And then I saw him . . . hanging there. I mean, who else but the devil would do that to a priest?"

The beat cop, Jack Murphy, was ranting to Fio. "Must be a trial, having a guy like him for a partner—a pretty boy with a la-di-da college dee-ploma. Guy who just because he's got an angel in high places and he's banging a movie star, he thinks his shit smells like roses. I bet you do all the work, only he's the one all the time gettin' his mug in the papers."

"Yeah, well it ain't always a fair or gentle world," Fio said. He met Rourke's eyes and he wasn't smiling. They'd been working together for almost a year now and their partnership wasn't easy. Mostly because Fio was more than half convinced Rourke knew and was sitting on the truth about who had really slashed Remy Lelourie's husband to death with a cane knife that hot night last July, and Rourke couldn't make it right with his partner because Fio was dead-on with his suspicions. Rourke did know the truth and he wasn't talking, and so distrust lay between them like a sore tooth you poked and worried with your tongue, and just couldn't let alone.

The parish coroner, Rourke saw, was peering closely at the victim's mouth and muttering to himself around the cigarette he had clamped between his teeth. He turned as Rourke came up. "Ah, Lieutenant, so this one is yours. Splendid. Splendid."

Moses Mueller was a short, fat man who wore old-fashioned frock coats, arrived at the crime scene in a chauffeured green Packard, and spent his own money on the latest forensic lab equipment. He was called the Ghoul by everyone who worked with him because of his passionate interest in death and because of the rank odor that always hovered around him and that no amount of Lucky Tiger cologne could overcome. The Ghoul in his turn despised all cops because they were, he'd once told Rourke in his pedantic manner with its old-world accent, "ignoramuses who think a postmortem is the equivalent of a cigarette after sexual intercourse."

Only Rourke seemed to have escaped the Ghoul's contempt and that had brought him a lot of razzing from his fellow cops, who were making bets on when the Ghoul would invite him over to his dungeon for supper.

For the moment, though, the Ghoul was straining on tiptoe for a closer look at where the nail had been driven through Father Patrick Walsh's right wrist. "Now this is indeed interesting," he said. "I see that your murderer has done it properly."

"What?" Fio laughed and Jack Murphy joined in. "There's a fuckin' manual for doing something like this?"

The Ghoul blew out a deep sigh, his chins rattling. "You misunderstand as usual, Mr. Prankowski. Look at many sculptures and paintings of Christ's crucifixion and what will you see? Nails through the palms. That was not how it was done, however. Usually the condemned man's outstretched arms were bound to the horizontal beam, the *patibulum,* with ropes, or nails were driven through his wrists. Between the radius and ulna bones of his wrists. Cicero considered it the most horrible of deaths."

Rourke made himself look at the nails. They more accurately should have been called spikes, he thought, for their heads were the size of a thumbnail and their shanks had to be at least seven inches long to drive through the width of the wrist and deep enough into the beam to bear the body's weight. Where they pierced the flesh, the skin was discolored blue, and rivulets of blood ran down the priest's arms to be soaked up by his sleeves. Not enough blood, though, to indicate that he'd bled to death.

"What was the actual cause of death?" he asked aloud.

The Ghoul came close to smiling—a rare event. "Ah, that I cannot tell you yet. The medical reason for death by crucifixion has never been fully understood. Perhaps it happens with heart failure or a form of suffocation. Or perhaps sheer exhaustion if one hangs long enough."

"Our witness says he heard screaming and then a gunshot not long before he found him."

"Oh, sure," Fio said. "That makes a whole lot of sense. Go to the trouble to nail a guy to a pasta drying rack and then shoot him to death."

"Yeah," Jack Murphy chimed in. "Maybe he was shot while trying to escape."

The Ghoul gave them both a sour look. "A *coup de grâce,* perhaps you are thinking," he said to Rourke. "I am not seeing any bullet holes, but nothing can be a certainty until I can have a good look at him back at the morgue."

He stepped back, his gaze sweeping slowly up and down the body. "I wonder why he was not stripped naked. They always stripped them, the Romans did, before they nailed them to the crossbeam."

A thick mist was rising off the river and winding like strips of wet gauze through the close, narrow streets of the Quarter. Rourke stood outside, beneath the macaroni factory's arched portico, and breathed deeply of the cool, damp air, trying to get the smell of blood and burnt flesh out of his throat.

The meat wagon had come and Father Patrick Walsh had been taken down off his cross, wrapped in a gray blanket, and carried away on a stretcher. The Ghoul had left in his chauffeured green Packard. Fio had taken a couple more photographs and finished dusting for prints, and the beat cops had been left inside in case the killer came back. It had been known to happen, Rourke thought, but he himself had never been so lucky on any of his cases.

Fio came out of the factory now, pulling the door closed behind him. He held his shoulders high and his head low, as if he was ducking a punch. He cast a long glance at Rourke's averted face, then went through the motions of lighting up a Castle Morro.

"Man," he said once the cigar was finally drawing, "I've seen some bad shit, but that . . ."

The wind blew the sweet perfume of Havana tobacco in Rourke's face, and he closed his eyes for a moment. Across the street, at the raided hot car farm, a gust slapped a sheet of newspaper at the chicken wire fence and set a Victory Gasoline sign to swinging on its chains with loud creaks. An empty pork 'n' beans can scraped along the gutter.

Fio pushed a heavy breath out through his teeth. "Don't go all moody and crazy on me, Day."

"I'm okay." Rourk's hands were shoved deep in his pockets, clenched into fists. He made himself open them, made himself breathe. Everyone was always telling him that he took each battered, butchered, and mangled corpse too personally. He was starting to believe that maybe everyone was right.

Fio gave him another long look. "Fine, then let's talk about the case. You see a guy who's had his feet burned and you think Mafiosi, only I can't see the outfit capping a priest."

"They go to Mass every Sunday and baptize their babies in the faith and get the archbishop himself to deliver the eulogies at their funerals, and they'd still off the Pope if it was good for business." Rourke shook his head. "Not like this, though. The guy who did this wasn't a mob enforcer. That beating to the face—it was personal. The killer knew Father Patrick Walsh and he was mad as hell at him."

"And nailing him to a fucking beam wasn't personal?"

"No, the nails and the votive candles, they were something else."

Rourke had thought he could almost feel it in there, a miasma left behind by the killer, but he couldn't put a name to it yet. Fury. Frustration. Despair. Desperation . . . Something.

Fio was rubbing his eyes, as if trying to wipe away the images of what he'd seen. "We keep saying *he,* but you'd think it would take two guys to nail a man to a beam."

Rourke shrugged. "It would be hard for one guy, but not impossible. If he knocked his victim out first."

"There was that big spread in the paper about Walsh a few weeks back," Fio said. "Maybe the guy who did this has a vendetta against the Catholic Church and he picked the good father to be like his punching bag. Someone to be at the fist-end of all his hate."

"Except the body wasn't naked."

"Jeez. You're worse than the Ghoul. What does it matter if he left the poor bastard's clothes on or took them off?"

"He had the nailing part right. Through the wrists. Yet he didn't strip him. If it was some kind of symbolic crucifixion of the Church, he would've followed the ritual to the letter."

"If you say so. It probably wasn't a sex thing then either. I had me a case back in Des Moines a couple of years back. Guy got his jollies doing nuns, but he took off their clothes before he fu— he did them."

Fio flipped his half-smoked cigar into the street. It landed with a shower of sparks and then it lay there, still burning, its tip glowing red.

It would take a while, Rourke thought, for votive candles to burn the soles of a man's feet badly enough to leave charred flesh and running blisters. The killer had gathered together what he would need ahead of time and brought it with him: the candles, the nails, and whatever he had used for a hammer. Then he had brought his victim here for the purpose of doing what he had done, and he had been prepared for it to take time. "He must've known about this place," Rourke said aloud. "Maybe he worked here before it closed down."

"Or he lives in the neighborhood." Fio pushed his arms out into a stretch, popping the joints. "Oh, joy. Think of all the gin and hot pillow joints we get to visit. I'll come home smelling like sour mash and cheap perfume, and the wife'll have me sleeping on the sofa for a week."

The men's gazes met and they shared a smile, and the edginess that had been coiling between them all night began to loosen a little.

"I've still got one question that's been nagging at me, though," Fio said.

"Yeah? What's that?"

"How do they make macaroni, anyway?"

Rourke had to laugh. "Beats the hell out of me."

He took one more slow look around. Tomorrow . . . no, this morning, for it was almost dawn, they would go all over the scene again. His sneering heart of hearts told him that people died all the time in obscene ways for obscene reasons and that iniquity and suffering flourished in the world, but he wanted a righteous justice for this one. He wanted it bad.

"Why do you think," he said aloud, "that hobos would want to avoid an abandoned factory that is dry inside and with plenty of wood to burn if the night turns cold?"

Fio, who had started to walk away, turned back around. "Huh?"

Rourke pointed at the graffiti chalked on the door. "Some tramp left a warning for other guys passing through that this place is unsafe."

Fio stared at the marks a moment, then shrugged. "Let's face it—this ain't the Ritz."

At the car, Rourke stopped and looked up at the infinity of the sky, where little was left to the stars, and the black holes between them were filling with light. He let his mind go, seeking a connection, and he smiled . . . The killer had had a plan, and the guts to see the plan through no matter how messy things got, and he was smart. Smart and careful and arrogant. Smart and careful enough that he would try to get away with this, and arrogant enough to believe that he would succeed.

"We'll get him, Day," Fio said, his craggy face creased with worry, for he'd seen the cruel edge on Rourke's smile and knew what it meant.

"We," Rourke said, "are going to nail his fuckin' ass to a crossbeam."

CHAPTER FIVE

The party had flapped on until five-thirty in the morning, when the hooch ran dry and the band packed up and went home. It seemed then that everyone left all at once and Remy Lelourie was alone.

There was no sadder sight, she thought, than a room after a party is over. The chandelier lights blazed too brightly on the silver trays littered with crumbs and on the crystal glasses with their melting ice and lipsticked rims. Wet rings marked the tables, and cigarette smoke hazed the air. The house smelled of flat champagne and sour gin.

She paid off the hired waiters and told Miss Beulah, her housekeeper, to leave the mess for later and go on down to bed.

Alone then, truly alone, she walked the cypress boards of the upstairs gallery for a while, where the women of her family had once walked with their hooped skirts and fluttering fans. The rising sun glazed bronze the water of the bayou. Wisps of mists writhed among the canebrakes, only to be snatched up and blown away by a strong rising wind.

The wind felt cold on her bare arms and she rubbed them, shivering a little. Her body had the same exposed-nerve feeling that sometimes came over her after shooting a scene, when she got too *into* a part and lost herself. The world would get like a piece of overexposed film then: bright, jagged, raw.

The wind gusted again, pulling the moss off the oaks and lashing at the dead black branches of the drowned cypress trees. She gripped her arms tighter, as if she were trying to hold herself together, to keep the wind from pulling her apart. Her friends and enemies both claimed that she could be more than a little crazy sometimes, and she believed that of herself. She had an emptiness inside of her that was a living thing—a yawning hunger that constantly needed filling. The emptiness made her act wild and reckless; it made her crave things, made her want to do things she knew would be bad for her.

The devil had come into her house tonight, the devil in the form of Max Leeland, the head of Bright Lights Studios. He had taken the train all the way out from California, to tempt her with more money than God could mint and with complete creative control of whatever film she next chose to star in. Nobody had complete creative control. Not even Mary Pickford. People thought that the movies were all about fame and money, but people on the inside knew that the fame and money were only tools to bring you the one thing that really mattered: power.

So Max had come, bearing gifts and a contract that would make her the most powerful woman in Hollywood. Because she'd been telling everybody for weeks that *Cutlass* would be her last picture, and because she'd come home and she had her man back and she was happy, happy, happy—they must have finally believed that she really would walk away from the movie business, if Max had come all the way out here to talk her out of it. Which was funny, because even before he'd arrived the old restlessness and craziness had already been creeping up on her once again.

A floorboard creaked behind her, and she turned around slowly, smiling. Not scared, because a little ol' bump in the night would never scare Remy Lelourie. She'd worked hard at inuring herself to fear a long time ago, by flirting with it and embracing it, facing up to the worst that fear could do to her by spitting in its eye.

The length of the gallery was empty, though, except for the gauzy curtains that floated out the open windows of her bedroom. For a moment it seemed that a shadow walked there, appearing in one shaft of light and then another, and then disappearing suddenly like a jump shot on a piece of film.

Day.

She felt a wrench of excitement and need, and yet even as it was happening she was thinking: Remember how this feels, Remy girl. Remember this for later, when you have to play a woman so in love with a man that just seeing his shadow cross her window makes her heart ache.

She must have been wrong about the shadow, because he wasn't there.

The bell ringer for the telephone on the desk was chirping, though, and she reached to answer it just as her gaze fell on her bed. It was a Louisiana Sheridan bed that sat well off the floor with posts ten feet high and decorated with wooden pineapples that were supposed to symbolize hospitality. The rice-patterned spread was turned down, and although the bed had yet to be slept in, the silk sheets were wrinkled and the pillow indented as if an invisible man already lay there.

Remy Lelourie stared at the vibrating bell ringer, her breath tripping suddenly.

Slowly, she lifted the handset and put the receiver to her ear. The line crackled, and she thought she could hear breathing, or perhaps it was only the soughing of the wind on the gallery.

Slower still, she brought her lips to the mouthpiece. "Hello?" she said.

The breathing quickened, as if excited, and then a voice low and muffled, "Did you get my letter, Remy?"

She saw it then—a creamy white envelope lying on her dressing table, propped up against the round, beveled mirror. Her name was written on it in a fat script with a strange rusty-brown ink.

She tried to hang up, but the handset slipped off the hook and clattered onto the desk. She went to the dressing table, floating now, as if she played a part in one of her movies. She stared at the envelope a long time before she picked it up. She slit open the seal with a scarlet nail.

Are you scared yet, Remy?

The last shreds of the stars had gone, and the sky was tinged on the edges by a rising saffron sun. Detective Daman Rourke drove his Stutz Bearcat along the river, past bags of coffee stacked on the wharf, past wagons piled with bananas and oyster luggers that rocked in their moorings. Tugboat horns moaned in the thick mist rising off the water.

He thought his partner was dozing, until the big cop sat up and tapped a thick finger on the windshield. "Hey, how come we didn't turn up Canal?"

"Because we're going to Our Lady of the Holy Rosary."

"No, we're not. Uh-uh. No," Fio said, staring hard at the side of Rourke's face. "You're going to get us fired," he went on when Rourke neither answered him nor turned back downtown toward the Criminal Courts Building, where the detectives' squad room was and where they should have been going. "Only you won't be fired because you've got an angel in high places and you're banging a movie star. I'll be fired, and the wife'll have me sleeping on the sofa for a month."

"If a cop was found like that, what is the first thing we'd do?" Rourke said.

"Aw, man. I don't want to hear this."

"We'd see if he was dirty and then cover it up."

"You saying you think Father Patrick Walsh was dirty?"

Rourke shrugged. "I'm only saying I want to get a handle on his life before the archbishop rings up the other good fathers at his rectory with the news that he's dead and everybody starts covering their asses." Rourke cut a glance at his partner. Fio was giving him that wild-eyed look again.

"You want me to come along with you while you roust some priests," Fio said.

"I'll roust them nicely."

"Hunh." Fio pushed back his cuff and tried to check his watch in the intermittent light of the street lamps. "It's ten minutes of six."

"Priests get up with the dawn. It's only sinners like you and me who've got to sleep off what we did the night before."

"You want me to come along with you while you go knocking on the door of Our Lady of the Holy Rosary rectory at six o'clock in the morning and tell 'em that one of their priests has been murdered and then ask them if they did it."

Rourke smiled. "Well, my daddy always said if it looks like a fight is coming, be sure you get in the first lick."

Fio showed his teeth in an answering smile. "You said you were going to be nice."

"Maybe I lied." Rourke was quiet for a while, then he added, "Did I ever tell you that I have a brother?"

More silence filled the car and two blocks rolled by before Fio said, "Eleven months we've been partners, I've told you stuff I've never even told my wife, and this is the first time you mention a brother."

"Yeah, well, he's a priest at Holy Rosary."

Our Lady of the Holy Rosary was on Coliseum Square in a neighborhood that was mixed like gumbo, with Negroes, Irish and German immigrants, and old American families who could trace their lineage back to before the Civil War.

The square was actually shaped like a triangle with the Gothic-style church on Race Street anchoring its base. Holy Rosary's school was on the church's lakeside and the rectory was on the riverside, and all had been built in the middle of the last century out of the same Louisiana brick that was glowing bloodred in the early morning sunlight. A milk wagon was pulled up to the curb.

Rourke and Fio sat in the car while the milkman ladled milk from a big tin can into a couple of glass bottles and carried the bottles through the gate in a black iron picket fence afroth with honeysuckle. He blessed himself as he passed through the shadows cast by the church's octagonal bell tower and then left the milk at the rectory's kitchen stoop.

Fio watched the milkman; Rourke watched the priest who was cutting through the green of the square, moving fast and looking back over his shoulder. Rourke watched as the priest, almost running now, crossed the street, climbed the portal steps, and entered the church through the iron-banded wooden doors.

"Wait for me," Rourke said to his partner, and got out of the car.

Rourke hurried up the root-cracked walkway, with the wind skirling yellow leaves around his feet. The knifelike fronds of the banana trees rattled above his head, and the waving knotted branches of the old figs threw shifting shadows on the red-brick walls.

Rourke's father's mother had carried bricks in her apron to help build St. Alphonsus, the church he'd grown up with as a boy in the Irish Channel. The women who had lived in this neighborhood generations ago would have done the same thing for Holy Rosary. Today the young sons of their line would be serving at the Mass in the way that Rourke had done. The sons and brothers and uncles of these families would become their priests.

Inside, the church was cool and dark and smelled of burning candle wax and incense. He found the priest standing before a small altar in the north transept. With his black cassock, the father blended in with the long shadows cast by the presbyter arches, except for the white of his hands that were folded before him. His head was not bowed, though. He looked up instead at the marble pietà on the altar, and from the taut set of his shoulders and back and the tight grip his two hands had on each other, it seemed that whatever this priest was asking of the Virgin Mary, it was more a scream of desperation than a prayer.

"Does she answer when you speak to her?" Rourke said.

Father Paul Rourke whirled, blinking as if a flash lamp had gone off in his face. "Day? What are you doing here?"

His voice echoed, then fell in the thick, black silence of the church.

Rourke searched his brother's face. The round Irish chin and plump cheeks were unshaven and with his dark beard they looked dusted with soot. His eyes had always drooped at the corners, giving his face a melancholy cast even as a boy, but this morning the shadows under those eyes were dark as bruises.

"What's happened?" he said when Rourke went on staring at him, saying nothing.

A rack of votive candles burned at the pietà's marble feet. Rourke went up to it and held his palm out close over one of the flames. He felt the warmth at first, and then the pain. "Do you know what happens when you put fire to human flesh long enough?"

His brother, the priest, watched as if mesmerized. The candle flickered and danced and burned beneath Rourke's open palm, and the pain reached a pitch that was like the blare of a locomotive horn.

"Stop it!" Rourke's brother seized his wrist, pulling his hand away from the flame.

"It cooks," Rourke said.

"My God, Day. What kind of trouble are you in?"

Rourke laughed. He took out his handkerchief and wrapped it around the throbbing burn on his palm. "Are you offering to hear my confession? From my lips to God's ears. Or maybe it's time I heard yours. After all, any priest who comes sneaking back to the rectory at dawn and wearing yesterday's cassock probably hasn't been keeping all the Lord's Ten Commandments."

Even in the wavering candlelight, Rourke caught the fear in his brother's eyes, and suspicion passed through him like a shudder.

His brother shifted his weight from one foot to the other, his gaze drifting off Rourke's face to the distant recesses of the nave, the empty pews and pulpit and altar. "I have the eight o'clock Mass this morning," he said, "and you know how my stomach gets into knots over the homilies. I always spend hours on them. I pray and sweat, and I am ashamed to say sometimes I even curse. I was up all night fretting over this one. There's a park bench beneath an old bent fig tree out in the square, and I go there often to meditate. You must've seen me coming—"

Rourke gripped his brother's face with his two hands. He dug his fingers into the soft flesh and gave him a rough shake, and then he lowered his head until their foreheads touched and the moment became an embrace.

"Paulie, Paulie, Paulie. You always were such a lousy liar."

Chapter Six

Pink tea roses on trellises framed the rectory's kitchen door. Fio was waiting for them there on the stoop, holding the milk bottles by their necks, one in each hand.

"Somebody's already up inside and making breakfast," he said. He'd picked one of the roses and stuck it in the brim of his hat. "Maybe whoever it is has made some coffee to go along with that lost bread I smell frying, and so maybe he could use some of this nice, fresh milk to put in his coffee. That's what's known as deductive reasoning. It's what detectives do, isn't that right, partner? We deduce stuff." His broad grin shifted from Rourke to the priest hovering behind him. "Say, do you by any chance got a brother who's a cop?"

Paulie's gaze clicked back and forth between the two detectives. "Day, for God's sake. What's going on?"

"Let's go inside," Rourke said, pulling open the screen door and then standing aside so his brother could go ahead of him. "I could use a cup of coffee."

The kitchen in the Holy Rosary rectory was big and bright with yellow chintz-curtained windows that opened onto a garden. It smelled good, of freshly brewed chicory coffee and boiled milk, and of cinnamon from the bread dipped in batter that was frying on the stove.

A priest sat at a beautifully polished round oak table with his elbows bracketing a steaming cup of café au lait and his head buried in his hands. "I guess you didn't sleep well either," he said without looking up as the door opened.

"Father," Paulie said, a bit too loudly. "The police are here."

The other priest's head snapped up, and Rourke saw shock register deep in his eyes. Shock and a bludgeoning fear.

Father Frank Ghilotti wore thick eyeglasses and he had large, slightly protruding teeth that gave his mouth a perpetually pursed look. His near-black hair was curled into corkscrews and plastered down wet over his skull. His olive skin had that freshly scrubbed look, as if he'd just stepped out of a bath or shower.

Father Ghilotti was the pastor of Our Lady of the Holy Rosary and as such he had authority over all the priests in his church. Rourke had met him only once, and briefly, about a month ago, the one time he had come to hear Paulie celebrate the Mass in his new assignment as Holy Rosary's assistant pastor. In New Orleans, family and connections were everything, and Father Frank Ghilotti had family connections of his own. He was the only son of the city's laundry racket boss.

And as that son, he had grown up in a world where polished wealth and polished power hid a rough street toughness. He showed some of that toughness now as he calmed his face and stood up, holding out his hand. "Detective Rourke. This early in the morning it can only be bad news."

His gaze shifted to Paulie, and something unspoken seemed to pass between the pastor and his brother, and Rourke thought, *Oh, Christ.*

"I don't know what it is," Paulie said, his voice still hitting that high, strident note. His face was flushed and spotted, and sweat glistened on his temples. "They haven't said."

"I'm afraid that our bad news is for the both of you, Father,"

Rourke said. "Father Patrick Walsh was found dead around two o'clock this morning in an abandoned macaroni factory in the Quarter."

Paulie let out a cry and stumbled backward, collapsing into a chair, jolting the table so hard that café au lait slopped out of the forgotten cup. Behind him, on the stove, the frying lost bread started to smoke.

Shock had whitened Father Ghilotti's face again, too, only this time Rourke thought the reaction came purely from surprise. There was still a wariness, though, in the wide-open eyes that stared out at them from behind the thick lenses. Wariness and a quick, calculating mind.

"But I don't understand," he said. "What was he doing down there in such a place in the middle of the night?"

"We were hoping you can tell us," Rourke said.

"Well, I can't. I can't even imagine."

Rourke's gaze went back to his brother. Paulie was staring down at the table, his face wet from crying, his hands gripped together in a tight fist in front of him. *How about you, Paulie? Can you even imagine?*

"Have you all been here at the rectory the whole night, Father?" Fio said. He had set the milk bottles down on the drain board and turned around to lean against it with his arms folded across his chest. As big as the kitchen was, he seemed to fill it.

Father Ghilotti stared at Fio a moment, then made an odd, abrupt movement with his shoulders and turned toward the stove. "My breakfast is burning." He started to reach for the handle of the fry pan with his bare hand, then pulled it back at the last second and used a folded-up dish towel instead. He wiped his hands carefully on the towel, before he turned to face them again.

"Last night, we'd all been invited for family suppers at the homes of our parishioners," he finally said. "We even made a joke about it—about how our popularity was going to make us all fat and save the Church money for our board. I ended up playing a game of chess with my host and it was late when I got home. Everyone else had already retired."

"Does that everyone include Father Pat?" Fio asked.

"I didn't check their beds, if that's what you're asking. I'm the pastor here, not a warden."

Rourke waited for his brother to say something about his own supper invitation, but Paulie only stared down at his fisted hands, running away inside himself the way he always did when things got bad.

One Sunday when they were kids, before Paulie had left home for the seminary, he'd invited his favorite priest from St. Alphonsus over for a chicken supper and somehow Paulie had gotten their daddy to promise that he would stay sober through the evening. Rourke had thought his big brother was a fool for not recognizing a vain hope when he saw one, for Mike Rourke had been the kind of cop who could wade into a bar fight with nothing but his fists and an attitude, and yet at the same time he had lived every day of his life scared. Looking back now, Rourke believed that what their daddy hadn't been able to face was the loneliness he carried around in his gut every waking moment. The booze couldn't completely banish the loneliness, but it took the edge off.

It was always worse in the shank of the day, when the night stretched before him, hollow and empty. He would begin with his shaking hands wrapped around a full shot glass, a freshly opened bottle at his elbow, and he would end up with his head on the table, passed out and drooling spit in a puddle beneath his cheek. Yet to everyone's surprise, maybe even his own, Mike Rourke had come sober to the supper table that one evening. He'd even put on his one good civilian suit, the one he wore to all the neighborhood's weddings and baptisms and wakes. He'd gotten a lot of wear out of that suit over the years, the Irish Channel being a place where living came hard and dying came often.

It was an irony most appreciated by those who lived in the Channel that the priest Paulie had chosen to invite to supper at the

Rourke house that evening was a secret boozer himself, was in fact as big an alky as their daddy ever was. Father Josey O'Connor, his name had been, and he'd brought along his own bottle and it wasn't long before the the two of them, priest and cop, were tying on a big one. Their drunk started out happy, took a turn into maudlin, and ended up mean. By one in the morning, they were out in the front yard swinging fists at each other's heads. The neighborhood had gotten a good laugh out of the sight, but Paulie had gone and lay down on his bed with his face to the wall and stayed that way for three days. Running away inside himself.

Rourke looked down now at his brother's bent head, noticing how the once thick brown hair was growing thin on the crown. Yet there was still that familiar crescent pock of a scar on his right temple from where he'd fallen off a pier at the lake one summer. Rourke ached for his brother suddenly, as if the humiliation and disappointment of that long-ago evening were still fresh.

Fio uncrossed his arms and straightened, filling even more of the room. "What family did Father Pat have supper with last night?"

Father Ghilotti's shoulders came up and he rocked forward on the balls of his feet, as if his first thought had been to meet Fio in the middle of the room and have it out with his fists. "The Albert Payne Laytons," he said instead, but with an edge to his voice now. "Mr. Albert is Holy Rosary's financial advisor, and Floriane de Lassus Layton is chairwoman of the board of our Catholic Charities."

Rourke knew of the Laytons. He'd come into contact with the family peripherally while investigating a case last spring, where a young Negro chimney sweep by the name of Titus Dupre had been accused of the rape and murder of a sixteen-year-old white girl and suspected in the disappearance of another. The Laytons' daughter, Della, had been a classmate of the two victims, and Rourke had interviewed her briefly at their school, the St. Francis of Assisi Academy for Girls.

"If he had an appointment after that," the priest was saying, "it would probably be in his book and that's upstairs in his bedroom. I'll get it for you."

"No," Rourke said. "We'll get it."

The bedroom smelled of cigarette smoke.

It was the only vice they were to find among Father Patrick Walsh's few personal things. The bedroom itself was sparsely furnished, with a narrow iron bedstead painted white and a pine chest of drawers with a small matching rolltop desk. An electric fan was the only concession to comfort.

A prie-dieu stood in one corner, with a picture of a bleeding Sacred Heart tacked unframed above it. Rourke saw where the cushion on the prie-dieu had been removed, which would have made kneeling on it uncomfortable, even painful after a time. An act of penance, then, as well as prayer.

On top of the chest of drawers was a faux tortoiseshell-backed brush and comb set, but no matching mirror. No mirror anywhere in the room, Rourke realized. Nothing on the walls at all except for the picture of the Sacred Heart and a wooden crucifix above the bed. Nor were there any framed photographs on the surfaces of the furniture, or remnants of a life before the priesthood.

Rourke peeled back the coverlet on the bed. The sheets were of a rough, fibrous cotton, and the mattress he looked under was little more than a thin pallet lying on top of a thick board.

"He lived like a monk," Rourke said.

"What'd you expect?" Fio said. "A Hollywood boudoir?" He was skimming the titles of the books on the shelf above the desk. He plucked one off and read the spine. "St. Thomas Aquinas." He shook it to see if anything fell out.

"He was a diocesan priest, though," Rourke said. "They take vows of obedience and celibacy, but not poverty. And the Church not only provides room and board, but also a salary. So what did Father Walsh spend his paycheck on?"

Fio slid the book back on the shelf. "Maybe he played the ponies.

Or maybe he's got a woman or a Nancy-boy tucked away somewhere. Wouldn't be the first time."

On the stand by the bed was a Bible, a breviary, and a goose-necked lamp. Its single drawer held a couple of packs of cigarettes, matches, a pencil, and a cheap spiral steno pad in which the dead priest had jotted down fragments of thoughts and ideas for future homilies. Rourke slipped it in his pocket.

The drawers in the chest held nothing but clothes, except for the top one where Rourke found the promised appointment book. It was bound with embossed green leather, its pages edged with gilt—a surprisingly expensive item, given the spartan existence revealed by the rest of the room.

Rourke flipped through it. Father Walsh's days had been full, so full that he'd made sure to schedule in his book an hour at two o'clock every afternoon for prayer. Alphabetized pages in the back of the book were crammed with names and phone numbers and addresses.

Rourke went back to yesterday's date. The last entry, scrawled through the hours of seven to ten in the evening, was simply the name Flo. Not Floriane de Lassus Layton, nor Mrs. Layton, but Flo. Rourke noticed how the entries from that day had been neatly printed, but "Flo" had been written with a flourish, as if the hand that held the pen had been excited, happy. Or maybe, Rourke thought with an inward smile at his own fancifulness, the hand had simply been in a hurry.

The book was too big for his pocket, and so Rourke tucked it into the crook of his arm. "Anything?" he asked Fio, who had been going through the small rolltop desk.

"Just the usual," Fio said. "Receipts, stuff like that. And a lot of letters from people who'd read his book. 'Dear Father Pat, You've changed my life,' and all that baloney."

"Let's bring those, too. Maybe somebody's life didn't get changed for the better."

Leaving Fio to finish up with the desk, Rourke started out the door, but he stopped on the way for a closer look at the crucifix over the bed. The tiny brass nails were driven through the Christ figure's palms, not his wrists.

At the end of the hall a small chapel had been built into a window alcove overlooking the garden. The window was set with beveled glass, and fragile ribbons of early morning sunlight shone through it onto the mahogany altar and bronze crucifix. Rourke looked at the nails.

Through the hands.

He heard a step behind him and he turned. An old man stood in the arched doorway of the chapel, wearing nothing but an old-fashioned pair of long johns. His hair, the color of dirty snow, grew in a circle of wild drifts around his head. His face was thick with sleep.

"You shouldn't be in the chapel," he said. "You get out of here right now."

Father Ghilotti appeared beside the old man to slip an arm around his shoulders. "It's all right, Father," he said, leading the old man away. "Why don't you get dressed and we'll have some breakfast together. I'll fry us up some more lost bread."

Rourke looked out the window, waiting while Father Ghilotti took the old priest back into his bedroom. The garden below was abloom with hibiscus and blue and pink hydrangeas. A plaster statue of the Virgin Mary sat in a niche in a stone wall surrounded by white blossoms of tea olive. A stone bench faced the statue and was shaded by a mimosa tree whose branches swayed in the wind. On the bench sat Rourke's brother, hunched over and with his hands gripping his thighs.

"Please forgive Father Delaney," Holy Rosary's pastor said, appearing back in the arched doorway. "He has these bad turns lately. He's long retired, of course, but he was the pastor here for forty years before me. This is his home and I couldn't bear to send him to another." He genuflected before the altar and then turned to face

Rourke. "Don't you think I deserve to be told how my priest was murdered."

"I haven't said he was murdered."

"Don't be coy, Detective. He wouldn't have died a natural death in a macaroni factory in the Quarter at two in the morning."

"The coroner wasn't sure about the exact cause of death. He's doing a postmortem."

A strange smile—one that Rourke couldn't read—pulled at Father Ghilotti's small mouth. "It's your roll, Detective, so I guess all I can do at the moment is sit back and wait for you to crap out . . . I see you've found Father Pat's appointment book without any trouble. It was a Christmas gift from me to him, the book. He rarely spent any money on himself, but then he grew up poor and he never seemed to pine for the finer things."

"And what do you pine for, Father?"

"Just what you would expect, of course," he said, the irony deliberate and thick now in his voice. "Wine, women, and song."

He put his hand in the pocket of his cassock and pulled out a rosary. He stared down at it, watching his own fingers rub the ebony beads. "I might as well tell you then, since you'll learn of it soon enough. Father Pat and I had quite a noisy disagreement yesterday afternoon."

"How noisy?"

Again that strange smile. "Holy water doesn't flow in our veins, you know. There was some shouting. Some name calling. A rectory is like a family and all families have their spats."

"In my family, when there was a spat, somebody usually got the crap beat out of him."

The priest's hand closed hard around the rosary's crucifix and his head snapped up. "Was Father Pat beaten?"

"What was your disagreement about?"

A few seconds of silence ticked by before he answered. "As a preacher, Father Pat had a style that was . . . unorthodox. It's hard to describe if you haven't heard it. It was joyful, exuberant, and loud.

Really loud. It wasn't exactly like a holy roller prayer meeting, but it was close."

"So what if he had 'em shouting hallelujahs, as long as he was packing them in? And filling up the collection basket."

"Yeah, well, there was that. He probably got twice as many worshippers at his Masses as the rest of us did put together. But lately some of the stuff he was saying in his homilies was flat-out contrary to the teachings of the Catholic faith, and so I forbade him to preach. I told him he could celebrate the Mass for the sisters in the convent, but no longer for the laity. And no more preaching. I told him a priest calls people to holiness and challenges them to a better life, but he does not make the Church about himself. Father Pat took offense and we ended up hollering at each other like a couple of guys at a boxing match."

"Do you think someone hated this style of his enough to kill him for it?"

The pastor blew out a hard breath, as if he'd just been punched. "Oh, God. I would have said until this moment that everybody loved Father Pat. And he was especially beloved in the eyes of our Lord, I do truly believe. Beloved and chosen." He turned his head and his gaze lifted to the bronze crucifix above the altar, and Rourke thought he saw a painful light like a burning match in his eyes. Or it could have simply been sunlight from the window glancing off his thick glasses.

"When I was a kid," Father Ghilotti said, "I had a favorite uncle who was also my *parrain.* He stood up for me at my baptism. He gave me expensive toys on my birthday and took me places, just the two of us together, like to West Park and the zoo. On the day of my confirmation, when I was twelve, my family had a big celebration and as my godfather he was there, of course. After the party was over, he left in a car with a couple of my old man's goons and he was never seen or heard from again."

He stopped, closing his eyes, and he might have been praying, or he might only have been remembering. "I saw them looking at each other," he went on, and his voice had taken on a street flatness. "My *parrain* and my daddy, before he got in the car. He knew what they were going to do to him and he knew why. They were brothers, but it was business."

He looked down and saw that he still had the rosary in his fist and he thrust it back into his pocket. "Nobody's safe," he said. "Not even a beloved priest."

"Did you kill him?"

The face he showed Rourke was both tough and open. "No, I didn't kill him. When I took my vows, I stopped being my daddy's son."

Rourke looked back out the window, where his brother still sat on the stone bench, curled in upon himself as if waiting for a reckoning that was sure to come, and sure to hurt.

It isn't true, Rourke thought. We are always and forever our father's sons.

The old priest, Father Delaney, was sitting at the kitchen table cradling a cup of coffee, a cigarette burning between yellowed, palsied fingers. He looked up as Rourke passed through on his way to the garden.

"You are the new assistant pastor," the old man said. "Father Paul, is it?"

Rourke paused, his hand on the doorknob and turned back. Father Delaney tugged at that place in Rourke that wanted to save the world from all pain and folly. He couldn't imagine a worse horror than to grow old and go on living while your mind broke off of you in pieces and melted away.

"No, Father," Rourke said. "Paul is my brother."

The old man's watery blue eyes, vague and trembling, creased with his smile. "Two priests in one family. Your mother must be proud."

"No, I'm not . . . Yes," Rourke said, smiling back at him. "She's proud." He'd never thought of himself as being like Paulie, not in looks nor in any other way that mattered. He wondered what connection this old priest, in his dementia, was seeing.

The old priest pointed his cigarette at the appointment book in Rourke's hand. "So now you've come for it, then. Because Father Pat is dead."

"Yes. I'm sorry."

"He was a good man, and he was particularly blessed, but he was . . ." His voice trailed off and he looked down at the coffee and the cigarette as if he suddenly couldn't remember how he'd acquired them.

"What was Father Pat?" Rourke prompted. He wasn't really expecting a coherent answer, but the gaze the old priest turned back up at him had cleared some.

"Lonely," he said, in a voice that was stronger as well. "Oh, we're all lonely in a way, because our hearts are restless until they rest in peace with God. But this priest, he had a loneliness of the soul."

Rourke followed a flagstone path and the smell of the tea olive to the stone bench where his brother sat. The morning sun was almost full up now and so bright it struck his eyes like shards of a broken mirror, making them shudder.

Paulie looked up at him with eyes that were swollen and red, then looked away. Rourke sat next to him, saying nothing. The plaster Virgin was wearing a blue robe and she had her hands pressed together palm to palm and tucked beneath her chin. She had a sweet look on her face. Rourke could imagine praying to her and the thought disturbed him. It had been a long time since he'd been on speaking terms with the icons of his faith.

He studied his brother's averted face a moment, then leaned over, bracing his forearms on his spread knees. "Paulie—"

"So how was the party of the century?"

It was the last question he would ever have expected to hear coming out of his brother's mouth. The movie studio's big to-do had been in all the papers, true enough, but he wouldn't have thought his brother would be one to follow the high and low drama of the city's flapper set.

"Why, Father, it was all the excitement you could ask for," Rourke said, drawling the words a little. "The booze was bountiful, the band was jazzy, and the mamas were hot."

Paulie's eyes squinted half closed and one corner of his mouth deepened into a dimple—his version of a smile.

"What?" Rourke said, when his brother went on smiling and saying nothing.

"I was just wondering what it's like to make love with a sex goddess. I'm not asking for particulars, mind you," he added quickly. "But apparently even the presence of the Virgin doesn't keep me from wondering."

A laugh sprang from Rourke's chest, taking away with it some of the ache. "Jesus," he said, shaking his head.

Paulie reached down and took Rourke's hand by the wrist, turning it over. An angry red burn marked his palm. "And what was that all about? Still shaking your fist in the face of God?"

Rourke pulled his hand free of his brother's grasp, curling his fingers over the burn. He saw where blood stained his cuff and yet he couldn't remember getting close enough to the body to have brushed against it. "I used to know a woman who hooked in a hot pillow joint," he said. "She had this philosophy that the good Lord got bored on the seventh day and that's why He created sin."

Paulie shook his head. "There wasn't any prostitute who said any such thing. I remember you trying out that blasphemous theory on Sister Mary Joseph in fourth grade. You got sent home, which was why you did it in the first place. There was some exhibition baseball game that day, out at City Park, and it spared you from having to suffer the consequences of playing hooky."

"Hey, now, I suffered. She must've whacked me a good half dozen times on my hand with her ruler and she had a swing Babe Ruth himself could admire."

Paulie smiled again, then the smile dissolved into a wincing twist of his mouth. "It was terrible, wasn't it? How Father Pat died. I can tell by your face."

"Yes."

Paulie's head fell back and he stared unseeing through the branches of the mimosa tree. White clouds tumbling across a sky the smoky blue of oyster shells. "God help me, Day. Why did I become a priest when I can't—"

He cut himself off, pressing his lips together tightly in that way he'd always done whenever he was facing something distasteful, as if the taste of it was in his mouth. "I was jealous of him, of Father Pat, only not for any reasons you're thinking. It's possible he might have been a saint, a real saint, only I would never want such a burden for myself, because sainthood is an awful burden—don't you think it's not. And I didn't mind either that he was everybody's favorite priest. Even Father Frank's and the archbishop's, in spite of all the trouble he was always getting into for disobedience, but I didn't care about that because he was my favorite, too . . ."

The tears were running freely down Paulie's face again, and Rourke couldn't help feeling a tinge of shame for his brother's sake. A legacy from their daddy, he supposed, who when they were boys had always laughed at them and called them sissies whenever they cried.

"Only I think I hated him sometimes, Day," Paulie was saying. "I was just so jealous of him. Jealous of his being so in love with God and with His world, and for always being so darn *certain.* Certain of what it meant to be a priest, of getting it right, when I can't even . . ."

He clasped his hands together and his head fell forward in such a way that Rourke thought he was praying until he began to talk to the ground between his spread feet. "The first time I was called upon to administer the last rites, a ten-year-old boy had pointed a shotgun at his daddy's face and pulled the trigger. Someone had covered the man with a sheet and I lifted it to anoint his forehead with the holy oil and there was no forehead there to anoint. There was no head at all, and that was when I knew I was always going to make a lousy priest. I couldn't forgive that boy for doing that to his own flesh and blood, and I couldn't forgive the father for what he must have been doing to that boy, and I couldn't forgive God for allowing any of it to happen."

He looked up at Rourke again, and his soul's pain showed on his face. "A priest is supposed to be God's instrument of forgiveness, but I can't forgive, Day. I can't forgive."

Rourke wanted to say something to make it right, but there were no words. His brother carried a grief against himself for what had been done to them when they were kids. Rourke knew it, for he shared it. Only for Paulie the grief had driven him into a life of celibacy and obedience and prayer, a life that had welcomed him, perhaps, but not saved him. For Rourke, whenever the craziness took hold of him, he had gone looking for those sweet, seductive paths of self-destruction. And sometimes—most of the time—he found them.

"Tell me what happened with you last night, Paulie."

His brother was holding himself stiff now, as if he feared that he would fly into pieces. "I'm not going to tell you that priests don't commit sins," he said. "Even the sin of murder. But no one at this rectory would ever have hurt Father Pat. We loved him."

Rourke said nothing.

Paulie pressed his lips so tightly together that a muscle spasmed in his cheek. "I'm your brother," he said.

"Tell me where you were last night."

The taut silence stretched on between them, until it was filled with the chatter of the mockingbirds and, out on the street, the roar of a car with a hole in its muffler.

"I can't," his brother finally said, so softly Rourke barely heard him.

"I'll find it out. Eventually."

"God," Paulie said with a torn laugh. "Do you have any idea what you look like when you smile like that? You'd *scare* the truth out of a body if there was any truth to be had."

"I've always been able to scare you, Paulie. After a while it got to where it wasn't even fun anymore."

"And you always have to win. Every game we ever played, you always won."

Rourke searched his brother's face a moment longer and then he looked away, and the other man breathed a sigh as if he'd been given a reprieve. They sat together for a small while in silence, both lost in memories that were oddly comforting in spite of all their pain, perhaps because they were shared.

"Remember," Paulie finally said, "how our daddy used to always say, 'This is such a sad and sinful world'?"

"Yeah. And he sure enough contributed his share of both sadness and sin."

"Did . . ." The word caught in his throat as if he'd swallowed a large bubble of air. "Did you hate him?"

"Sometimes."

Rourke waited for the rest of it, waited for his brother to ask if he forgave their father. And their mother. Paulie had never even been able to speak aloud about their mother and what her leaving had done to them.

Rourke wasn't sure what his answer would be and it didn't matter anyway, because his brother didn't ask.

Father Paul Rourke watched his brother walk away with that hard, confident way of his. It had never struck him before this moment how much Day had grown up to be the image of their daddy. The sun-tipped hair, the startling dark blue eyes, the wide mouth with its promise of cruelty. Tall and lean, but not thin, with a boxer's shoulders and a boxer's way of carrying himself, on the balls of his feet, as if spoiling for a fight.

Always so sure of himself. Always so tough.

Mike Rourke had tried to raise both his sons to be tough, and then he'd worked hard at showing them that no matter how tough they ever got their old man would always be tougher. The toughest Rourke of them all. He had made his point easily with Paulie, who had always felt powerless before his father. Day, though, just wouldn't stay down. No matter how hard or often he was hit, he kept getting up and coming back for more.

Only two years separated them, but Paul Rourke had never understood his little brother, never known where Day got his snarling courage, although he'd always felt that one of life's great mysteries would be solved if he could. All those shared hours of their boyhood, they had fought and dreamed and sinned together, and he had never really *known* his brother.

But then, how well can you ever really know someone? he wondered now. How much can you ever know of that place deep inside a man's guts where he lives? Certainly, Paulie thought, he had never really known himself.

Above the door to the seminary that he had run away to as a boy were inscribed the words of Jesus Christ: *Anyone who does not take up his cross and follow me cannot be my disciple.* When he walked through that door he had thought he could lose all memory of where he had come from, and he had truly believed that all he had to do was take up the cross and joy would come. Only he had been wrong. He loved the Church, with all its holy mysteries and ceremonies, but he hadn't forgotten and the joy hadn't come, and he had hidden this shameful lack from himself and from the world like a sin concealed in the confessional.

And now, because of what had happened, because of what he had done, what he was *doing,* his sin would be found out.

He had heard the slam of the kitchen's screen door and footsteps on the flagstone path, and still he jumped when his pastor laid a heavy hand on his shoulder.

"What are we going to do now, Paul?" Father Ghilotti said.

Paulie wanted to laugh, but he was afraid that if he unclenched his throat he'd start to bawl like a child. "Pray?" he finally said, his voice breaking on the word.

"We're going to have those detectives snooping around us for a while, and we know what-all they could find. If something isn't done."

Paulie shook his head, and this time he did laugh, although it was more of a gasping noise. "What *something* are you suggesting that we do, Father? One thing you ought to know about my little brother—our daddy used to beat on him with a bicycle chain and he could never break him. Day won't back down before anyone or anything."

Father Ghilotti's words were nearly overcome by the rush of the wind through the mimosa branches above their heads. "We've got to trust, then," he said, "that God will give us the grace for every possible circumstance. Foreseen or unforeseen."

"With God's grace," Paulie repeated obediently, but he didn't believe it. There would be no grace, no expiation for him now. No forgiveness.

CHAPTER SEVEN

The crack of billiard balls and the strum of a banjo leaked out the rotting shutters of the speakeasy on the corner as Daman Rourke passed by on his way home from the garage where he parked the Bearcat. He lived in a Creole cottage on Conti Street in the Faubourg Tremé, an old New Orleans neighborhood where white plantation owners had once kept their colored mistresses.

This early in the morning the street was cool beneath the scrolled iron colonnade, and the wet sheets hanging over the iron balcony of the brothel next door flapped in the wind. As Rourke walked along the brick banquette, he thought about his brother . . . His brother, who seemed more than happy to break bread with the families of his church, had never accepted any of Rourke's supper invitations.

Paulie had refused even to set a foot inside the cottage because it was the place where their mother had come to live after she had deserted them. Where she had come to live in sin for thirty years with her married lover. Their mother was gone now and the cottage was Rourke's, and he supposed that meant he must have found a way to forgive her. Not that she'd ever asked for his forgiveness. In one of the last conversations they'd had together, she told him she regretted nothing.

The colored woman who lived across the street and dabbled in voodoo was scrubbing down her front stoop with powdered brick and water. "You goin' to spend all night long at the *bourré* tables, you," she called out to Rourke, "you better be buyin' some of my good-luck *gris-gris.*"

"How do you know I didn't pass the night with a lady?" Rourke called back.

"I got somethin' for that, too. Make that bone o' yours stand up tall and salute the flag."

Rourke laughed and blew her a kiss as he pushed open the cottage's lacy iron gate. He walked down a domed brick carriageway and entered into the courtyard, where Remy Lelourie was showing a little girl in a blue jumper and a Pelicans baseball hat how to make a yo-yo walk the dog.

Rourke paused within the purple shadows of a bougainvillea vine to watch. Sunshine splashed yellow puddles on the cobblestones around them, and their laughter made melody with the rattle of the banana leaves and the water ringing in the iron fountain.

The little girl saw him first. Her full mouth burst open wide, and her smile, as it blew through his chest, was devastating.

"Daddy!"

She ran at him full tilt and he scooped her up into his arms, hugging his daughter, Katie. Hugging her tight. She smelled sweet, like crushed strawberries.

Remy Lelourie came, too, more slowly. She looked bright as a sunrise, in an orange and red patterned pullover and something that looked like men's trousers. Only they'd been cut to cup her slender hips and bottom like a man's hands, and they were sexy as hell.

"Hey," he said.

She lifted her chin and tilted her head to the side in that way she had. A red beret was perched on her shingled hair at a rakish slant. "Hey, yourself," she said.

Katie twisted around in his arms. "I told you, Miss Remy. I told you he would be coming home soon."

"Why, so you did, honey," Remy said, drawling the words, having fun. "And now here he is, just like you said, and grinning like a possum eating a yellow jacket."

Rourke laughed. As he set Katie back on her feet, he knocked off the grimy Pels cap that she wore everywhere, including to bed. He caught it before it hit the ground and he went to put it back on her head, and that was when he saw that her braids—her beautiful thick brown braids that hung all the way to her waist—were gone.

"Jesus. What happened to your hair?"

She laughed, a little girl laugh full of ruffles and bows. "I bobbed it. Just like Miss Remy's."

"She bobbed it," Remy said, laughter in her eyes. "All by herself."

It looked as though his child had taken a pair of sheep shears to her head. God, he could see the pink of her scalp in places. *It'll grow back,* he told himself. He wanted to weep.

"Don't you like it, Daddy? I think it looks spiffy."

He bent over and kissed the top of his daughter's ravaged head. "It's the bee's elbows," he said.

Laughing, she punched his belly lightly with her fist. She loved the slang she picked up on the radio and she used it whenever she could. "You're being goofy. And you're getting it all wrong. It's the bee's *knees.*"

"You're sure it's not the monkey's banana?"

She punched him again, harder this time. "Mrs. O'Reilly says it's a good thing I got a hat." She threw a scowl in the direction of the kitchen, where the latest nanny was bustling about behind the green jalousied windows. "I don't like Mrs. O'Reilly."

Rourke could have predicted this was coming. Mrs. O'Reilly was a forty-year-old widow from County Kerry with a way about her that was as soft as an Irish morning, and so he'd had high hopes for her when he'd hired her only three days ago. Lately, though, his daughter had been going through nannies so fast the sheets on their bed didn't get changed before they were gone. Katie, who had been waging campaigns of annihilation against these women, had proven herself to be a real little Napoleon.

He had an uncomfortable idea why she was doing it. He had no idea what to do about it. Katie's mother, his wife, had died six years ago, only a year after Katie was born, and most days it seemed to Rourke that being a father was the most terrifying challenge he'd ever faced in his life.

Katie had taken his hand and was trying to pull him toward the bench by the fountain where there lay a box kite patterned in the Stars and Stripes. "Let's go now, Daddy, before all the wind goes away."

"Katie." He gripped her shoulders and turned her around, then squatted down in front of her so he could look her in the eye. They'd made plans to fly her new kite in Congo Square this morning and now he was going to have to disappoint her. Again. "I can't do it today, after all, baby. I caught a big case last night, and I'm probably going to be working on it all this weekend."

Her lower lip trembled and she pulled away from him.

"Katie, how would you like to be my guest on the set of *Cutlass* later on this mornin'?" Remy said, taking her hand. "We're going to be shooting the big sword fight."

Katie jerked her hand free and crossed her arms over her chest. "No. I'm flying a kite with my daddy."

Rourke brushed her cheek with the back of his hand. "We'll do it another Saturday soon, I—" *Promise.* He caught back the word before it could come tripping so lightly out of his mouth. Katie had a tendency to keep a strict accounting of his promises, and so far he was deeply in the red.

"Tell you what, though," he said instead. "I can't catch any bad guys on an empty stomach. What do you say we go get us some waffles from Buglin' Sam?"

He smiled and hoped she'd send a Katie-smile back at him, but it didn't come.

Buglin' Sam put his regulation Army bugle to his lips and blasted the brassy notes of reveille out over Jackson Square. Katie, laughing with delight, ran up to the horse-drawn wagon and by the time Rourke and Remy got there she already had her face buried in a sugarcoated hot waffle.

Buglin' Sam, the waffle man, had parked his wagon across from St. Louis Cathedral, alongside the iron fence that surrounded the square, in order to entice the worshippers on their way home from Mass into breaking their fast with his delectables. He had some competition, though, for the air was rich with tempting smells: of coffee, bread, and strawberries from the nearby French Market stalls, of *boudin* and cheese from the Central Grocery. Right next to Buglin' Sam himself, a woman in a red turban was frying oysters, ham, and eggs over a fire in an oil drum.

Rourke bought more waffles for him and Remy. They strolled slowly hand in hand, looking at the watercolors and charcoal sketches that hung on the fence near Buglin' Sam's wagon, put there by aspiring artists. This early on a Saturday morning only a few people were about, but they all had noticed the movie star in their midst and they were staring and pointing and whispering. Rourke hated this about their lives together, but he didn't see how there was ever going to be an end to it.

He didn't know what had brought her to his house this morning, and he didn't ask. Her hand felt so fine in his. No, more than fine. This is ecstasy, he thought. The grown-up version, where contentment and tenderness are mixed with a sadness that comes from knowing that the good moments, the sweet moments, can't be held on to forever, but only felt brushing by.

"After you catch the bad guys, Daddy," Katie said, touching his other hand with sticky fingers, "will you roast them alive?"

Startled, Rourke looked down into his little girl's face, with her sugar-rimmed mouth and the bill of her Pels cap shading her eyes. Her mother's eyes, grayish green with golden lights and as changeable as the lake on a cloudy day.

"Katie, where . . ." He knew where, though. Not even twenty feet away from them stood a news kiosk with a blown-up poster of the

Morning Tribune's front page—the banner headline, ROASTED ALIVE IN A CHAIR OF DEATH, above a composograph of a Negro boy's head on the body of a man in the electric chair. The head belonged to the chimney sweep Titus Dupre, and tonight, at the stroke of midnight in the New Orleans Parish Prison, he was going to be executed for the raping and killing of Nina Duboche. For killing two girls, or so the world believed, although he'd been tried and convicted for only the one because the other girl's body had never been found.

All executions were performed in the parish where the prisoner was convicted, and so sometime this morning a portable electric chair would be arriving by truck, along with the generator needed to power it. Normally, Louisiana's condemned men met the state's executioner at the gallows, but proponents of the chair, arguing that hangings were gruesome and archaic, had convinced the legislature to give the newfangled machinery a test run on seventeen-year-old Titus Dupre.

At a loss for what to say to his daughter, Rourke looked over at Remy for help, but her attention had been caught by a Negro spasm band that was dancing for pennies beneath one of the stucco arches of the French Market, making music with a washboard and pot covers.

Katie, her question already forgotten anyway, was showing Buglin' Sam how she could make her yo-yo go 'round the world, and so he was spared for the moment having to explain to his seven-year-old daughter why the state of Louisiana was going to strap a boy into an oak chair and shoot two thousand volts of electricity through his body.

Rourke's own gaze went back to the spasm band. The dancing boys' shoes blurred over the banquette, the bottle caps on their soles striking sparks off the bricks. Behind them, a butcher under the eaves of the French Market was hacking at a bloody side of beef.

Sweet Jesus, he'd been hanging from a crossbeam, nailed through the wrists like an animal carcass. A priest. And where had God been when that was being done to him? Where was God?

Rourke pulled in a deep breath then let it out slowly, feeling tired. Katie was now feeding bits of waffle to the pigeons, and he called out to her, telling her it was time to head home.

"Wait, Day. Before we go . . ."

The intensity in Remy's voice raised the hairs on the back of his neck, even before she handed him the envelope. Her name was written on the outside of it, in a flowery script, but there was no address or stamp. It had been opened, and inside was a single sheet of paper.

"What's this?" he said.

"I found it on my dressing table last night," she said. "Or rather, early this mornin'. He must have gone into my bedroom during the party. And then, after everyone had left, he rang me on the telephone and said, 'Did you get my letter, Remy?'"

Rourke unfolded the paper and read the single, finely calligraphed line: *Are you scared yet, Remy?* And the signature, its letters larger, bolder.

"Who's Romeo?"

"That's just it, Day—I don't know. I've never heard of the name outside of the play, and that's one of the few Shakespeares I've never done. The closest I've ever come to it was an audition years and years ago, back when I was trying to break into the stage in New York. But I didn't even get a callback."

"You didn't recognize his voice?"

She shook her head. "No . . . Maybe. It was muffled, like he was speaking through cotton, but there was something in the way he said my name . . . I don't know. It's mostly just a feeling."

Rourke tilted the paper up to the sunlight. It had a watermark, which might make it traceable, and the ink was strange.

"Whoever he is, I think it's a game he wants me to play," she said.

He thought he'd heard the whip of excitement in her voice, and that scared the hell out of him. In some ways he knew Remy Lelourie better than he knew himself. Together they had once played

Russian roulette with a loaded revolver; they'd once tried to outrun a train. Neither one of them had ever met a dare they didn't take.

"Don't play it, Remy."

She laughed, the bright, brittle flapper-girl laugh that he didn't always like. "And this advice is coming from the man who almost drove into a tree last night? I thought Hollywood was a thrill a day with its champagne baths and tango dancing and petting parties in the purple dawn, but they got nothing on New Orleans. I come home and the first thing that happens is I get thrown in jail for murdering my husband, and now someone might have it in his mind to murder me."

"Dammit, Remy," he said, lowering his voice because Katie was coming toward them now, trailing pigeons and crumbs. He tucked the letter and envelope into his coat pocket. "What this guy is after is your attention, so don't give it to him. Let me take care of it."

His last words had sounded idiotic to his own ears: *Let me take care of it.* Daman Rourke, champion cop. Remy Lelourie had spent the whole of her life taking very good care of herself and with a frightening ruthlessness; she'd never once looked for help from any man, nor needed it. He expected her to jump on him now for implying otherwise, but instead she only smiled.

He stared at her, at the face that was so otherworldly beautiful it hurt sometimes to look at it. Like staring directly into the sun.

She must have thought he was about to tell her something she didn't want to hear, because suddenly she covered his mouth with her hand to stop the words.

"I love you, though," she said.

Though? I love you, *though.* Jesus. What in hell was that supposed to mean?

He took her wrist and held her fingers to his lips and kissed them, and then he let her go. Her hand curled around the kiss he had given her, and then she looked away and up, to the twin spires of the cathedral shining sequin bright in the sun, and she did a strange thing. Slowly, she lifted her hand into the air and uncurled her fingers, as if she was setting free a handful of butterflies.

In that instant, the cathedral clock began to chime and the flock of birds around Katie rose up in a great flap of wings, blocking out the sun.

Rourke's eyes ached from a night of no sleep, and even though he'd showered and shaved and changed out of his tuxedo and into a cream linen suit, he still felt grimy. The last few days had been cool for so early in October, but the sun seemed to be outpacing the wind now and the morning was turning hot. Beneath his coat, his shirt was already sticking to his back.

His aggravation wasn't helped by the fact that he couldn't seem to get near his office because of the mob scene at the Criminal Courts Building and the adjoining Parish Prison. Most of the noisy, rambunctious crowd was probably there out of curiosity, to see the novelty of the chair of death arriving at the prison, but an angry element was fermenting right in front of the Tulane Street entrance to the Courts Building, which housed, besides the courts, the city's police headquarters and the detectives' squad room where Rourke worked.

Rourke found a parking place on Canal Street, across from the new Saenger Theatre, and as he got out of the car a scrawny kid with freckles and elephant ears who sold newspapers on the corner came running up to him. "Watch your car for a dollar, Lieutenant," the kid said. He was in love with the 'Cat.

"Sure," Rourke said. "Only watch it from the outside. The last time you got something sticky all over the steering wheel."

Rourke gave the kid four bits and started to walk away, but then he stopped and looked up at the enormous billboard on the roof. It took twenty-four sheets to cover the board and at night a powerful searchlight threw on it the illumination of "a hundred suns," so that it could be seen from practically every downtown street corner.

Remy Lelourie larger than life.

He was losing her, he could feel it. Once they were done filming

Cutlass, she would go back to Hollywood and to her life of champagne baths and tango dancing and petting parties in the purple dawn. And if she left him this time the way she did the last time, then it would be without so much as a so-long, darlin'.

With its rusty brick and sandstone towers and turrets, the Criminal Courts Building looked like a medieval castle and this morning it was under siege. Many of the men in the mob out front sported white, caped robes with black crosses on their breasts. Their conical hats bobbed in time with their chants and the beat of a drum. The placards they thrust into the air read "Burn, nigger, burn" and other, worse, epithets.

The Ku Klux Klan was back, and with a vengeance.

The triple-arched entrance was blocked by sawhorse barricades and ringed by a handful of nervous foot cops in wet, clinging blouses. A thick-necked, buck-toothed man wearing yellow linen shoes and purple suspenders over a yellow shirt was thumbtacking to the sawhorses crude posters of a black man hanging from a tree. None of the cops was bothering to stop him.

Some of the Klan boys were engaging in ugly name calling with a woman sporting a white Humanitarian Cult sash across her chest. She was trying to distribute her abolition of capital punishment literature, and while no one was willing to take her leaflets, she was giving back with a smart mouth as good as she got.

Rourke had pushed his way through the crowd to the barricades, when he saw someone out of the corner of his eye—a tall, gangly Negro boy with long matted locks of hair, who was dressed in the top hat and black frock coat of the chimney sweep. Cornelius Dupre, Titus's younger brother.

Forty percent of the city had colored skin, but Cornelius Dupre seemed to be the only one of them in this crowd, and Rourke didn't think he'd come for an up-close look at the electric chair that was going to kill his brother. Their gazes connected, Rourke's and the boy's, and the look Cornelius Dupre gave him was flat and hard with hate.

Rourke was about to go have a word with him, but just then the Humanitarian Cult woman made the mistake of pulling one of the lynching posters off a sawhorse, and the buck-toothed man in the yellow shirt and purple suspenders turned on her with a growl. One of the foot cops grabbed the man's arm, but he threw the cop off him. The cop staggered backward into Rourke, and he would have fallen on his butt if Rourke hadn't caught him.

"Hit him with your stick," Rourke said, pushing the cop back onto his feet.

The young cop looked around, his eyes bewildered and scared. "What?"

By now the woman had dropped the poster, but the buck-toothed man still came at her. Rourke could feel the raw energy of the crowd around them, mostly Klan men, ratcheting up and turning ugly. The buck-toothed man snatched the woman's leaflets out of her hands and began to rip them up. Spit sprayed from his mouth as he screamed at her, something unintelligible except for the words "nigger-loving bitch." The woman spat back, a big globule that landed smack in the man's eye, as she tried to wrestle her leaflets away from him. The man roared, dropped the leaflets in the gutter, and cocked his fist.

Before he could let fly with a punch to the woman's face, Rourke had taken the cop's nightstick out of his belt and clipped the buck-toothed man behind the ear, stunning him just hard enough to send him to his knees.

"You get up," Rourke said, "and I'll hit you again. Only this time you won't be seeing straight for a week."

One of the Klan men took a threatening step toward Rourke, met the promise of violence in his eyes, thought better of it, and turned away. Rourke stared down the other Klan men until their gazes dropped and they began to shuffle away from the woman, who was on her hands and knees in the street calmly gathering up what was left of her anti-capital punishment leaflets.

Rourke handed the stick back to the foot cop. "Anybody causes any more trouble, you arrest his ass for assault, inciting a riot, resisting arrest, and anything else you can think of."

The young cop's eyes widened even more and he wiped his mouth with a shaking hand before he took back his stick. Rourke looked around for Cornelius Dupre, but the boy was gone.

As Rourke passed between the sawhorse barricades and climbed the shallow steps of the Courts Building, he looked up and saw that Fiorello Prankowski waited for him at the door, wearing his long-suffering look.

"Man," Fio said. "It's gonna be a long, ugly day."

In the squad room Detective Nate Carroll was regaling his fellow cops with a description of his own exciting night.

"Now I'm looking at this guy and he's sitting at the kitchen table with a knife stuck in his head the size of an elephant's dick, and I hear a noise behind me. So I turn around and there's the dead guy's wife and she's got a very big fucking ax in her hands and she's got murder in her eyes . . ."

He paused, letting his tale dangle and waiting for a straight man to feed him a line.

The desk sergeant, grinning around the tobacco chaw he had stuffed in his cheek, obliged. "So you sweet-talked her into putting down the ax, and now the mayor's gonna give you a medal."

Nate Carroll's cherub face was set serious and his bright red curls bounced as he shook his head. "Hell, no. I got my ass outta there fast and called the cops."

The desk sergeant shot a stream of brown spittle into the coffee can next to his desk before he laughed. He saw Detectives Rourke and Prankowski and he stopped them on the way to their desks. "The Ghoul wants to see y'all before he does the cut on your crucifixion killing. He's got a bee up his ass about it, too. Been calling up here every five minutes."

The stench of the coroner's laboratory hit Rourke in the face like a slap, making his eyes water and his nose burn. The Ghoul stood in floating layers of cigarette smoke, pinning the photographs of the crime scene to a large corkboard that nearly covered one of the puke-yellow walls.

"Ah, yes, Detectives," he said as the two cops entered through an iron-banded door that could have come from a dungeon. "Thank you for coming." He waved his hand at a steel dissecting table upon which lay the remains of Father Patrick Walsh. A stained sheet covered the body, except for the head. "You must have another look at the *corpus delicti.*"

The two detectives followed the coroner as he made his lumbering way to the table. The tile floor had recently been hosed down, but no amount of soap and water, Rourke thought, would ever be able to scrub the blood and body fluid stains out of the grout.

The Ghoul reached for the sheet and began to pull it back, and Rourke shoved his hands deep in his pockets and set his jaw. He really hated looking at dead bodies, especially dead bodies on slabs in the morgue.

The sheet was off and Rourke looked down at the naked white corpse. "Sweet Jesus," he said.

"Whoa, Nellie," said Fio.

"Indeed," said the Ghoul. "Your murdered priest is a woman."

CHAPTER EIGHT

Father Patrick Walsh had been tall and raw-boned for a woman, with wide shoulders, narrow hips, and small breasts. She'd had a plain face, its features arranged in square, blunted angles. Her hair, the color of dead leaves, had been barbered close to her bony skull. Rourke could just about see how she'd gotten away with the deception, as long as she was careful never to allow anyone to see her naked.

"She had small breasts as you can see," the Ghoul said, "but she'd also flattened them by wrapping an athletic bandage around her chest. She had on a man's undershirt and drawers beneath the priest's cassock. The drawers were undisturbed."

"Then she wasn't raped before the killing?" Rourke said, following the coroner's train of thought.

"I've found no evidence of it, neither rape nor consensual sexual intercourse. She had been about to start her menstrual flow, though. She was a fully developed and normal woman. Physically, that is. With an apparently functional uterus and ovaries."

Rourke looked at the juncture of her legs, at the sparse pubic hair covering what was definitely a vulva. Thin, shiny white lines veined her flat belly. "It looks like she might've had a baby at some time."

"Ah, yes, indeed," the Ghoul said. "Her perineum is scarred from a birth tearing, but it was not a recent occurrence." The coroner always became engaged by his cases, but Rourke had never seen him so excited. His bulk rolled like sea swells as he rocked back and forth on his toes. "I would estimate her age to be early forties. If she had the child in her youth, he could be a grown man by now. Or grown woman, of course."

Fio rubbed a big hand over his face. "Aw, jeez. This is bad. This is worse than a political hot potato, this is a friggin' . . . I don't know what. Bad."

"Oh, I love this. I just abso-lootin'-tutely love this."

Captain Dan Malone rested his elbows on his gray metal desk and thrust his fingers through his rumpled sandy-blond hair. He was an amicable man with Southern-gentleman good manners and a high tolerance for aggravation. None of his men had ever known him to use a foul word, not even in a squad room full of cops who couldn't make it to the end of a sentence without one.

Still, even the most easygoing of men had their limits and Malone looked as though he was about to reach his. "This crucifixion killing—a priest, heaven help us all—has already caused a real rumpus among the powers that must be obeyed. The wires between here and City Hall have been buzzing all morning, and now you tell me he is a she. Lord love a duck."

He dropped his hands and raised his head to glare at his two detectives, as if they—by bringing him the news—were now responsible for all its repercussions.

Rourke slouched on his tailbone in the visitor's chair. Fio stood with his shoulders pressed into the door jamb, his arms crossed in front of his chest. They were inside Malone's office with the door shut and the Venetian blinds closed on the window that looked out on the squad room. The blinds were up, though, on the open window that overlooked the street below. They could hear hoots and jeers from the crowd and a lone voice with a bullhorn calling for a prayer.

"You sure y'all saw it right?" Malone said.

Rourke and Fio both gave him a wounded look.

"Okay, okay. So who knows about it? Tell me the whole world doesn't know about it."

"Just we three in here, boss. And the Ghoul," Rourke said. "And maybe whoever killed him."

"Her," Fio said.

"He spent over half his life being Father Patrick Walsh," Rourke said. "I would think that's how he'd want us to think of him."

Fio tilted his head back and rubbed his hand over his face again. "This is nuts."

Malone pointed a finger at Rourke since he was closest. "And that reminds me. The archbishop was all over my caboose earlier this morning because y'all went and rousted the good fathers of Our Lady of the Holy Rosary like they were goons. And the sun was barely even up."

"That was Fio," Rourke said. "I was nice."

Fio gave him an up-yours look, then grinned.

Malone pulled a battered cigarette out of his shirt pocket so that he could think. He hadn't smoked in fifteen years but every day he hand-rolled himself a few fresh ones to play with. He claimed the smell of the tobacco stimulated his brain cells. "Tell me what y'all got so far," he said.

Rourke told him about Carlos Kelly and Tony the Rat and his goon, Guido the Rat, and the shot and scream, and the bats, and Father Pat's dying plea for mercy. "We think the killer might've once had a job at the factory," he said. "So I got someone working on getting the payroll lists."

"And we already checked the incident reports for shots fired in the area," Fio added. "It turns out a sister shot at her pimp. Shot his ear off. He was the one doing the screaming."

Malone shook his head. "Ye gods. What was done to her . . . him. Father Pat. You'd think he'd've been hollering like a pig caught under a gate."

"There was a gag near the body, but he wasn't wearing it when the kid found him," Fio said. "We'll do a canvas. See if anyone else saw or heard anything."

Malone rolled the cigarette back and forth on his palm, not meeting their eyes now. "You think one of his own did this? Another priest?"

Fio glanced at Rourke, waiting, and when Rourke said nothing, he answered, "Something dicey is sure enough going on in that parish. They spooked soon as we even showed up." Fio shook his head, scratched the back of his neck. "I don't know . . . Could be they knew this Father Pat was a woman." His gaze slid over to Rourke, then fell to the floor, a flush staining his broad cheekbones. "Could be they were, uh, you know . . . doing her."

"There was nothing in his life at the rectory to give even a hint that he was female," Rourke said, thinking out loud. He remembered the monastic room with its plain furniture and the lack of mirrors. And she'd been about to start her monthly, yet they'd found no drugstore pads. So what had she used? Rags, maybe, that she washed out every night in secret. "To live that kind of lie for twenty years—you'd have to be committed to it. Deep in your heart committed."

Fio made an abrupt movement of impatience, pushing himself off the wall. "Whoever did the killing knew Father Pat was a woman—I'd bet a month's salary on that. It was all about either covering up or getting even."

"Except there was no rape. And the killer crucified him without taking off his clothes."

Fio rolled his eyes at the ceiling, beseeching the water-marked plaster for divine assistance. "There he goes with that again."

Malone's gaze, which had been bouncing back and forth between his two detectives, settled on Rourke. "What?"

Rourke shrugged. "Just a feeling I keep getting . . . People trust priests with things they would never reveal to anyone else. They let priests into the deepest part of their lives. Father Pat wasn't just killed, he was tortured. Maybe someone let him in too deep."

The crowd below erupted into a roar. Fio went to the window to have a look. "Ol' Sparky has arrived," he said.

Malone threw his cigarette at the wall. "Oh, swell. That's all we need." He bent over and yanked open the bottom drawer to his desk. He produced a brown bottle that didn't have a label and three battered tin cups. He filled the cups to the brim with the bootlegged bourbon and passed them around.

Even so early in the morning, the booze tasted good to Rourke. Too good. He made himself quit after one swallow.

Malone up-ended the bottle, topping off his own cup. "This pastor at the dead priest's— Sweet mercy, should we even be calling her a priest? Anyway, this pastor at her parish . . . "

"Father Frank Ghilotti."

"Isn't his daddy the Ghilotti of the laundry rackets? Maybe the dicey feeling y'all were getting is that they're all mobbed up there at Holy Rosary. Stranger things've happened, I suppose. There's that scut going 'round that some outfit from the outside is going to try to muscle in on our rackets now that the Maguires are out of the picture. We could start to get all sorts of strange hits from that."

"We'll round up all of the known goons and jump up and down on their nuts," Fio said. "See what shakes loose."

"Yeah, do that. It'll give me something concrete to tell the brass."

The bell ringer for the telephone on Malone's desk let out a shrill peel. He stared at it while it rang twice more, then he sighed and lifted the telephone's handset off the hook.

"Captain Malone here. Yes, sir, Superintendent. Uh, yeah, there've been some new developments . . ." He pulled a God-help-me face and waved the detectives out of his office.

They filed out, only to be called back inside a few moments later.

"The papers just broke the story of the murder," Malone said. "They're selling extras on the street corners right now and they got all the gory details: crucifixion, feet burning—everything but the fact that he is a she. The super's going to get together with the archbishop and talk over what do about this latest wrinkle in this plum-awful nightmare. He wants the meeting done on the hush-hush, and both City Hall and the cathedral chancery are swarming with reporters, so it's going to be at his house on Rosa Park, and he wants you there."

"Oh, joy," Fio said, turning on his heel and going back through the door. "There's gonna be enough juice in the room to fry us all."

"Which is why," the captain said, "the only two words you need to know are, Yes sir."

Rourke was about to follow Fio when the captain stopped him. "And that goes double for you, Day," Malone said. "Don't give them any of your you-can-kiss-my-caboose bullshit. Whatever they tell you to do, you do it."

Rourke smiled and touched the brim of his hat in a mock salute.

The sawhorse barricades were still up in front of the Criminal Courts Building, but the crowd had surged out into the street to surround a flatbed truck, whose load was covered with a black tarpaulin. The truck driver was leaning on his horn to no avail, and the traffic backing up behind him was honking as well, and the constant, discordant blaring jangled Rourke's nerves.

Several of the Klan men had jumped on the back of the truck and were unrolling the tarpaulin cover. Alone in the Courts Building's brick arched entrance, Rourke and Fio paused for a moment between the stucco pillars to watch. The tarp came off to reveal a high-backed oaken chair with leather straps, and the generator to power it.

"It's not as big as I thought it would be," Fio said.

It looked plenty big enough to Rourke. The cheers of the crowd were suddenly like hard fists beating against his temples, and then somebody set off a string of firecrackers.

He wasn't sure what made him look up to the roof of the Blue Bayou Hotel across the street. What he saw when he did look, though, was a flash of sunlight off a rifle barrel.

Rourke threw his shoulder into Fio's chest, sending them both to the ground. Firecrackers were going off all around them now, horns blasting and police sirens blaring and people chanting, "Burn, nigger, burn." They couldn't hear the shots, but pieces of the stucco pillar exploded into fragments above Rourke's head.

Fio's hat blew off. He snatched it as it rolled away from him and slapped it back on his head.

The pop of the firecrackers petered out, although the chanting and the blare of horns went on. Rourke and Fio crouched behind the pillars with their guns drawn, scanning the hotel's rooftop.

A shadow of movement passed across a chimney.

"The bastard's getting away," Fio shouted.

They rolled to their feet and took off running across the street, dodging cars and wagons and stragglers from the crowd around the truck with the chair. No one else seemed to have even realized that the shots had been fired.

The hotel was small, only six stories, with a fire escape that let down into an alley. Rourke went through the hotel's revolving front door, while Fio ran around to the alley to cut off an escape at the rear.

The lobby had an elevator, a small black wrought iron cage, but the car was already on the top floor. Rourke disabled it by propping open the door, and took the stairs two at a time all the way up to the roof.

The hotel roof was flat, covered with tarpaper and gravel, and it was empty. However, he could see by the chimney a place where the shooter could easily have made the leap onto the lower roof of the apartment building next door. Rourke called down to Fio, telling him to check that building as well, but he knew they were already too late.

He went to the ledge that overlooked the entrance to the Criminal Courts Building. The area was littered with .30-caliber shell casings, from a Springfield rifle, maybe. Using his handkerchief he picked the casings up and dropped them in his pocket. The Ghoul had recently bought a new invention called a comparison microscope for conducting ballistics tests. They hadn't used it much yet, but Rourke still had high hopes for it.

The door to the stairwell squealed open behind him, and he whirled.

Fio emerged, panting hard, his face red. "What in hell is going on here?"

"What are you asking me for?" Rourke said. "You're the one whose hat got shot."

"My hat got shot 'cause you ducked." Fio took off his hat and poked his finger through the hole in its crown. "Shit, man, this was a good hat."

Rourke laughed because the hat in question was ten years old if it was a day. The crown had broken down in the center even before it had gotten shot, and the brim had a tendency to curl up on the edges in damp weather.

Fio gave him a withering look. "My hat gets killed and you laugh."

Fio placed the hat on his head with exaggerated dignity. He started to turn back toward the door, and Rourke saw that the left upper arm of his partner's beige pongee suit coat was wet and red.

"It looks like more than your hat got hit."

"Huh?" Fio looked to where Rourke was pointing. He prodded the blood-soaked hole in the sleeve of his coat. "Ow, Jeez Marie and all the saints. I think the bullet's still in there."

"I told you he was shooting at you."

"Yeah, well, who is he and what did I ever do to him?" Fio said, looking around the rooftop as if he expected the shooter to leap out from behind the chimney and explain everything.

Weldon Carrigan, superintendent of the New Orleans police force, lived in a gracious antebellum mansion on Rosa Park in the uptown silk stocking district. It was a house he had acquired through marriage, along with a modest fortune that he'd long ago turned into a very large fortune. From the lowest beat rookie to precinct captain, most of the cops in New Orleans were on the pad, and as superintendent, Carrigan's pad was the biggest of them all. All the rackets in the city—bootlegging, prostitution, loan sharking, protection and extortion—they all had Weldon Carrigan, along with much of City Hall, on their payroll.

Weldon Carrigan was other things to Rourke, besides his superintendent. He was father to Rourke's dead wife, Jo, which made him Katie's grandfather, her beloved paw-paw. He was also Rourke's angel, under whose sheltering and uplifting wings Rourke had been given the plum of homicide detective and early promotion up the ranks. Theirs was an elastic relationship, though. Weldon Carrigan had once offered Rourke fifty thousand dollars not to marry his daughter, and Rourke had once let his father-in-law get away with the murder of a crooked cop in exchange for being allowed to keep his own job, and a relatively free hand at running his cases however he saw fit.

Parked in front of the Carrigan mansion was the archbishop's black Jackson Touring Car, and a uniformed chauffeur was rubbing a rag over brass trim that was already bright as a mirror. What with the shooting and then taking Fio to the hospital to get the bullet dug out of his arm, Rourke had been keeping two of the most powerful men in the city waiting for the better part of an hour.

He climbed white marble stairs to the wide, pillared gallery and rang the bell of a door that glittered with beveled glass. A butler showed him down a long hall of black and white marble tiles and into a cozy rear sitting room whose tall windows had a view of the swimming pool and his mother-in-law's splendid garden.

Weldon Carrigan struck a presence equal to his position, with his thick shoulders, his large graying head, and his contrasting black eyebrows that grew like a hedge over gunmetal-gray eyes. He stood at one of the windows with his hands gripped into a fist behind his back.

He waited until Rourke was all the way in the room before he turned. "About goddamn time," he said.

"And here I was thinking you'd be grateful that I bothered to show up at all," Rourke said, smiling as he shook his father-in-law's hand. Weldon Carrigan's grip was hard enough to fuse flesh to bone. Rourke took it like a man.

Archbishop Peter Hannity sat by the fireplace in a tapestry chair that had a back like a throne. He was a diminutive man with a nose hooked like a crow's beak, and hooded, piercing blue eyes. He might have been small in stature, but he held a power even greater than Carrigan's, and Rourke knew he would marshal the full extent of that power to preserve the sanctity of the Catholic priesthood, the long black line. Even if that meant protecting a killer.

Rourke bent over and kissed the ring on the fine-boned hand. "Good morning, Your Grace," he said. He got a stern-lipped, monsignorial nod in return.

A maid in a stiffly starched cap and apron wheeled in a Sèvres coffee service on a silver-plated cart. Rourke sat down in a chair opposite the archbishop, the tufted leather sighing beneath his weight. He studied the man openly as they sipped coffee sweetened with sugar and cream. The sun shone through the tulle-curtained windows, throwing shuddering light onto the priest's face, and Rourke could see the shock there now. He looked fragile as heirloom china, older than his seventy years.

As the archbishop spoke, though, his voice betrayed nothing, and Rourke could almost see the scales tilting back and forth behind the penetrating eyes: what to give away, what to trade. And what to bury deep.

"Do you appreciate what is at stake here, Detective?" the archbishop said.

"I got an idea."

The mouth softened a little, almost smiling. "Yes, I rather suspect you do. The question, of course, is whether you are right in your idea." His gaze searched Rourke's face and the scales tipped some more, judging, weighing. "Tell me, then: Do you love God above all else?"

Love? Laughter welled up in Rourke's throat, but he didn't let it loose because he was afraid it was something else. Most days it seemed to him a test of faith just to go on believing in the existence of goodness.

"It is possible, you see," the archbishop went on as though Rourke had answered aloud, "to love a thing that keeps on breaking your heart."

"I don't want to be telling you your business, Your Grace," Weldon Carrigan said. He'd been busying his hands with lighting a long, narrow cigar. He blew its sweet smoke out in front of him now and looked into it with amused eyes. "But if you're going to bribe a man's soul, then you need to know his price. What my son-in-law loves above all else is being a cop."

Rourke's gaze had gone to the window, to watch a blue jay take a bath in the fountain. The bird was really going at it, flapping its wings and shaking its head, spraying water all over the place, and he wondered if a bird could feel happiness.

"Your priest was tortured," Rourke said. "The soles of his feet were burned with votive candles and he was hung from a crossbeam in a macaroni factory, with nails through his wrists."

The archbishop sought Rourke's gaze again and held it while he let a silence build for one beat, two. "And the one who did this evil will face a day of reckoning more terrible than any we on this earth can provide. Vengeance is mine sayeth the Lord."

"I'll concede the Lord His vengeance," Rourke said, and that time he almost did laugh aloud at his own arrogance. "The truth is what I'm after. Had you known Father Pat was a woman?"

The archbishop's hand jerked up, as if he was reaching for his own throat. Instead, he wrapped his long, thin fingers around the large crucifix he wore around his neck. He closed his eyes and gripped the cross so hard his knuckles whitened. "Known? How could any of us have known? Known and then allowed it to go on and on, all these years. Even now it seems a thing that defies belief and acceptance."

He opened his eyes and let his hand fall back into his lap. "Yet I should have seen that he was not a true priest. He had a way about him . . . her. Rebellious, flamboyant. The things he would say sometimes during those homilies of his, and that way he had of celebrating the Mass, throwing open the doors of the church and inviting Jesus on in as if the consecration of the body and blood was some kind of salvation show. He—" His lips pulled back from his teeth as if the word had suddenly burst sour on his tongue. "She . . ."

He. She. Until Rourke had walked into the morgue this morning and looked down on the naked body of Father Patrick Walsh, he had never truly understood before how the collection of tissues and corpuscles and bones that made a human being was so defined by a pronoun. He. She. To know Patrick Walsh as a priest was to think of him in one way. To know this priest was a woman was to think of him in a wholly different and seemingly incompatible way.

"Yet I've been told Father Pat was well liked, even loved, by all those who knew him, including yourself," Rourke pressed, feeling a little mean as he watched the skin jump in the papery cheek, the aged hands tremble. The archbishop must have been feeling betrayed by Patrick Walsh in the same searing, elemental way a wife would feel betrayed to discover that her husband had been married to another woman for the last twenty years.

The trembling was in the archbishop's head now as he shook it. "You must stop calling her Father. Patrick Walsh, or whatever this . . . person's name turns out to have been, was never Father to any Catholic. Priests act in the person of Christ Jesus in the lives of the faithful, they are Christ's disciples on earth, and woman was not created to serve in this role."

"Perhaps an exception was made."

The archbishop's mouth tightened and he averted his eyes. "You mock what you fail to understand. If our Lord had wanted women ordained, He would have ordained his own blessed mother, Mary, who was free of sin, but He did not. Patrick Walsh was no priest."

"And what then of the babies he baptized, the sinners he absolved? He celebrated the Mass, married the faithful, comforted the grieving, and buried the dead. He did those things for twenty years. If he was not a true priest, then in whose name were all those acts of faith and sacraments made?"

The archbishop brought his gaze back to Rourke, and all the fear and anguish he felt was betrayed now by his face. "And so you see why this must never become known," he said. "Never. For it may be a test of faith that is too difficult for some to bear. Surely it is possible that this woman was the devil in disguise, or one of his minions sent to betray the priesthood, to make a mockery of it? She has done grave harm to God's Holy Church, and the peril to more souls should be weighed against this truth you seek. We must have a care that in an effort to find her murderer, a further, greater harm is not done."

Weldon Carrigan threw his cigar into the empty fire grate with such force it exploded into a shower of sparks. "Right now we've got a lid on this mess, and that lid is staying on." He smiled, a good ol' boy smile that didn't even try to hide the brass knuckles. "You're going to play ball with us on this, Day, or I'll be on your ass like a rabid dog, and the good archbishop will have your brother sent to a parish so far out in the boondocks he'll be grubbing sweet potatoes with his toes."

Rourke smiled as well, for they had done this dance before, he and his angel.

He set his coffee cup down on a pearl inlaid table and stood up. When he spoke it was to the archbishop. "I'm not going to sandbag this investigation, Your Grace, just because *he* has become a *she* and we're all too scared now of what that really means and of what more we might find when we start kicking over rocks. Whatever else Patrick Walsh was, he was a human being and he deserves for someone, even if it's only the three of us here in this room, to know who killed him and why."

The archbishop stared at Rourke, searching his face. "You can be a cruel man, I think. But you also have courage and you have honor, and when the time comes you will know what is the right thing to do and you will do it. Come here, my son." His mouth quirked with a slight smile, as he raised his ringed hand, beckoning. "Come and kneel to receive the blessing of God and your Church, and do at least try to appear a little humble while you are doing so."

Rourke sat in his car, thinking.

The live oaks cast cool green pools on the velvet lawns and deep galleries, and he could hear the lilting piano strains of a Brahms waltz coming out an open window of the house next door. Two little girls about Katie's age were playing beneath the shade of the trees in the neutral ground. They'd dressed up a big tabby cat in a doll's nightie and were trying to put him in a buggy, but he wasn't having any of it. The cat squirmed, trying to get away, until one of the little girls brought it to her breast, cradling and rocking it like a baby.

Little girls. His Katie loved baseball and played a mean game of street hockey, yet just the other day he'd noticed her talking to the boy who did odd jobs for the speak on the corner and she'd been all giggly and flirty with him, seven going on seventeen, and scaring the living daylights out of her poor old daddy. Rourke wondered now what kind of little girl Patrick Walsh had been, growing up—if the *Times-Picayune* article had gotten it right—in that orphanage in Paris, Louisiana. Whether she had played with dolls and flirted with the boys. At what point in that life had she become he?

Nobody is wholly who they say they are; even in the confessional you can end up lying to yourself and to God. Yet what was that Paulie had said? *I was jealous of his being so in love with God and with His world, and for always being so darn* certain. *Certain of what it meant to be a priest, of getting it right . . .* What if Father Pat had taken up holy orders not to hide what he was, but rather to be more fully what he was in his heart? A spiritual being in love with God and His world.

A murder victim could be like a kaleidoscope, Rourke thought. You do a little twisting and you get a whole different picture. Ever since he'd looked down on the crucified corpse in the morgue that morning and seen a woman, Rourke had been thinking of the dead priest as someone who had perpetrated an enormous, elaborate, and desperate lie upon the world, but maybe Father Pat hadn't seen it that way. Maybe to Father Pat the terrible lie was the one that God or chance or biology had perpetrated on him, the lie he must have felt like a physical blow every time he looked at his naked body in the mirror and saw an image that didn't match the one he had of himself in his head. He. She.

So who had the killer nailed to the crossbeam last night, he or she? Priest or woman?

Rourke sat in the car, watching the little girls play with their cat, and he felt a sudden rush, like the pop you get from a snort of cocaine. Most murders were spur-of-the-moment, crimes of passion, or crimes born of stupidity, and easily solved. Every now and then, though, he would catch a case like this one, where the killer had nerve and brains and a plan.

He was beginning to know Patrick Walsh now, know him from the inside out. It was like developing a photograph—get the image sharp enough, and then you can see, emerging out of the background, the murderer holding the knife, or the gun, or the nails, in his hands.

Nails. Nails through the wrists.

"I'll get you, you sadistic son of a bitch," Rourke said aloud, and he smiled.

He wanted to shake up the priests of Our Lady of the Holy Rosary some more and see what fell out. He wanted to have a talk with Floriane de Lassus Layton, the "Flo" written with such an excited flourish in Father Pat's appointment book. And he wanted to take a good long look at the crime scene in daylight and talk with a few of his contacts on the street. A good cop knew all the bad weasels in town. Sometimes it was simply a matter of getting the right weasel to tell you who'd done it.

He punched up the engine and slipped the 'Cat into gear, singing "Sweet Georgia Brown."

It was like the super had said: He loved being a cop. Fucking loved it.

CHAPTER NINE

Fifteen minutes later Rourke was sitting in his car in front of Our Lady of the Holy Rosary, watching in astonishment as Tony the Rat climbed the portal steps and went through the heavy, iron-banded front doors. Rourke waited just long enough for the doors to close behind the loan shark's back, then followed him.

Sunshine streamed through the stained glass of the rose window, casting red and blue blossoms of light onto the interior arches and columns and pilasters. A young woman in a bright pink hat and an older one in widow's black knelt in prayer in the pews closest to the chancel. In the choir above, a chorus of schoolgirls sang the *Kyrie Eleison,* practicing for tomorrow's High Mass. Their voices rose to the vaulted, frescoed ceiling, hauntingly clear and beautiful, like bells peeling over snow.

Rourke spotted Tony the Rat at the south end of the nave. The loan shark paused to pull a red silk handkerchief out of his sleeve, and pressed it to his perpetually leaking nose. Then he genuflected at the chancel rail and headed for the confessional in the west transept.

The door to the confessor's box was closed and the green light above the lintel was on. Both of the penitent's boxes were empty;

Tony went into the right one and pulled the red velvet curtain closed.

Rourke sat in a pew and waited. Five minutes later Tony the Rat, apparently cleansed of all his many sins, pushed open the curtain of the penitent's box and came out. He genuflected at the chancel rail again, and left the church the way he'd come in, blessing himself from the holy water fount on his way.

Rourke thought about following him outside and bracing him, but then decided against it. A guy like Tony couldn't be cracked open without some kind of handle, and Rourke didn't have one yet.

Rourke waited around the confessional a half a minute for the priest to emerge, but instead of the priest coming out, the young woman in the pink hat went in, snapping the red velvet curtain closed behind her.

A stooped old man came out of the sacristy just then, carrying an armload of hymnals that he dumped on a table beneath the church bulletin board. Rourke figured he must be the sexton and he approached the man, showing him his detective's shield. He asked where he could find his brother.

The sexton adjusted the glasses at the end of his nose, sucked on his false teeth, and peered long and carefully at Rourke's credentials. "Father Paul's not here," he finally said. "He got called up to Charity Hospital to give old Mrs. Furillo the last rites."

"Yeah, okay," Rourke said, surprised at the depth of the relief he felt to know the priest who had just had a little private meeting with Tony the Rat was not his brother. Because he figured there was as much likelihood of the loan shark coming to Holy Rosary for genuine absolution as there was of the Yankees trading Babe Ruth. "So how much longer, then, will Father Ghilotti be hearing confession?"

The sexton fiddled with his glasses, sucked some more on his teeth, then said, "Father Frank's out back in the boys' clubhouse right now. Confession's not till this evenin'. Five o'clock."

Rourke went back to the confessional at a run, but the priest's box was empty.

Rourke found the sexton again and got access to the chancery office telephone. He called down to the precinct station house and arranged to have Tony the Rat picked up for jaywalking or spitting on the sidewalk, or whatever it took. Rourke was wishing now that he'd followed Tony out of the church and asked him a few pointed questions, but there was still time for that. Besides, a few sweaty, itchy, coke-hungry hours in a cage might help the loan shark see the value of cooperation.

And in the meantime Rourke was going to have a little heart-to-heart with Father Frank Ghilotti.

Rourke opened the door of the clubhouse to the smack of a fist hitting leather and the squeak of rubber-soled shoes on the old puncheon floor. The priest steadied a punching bag that was almost as big as the scrawny boy facing it. The boy's arms were skinny as broom handles and the big padded leather gloves made his hands look too heavy to hold up.

"You're pulling back on your punches soon as they land," Father Ghilotti was saying. "Push your fist all the way through the bag and do it like you mean it."

The boy cocked back his gloved hand and was about to let fly when he heard Rourke's footstep and whirled.

"Cheese it, it's the cops," Father Ghilotti said.

The boy's eyes widened and he backed up until he knocked into the punching bag. "I didn't do nothin'," he cried. "Honest, I didn't."

Both men laughed, and the boy jumped in the air as if he'd been goosed with a hot poker.

"Now there speaks a guilty conscience if ever there was one," the priest said. He touched the boy lightly on the shoulder. "The policeman is here to see me, Bobby Lee, so why don't we call it quits for today."

The boy nodded, swallowing hard. He gave Rourke a wide berth and then took off for the door, running.

"He was nabbed not too long ago trying to lift a ham at the Poydras Market," the priest said. "The butcher let him off with a warning, but with a threat to bring in the law next time he caught the boy stealing. They've five kids in that family and their daddy's gone." He held out his hand to Rourke and then realized there was a boxing glove at the end of it. "Sorry," he said, smiling a little, shrugging. "I have this theory that it helps boys like Bobby Lee, boys who are angry at the world and hurting inside, to hit on something that won't hit back and can't be hurt in turn."

He looked Rourke over, as if reassessing his first impression. Or confirming it. "You look like you might do a bit of boxing yourself," he said.

"I do some sparring at the Athletic Club as many times a week as the job'll let me."

Father Frank Ghilotti made an incongruous picture himself, with the sleeves of his cassock rolled up to reveal the fat, padded gloves, and yet once again Rourke was struck by a sense of the man's inner toughness. Having a couple of homicide detectives appear at his rectory so early this morning with the news of Father Pat's death might have put the pastor off his stride, but he seemed to have regained his balance.

"Father Pat was hurt," Rourke said, trying to throw him off again. "He was crucified."

Genuine anguish, or so it seemed, filled the priest's face. "Yes, I know. Archbishop Hannity telephoned a little after you all left this morning and gave us the details, but to be honest I had a hard time believing what I was hearing. How could such a thing have been done to him? And why?"

"Most killings are done out of greed or fear or passion," Rourke said. "Likely the why will end up being one of those."

He looked around the clubhouse, a temple to emerging manhood with its canvas sparring ring and barbells. The place smelled like a gymnasium—sweat and damp towels. "Did Father Pat help you teach the boys how not to pull their punches?"

In the silence that followed his question, Rourke could hear water dripping somewhere, and the bounce of a basketball on the pavement outside.

"Was he a chicken hawk?" Father Ghilotti finally said. "Is that what this is all about?"

Rourke's gaze came back to him, but he saw on the priest's face only pain and a kind of wary distaste. It would be a clever, disingenuous question to pose, though, if you were the killer and you'd known all along that Father Pat was a woman.

"Do you have reason to think he was?" Rourke said.

The pastor took his time answering, as if he were picking his words out of a minefield. "Father Pat was a well-loved priest, very popular, and because he was human that popularity gave him a certain pride and made him ambitious. I would have sworn, though, that he was chaste."

"And yet now you're wondering."

He lifted his shoulders in a small shrug. "It's just that when your archbishop does the kind of soft-shoe shuffle that I got from His Grace this morning, it's usually because one of your own has been caught diddling little boys. Or girls."

"What kind of soft-shoe shuffle?"

"The don't-tell-anybody-anything-and-don't-ask-any-questions kind."

"Yet here you are, telling me stuff and asking questions."

Behind the thick lenses, the priest's eyes blinked once, twice. "Baseball ruled spitballs illegal back in '08. That doesn't mean they still don't pitch them."

They shared a smile, and Rourke found himself liking the other man. He seemed an odd, yet, genuine, mixture of spiritual devotion and that street toughness. Rourke thought it was possible that under extraordinary circumstances Father Frank Ghilotti could kill, but it was hard to imagine him doing it any other way but cleanly.

"You said Father Pat was ambitious," Rourke said. "Did his ambitions clash with yours?"

Something that seemed to be amusement flickered across the priest's face. "I want to be archbishop myself someday. Father Pat wanted to save the world."

"And what were some of the ways he went about trying to do that? Saving the world."

The priest tapped the punching bag with the nose of his gloved fist, hard enough to make it swing with a squeak. "In some ways, being a priest isn't a whole lot different from being a cop. To get ahead you need an angel, and a knowledge of where the bodies are buried. So how about a trade? A body for a body."

"You go first," Rourke said.

A half smile pulled at the other man's mouth. "A few months ago, Father Pat had this thing going. It was a kind of club. He called it the Catholic Ladies Social, but its purpose was to help wives work through the troubles in their marriages. I'm not sure what all went on in those meetings, but some of the husbands complained to the archbishop, and that was the end of Father Pat's experiment with female self-determination."

"Only you don't think he ended it."

"On the contrary, Detective. If I had thought he was disobeying the archbishop, it would have been my responsibility to do something about it."

Rourke felt a little tug in his guts that was a hunch taking root. There was something going on here. It was too soon to tell just what yet, but there was something . . . something . . .

"Now it's your turn," the pastor said.

"Okay. We don't know what Father Pat was doing in that macaroni factory last night, but we think he may have accidentally stumbled onto something he shouldn't have. We're liking a bottom-of-the-rung hood by the name of Tony Benato, either for doing the killing himself or for having ordered it done."

Rourke saw nothing on the priest's face, no telltale flicker in the eyes behind their thick lenses, no tightening of the muscle along the jaw. Which meant either that Frank Ghilotti's father had trained him well, or that he had no idea who had been using his confessional for a private meeting with Tony the Rat.

Rourke had lied to the pastor, anyway, for he didn't really like the loan shark for the killing. It was out of Tony Benato's league, or should have been. It seemed, Rourke thought, as though he was being given puzzle pieces that fit together perfectly, but the picture he got made no sense at all.

As Rourke was leaving the clubhouse, he paused at the door and looked back. The priest was laying into the leather bag now with a blizzard of punches, his shoulders bobbing and weaving, his feet dancing.

Outside, Father Delaney was deadheading the tea roses that climbed the trellises framing the rectory's kitchen stoop. "Mornin', Father," Rourke said, passing by him on the path.

The old priest looked up and smiled at Rourke from beneath the frayed brim of a floppy straw hat. "I know you," he said. "You're Father Paul's brother. The policeman. And you've come for the book."

"Yes, I've got it now, Father. Thank you."

The old priest dropped the corpse of a brown, withered blossom into a basket between his splayed feet. "I hope there won't be more trouble."

The tea roses were the pink of a girl's blush, and Rourke got a sudden rush of their scent as he came closer. "What sort of trouble do you mean, Father?" he asked.

"More trouble between Father Frank and Father Pat—they were arguing. Shouting. Only Father Pat's dead now, so I suppose . . ." The old priest's head began to tremble and his gaze jittered away. "I get so confused anymore."

"Did you hear what they were saying?" Rourke pressed, although he kept his voice gentle and easy. "When they were arguing?"

"Devil's bargains—that's what he said. He wouldn't make any more devil's bargains."

"Who said that? Father Pat?"

"We thought he was a saint and he was afraid he might be, but all of us were wrong. There wasn't any miracle. It was all in his head."

"Father Pat thought he was a saint?"

The old priest's head shook harder and his mouth opened as he tried to grasp on to the sliding memory. "I don't know . . . I get so confused anymore."

He reached for another dead rose and jammed his finger down hard on a thorn. He exclaimed and thrust the finger in his mouth, sucking on the wound. He looked at Rourke, blinking hard, and Rourke could see the vagueness settling over his mind like a fog. "My mother grows roses," he said. "American Beauties as big as soup bowls. She's coming to my ordination tomorrow. She wasn't happy when I chose to become a priest, but she's reconciled now . . . I'm sorry, but have we met before?"

"I'm Father Paul's brother." A pair of gloves lay next to the basket of dead blossoms, and Rourke stooped to pick them up. "Here, let's put these on," he said, "so you don't get pricked again."

A Solano Ice Company wagon had pulled up to the curb in front of the rectory, and a man in green overalls was wrestling a block of ice onto the tailgate with a giant pair of hooked tongs. Across from the church, a handful of reporters had gathered on the green of Coliseum Square.

Rourke walked to his car. The old priest had said something, and now it was dancing on the edge of Rourke's consciousness, a little inkling that was about to become a full-blown thought, when one of the reporters called out, "Hey, Mr. Rourke. I got a question for you."

And the thought was gone.

The reporter jogged across the street, taking awkward, hitching strides. He dodged the ice man, who was setting his feet, getting ready to swing the block of ice up onto his shoulder. "Hey, Mr. Rourke. Garrison Hughes of *The Movies* here. I got a question for you. Remy Lelourie and Alfredo Ramon are supposed to have some hot love scenes in this latest flick of theirs. How do you feel about that?"

Rourke's answer was to jab his middle finger into the air.

Garrison Hughes of *The Movies* here showed his yellow corn teeth. "You do know he slashed his wrists when she jilted him after their first picture. The studio hushed it up, but next time you get a chance take a look at the scars."

Are you scared yet, Remy?

Rourke turned and went after the guy. The letter Remy had gotten, the threat implicit in it, had been in the back of his mind all morning long, like a nerve-jangling whine. He wasn't going to hurt the reporter, only ask the man some questions of his own, but he wanted to hurt somebody, and that desire must have showed on his face, because Garrison Hughes whirled to run and smacked hard into the ice man.

The reporter took a flailing step backward, tripped on the curb, and landed on his butt in the gutter. The ice man, off balance under his load, staggered backward as well, knocking into the tailgate of his wagon and sending another block of ice sliding off the end of it. The ice block fell with a vibrating thud onto the reporter's sprawled left leg, and Rourke heard a crack, like a hickory stick breaking.

"God almighty," the ice man said. "His leg just got busted."

The reporter, his leg pinned under the block of ice, was trying to push himself up onto his elbows.

"Lie still," Rourke said.

"My leg's busted," the reporter said. Rourke was impressed that the guy wasn't screaming.

"His leg is really busted," the ice man said.

"Lie still," Rourke said. With the ice man's help, he was able to lift the block of ice off the reporter's leg and shove it aside. He was relieved to see no blood or jagged bones. Because, Jesus, after the way it had cracked . . . "I'm going to call an ambulance."

"Naw, no need to bother with that. I got another one in the trunk of my car."

"Huh?" the ice man said, then, "Whoa," when the reporter reached up his pants, gripped himself by the ankle, and pulled off the splintered bottom half of his leg.

"I lost the original in the Argonne," he said. "Now I got myself a wooden one and a spare."

Rourke helped Garrison Hughes hop to his battered Model T and strap on his spare wooden leg.

"Is there a list somewhere," Rourke asked him, "of all the movies ever made and who starred in them?"

Hughes thought about it a minute, then shook his head. "Naw, I don't think so. Why? What are you on to?"

"Nothing you're ever going to know," Rourke said. "And you're going to quit following me around with that fuckin' camera, or I'll bust your balls next time, instead of your leg."

Rourke didn't laugh until he got back to his own car and then he thought about the wooden leg and the way it had cracked when the ice fell on it, and he laughed so hard his ribs hurt and he had to lay his head on the steering wheel.

It felt good though, the laughter, so that he was still smiling when he punched on the ignition and pulled away from the curb. He drove a little too fast down Race Street and turned uptown at the corner of Coliseum. He needed to hook back up with Fio at the hospital, but first he wanted to have a talk with Floriane de Lassus Layton.

Well-off, old family, so she'd have connections and all the social graces. Chairwoman of Holy Rosary's Catholic Charities, which put her in the Church's inner circle. She'd know of some scandals, maybe know where some bodies were buried. Rourke wasn't acquainted with her personally, only by name, but he remembered the impression he'd gotten of her daughter last summer, when he'd interviewed the girl for the Titus Dupre murder case. What was her name? Darla . . . No, Della. An astute girl, with one of those effervescent personalities that had a little tartness underneath it. Like lemonade. Pretty in a wholesome way, with big hazel eyes, but trying too hard to grow up fast. A handful then, maybe, for her mother.

"Flo," he said aloud. Getting a feel for her.

CHAPTER TEN

She had already heard about the murder. News, especially news of the gory or scandalous sort, could spread through New Orleans faster than the yellow fever had done in the old days.

She had been about to host a mah-jong party when the first telephone call came, and so she was wearing a red dragon robe and elaborately embroidered Chinese slippers when she met Rourke in her parlor. She had been crying.

The Laytons lived in a handsome Greek Revival raised villa on Prytania Street. Albert Payne Layton was a stockbroker and he had recently made a killing in the market, but the house had the look and smell of old money. De Lassus family money, from sugar refineries going back to before the Civil War.

Floriane de Lassus Layton was in her late thirties, perhaps only seven or eight years older than Rourke, and her face while not beautiful was smooth and round and full of warmth. She had deep mahogany red hair, magnolia-white skin, and an air of eggshell delicacy that couldn't be cultivated or affected. You had to be born to it.

Rourke thought her eyes had a look of shame in them, though, dark as a bruise, that you didn't often see in women of her kind with their heirloom homes and bell jar lives.

"Mrs. Layton," Rourke began, after she'd offered him coffee and they'd settled across from each other in matching green and cream silk chairs, "I wonder if you could tell me what time Father Pat left y'all last night, and if he told you where he was going afterward?"

She stared at him for a moment, as if uncomprehending, then she folded her arms over her belly and bent over, holding herself as if she'd just been gutted. "Oh, God. It's really true, then. I couldn't bear to believe . . ."

She held herself tighter, rocking back and forth, and a good while passed before she straightened and wiped the wetness off her cheeks with the back of her hands. "I am so sorry—where are my manners? And what must you think of me, to be indulgin' in such a shameful display of weeping?"

"I'm thinking," he said, "that you've just lost a very good friend."

Her mouth quirked up in a pained smile, as if she thought his sympathy nothing but a policeman's ploy but was too polite ever to say so. "Father Pat was here last evenin', of course," she said. "We had red snapper because it was Friday, and then afterward we played Gilbert and Sullivan on the phonograph and he sang along. He has a beautiful countertenor voice . . . had. It was ten o'clock when he left. I remember the clock in the hall striking the hour while we were saying our goodbyes at the door."

"Did Mr. Layton have supper with you all?"

Her fingers, which had been making little pleats of the kimono in her lap, stilled. "Albert? Yes, of course, he did. He's . . ." Her gaze fell to her hands. She toyed with her wedding ring, twisting it around and around on her finger. "He isn't here right now, though. He always plays golf on Saturday mornings."

"Did you belong to Father Pat's club?"

Her hands clenched together hard in her lap. "Club? I don't know . . ."

"The Catholic Ladies Social."

"Oh, that." She relaxed some, lifting her shoulders in a little shrug. "I did for a while. But I got so busy with other things, I had to quit it. The Charities takes up so much of my time."

Rourke asked nothing more, and after a moment she lifted her head and her gaze met his, and a faint blush crept up her neck.

She jerked to her feet, turning away from him. She rubbed her hands up and down her arms as she walked to the French doors opening out onto the wraparound gallery. The purple wisteria that climbed the columns trembled in the wind. A pair of mockingbirds flicked in and out of the sunlight.

Rourke watched her, and in the quiet the wind pushed against the window sashes.

"Did you know that you and my husband have Loyola in common, Detective Rourke?" she finally said, drawing on the Southern etiquette of making a connection, however small or tenuous.

Even before he began keeping company with a movie star, Daman Rourke's life had been spread through the pages of the tabloids because of the high-profile murder cases he had solved. He'd gotten used to people he'd never met before knowing the kind of details about his life that he usually pried out of others. That he'd grown up rough in the Irish Channel, the son of a cop. That he'd been an air ace in the Great War, joined the police force afterward, and gotten a law degree from Loyola while walking a night beat. Mostly, though, the papers wrote about the scandals and the tragedies. His mama deserting her man and babies to go live with her married lover, his daddy dying in a knife fight in a Girod Street dive. His high-society wife dropping dead at the age of twenty-two because of a hole in her heart.

That they hadn't uncovered all his secrets yet seemed only a matter of time and serendipity, and that, Rourke reflected, was the nature of secrets. You thought you had them deeply buried, and all the while they were working their way through to the light. He could have told Floriane de Lassus Layton that. Perhaps he would before this case was through.

He wondered about her secrets as she prattled on. "Of course, Albert was there before your time, so I suppose your paths never crossed." She rubbed her hands up and down her arms some more, as if she'd suddenly taken a chill. "Is it hot outside? It looks like it's getting hot."

"Some," Rourke said. "The wind's still blowing though."

She turned away from the French doors and went to a phonograph that sat on a marble-topped console table next to a cocktail tray. She took a record out of its jacket and put it on the spindle. She lifted the needle and started to place it on the record, then set it back down again. Her eyes grew bright. She closed them to hold back the tears.

"Your husband wasn't here last night, was he?" Rourke said. "And neither was your daughter. It was just the two of you having supper, playing Gilbert and Sullivan, you and Father Pat."

Her eyes tightened at the corners as if she was wincing deep inside herself. "Nothing happened, though. I would swear that to you on a Bible if I must. We ate supper and played the phonograph, and he left at ten o'clock. I will swear it."

Rourke got up but he didn't go too close to her just yet. She had laid out the mah-jong game on a low table in front of the fireplace. The room smelled of the incense that had been burning in the belly of the plaster Buddha on the mantel. Mah-jong parties were all the rage now, and you could buy a cheap set made out of celluloid in any dime store, but these tiles looked like the real thing. Made in China out of the shinbones of cows.

Rourke felt her presence as she came up next to him, but he was careful for the moment not to look at her. Hunger and wanting and need can live in you, he thought, hide in you, and then come out when you least expect it, when you don't want it, and the hunger to possess another's body doesn't always come with love. When you are in love, though, then your hunger is for your other's whole being: heart and mind and soul, as well as body.

So if you are Flo Layton, wife and mother, chairwoman of the board of Holy Rosary's Catholic Charities, if you are she and you've summoned the courage at last to take your priest, the object of your love and hunger, up to your bed, and you embrace and kiss him in the dark, maybe, and you take off his clothes, touching him now, touching him all over and you reach for him like you reach for your husband, and your priest, your lover, your he, becomes a she . . . If you were that woman, would you fall out of love in an instant? Would you fall out of hunger?

"It's a silly thing, isn't it," she said, "to play this game just because everybody else is doing it. Truth to tell the rules are so complicated, I'm not sure any of us even knows what we're about most of the time. Do you play, Detective?"

"No. *Bourré* is my weakness, I'm afraid."

"That was also my daddy's game. He used to say that how a man behaves at the *bourré* table is how he behaves in life. The cutthroat play, that pure crazy courage to risk it all. The ability to bluff and detect a bluff."

Rourke looked up from the mah-jong table, looked at her, and he saw that she was crying again.

She exhaled a deep sighing breath, like someone who had been waiting a long time for a dreaded moment and now finally it was here. "So I would be a fool to try to lie to you, wouldn't I? A police detective who plays *bourré.* We were friends, Father Pat and I. Good friends, and close in a strange way. Almost as if we were . . ." She trailed off, searching for a way to convey her thoughts, shrugging when she couldn't. "You could say I loved him, but it never became the worst of what you are thinking. He wasn't a priest who would ever betray his vows, and I'm not a woman who . . . I'm not that kind of woman."

He didn't know if he believed her or not. His gut would have believed her, if not for that look of shame he saw in her eyes.

As Rourke was leaving the Layton house, he noticed that from the gallery you could see the octagonal tower of Our Lady of the Holy Rosary, thrusting up through the trees and over the roofs of the neighboring houses. If you had a fanciful imagination, he thought, the tower's clock might seem like a large unblinking eye, a witness to all the lives, both sinful and virtuous, that went on in its long shadow.

He heard the creak of wood rubbing on wood and he turned. A young woman sat in a white wicker rocker among large terra-cotta pots of red and white hibiscus as if she was posing there.

She stood and came toward him. "Detective Rourke?"

Rourke shoved his hands in his pockets, rocked back on his heels, and smiled. It was the smile he'd used unconsciously on all women since he'd grown old enough to figure out how far it could get him. "Mornin', Miss Della."

She blushed a little, but at the same time there was some kind of calculation going on behind the big hazel eyes that studied his face. "You remember me," she said. "I wasn't sure you would."

She looked different than she had on that afternoon six months ago, when he'd interviewed her for the Titus Dupre case. That day she'd been the picture of the Catholic schoolgirl in her wool blue plaid skirt and cardigan sweater. This morning she was all baby vamp in a peekaboo hat, long knotted beads, short pleated skirt, and nude hose rolled down to reveal her rouged knees. She'd rimmed her eyes with a black pencil and greased her eyelids to make them shiny, and painted her lips a bright red, the color of the hibiscus in the pots.

"I remember," Rourke said, "that you think the classes they make you take at school are nothing but 'bushwa' and that you like tennis and going to the movies, and that your favorite film star is Remy Lelourie."

She laughed and fluttered her greased eyelashes, flirting with him a little, trying out her newfound womanhood. "I bet everybody tells you that, though," she said. "About being a fan of Remy Lelourie, since the whole world knows that you're her lover."

Rourke looked around the porch, then leaned into her, lowering his voice almost to a whisper. "Most of that stuff that they put in the magazines . . . it's all made up."

"I know," she whispered back at him. She giggled, catching it with her hand, and she seemed more her age now. Not sixteen going on twenty-one. "Still, a bunch of us girls at school, we belong to the Fantastics in honor of Remy Lelourie. It's like a fan club thing? And I was wondering . . . I mean, since you do know her . . . Do you think she'd be willing to give us her autograph?"

"Sure," Rourke said. "I'll even get y'all some signed photographs. How many of you are there?"

"There's seven of us now."

Rourke took out his notebook and fountain pen and handed them to her. "Why don't you write down all your names and that way she can personalize the salutations."

"That'd be swell. Thanks." She smiled, but that calculating look was back in her eyes, and Rourke had a feeling that she wanted more from him than a little flirtation and a movie star's autograph.

As she took the notebook and pen from him, she looked back over her shoulder as if she'd felt someone spying on them from the parlor windows. Rourke could see Flo Layton, though, and she wasn't at the windows. She'd gone back to the console table with the phonograph, and as they both watched she put a record on the spindle. This time she spun the crank and let the needle touch the disc, and the brassy chords of "The Lord High Executioner" spilled out of the horn.

The girl had a strange look on her face as she watched her mama. Rourke would almost have described it as a look of horrified glee.

"I heard about Father Pat," Della said, and her voice, oddly flat, did not go with that face. "I heard that he was murdered. Did you come here to talk to Mama about him?"

"It's part of a routine we do," Rourke said. "Tracking the victim's last hours. I guess he was here last night, but you weren't home."

"I ate supper at Mary Lou Trescher's, and then I slept over." She turned away from the window, and Rourke thought he might have seen a shudder pass through her. "I don't like to have supper at home on Fridays 'cause I hate fish. Mary Lou's mama always fixes macaroni and cheese."

"Did Father Pat come over to you all's house very often?"

She was writing in his notebook now, pretending maybe not to have heard him, but then she shrugged. "He and Mama worked together a lot on the Catholic Charities."

She gave him back his notebook and pen and then followed him down the gallery steps out to the corner where he'd parked the Bearcat beneath the shade of an elm tree.

She walked all around it, trailing her fingers lightly over the domed hood with its flying chrome ornament and the rakish yellow fenders. "Wow," she said, genuinely excited now, bouncing up and down on her toes with it. "Is this your car? It's a darb."

"Yeah?" Rourke laughed. A darb. He'd have to remember that one for Katie.

When the song had fallen into a scratchy silence, Floriane de Lassus Layton cranked the phonograph and set the record to playing all over again. She didn't sing along; she really wasn't that good a singer. Not like Father Pat.

Once, last night, he had tried to do a sailor's jig along with the song. He'd been clumsy on his feet, though, all knocked knees and pointed elbows, and so she had laughed at him and he'd laughed at himself, and she remembered thinking afterward, after their laughter had wound down, This is what it is to be happy.

It had been like looking at the sun through the spray of a fountain, though. Almost too bright to bear, and you think you're seeing rainbows, all dazzling prisms of color and light, but it's all only an illusion. You look away and the rainbows are gone.

An illusion, and a cruel one, in the way that you can fool yourself for one sweet moment into believing that you are not who you are, Floriane de Lassus Layton. Mother to Della, wife of Albert Payne Layton. Lover of a . . .

The record wound down and she cranked the phonograph and brought the needle back to the beginning again.

Lover of . . .

She watched the record go around and around and around.

Lover . . .

Her hand lashed out, knocking the needle, and sending it scratching across the grooves in the vinyl with a loud, grating screech.

"Now you've gone and ruined it."

Floriane de Lassus Layton whirled, her hand flying to her throat, as if to stop a scream. Her husband stood in the doorway. He was a tall, redheaded, freckled-faced man, and when he was angry his freckles stood out on his fair skin like flecks of orange paint.

He had stopped within the shadows of the hall, almost as if he knew how she tried to read his moods, and so she couldn't see his face.

"Bertie," she said, hating the fear she heard in her own voice. "I wasn't expecting you home until this evenin'."

He stood where he was for a moment longer, saying nothing, and then he came into the room. He came right at her and she stood rooted to the floor, waiting for him. He went to the phonograph instead, and he put the needle back on its arm lock, and then picked the record off the turntable with both hands.

"I'm afraid, my dear," he said, "that if you were to try to play this now, every note would sound like a stuttering hiccup." She watched his big hands, the sinews and muscles in the back of his hands, with their red hairs coarse and stiff as copper wires, watched them tightening until the record broke in two with a loud snap. "Oops, now I've gone and really done it." He looked at her and smiled, and the freckles were dark on his face. "Never mind, though. I'll buy you another."

She could feel herself hunkering down inside, even though he hadn't hurt her yet, and might not even hurt her at all. Sometimes when she expected him to hurt her, when she had herself all steeled to bear it, he would treat her so gently, as if she were made of spun glass, and that was the true horror of life with Albert Payne Layton. He was wholly unpredictable.

He dropped the pieces of record on the floor and turned toward her, and this time she would have run if there had been any place to run to, and if a part of her didn't believe that she deserved this, deserved every bit of it, because she was Floriane de Lassus Layton and she had betrayed him, and betrayed herself.

"I heard about Father Pat," he was saying, "about how he was found murdered early this mornin', and in such a terrible way, too. Crucified on a cross like Christ Jesus himself. Knowing how fond of him you were, I thought you might need comforting."

He said the words sweetly, but he had taken her hand and his fingers were gripping hard enough to bruise bone. He had done this once before, only that time he'd squeezed until three of the bones had broken.

He brought his face close to hers, close enough that she could have counted his freckles, dark now as spots of blood. She could see traces of talcum powder on his shirt collar. A pimply shaving rash spread up his throat like a blush.

"A homicide detective was just here," she said, trying to sound normal, as if the tears weren't crowding the corners of her eyes from the pain in her hand. "He wanted to know what time Father Pat left after supper last night. I think he might still be out in the street by his car, talking to Della."

Albert laughed, but he let go of her hand. "Oh, dear. Poor Flo. Was he so crass as to ask if you and your priest were sleeping together? How humiliating that must have been for you. Don't you just know it, though, that when something like this happens, people's minds always drop right into the gutter."

He turned away from her and went to the cocktail tray. He picked up a cut glass decanter that had once belonged to Flo's great-grandmama and poured bourbon into a large tumbler. "How about a drink, darling?" he said. "You could probably use one. I know talking to the police always makes me feel like I'm about to break out all over in hives."

She'd been too scared to notice it before, but she heard it now—

the triumph in his voice. His whole body vibrated with it. "Bertie," she said softly, and unconsciously, she put her hand to her throat again. "What have you done?"

"What?" He had brought the tumbler up to his lips and now he held it there and looked at her over the rim. He'd made his eyes go wide with surprise, but then he could make his face show you anything. "You're thinking I killed him now? God, that is rich," he said, and he laughed. An excited, surging laugh that brought a burn of vomit rising up into her throat.

She took a few steps back, out of the swinging reach of his fist, even though he'd actually never struck her in the face before. He found other ways to hurt her, ways that most times didn't even leave bruises.

He was acting so smug, though, like he knew something. Maybe he hadn't been with his latest floozy last night, after all. Maybe he had waited outside until they'd left the house and he'd followed them instead, and if he had followed them then he was smart enough to have most of it all figured out by now. Albert Payne Layton was a very smart man, and practicing cruelty was a pleasure to him, a pleasure and an art. He would enjoy ruining everything just for the practice.

She'd become so lost in her thoughts she hadn't noticed that Bertie had come up to her again, was looming over her. "You're looking quite pensive, my dear," he said. "Are you doing some mental embroidering on your alibi, going over all the lies you told that cop to see if you might have slipped up, maybe revealed one of those deep dark secrets of yours? Did he ask you, for instance, where you were at two o'clock this morning?"

"Where were you?" she blurted, and was instantly sorry.

But he only smiled and made a tsking sound with his tongue, shaking his head. "Now, now, Flo. Remember the rules. I get to fuck whomever I want, while you stay at home and do your penance."

A small gasp came from the doorway, and they both jerked around. Their daughter, Della, stood there and she had herself all dressed up like a flapper, with too much makeup around her mouth and eyes and a skirt that was way too short.

"Hey, honey," Albert said. "You look nice."

"Thanks, Daddy."

She gave him a bright smile, and then her gaze went to her mama, and Flo expected her daughter to look almighty pleased with herself because she always could wrap her daddy twice around her little finger. Only on Della's face, as the girl looked at her, was contempt and a strange kind of horrified disgust.

She knows, Flo thought. She looked at her husband and saw that he was laughing at her, laughing with his eyes. *Dear God in heaven, she knows. He has gone and told her everything.*

CHAPTER ELEVEN

Sixteen-year-old Mary Lou Trescher was having the best day of her life.

Before her dazzled eyes was the deck of a pirate ship awash with sea foam. Blood ran through the scuppers, and battle smoke drifted through the broken spars and masts and tangled rigging. The wooden hull groaned with the rocking waves. The air smelled of salt and cordite, and adventure.

The ship looked so real; big as life, even though it was indoors, inside a giant river warehouse that had once stored bananas and coffee off the boat from South America. Bright Lights Studios had taken over the cavernous building and turned it into a place where a ship floated in a huge tank rather than the sea, and the cypress swamp onshore had been painted on a canvas backdrop. A giant screen that looked made out of tinfoil arced over the ship, where the sky should have been.

It was all so amazing she had to pinch herself to believe that it was real. Yet here she was, Mary Lou Trescher, on a movie set, watching a Remy Lelourie picture being made. Reginald Trescher, her second cousin on her daddy's side—who had worked for the electric company until by some miracle he had landed a job working the *Cutlass* set lights—had used his connections to get her a pass into the warehouse this morning, so that she could watch them shoot the sword fight scene.

The other Fantastics were all just going to be *so* jealous when they heard. Mary Lou wanted to rush out right now and tell them what she was seeing and doing, even though nothing much had happened yet. A few men walked about, carrying clipboards and picking their way through the heavy electrical cables that snaked all over the floor. A small orchestra was tuning up their instruments; Reggie had told her they played mood music suited for each scene to inspire the actors. Someone turned on a giant fan and the sails flapped and waves splashed up over the ship's rails, but after a few moments of that the fan was turned off.

Seven cameras on tripods had been placed around the ship, and a bearded man dressed in an open-necked shirt, jodhpurs, and riding boots kept going from one to the other, peering through the viewfinders with a monocled eye and making notes on the scenario he carried rolled up in his hand.

Her cousin Reggie had pointed him out to her as the famous German director Peter Kohl. Reggie had said Mr. Kohl was a man painstaking with details: clothes, makeup, lighting—it all had to be just so, which was why everything was taking so long. "It takes us hours," Reggie had said, "just to set up and shoot a couple feet of film."

What Mary Lou most wondered, though, but hadn't dared to ask, was why Mr. Kohl had dressed himself to look like he'd just gotten off a horse when they were making a pirate movie.

So far Mary Lou had only gotten a glimpse of Remy Lelourie herself, when the movie star had stuck her head out the door of her portable dressing room and asked if they were ready for her yet. The dressing room itself was a marvel, for it was on wheels. It made Mary Lou think of the Gypsy wagons she had seen in countless movies.

After several more long minutes when nothing was happening, Mary Lou drifted over for a closer look at one of the cameras. It was smaller than she would have imagined, not much bigger than her school satchel, but with two spools the size of phonograph records fastened onto the top.

"Touch that and you're dead."

Mary Lou nearly leaped out of her skin, and then she nearly fainted when she turned and got a look at the man who had spoken. She thought for a minute he was wearing costume makeup, or a mask, so hideously scarred was half of his face.

If he was insulted by how she was staring so wild-eyed at him, he didn't show it. It was hard to tell from his expression, for the skin on the scarred side of his face was thick and stiff as leather. "I'm Jeremy Doyle," he said. "The chief cameraman of this extravagant fantasy. And that's my camera you were about to touch without permission."

Mary Lou stuttered an apology. She was having a hard time deciding where to look. It seemed an insult to look away, as if she couldn't bear the sight of him, and yet to look at him was to give the impression of staring. It seemed that whatever she did, look or not look, was liable to hurt his feelings and then suddenly it struck her: this Jeremy Doyle had said he was a cameraman. A *cameraman.* Somebody . . . who was it? Hedda Hopper? Norma Shearer? had been discovered sipping a nectar soda in a drugstore by a Warner Brothers cameraman.

So she made herself look at this cameraman full in his scarred face and held out her hand, palm-side down. "Mary Lou Trescher," she said, and then she gave him the jaded flapper girl pout that Remy Lelourie had made famous in *Jazz Babies.* "I was only trying to amuse myself while I waited for something to happen. Are movie sets always this dull, Mr. Doyle?"

His mouth screwed into a fearsome grimace, and it took Mary Lou a moment to realize it was his version of a smile. "Listen to yourself. You're not going to tell me you don't find this glamorous." He waved his hand, encompassing the set, and as if it had been a cue, the banks of incandescent lamps in back of the pirate ship flooded on, bathing the deck in a wash of white light.

Mary Lou's breath left her in a soft sigh, for what had seemed spectacular before was now otherworldly. The open warehouse rafters faded away, and the cables and dollies and folding chairs and arc lamps—they all disappeared and suddenly she was a lady pirate at sail on the high seas.

She felt the cameraman's gaze on her and she blushed, although she was pleased, too, of course, for it must mean he thought her pretty. Of all the girls in the Fantastics, Mary Lou was the one everybody said most looked like Remy Lelourie.

"Oh, Christ," he said. "Now I suppose you'll be packing your bags and running off to Hollywood." He reached around her and did something to his camera, snapping a cap off the lens and winding a crank. "Let me give you some advice, baby doll, even though you won't take it and you sure as hell won't like it. The studio lots are already full of girls like you, with your simpering lollipop faces. I can tell right off you haven't got what it takes to make it, so save yourself the price of a train ticket and a broken heart."

Mary Lou stared at his ravaged face, hurt and stunned breathless, and then something seemed to crack loose inside her and her eyes welled with tears.

"I knew you wouldn't like it," he said, and he turned on his heel and walked away from her.

Mary Lou took off running in the opposite direction. Tears blurred her eyes so, she nearly ran smack into an open door. She stopped, her chest heaving with pent-up sobs, trying to hold back the tears with her hands and getting mascara all over her white gloves, when she realized that the door she'd almost run into was Remy Lelourie's dressing room. The movie star was not inside, but Alfredo Ramon's dressing room was pulled up next to it and its door was also open, just a crack, but enough for Mary Lou to climb the two steps and take a peek. She almost gasped aloud at what she saw.

Cutlass's leading man was leaning against a beautiful cherry wood dressing table, one heel braced on a small red and blue Oriental carpet, the other leg sharply bent at the knee. The sleeve of his black pirate's shirt was rolled up, and his bare arm rested against his thigh. His fist was clenched, the sinews rigid. Rubber tubing bit into the muscle of his forearm. He was injecting something into his wrist with a hypodermic needle.

His full lips fluttered with a sigh as he pressed down on the plunger. His head fell back, his eyelids squeezing shut, and his face tightened as if in a rictus of pain. He stayed that way, frozen, except for the shudders rippling over his taut muscles and the harsh shocks of his breathing.

After a while his breathing eased and he straightened slowly. He untied the rubber tubing and pulled the glass syringe out of his arm, dropping it on the dressing table, shaking his hand. He turned his head, and the blurred focus of his eyes brightened with amusement. "Hey, baby, what're you looking at?"

Mary Lou's face burned with embarrassment because she thought he was talking to her, but then she realized it was Remy Lelourie, who must have been standing on the other side of the partly closed door, for he said, "Come on, Remy, don't frown like that. You'll put lines in your beautiful face and it is such a beautiful face, too. More beautiful even than mine, I think . . . Or maybe not." He laughed suddenly, wildly. "Whooh. This horse I scored is something else. You sure you don't want some?"

Remy Lelourie came further into the room, enough for Mary Lou to see her now. She was wearing her pirate's costume: black satin shirt, tight black leather pants, and knee-high boots. She had a sword buckled around her waist. A bloodstained bandage was wrapped around her head.

"God, Freddy, we're about to go at each other with swords and you're flying to the moon. Does Peter know you're using again?"

"He doesn't care." His words were slurred, but an edge was there, cutting through. "You're the box office, baby. 'Long as you behave, everything is copacetic."

Remy started to turn away from him but he grabbed her arm and jerked her back around to face him. "Are you fucking him yet?"

She tried pulling free of him, but his grip tightened. "Freddy, don't be like this."

"The last picture we made together, you started out in my bed and ended up in his. I was thinking that maybe this time if you started out in his, you'd end up in mine."

"Freddy, you are being pathetic. Let go of me."

He looked down at her with half-open eyes, the flesh beneath his sharp cheekbones quivering with tiny tremors. Then he dropped her arm and took a step back.

Mary Lou barely got down off the stoop and around the corner of the wagon before Remy Lelourie came through the door.

A heavy hand fell on Mary Lou's shoulder and she whirled so fast she almost stumbled. She half expected to see the cameraman with the scarred face, back to torment her some more, but it was her cousin Reggie.

"Hey, why so jumpy, kid?" he said, laughing. "They aren't real pirates, you know. Come on. I'll introduce you to Miss Lelourie."

"No, Reggie, wait. What are you doing? She's a movie star, for God's sake. We can't just go right up to a movie star like she's just any-old-body."

Reggie wasn't listening. He was pushing her forward and calling out to Miss Lelourie, and before Mary Lou had time to take a breath she found herself standing in front of an honest-to-goodness movie star, shaking the woman's hand, and mumbling something that sounded incoherent even to her own befuddled ears.

Remy Lelourie seemed smaller than she did on the screen, but her face was almost too beautiful to be real. No, not so much beautiful as something else. Looking into that face reminded Mary Lou of a summer thunderstorm, of that first instant after the lightning strikes and the air is alive with electricity, and you wait with tingling breath-held anticipation for the explosion of thunder that is coming, and the pouring rain.

"I'm so glad Reggie thought to bring you here this mornin', Miss Trescher," Remy Lelourie was saying in a voice that was husky and surprisingly shy. "Make sure he puts you right up in front of the set, where I can see you. I'm going to need a friendly soul out there cheering me on when they all start to bully me for missing my marks."

Mary Lou doubted that Remy Lelourie had ever missed a mark in her life. She wanted to say something to that effect, about how much she admired Miss Lelourie's talent and how she'd seen every one of her films at least a half dozen times each, but she couldn't seem to unlock her jaw and get her tongue to move.

"Breathe," Reggie said in her ear, but Mary Lou couldn't seem to do that either.

Miss Lelourie had leaned in to her and looked about to say something else, when her attention was caught by Peter Kohl, the director, who bore down on her, his jutting, pointed beard leading the way.

"Remy, Remy, my beautiful, fiery pirate. There you are." The director's gaze passed over Reggie and Mary Lou as if they were no more than props on his set, and fastened onto the face of his leading lady, warm and intimate, and more like that of a loving father than a man who had apparently once shared her bed.

"Now, this is what I want from you, Remy darling," he said. He draped his arm over her shoulder, steering her toward the ship. "You are angry, and the anger is like an inferno inside of you. You are an outlaw. An outlaw who has undergone moral reparation of a sort, this is true, for you are in love. In love!" He flung his arms out in a flamboyant embrace of the word, held them in the air a moment and then let them fall with a sag of his shoulders. "But, still, you are an outlaw. Let me see the outlaw, darling. Let me see it."

To Mary Lou's surprise Miss Lelourie turned and smiled at her before allowing herself to be led away by her director. Mary Lou hesitated, not sure if she was supposed to follow, and then she got the strangest feeling that someone was watching her.

Alfredo Ramon leaned against the door to his dressing room, looking handsome and piratical. His dark eyes stared at her wide open, intense and unblinking, like those of a cat about to pounce on a mouse. Mary Lou wasn't sure, though, if he was really looking at her or simply through her.

She started to smile at him and then she remembered suddenly how she had spied on him while he'd been thrusting that needle into the bulging blue vein in his arm. She looked down at her feet, instead, feeling vaguely ashamed, and when she looked back up again, he was gone.

"Hey, let's go, kiddo," Reggie said, grabbing her arm and pulling her along after him. "Are you putting down roots? We're about to shoot."

Remy Lelourie walked across the gangplank and climbed onto the ship's poop deck. She simply stood there, with her arms down straight at her sides and her head slightly lifted, and though Mary Lou could see no overt change in her expression, her very presence seemed to alter from the inside out, and suddenly it was all there, in her eyes and mouth, in the set of her shoulders and the arch of her neck. She was a pirate, an outlaw.

Peter Kohl had been watching her through a camera's viewfinder and now he stepped away from it and clasped his hand over his heart in a mockingly dramatic gesture that seemed oddly sweet. "*Lieber Gott,* Remy darling. You have slain me."

She broke the pose in an instant, becoming herself again. She leaned over the rail, laughing at him. "You mustn't succumb to my charms yet. The picture's only half finished." She lifted the edge of the bloodstained bandage and scratched her scalp. "Why am I wearing this thing around my head?"

"Because you are wounded, Remy darling."

"Peter, darling. I was stabbed in my arm, not my head. I distinctly remember being stabbed in the arm."

He came to the edge of the giant tank and stood staring up at her, with his hands on his hips. "But the bandage around your head looks so romantic. What is a bandage around the arm? Nothing. A bore. Leave it as it is and we'll worry about fixing things later."

He picked up a megaphone from off his director's chair, and somebody yelled out, "Ready on the set." The orchestra launched into "The Ride of the Valkyries." The giant fan started up, and waves slapped against the sides of the ship, the sails billowed. Somebody yelled, "Smoke! Let's have some smoke!" and the fireworks man shot smoke bombs over the masts, and a white haze began to drift through the rigging.

Remy Lelourie laughed and drew her sword, and magic happened.

Remy Lelourie knew that a scene was working when she could feel herself being seduced by the magic of her own image in the camera's eye. She gave herself to the camera, gave every breath and drop of sweat, pried herself wide open for the camera. She loved the camera with a hungry, grasping, needy love, and the camera responded by loving her back.

They did twelve different takes: all with long shots, mid shots, and close shots, the seven Mitchell cameras all grinding away simultaneously, shooting hundreds of feet of black and white film. Then Jeremy Doyle climbed on board and did the innovation filming with his 35mm Eyemo handheld camera, lying on the deck on his back and shooting up, climbing up to the crow's nest and shooting down, dangling from the ship's rail by his legs and shooting sideways—while she and Alfredo Ramon clashed swords and romped across the deck again and again, leaping over broken spars and burning hatches, and swinging from the rigging, and Peter Kohl conducted the tempo like an orchestra leader, moving it up, bringing it down.

Light from the mercury vapor tubes bounced off the overhead diffusion screen, turning the ship's deck into a sauna. Smoke from the bombs and hot ash from the Klieg lights floated through the air, turning their eyes red and swollen and searing the breath from their lungs. By the fifth take, Freddy was so badly winded his breath was singing and he was cursing under his breath in his nasal Bronx accent.

"Cut," Peter finally bellowed through his megaphone. "That, ladies and gentlemen, is a wrap."

Jeremy Doyle swung down off the rigging, landing feet-splayed in front of her. He was holding his camera, Remy realized, the way she had held the sword.

She pulled off the bandage and tilted her head back, pushing her fingers through hair damp with sweat. "Well, Jere?" she said, smiling, exhilarated, still half in the part. "Was I enough of an outlaw, do you think?"

The cameraman gave her his fearsome, lopsided grin. "A real firebrand."

Laughing, she blew him a kiss as she trotted down the gangplank.

Peter Kohl was pacing the edge of the tank, blue penciling the photoplay, already preparing for Monday's filming. He was vibrating now with nervous energy, which meant that he was feeling good about the scene they'd just shot. After a string of flops, he needed this movie, needed it badly, and the more brilliant the daily rushes were looking, the more scared he became that something would happen to ruin it all for him.

Remy took a slow, circuitous route back to her dressing room, stopping to thank everyone who'd been involved in the shoot. Her skin itched beneath the heavy makeup. She was dying to get her hands on some cold cream.

The smell hit her in the face when she opened the door to the little caravan. Crushed rose petals—hundreds of them, it seemed—were strewn all over the floor, filling the small space with their sweet, overripe smell. And written in lipstick across the dressing table mirror in that same elaborate hand:

Are you scared yet, Remy?

* * *

Mary Lou Trescher was amazed at how fast the studio emptied out once the shooting was done. It was barely coming on to lunchtime when the last bank of lights was shut down and everybody who was anybody had already disappeared into their dressing rooms and offices. Reggie told her that later this afternoon, after the film was processed, they would all get back together again to watch the dailies, which meant, he said, that they were going to screen the footage just shot that morning.

Mary Lou didn't want to leave, but of course nobody was going to invite her to watch any dailies, and so she wasn't either surprised or disappointed to find herself back out on the docks, among hogsheads of sugar on flat wagons and oystermen unloading their luggers.

Reggie was going to a speakeasy to celebrate the end of the day's shooting with some of the other electricians. Mary Lou gave him a big hug and kiss as a thank-you for so special a morning and then she walked alone to the corner where she could catch a streetcar going toward home. The riverfront was crowded with traffic this time of day, but Mary Lou was still caught up in the magic and she floated down the sidewalk with stars in her eyes and a head full of dreams.

It took her a moment to realize that someone was calling her name and another moment to figure out where the shout was coming from. Then she noticed that a man was waving at her from a car that was idling at the red streetlight. She recognized him right off and so she waved back at him and smiled.

He stuck his head out the window and motioned her over. "Can I give you a lift somewhere?"

Mary Lou looked down the block, but the streetcar was nowhere in sight. She was afraid the light was about to change, and so she made up her mind fast, stepping off the curb and almost into the path of a bicyclist who bellowed at her to get out of the way.

She had to run then to dodge an oncoming beer truck, even though her mama would have probably died to see her only daughter running across the street like a hooligan. The man got out of the car to open the door for her, and she used her best smile on him, the one everybody said was so much like Remy Lelourie's. "This is swell, thanks."

It was his silence, the strange rudeness of it in the face of her own courtesy, that made her pause as she was climbing into the car, and turn half around to look at him. Which was why she saw, for just that split second, the edge of his hand slicing through the air, before it slammed into the side of her neck.

Her legs buckled and the world blurred, and he caught her beneath the knees and slid her onto the car's seat. His mouth brushed against her ear, whispering.

"It's going to feel good, baby. So good."

Chapter Twelve

I did some thinking," Fiorello Prankowski said, "while that goon in a white coat was digging the bullet outta my arm with something that felt like a shovel. I decided the guy was shooting at you. Yeah, it was you he was after and all's I did was get in the way."

They were having lunch at the soda fountain in Kress's Five-and-Dime, sitting before a marble-topped counter, on swivel stools, beneath a canopy of hanging ferns. Since Rourke had said he was treating, Fio had decided they ought to splurge and go to some place classy for a change.

"Go ahead and figure it that way," Rourke said, "if it makes you feel any better. And since you're the guy with his arm in a sling and a hole in his hat, I can always console myself with the thought that whoever he is he's a hell of a bad shot. So as long as I keep you alongside me, give him something to hit when he's aiming at me, then I'm safe."

Fio had finished off two cherry cokes, a muffaletta, and a plate of soufflé potatoes, and now he was eyeing the banana cream pie. "Yeah, well what you got to do is look at the big picture, and in the big picture, in the grand scheme of things, so to speak, you're the one who's always getting shot at. You had them Chicago outfit guys after you all last summer. Tossing pineapples around and ripping up the place with machine guns. Maybe they've come back down for a second go at you."

Rourke washed down the last of his oyster sandwich with a swig of coffee so hot it burned the roof of his mouth. "You done eating?" he said to Fio, reaching for his money clip. "Because if you're done—"

"Nobody said done. Done is after I have dessert. Done is after the piece of banana cream pie I deserve on account of all the blood I lost when my arm got in the way of that slug meant for you."

Rourke drank more coffee while the soda jerk brought Fio his pie. He started eavesdropping on the conversation of the two young women sitting on the stools next to them. One had just gotten engaged and she was telling her friend all about it. Her fiancé had stuck the ring in a chocolate ice cream cone and she had almost swallowed it.

Remy Lelourie, he thought, wasn't ever going to marry him, and he had been a fool ever to entertain the fantasy. She was scared of almost nothing in this world, but she was terrified of that. He had asked her once. Her answer had been to cry and then to make love to him and then to give him no real answer at all.

"Before you got shot at," Fio was saying, "when you were coming to the gallant rescue of that Humanitarian Cult woman, I thought I saw Cornelius Dupre hanging back on the fringes of the crowd."

"He's just a kid, Fio."

"He's only two years younger than his brother, and that Titus is old enough to have raped two girls, then strangled them and dumped their bodies in the river . . . or wherever he put the first one. That boy is probably thinking his brother wouldn't be getting electrocuted tonight, if it weren't for you. I was up at the lake, fishing and getting a bad case of sunburn on the back of my neck when all that was going down, so the Dupres can't be blaming me for all their troubles."

Rourke drank more coffee and let it go. Fio's way of working through a case was to rattle off at the mouth, while his brain percolated and sifted through the details. He was one of the best homicide detectives New Orleans had, even though he'd been born and raised and had spent most all of his years on the job in Des Moines, Iowa. He'd come to New Orleans on a case seven years ago, met the woman who sold hats in Maison Blanche, married her, and tried bringing her home to Iowa. New Orleans girls didn't transplant well, though, and so last year he'd ended up coming back here for good.

Maybe, Rourke thought, he should just go ahead and buy Remy a ring and give it to her in an ice cream cone.

"What I don't want to be thinking," Fio went on after a few moments of blessed silence had passed, "is that the shooting had squat-all to do with our crucifixion killing, because that case is already so balled-up it's making my head hurt. And everybody is behaving like they're trying to run a shuck on us. I don't know if I want to be the first to say it out loud, Day, but just who are the bad guys here? A bunch of priests? I'm having a hard time getting my head around the notion that the Church found out Father Pat was a woman, panicked at the thought of the scandal, and put a hit on her. Him."

"You ever heard of the Borgias?"

"They some old New Orleans Mafia family?"

"Some old Italian family," Rourke said, hiding a smile. "In the fifteenth century one of them became Pope. Poison was his preferred method of doing a hit, but sometimes he had his enemies tortured to death in a dungeon he had built for that purpose. He was also maybe screwing his own sister. Our archbishop is another tough old bird, who didn't get where he's at making nice. Contracting for murder is a big line to cross, though. And, besides, it wouldn't make sense to take care of the kind of problem Father Pat presented for the Church in such a way that the problem called attention to itself. It wasn't until he turned up dead and an autopsy was done that Father Pat's secret came out."

"Aw, man. Don't start in again with that stuff about him not being naked." Fio pushed back his clean pie plate, belched, and patted his gut. "What we need to do is have a heart-to-heart with Tony the Rat. Call me a cop, but I don't believe the man went into that confessional for the good of his immortal soul."

"Yeah. Probably not. Anyway, I already called down and had him picked up, so let's let him sweat some more. I want to have another look around that factory in the daylight."

Back outside, beneath the shade of Kress's fancy mosaic tile arcade, Fio paused to light up a cigar. "Did you ever think about it?" he said to Rourke. "About becoming a priest?"

"Sweet Jesus, no. You?"

"My Polish old man liked to say he was an atheist just to get a rise out of my Italian ma, who was as devout as they come. She was all the time praying to God to make one of her sons a priest. Growing up, I got this picture in my head of God's arm reaching down from heaven to smack me in the face with a vocation, like it was a pie. It got to where I was scared even to set foot in a church in case her prayers were answered."

"So you became a cop instead."

Fio grinned around the Castle Morro clamped between his teeth. "Yeah. I guess the joke was on me."

Rourke laughed and then he started down the street. Fio stayed where he was and so Rourke turned back around. "What?"

"I don't want to ask this, partner, but I got to. Do you think your brother—"

"No," Rourke said, and then, "I don't know. Maybe."

Fio gave him a long, hard look, but said nothing more.

"I would say it's not in Paulie's nature to kill," Rourke said after a moment. "My brother hasn't got it in him to either hate or love that much. He hasn't got the *intensity*."

"I don't know, man . . . People commit murder for other reasons besides hate or love."

Rourke shook his head. "Not this killing. In spite of all the planning it must have taken, this one was done with the heart."

* * *

The macaroni factory looked even seedier in daylight.

It took up most of the block, except for a decaying old flophouse on the corner that was on the last legs of its existence. A couple of months ago, Rourke remembered, a body four days dead had been found there, strangled and stuffed under a bed. They'd been renting out the room through all that time and either the guests hadn't noticed the smell or had been too wasted to look and see what was making it.

Rourke parked the car across the street, in front of the raided hot car farm. The Victory Gasoline sign that hung by chains over the gate was still creaking in the wind, but something about the place seemed different today. On the other side of the chicken wire fence, a couple of pumps stood in an island in front of the garage's bay doors, their hoses dragging in the dust. The doors were well boarded up, though, and it didn't look as if anybody had been near them since the riot squad had broken through with axes and crowbars.

The wind gusted and the gasoline sign squealed on its chains, but it seemed to Rourke that he'd heard something else, something that sounded like a faint cry, and the back of his neck prickled. Then he heard the click of claws on pavement, and a mangy black dog appeared from the back of the building, growling and baring its teeth at them.

Rourke turned and started to follow Fio across the street. They walked past a tamale cart that nobody seemed to be tending. "Middle of the day, not a lot happening 'round here," Fio said.

Rourke looked back over his shoulder at the hot car farm. The dog stood guard at the fence watching them, the wind ruffling its fur. When the wind blew just right, you could smell the river from here.

An old bum had taken up residence in the macaroni factory's arched stone portico. He seemed to be sleeping, but as they came up he lifted his head off his chest and looked up at them. His face was creased like an old leather glove and one of his eyes was dead. An old sailor's hat testified to something he once might have been.

"Y'all don't want to go in there," he said. "It's a bad place."

"Yeah?" Fio said. "What makes you say that?"

A sly grin short of a few teeth spread across old bum's mouth. " 'Cause it's the doorway to hell."

"Is that why you chalked those hobo marks on the door?" Rourke said.

"I got something for y'all," the bum said. He pulled open his filthy, buttonless trousers and took out a limp penis, flopping it up and down on his hand. A string of saliva drooled from one corner of his mouth.

"Aw, man," Fio said. "We got us a weenie wagger. Put that pathetic thing away before we arrest it."

Inside, the factory smelled of dust and blood and feces. It didn't seem so hellish a place in the light of day, though. The large vats, the wheels and pulleys and giant fan belts were just heaps of rusting machinery. The only evidence left of Father Pat's terrible ordeal were the bloodstains on the drying rack's crossbeam and the globs of melted candle wax on the floor.

Rourke climbed up onto the catwalk and walked around it until he found, half hidden behind a pile of rotting cardboard boxes, the door that let out onto the fire escape. The padlock had been busted, and recently, judging from the raw marks on the wood.

The killer could have been up here on the catwalk that night, Rourke thought, when Carlos Kelly had come through the door below, looking for a place to hide from Tony the Rat's goon. Whatever had been going on that night between the murderer and his victim, it had the feel of an act interrupted. And so whatever Father Pat's tormentor had wanted from him—the thrill of listening to him beg for mercy, maybe, of watching him die an agonizing death—the killer's desire had been denied.

At least, Rourke thought with a wry inward smile, that was his own theory of the moment. To test it, he covered his hand with his handkerchief, pressed down on the door's latch and pushed it open. It squealed on its rusted hinges like the scream of a bat.

* * *

Across the street from the macaroni factory and down an alleyway that smelled of old brick and beer piss was a speakeasy called the Crazy Cat, known for its exotic dancers whose act was to take off all their clothes and do the bump and grind. The Crazy Cat was where Carlos Kelly had run for help after finding the crucified priest.

To get there you had to walk along a row of filthy cribs, where prostitutes stood naked or nearly so in the doorways and behind the slatted blinds in windows and called out to potential customers as they passed on by.

This time of day most of these ladies of the night were still sleeping, but one was sitting on her stoop, wearing a faded pink silk wrapper, smoking a cigarette, and working on a jug of sour mash.

She looked really young, no older than sixteen, and she hadn't been on the street long enough to have lost all her looks. She had long flaxen hair gathered into a thick braid that hung over her shoulder and curled around one breast, and a pixie face with freckles sprinkled across her cheekbones and nose.

Rourke stopped to talk to her, maybe because at the moment she looked as though she needed somebody to recognize her existence in this world. "Were you working last night?" he asked.

She looked him up and down, and then her lip curled into a beautiful sneer. "You cops ever think of spreading it around?" she said, in the slack-jawed slur of the addict. "I already gotta give one blow job on the house pret' near every night to that bastard bull cop Jack Murphy."

"So in between your tricks last night, freebies or otherwise," Fio said, "did you see or hear anything naughty or nasty going on?"

She pressed a hand to her breast, widened her eyes and opened her mouth in feigned shock. "What, you mean somebody was up to no good? Honey, how many law-abiding citizens you seen around here lately?"

Rourke gave her a dollar for her time, and Fio shook his head at him.

The speakeasy's door was shut, but its Judas eye was open, and with no bouncer on duty they were able to walk on in. They didn't see any exotic dancers doing the striptease, just a man behind the bar and a lone drinker occupying a table up against the back wall.

The air was thick with the nauseating smell of muscatel, stale smoke, cracklings, chewed tobacco, the jar of picked hogs feet and sausages that sat open on the bar, and the damp sawdust rotting on the floor. The tin-shaded lights were turned off, making it cool and dark, but a few bands of greasy sunlight spilled through the shuttered windows. It was the kind of dive where you fought with knives and bottles.

A man with milky eyes and a nose that looked like it had been smashed flat long ago by something the size of a baseball bat was wiping down the bar with a wet rag. He took one look at Rourke and Fio and turned his back on them.

Rourke had started for the bar when he got a better look at the lone drinker sitting along the back wall. The kid had a greasy, pocked face, mangy black hair, and shoulders so bony his shirt hung off them like off a wire hanger.

The kid spotted Rourke at the same time, and he bolted up from his chair, heading for the back door. Rourke chased him into a toilet that was little more than a hole in the floor and snagged his coat as he was about to crawl through the window.

"What'd I do? What'd I do?" the kid kept crying as Rourke hauled him out of the toilet, back into the speak, and threw him hard into the chair he'd been warming. His head banged on the greasy wall. "Ow. Jesus, Lieutenant. I didn't do nothin'. What'd I do?"

"You made me chase you, Eddie. You shouldn't have made me chase you."

Fio pulled up a chair and sat down at the table. "You shouldn't have made him chase you, Eddie. And into the can, too. You gotta be one crazy fucker to make him do that."

The kid looked back and forth between the two cops with wild eyes. "Who the hell are you?" he said to Fio. He pointed a finger at Rourke's face. "And he's the one who's crazy."

"I know," Fio said sadly. "That's why you shouldn't have made him chase you."

Rourke knocked the pointing finger away. "You make me crazy, Eddie."

"Aw, man, I didn't do nothin'. What'd I do?"

Edward Durango had been making a living by creeping houses since he was ten, and he was either real busy or not all that good at it, because Rourke had busted him more times than he wanted to remember. The kid was known as Dirty Eddie, because he always left a pile of shit on the bed of the homes he burgled.

The one thing Eddie Durango was good at, though, was being a weasel. For the price of a bottle of muscatel, he would squeal on his own mother, if he'd ever had one. The amazing thing was that, in spite of all his squealing, Dirty Eddie had a string of sources that had proven through the years to be almost infallible.

Rourke pulled up another chair and sat down, so that they made a cozy trio around the table. "Let's have us a little conversation, Eddie," he said.

Dirty Eddie didn't look too happy about it, but he nodded, wetting his lips. "I got a bit of a dry throat, though. A fella can't do a whole lotta conversing with a dry throat."

Rourke called out to the bartender to bring them some boilermakers. The man tried acting like he hadn't heard him, but then he put down his rag. He took a wooden mallet from behind the bar and laid it out in plain sight, before he started jerking beer into three schooners.

"Don't mind him," Dirty Eddie said. "He's only worried that you're here for some juice, and since he knows Jack Murphy don't share, he figures whatever he ends up paying y'all will only end up being extra to what he's already laying out to Murphy for protection."

It came as no surprise to Rourke that the foot cop he'd met at the crime scene last night was on the pad in a big way. Usually rookie cops were the ones given the night trick on the bad beats like the Quarter, but a crooked cop would consider this a sugar post, because the pickings were so good. A beat cop's salary was three hundred dollars a month. In the Quarter, he could pocket six hundred dollars shakedown money in a week, not to mention all the free booze and poontang that he could handle.

The bartender raked the foam off the beers with a ladle and brought them over to the table. When he came back a moment later with the three shot glasses full of whiskey Rourke asked him to bring Eddie a plate of dirty rice and beans.

"Not only is that badass cop Jack Murphy on the pad here," Dirty Eddie said once the bartender had disappeared into the kitchen behind a pair of swinging doors. "The two of 'em are in the dog fight business together. They got the pens all set up right out back." He pulled a sad face. "Man, I hate what they do to them dogs. Y'all oughta raid the place sometime."

He stared at the kitchen doors, watching them swing into a stillness and thinking, maybe, about the dogs. Then he sighed and poured the jigger of whiskey into the beer. He drank it down in three swallows and raised his eyebrows at Rourke, who said, "Talk first."

Dirty Eddie wiped off his mouth with the back of his wrist. "Okay, okay, I can guess what you're down here trolling for, and I got something for you. Something big." He looked around the joint, as if he weren't already aware that they were the only ones in it, then he leaned forward and lowered his voice to a whisper. "Word was out on the street last week that somebody wanted a priest worked over, only it didn't seem like the guy was getting any takers. I mean, a priest for God's sake. How sick do you gotta be?"

He rubbed his finger around the shot glass, picking up any stray drops, and stuck it in his mouth. He sucked and then stopped with his finger in his mouth as a thought occurred to him. "Jesus. I guess he did get a taker, after all."

Fio's breath had left him in a grunt. "Aw, man," he said.

Rourke stared at Eddie Durango, trying to understand why what the burglar had just said was making so much sense when it was flying in the face of everything his gut had been telling him all along.

"Who's the guy who bought the hit?" he finally asked.

Dirty Eddie shrugged his pointy shoulders. "I guess he's being careful, because nobody seems to know, and I never heard nothin' about it bein' a hit. Just whoever took the job was supposed to put a beating on the priest, and that Tony the Rat was fronting the money for it."

Fio slammed the flat of his hand down on the table so hard it jumped. "Goddammit. What'd I tell you?"

Rourke shot to his feet. He took a step, then turned around. "One other thing. Did Tony ever describe to anyone how and where the beating was supposed to be done?"

"You mean did he say to crucify the guy like Christ Jesus in a macaroni factory?" The burglar shook his head at the wonder of it. "Man, if that had been the word going through the street, even you cops would've noticed the stir it was leaving in its wake. Naw . . ." He belched and wiped the grease off his mouth with a grimy sleeve. "The only details I got—and it wasn't even a whisper, you know? More like a feeling you just pick up on the wind . . . was that Tony's client wanted this priest's ass kicked because the guy was fuckin' his ol' lady."

"Okay," Rourke said, and tucked five dollars under Dirty Eddie's shot glass. "You try and stay out of other people's houses for a while, you hear."

"Shit," Rourke said when they were back out in the alley. "We should've had that talk already with Tony the Rat."

They practically ran back to the car, only to find Jack Murphy there waiting for them. He was sitting on the 'Cat's fender, and wearing that smirk all over his face. "Evenin', Dee-tectives," he said.

Rourke tried to walk around the car casually, while looking for gouges in his precious wax and paint job, and he was so relieved not to see any that he almost forgot to put the mean in his smile. "Walking the beat when it isn't even your shift yet, Murphy?" he said. "Must be payday."

Murphy pushed himself to his feet. "Nice car you got here." He took out his handkerchief and pretended to wipe off any smudges he might have put on the pristine fender. "You shouldn't've left it all alone out here on the street, though." He sighed and shook his head. "Leaving a nice car unattended in a neighborhood like this . . ." He looked around, sighing and shaking his head again. "Full of lowlifes and as used and dirty as a whore's crotch—man, anything coulda happened to it. Good thing for you I came along when I did."

He started to walk off, swinging his nightstick, only to bring himself up short. "Oh, by the way . . . I heard you all called down to have Tony Benato picked up? Had cops all over town, chasing themselves looking for him."

This, Rourke thought, was not going to be happy news. "Yeah, so what happened?" he said.

"A couple foot cops found him for you all right, in a hookshop on Basin Street. Only they were too late. Ol' Tony finally packed so much coke up what was left of his nose, he damn near blew his head off."

Chapter Thirteen

The house on Basin Street was a Queen Anne that had been tarted up to complement the hookers who worked there. Red flocked paper on the walls, black horsehair sofas and potted palms in the parlor, and a lot of lewd oil paintings and fake gilded mirrors everywhere. A sign in the foyer promised: SATISFACTION GUARANTEED, OR SECOND TOKEN GIVEN FREE.

The madam was a plain woman, wearing a black dress that looked left over from the last century, with her gray hair done up in a tight bun and a heavy iron ring of keys fastened at her waist. She didn't bother to look at their shields and her voice said she'd seen it all before. "Top of the stairs on your left. Number thirty-three."

Upstairs a handful of uniform cops and half-dressed hookers milled outside a doorway in a gaslit hall lined with doors that for some curious reason all bore the number thirty-three.

"So what do you know, Sarge?" Rourke asked the cop in charge, a barrel-shaped man with a cue ball for a head, who sported sergeant's stripes on his blue uniform blouse.

"Tony Benato, that lowlife hophead you all been lookin' for?" the sergeant said. "He picks out a chippy downstairs and brings her up here, but then he decides he's going to snort a little flake first, before he gets down to business. The girl said he took a toot and it was wham, bam, goodbye, ma'am. She's still in there, the chippy is. They both are."

The bedroom was what you'd expect to find in a bordello that was struggling, unsuccessfully, to look classy. A lamp with a red-fringed shade, black satin sheets on the canopied bed. The whore sat on a purple divan in front of an empty fire grate, smoking a cigarette. She went with the decor: purple silk wrapper, red corset, and black silk stockings. She had curly red hair out of a bottle; her naked breasts were the size of cantaloupes.

Tony the Rat lay flat on his back on the red and gold Turkey carpet, his arms flung out from his sides as if he, too, had been crucified. His eyes bulged wide open, staring at the ceiling, and the skin of his face was the hot pink of a blush. White powder caked his ravaged nostrils and white, foamy vomit drooled from the corners of his mouth.

"Deader," Fio said, "than a can of corned beef."

The whore let out a little mewling sob. "What?" she said when the two cops looked at her. "I sorta liked the guy. Is that a crime?"

The cops exchanged looks, then Fio shrugged and said, "Musta been his inner beauty she was responding to."

Rourke squatted down next to the crumbling cake of off-white powder that lay on the floor next to Tony's outstretched hand. The piece of paper it had been wrapped in looked like a page torn out of a hymnal.

"A lot of coke," Fio said.

"Yeah. Probably more than Tony Benato ever saw all at once in his life before. He must've thought he'd died and gone to heaven."

"And then he died and went to hell."

Rourke leaned over the body and sniffed, and thought he caught a faint odor of burnt almonds. "Could've been laced with cyanide."

"Aw, jeez." Fio tilted his head back and looked toward the heavens, because only the good Lord could save them now. "Somebody," he said after a moment, "went and shot this ceiling full of holes."

"Some john did that last week," the whore said. "There was a fly buzzing around up there and he tried to kill it with a six-shooter. He said he was a revenue agent. The john did."

Fio snorted a laugh. Then he looked back down at the body sprawled on the floor. "Man," he said. "Are we ever fucked."

Rourke pushed himself back to his feet. He took a turn around the room and then pulled a spindle-backed chair with a crocheted rose seat up next to the hooker. Her gaze flickered nervously over his face, then settled on the smoking tip of her cigarette. Her breasts were enormous, with large rose-brown nipples. A man, Rourke thought, would need both hands to hold just one of them.

"Tony Benato," Rourke said. "Did you know him?"

"You talking about the dead guy?" Her gaze did a quick flash to the body and then cut back to her cigarette. "I never saw him before today," she said. Rourke thought she was probably lying, but more out of habit than guilt.

"So he comes in the parlor, picks you out, and y'all come up here . . ."

She shook her head hard, red curls bouncing. "That blow, I didn't have nothin' to do with that. He brought it with him. He offered me some, but I said no thank you, sugar."

"Yeah? Why?"

"I'm scared of it, you know? Scared I'll like it too much. I already got a zooful of monkeys hanging on my back, without having to go out looking for another one."

Rourke nodded; he knew. He'd done a little coke for a while after his wife had died and he'd liked it much too much. He still felt the hunger for it every once in a while.

"Did y'all talk a little before he tooted up?"

"I don't know . . ." She shrugged her shoulders and took a quick drag on the cigarette. She had a small scar next to her mouth that puckered and dimpled when she smoked or talked. It was sexy in a strange way. "He said he liked me, that he liked redheads with big tits. Then I kinda felt him up a little, you know, to get him going 'cause the clock was ticking and Mother Pearl gets sore when we run over. Then he sucked the blow up his nose and had a fit."

She leaned over to knock the ash off her cigarette into a tea saucer, her naked breasts swinging round and heavy. She glanced up at Rourke through thick clumps of black lashes, looked away, then came back at him. "He might've said something else . . ."

"What? . . . Come on," he said when she didn't answer. "Don't make me run your ass downtown."

She squinted into the distance, biting on her lower lip, and the little scar dimpled. "It didn't make a whole lotta sense to me, what he said, so I might not get the words exactly right . . . He said, 'Come on, blow a line. Hey, blow two, 'cause God's in his heaven and it's going to be snowing in hell, for as long as I can make it happen, baby.' "

"Hey, no, that's good. That helps a lot," Rourke said, smiling at her so that she smiled back and the sexy little scar dimpled again.

He tried a few more questions, coming at her from different angles, but he got nothing more. He took another look at the corpse and then went back out into the hall and found the beat sergeant.

"Stay with the body till the meat wagon comes," he told the other cop, "and warn everybody that there's cyanide in the coke. And make sure they believe it." Otherwise, Rourke was thinking, that cake of cocaine could lose a few flakes on its way to the evidence locker and they'd end up with a dead cop or two.

"The way you kept staring at her tits while you were conducting that official interrogation," Fio said, on their way down the stairs, "I thought your dick was gonna jump up and do the Charleston around the room."

"I was only carefully observing the scene of the crime like a good detective should," Rourke said. "She had a birthmark on the left one in the shape of a Valentine heart. You never know when that might turn out to be the important clue that cracks the case."

"Man," Fio said, shaking his head at the wonder of it, "I didn't think you could grow 'em that big."

"Aw, shucks," Rourke said, as he held the front door open. Fio had stopped at the parlor entrance for one last observation of the girls. Gathering clues. "I can grow 'em that big any day of the week."

"I was talking about tits," Fio said.

"Uh-huh. You say that now."

Outside, they stood on the brick banquette in front of the whorehouse, both feeling down and lost, the case having gotten away from them. Fio had his hat off and he was playing with the bullet hole in the crown, poking his finger in and out.

"Fuckin' Tony the Rat," he said. "Man, right now we don't even got what the little birdie left on the rock."

Rourke didn't say anything. In the harsh afternoon sunlight the Quarter looked seedier than usual. The jalousied blinds on the houses were all rotting, the paint on the doors peeling, the stoops littered with trash. The iron lace balconies sagged. It looked like nothing had been painted or repaired in fifty years. It looked . . . unloved.

Fio slapped the hat back on his head. "And to think the highlight of our day is yet to come. We still get to go break this happy news to the captain."

On the way back to the car they remembered that Tony the Rat had had an enforcer working for him. They spent over an hour looking for Guido the Rat before they found out that he was on his way to the morgue.

The five hand-rolled cigarettes lined up along the front of Captain Dan Malone's desk were all bent and twisted and leaking tobacco—a testimony to the kind of day he was having. His ear literally ached from all the telephone calls he'd been fielding on the crucifixion killing: from every newspaper in the state and a few others from as far away as New York City, from his own chief of police and the chief's assistant, from the superintendent of police and the super's two assistants, from the archbishop and his three assistants, from the mayor, and from all but one of the city councilmen. And the only reason Malone wasn't batting a thousand there was because Councilman Pellagro was in Florence, marrying off his daughter to some Italian count.

Meanwhile, the crowd outside the Criminal Courts Building had grown bigger and rowdier and noisier, even though the electric chair had long since disappeared into the bowels of the Parish Prison and Titus Dupre wasn't due to die in it for another seven hours yet.

And then to top it all off, some maniac was apparently out there on the loose, taking pot shots at his detectives. It was enough, he'd told the maniac's two targets as they'd filed into his office, to make a man want to shoot his own head off just so his ears could have a little rest.

The captain sat behind his desk now, cradling his head in his hands while he listened to a summary of how the crucifixion killing case had gone up Tony the Rat's nose. When he looked up from time to time to give his men a good glare, his hair would stick out from the sides of his head where he'd grabbed and pulled on it.

This time Rourke propped up the door jamb and Fio was in the chair, nursing his shot arm and doing all the talking. He had, Rourke noticed, put the sling back on that he'd so cavalierly taken off right after they'd left Kress's Five-and-Dime earlier that afternoon.

"Judas Priest on a sandwich," the captain said, when Fio was done. "Did you two wake up bored this mornin'? Did you decide to conduct an experiment, maybe, to see how much misery you could bring to my day?"

Fio shot a glance back at Rourke and cleared his throat. "It gets worse, boss. Tony's goon, Guido the Rat—when he fell off that pier last night, he must've hit his head on a piling or something and drowned. An oyster lugger found him washed up on a shoal downriver. The Ghoul said he had a lump on his head the size of a tennis ball and that he'd probably been in the water for over ten hours."

"Ye gods." Malone snatched up a cigarette and flipped it at the wall. "While you two've been out there chasing your tails and getting nowhere, your suspects have been dropping around you like rats . . ." His mouth relaxed suddenly into wry smile. "If you'll pardon the pun."

"It's all my fault," Rourke said. "I should've gone after Tony Benato right there at Holy Rosary, him and whoever was in that box probably waiting to pass him the coke. For acting suspicious or under the influence or some damn thing."

Malone had gotten up and fetched the cigarette he'd thrown. By the time he sat back down again and put the cigarette back in its place in line on the desk, he'd recovered his usual equanimity. "Don't beat yourself up over it, Day," he said. "How were you to know some kind of payoff or blackmail or whatever in tarnation you want to call it was going down in that confessional? What if it really had been what it looked like it was, and you ended up rousting some innocent priest who was only going about his holy business? The good Lord forgives anyone who repents, even hophead loan sharks with holes in their noses, and the powers that must be obeyed would've been all over our cabooses if that penitent act of his had turned out to be legit."

"So what do we do now?" Fio said. "We can't haul the archbishop and the priests of Holy Rosary down here and give them the third degree. We got nothin' to go at them with. A big fat goose egg is what we got."

Rourke pushed himself off the wall and prowled the small room, his hands in his pockets, jiggling car keys and change. "I just can't see the Tony Benato we all knew and loved agreeing to front money for a crucifixion killing on anybody, let alone a priest. Not even for a half a brick of coke. Whoever was behind the contract must've had leverage on him."

"The Ghilotti family's got plenty of leverage," Malone said.

"The Ghilotti family could've done it themselves and for a lot less trouble."

"So what are you saying?" Fio said. "That maybe we aren't totally fucked?"

Rourke stopped pacing to stare at a crack in the yellowed plaster wall. "We've jumped to some conclusions here. That Tony the Rat went into the confessional at Holy Rosary to get paid in cocaine for fronting some kind of hit on Father Pat, that the person doing the paying was another priest or connected with the Church in some way, and that Tony himself was killed in turn because of what he knew. Any one or even all of those conclusions could be wrong. We don't even know for sure if Father Pat was meant to end up dead. The word on the street was for a priest to be worked over, not killed.

"And besides . . ." He turned around and leaned back against the wall. "Besides, a guy like Tony the Rat goes soliciting murder, or even a beating, the somebody he's going to find to do the job would be more likely to use a brickbat in a dark alley somewhere, make it look like a mugging. This crucifixion thing—it's too . . . elaborate. And there was too much danger of the killer getting caught in the act—in fact, he almost did. It's like this guy had some kind of *relationship* with Father Pat."

"This mornin'," Fio said, "you'd decided it wasn't a sex thing."

"That was this morning and a man is entitled to change his mind." Rourke tipped his head back, lightly banging it against the wall a couple of times. "It's just . . . I keep thinking there's something we're not seeing, but maybe we're getting all hung up on the method when it's the motive we should be looking into. Dirty Eddie said he'd gotten a feeling there was a jealous husband in the picture somewhere."

"Hey, I can see that," Fio said. "Guy comes home and finds his wife in the sack with another guy who turns out to be a priest who turns out to be a woman. That'd be enough to rile the Pope."

"Yeah, well . . ." Malone pulled the bottom drawer of his desk out and propped his feet on it. He leaned back and laced his hands behind his head and cast a suspiciously benevolent eye at his two detectives. "Unless Tony the Rat ended up doing the killing himself—which I'm inclined at the moment to doubt—there's not only the somebody who wanted it done and put out the hit, or whatever it was supposed to be . . . there's the somebody who actually did do it. And what is going to happen here is that the two of you are going to find these somebodies, and then maybe I won't be firing your cabooses before the end of the week."

The captain had even been grinning when he'd said it, but there was a *tone* there they'd never heard before. Fio caught Rourke's eyes and shrugged his shoulders. Rourke looked away so that he wouldn't smile.

"Day, stay one more minute," Malone said as the two detectives were about to leave. He waited until the door had shut behind Fio's back and then he said, "Going through the file on this crucifixion case, I noticed that one of the priests at Holy Rosary—"

"Yeah. Father Paul Rourke is my brother."

"Is that going to be a problem?"

"No."

" 'Cause if it's going to be a problem . . ."

"It won't be a problem."

Fio was waiting at Rourke's desk, sitting in Rourke's chair with his feet up and his head back, studying the water marks on the ceiling.

"He wanted to know about Paulie," Rourke said before his partner could ask. "He wanted to know if it could turn out to be a problem. I told him it wouldn't."

Fio kept all expression off his face. Even his eyes were blank. "Okay," he said.

He let his feet fall with a thud and stood up. He picked his hat off the blotter and stared at it for a moment, playing with the bullet hole in the crown. "Since of the two of us," he said, "you're the one who's the hotshot dick with all the ideas and I'm just the dumb schmuck who goes along for the ride . . . it's your call. We could go roust Tony Benato's friends, except I don't think he had any. Or—"

"Why don't you call it a day?" Rourke interrupted. "You're looking about as beat as I feel, your arm must be hurting like the blue bejesus, and this case sure isn't getting solved tonight."

"Or," Fio went on, "we could both go home, spend some time with our families, get some shut-eye, and start all over again tomorrow, all bright-eyed and bushy-tailed, even though tomorrow's Sunday and Sundays are supposed to be our day off, but, what the hay, we're the city's finest and the city's finest never rests, and you're just like my wife, you never listen to a word I say."

Rourke was checking his watch for the time—it was coming on six in the evening; Father Pat had been dead for sixteen hours. Rourke hadn't been to bed since he couldn't remember when and he was dead tired, but he also had that nerveless, focused feeling that could keep him going through a marathon game of cutthroat *bourré.* "You go on then," he said to Fio, "and I'll catch you in the mornin'. I just want to spend a little time writing up reports for the case file, going over what we've got so far, and digesting all the pithy observations that I've been hearing you make throughout the day when you thought I wasn't listening."

"Pithy observations," Fio said as he wedged his hat back on his head and sauntered from the room. "Man, you'd think we could leave off discussing your dick for more than an hour or two at a time, but, no, it's always gotta be about you, you, you . . ."

The squad's desk sergeant was in charge of collecting the paper on the case. Rourke got the file from him and went back to his own desk. He poured himself a glass of rye from the bottle he kept stashed in his bottom drawer and settled down to read.

"Hey, Sarge," Rourke called out after a minute. "I don't see Father Walsh's appointment book in here. Big, fancy green leather thing . . ."

"Nate Carroll's got it," the desk sergeant said. "There were some phone numbers in there without names attached to 'em and he's running them down for y'all."

So far, Rourke saw, five people had confessed to the murder. The captain would have put one of the other detectives on chasing those down as well, but it would be a waste of time. Gory, sexy murders like this one always got their share of loony birds coming forward to claim that some voice in their heads had told them to do it.

Nate Carroll and his partner, George Lappin, had canvassed the neighborhood around the macaroni factory and gotten zilch. They'd also talked to the housekeeper at Holy Rosary's rectory and she'd confirmed that the victim and Father Ghilotti had had "words" yesterday. She wasn't sure what the argument between the two priests had been about, but she thought it might have been money.

The Ghoul hadn't submitted his autopsy report yet, but Fio's photographs had been developed and they were ugly. The killing looked worse in black and white, Rourke thought. More obscene. There was something almost symbolically sexual in the close-ups of the nails piercing the wrists, the priest's hand and arm ethereally white against the black beam. Soft, white flesh being penetrated by the phallic-shaped spike. The black blood.

In one of the close-ups it looked like the flash lamp had caught some markings on the beam, next to the hand. Rourke dug a magnifying glass out of his desk and looked closer, confirming to himself what he had suspected. He'd seen enough suicides by hanging to recognize ligature marks left by a rope wrapped around wood.

Rourke tapped the magnifying glass on the photograph, thinking . . . Father Pat had probably been unconscious then, when he'd been brought to the macaroni factory. The killer had tied him up to the beam with ropes first, but then he would probably have waited for the priest to wake up. He would have wanted his victim aware when he drove the nails in, wanted him to feel it. Wanted him to hurt.

For a criminal law course that Rourke had taken at Loyola, he'd had to read a thesis paper by a Notre Dame psychologist, *Man's Death at the Hand of Man: The Psychology of Murder.* The paper had been mostly academic hoodoo, but there had been an interesting premise at the heart of it: that murder usually resulted from urge colliding with resistance. It could have been like that this time, Rourke thought. The priest could have had something the killer wanted and he had resisted giving it over. Or he hadn't had it in his power to give it over.

Or hadn't had it in *her* power . . . It could have been about sex after all, if the killer or whoever was behind the killer had wanted a kind of love that Father Pat the woman hadn't had in her power to give. A woman wanting a man, say, or a man wanting a man.

And urge would have collided with resistance.

The desk sergeant had gotten the newspapers to send over any clippings they had of Father Patrick Walsh, and Rourke flipped through them. Attached to the article on the priest that the *Times-Picayune* had run a few weeks ago was a glossy photograph of him taken at the end of a Mass. In the picture he had just turned from the altar, one hand raised to bless his congregation, and there was some kind of a black mark on the priest's palm. Rourke picked up the magnifying glass for a closer look, but he still couldn't tell what it was. It was too dark to be dirt; an ink stain maybe, or a small cut. Or maybe there had been a flaw in the negative, a problem with the film or the developing process, and that was why the photograph had not been printed with the article.

Rourke moved the magnifying glass onto the priest's face. Father Pat had been wearing such a look of utter joy that day. He literally *shone* with it, like a beacon in a lighthouse in a black night, on black water. Rourke thought that such an ecstasy of spiritual joy would be considered by some to be a form of holiness, and holiness, surely, was a form of power.

His power. Her power.

Who were you really, Patrick Walsh?

Rourke had been carrying the priest's spiral notebook around with him all day in his coat pocket, and he took it out now. He saw that a telephone number had been scrawled on the back flyleaf. It wasn't a New Orleans exchange, and Rourke started to write a note to Nate with the number so that the other cop could follow it up, but then he decided that he would check it out later himself. He also wanted to take the time to read through every word in the notebook, but for the moment he turned to the last few pages. Father Pat had been drafting a sermon on free will, and his own thoughts and quotations from the Bible and other sources had been recorded in a jumble as they had come to him.

We wonder, he had written, *why God gave the human heart the power to feel pain. Surely an all-powerful God, a loving God, would have spared us that? Yet not only did God give our hearts the ability to suffer the unbearable, He gave our hearts a memory so that we might relive the suffering again and again. Why would God do such a thing to those He created in his image?*

But no sooner do I put forth the question and allow my heart to open up to the will of God, then there is my answer: I must give everything over to the Lord Jesus Christ, including my pain, especially my pain. Only then will I know peace.

Other words, quotations it looked like. Rourke recognized one from Socrates: "A life unexamined is a life not worth living." From the Psalms, from Job. From the apostle John: "Ye shall know the truth and the truth shall make you free."

Everyone, the priest had written underneath this quotation, *has one unalterable truth at their core, a truth that lives in the heart of their existence. Only the heart has a will and it guards itself well, and so it remains forever mysterious.*

Two of the night shift cops came in just then carrying buckets of fried shrimp and cartons of dirty rice, and the squad room began to smell like a greasy diner. The cops were indulging in a running argument about the new cushioned cork-centered baseball introduced last year.

"That's why the Babe was able to hit sixty home runs this season," the one cop said. "Fuckin' juiced balls are taking the sport out of the game."

"See, there's where you're wrong, my friend," the other cop said. "Babe Ruth might've slugged sixty homers, but he still struck out most times he went to the plate. Baseball isn't a sport, it's a metaphor for life. The diamond is eternity and the ball is the journey."

"Yeah? And what's the fuckin' bat then, huh? Can you believe his shit?" the first cop asked of the squad room in general, but he got no answer.

Rourke ignored the cops' banter. He flipped back through the pages of the notebook, skimming, and then his brother's name caught his eye.

It was a note, scribbled in the margin next to a draft of a homily the priest had titled "Seeing God for the Trees." The penmanship was ragged, the letters deep, desperate slashes across the page.

A wicked, wicked bargain. The woman can't be sacrificed on the altars of pride and faith. Must make Paul see.

Rourke braced his elbow on the desk and lowered his head into his hand, pressing his eyes closed with his thumb and two fingers. "Christ," he said aloud.

He opened his eyes and stared at the words etched deeply into the cheap paper, not really seeing them but seeing instead his brother's face from a long time ago when they were kids. Faded pictures in a scrapbook that was probably better left tucked away and forgotten on a closet shelf somewhere.

They'd had some good times, though, surely? Like that day on the Gulf Coast when a crab had gotten tangled in his hair, and Paulie had laughed so hard he'd started choking and nearly passed out. Or that time when he'd accused Gladys O'Toole of having cooties in her drawers and she'd pulled them down to prove she didn't and, God, the expression on Paulie's face as he got his first glimpse of naked pussy . . . Like he hadn't known whether to shit or go blind.

And the best day, maybe, a perfect summer's day, the kind of day made by God just for playing baseball, when Paulie had won the game for them in the bottom of the ninth by hitting one into the stand of cypress trees that marked the "she's outta here" line in right field. Paulie rounding third base and trotting home, his fist pumping in the air and a big grin cracking his face wide open. Looking like someone had just named him king of the world.

A wicked, wicked bargain . . . That doddering old priest, Father Delaney—hadn't he said something about a bargain? A devil's bargain.

Rourke put Father Pat's notebook back in his pocket and shuffled through the newspaper clippings, looking for one that he'd only glanced at earlier. It was a *Morning Tribune* article on a proposed renovation project for the roof of Our Lady of the Holy Rosary. The story was accompanied by a photograph of the four priests standing on the church's red-brick steps. It had been a sunny day then, too, the kind of day that would have been perfect for playing a game of baseball. They were all smiling wide for the camera, the priests of Holy Rosary, except for his brother.

The heart has a will and it guards itself well.

Rourke had just given the crucifixion killing case file back to the desk sergeant when the man and woman came through the door into the squad room, and he felt his heart sink even more.

"Mr. Bloom. Mrs. Bloom," he said as they came up to him. "What can I do for y'all?"

Otis Bloom was a big man, flamboyant in his dress and fussy in his mannerisms. His handlebar mustache and his bald head were both waxed, and today he sported a polka dot tie and a pink carnation boutonniere. He drove a taxcab for a living and ever since Rourke had met the man six months ago, he'd never seen him when he wasn't wearing a long, freshly laundered black duster.

He had an unusual and expensive hobby for a cab driver, though, Rourke remembered. He collected books, in particular signed first editions. Rourke had been in the Blooms' modest shotgun house a couple of times, working on the case of their missing daughter, and he'd envied the man his library, alphabetically arranged on handmade shelves lining the parlor walls.

Rourke had been impressed, too, by Otis Bloom's claim that he'd read all his books, cover to cover. By contrast his wife, Ethel, had always made Rourke think of the little brown wrens that flitted through the oaks at City Park, and Rourke saw now that in the months since the loss of their daughter she had shrunk even more. It was as if whatever had been inside her had gone away, and all the bones and muscle and sinew had collapsed in upon themselves. Her face was as gray as wet ash, and her eyes looked hollow, and a little unhinged. She had reached that place, thought Rourke, where she no longer cared about anything.

Otis Bloom was looking slowly around the squad room and his jaw flexed hard, as if he chewed on his unspoken words. From the little Rourke knew of him, he seemed to be a man who tamped his emotions deep and he'd always had to work at getting out what he wanted to say.

"Mr. Bloom," Rourke said. "It's hours yet before the execution. Maybe you all should—"

"Has he told you yet?"

Rourke put his hand on the man's shoulder and steered them back to his desk beneath the window. He settled them into chairs and then sat down facing them, leaning over to brace his elbows on his spread knees.

"I'm sorry," he said. "Titus Dupre hasn't told anyone what he did with your daughter. And the truth is I don't think he ever will now."

Ethel Bloom's face flinched as though he had slapped her. Otis Bloom stared at his lap, where his gloved hands gripped his black bowler so hard he was crushing the felt.

When he looked back up at Rourke, his eyes were dark with emotion, but his voice remained low and controlled. "Please, Detective, she was our only child. You've got to do something, you've got to make him tell you . . . because after tonight it's going to be too late. We'll never know what he did to her, where he's put her. We'll never see our little girl again and we'll have no peace the rest of our days."

Rourke could have told them that they didn't want to see her again. Six months dead, and after what had probably been done to her, no parent should ever have to look at that. Or rather that was what the cop in him thought. The father in him understood that the Blooms had to know what had happened to their daughter, even if that knowledge only brought them pain. Their lives were already one long road of pain, anyway. Everything they'd lived for, everything they'd hoped for, everything that had brought them joy—it had all gone away with their child.

One day last April, sixteen-year-old Mercedes Bloom and her best friend, Nina Duboche, had been seen laughing and talking with the neighborhood chimney sweep on the front gallery of Nina Duboche's house, engaging in a little forbidden flirtation, maybe, with the handsome colored boy who was supposed to have known that his place was to look and want, but never, never to think of touching. That evening Mercedes Bloom had disappeared off the face of the earth. The local precinct cops had put her down as a runaway, until another evening two weeks later when Nina Duboche had started to walk the six blocks from her house to the spring hop at her school's gymnasium and had never gotten there. The following morning, Nina Duboche's raped and strangled body had been found washed up on the riverbank.

Nina Duboche had had the life choked out of her with the kind of weighted rope chimney sweeps used with palmetto fans to clean the soot out of flues, and so Titus Dupre—the boy the girls had been seen flirting with on the day Mercedes Bloom had first disappeared—became an early suspect. Within hours, part of their school uniforms, two navy blue tasseled tam-o'-shanters, had been found stuffed beneath the boy's mattress, and colored gossip had him bragging to his friends at a Negro smoke joint the night before about how he'd been having himself some taste of white jelly and it was sweet.

It had taken the jury less than an hour to convict Titus Dupre of Nina Duboche's rape and murder. The whole city believed he'd raped and strangled Mercedes Bloom as well, although her body had never been found.

Ethel Bloom had been sitting quietly in her shell, almost invisible, while her husband and Rourke talked, but now she jerked suddenly and began digging frantically in her purse until she found what she was looking for. She leaned into Rourke to thrust a small, framed photograph into his hands, and he got a powerful whiff of dried sweat and sour gin from her body.

"Show that boy this, Mr. Rourke," she said, and her eyes held the bewildered horror of someone who thought she had awakened from a nightmare only to realize that the nightmare was really her life. "Show him her face one last time before he dies. If he has any heart left in him at all . . . Please."

Mercedes Bloom had had wheat blond hair and a sweet, heart-shaped face that wasn't quite pretty yet, but held a promise that it might become so. Rourke had looked at this photograph often during the early days of the case, and sometimes he'd thought he could see a sadness in her smile and a dark knowledge in her eyes. As if she'd always known that bad trouble would be coming for her someday.

Rourke set the photograph down carefully on his desk. "I was going to go on over to the Parish Prison this evenin' anyway, to see Titus Dupre before I head on home. I'll show him your girl's picture, but I just don't want you all to get your hopes up."

Ethel Bloom stared down at her hands, where they now clutched her purse with a death grip. Otis Bloom stared off into the distance, his jaw working. Then he got to his feet, gracefully for so large a man. "Come along, Ethel," he said. "I'm sure Detective Rourke has a lot on his plate this evenin'."

"But I had to give him the photograph," Ethel Bloom said in her tremulous, gin-sodden voice. "We decided I should give him the photograph—"

"Yes, darlin'. And so you have."

Otis Bloom leaned over and took his wife by the elbow, helping her to her feet. It had seemed the simplest of gestures, but for a moment Rourke thought a powerful emotion had flashed across the man's face. Horror, perhaps, that on top of having lost his only child, he was now losing his wife to grief and gin.

This kind of grief, Rourke thought, the bad kind that other people give you, that you don't see coming and never deserved—it ruins you inside. Ruins a marriage, a family, so that it is never the way it was before.

"You take your wife on home now, Mr. Bloom," Rourke said gently. "I'll see y'all later tonight."

Otis Bloom nodded, his eyes bright suddenly with held-back tears, his jaw working some more. "You wake up every day and you say, This can't be happening, this nightmare can't still be going on. And then the sun goes down and it's one more day she hasn't come home. She was our little girl," he said. "Our baby."

CHAPTER FOURTEEN

The raw, rancid smell of decomposing flesh bludgeoned Rourke in the face as soon as he opened the door to the morgue. Even with the recent addition of refrigeration in the last few years, the place always reeked. There was nothing like a trip down here, he thought, to remind you that what's left after death is a shell that rots.

The parish coroner was scrubbing blood off his hands at a gray-speckled sink, enveloped in wreaths of cigarette smoke. He looked up when Rourke entered and nodded almost happily. "Ah, Detective Rourke, what an agreeable but not unexpected pleasure it is to see you. I made a wager with myself that you would pay us a visit before the end of the day."

Since there was no one in the morgue but the Ghoul, Rourke figured the "us" the coroner was talking about was himself and his corpses. Three of the cutting tables were occupied, their contents covered with stained shrouds.

"You will be pleased to learn," the Ghoul said, drying off his hands on a foul-looking towel, "that I have indeed discovered a few additional things about your crucified female priest, although I do not know how useful they will be to you with your investigation."

As the Ghoul's bulk lumbered across the room, he waved his hand at an enshrouded body. "By the by, I also managed to squeeze in the preliminary on your Mr. Tony Benato, as per your urgent request. Death was due to internal asphyxia brought about by the inhalation of cyanide through the mucous membranes, along with a considerable amount of cocaine. You will be getting a more detailed report soon, but first things first . . ."

Rourke joined the Ghoul at the center table, which held the body of the woman known as Father Patrick Walsh. With a touch that bordered on the reverent, the Ghoul pulled the shroud down to her waist. Her torso, cut open from pubic bone to sternum for the autopsy, had already been sewn back together with crude, black stitches.

Rourke looked down at her battered face. The flesh resembled putty, the bruises were black, the cuts bloodless. She'd been a homely woman, but there was something compelling about the nature of her homeliness. A kind of defiance in the raw, brutal structure of bone and cold flesh.

"The direct cause of death," the Ghoul was saying, "was a coronary occlusion, no doubt caused by the trauma of the crucifixion. She had also—how do you police say it?—been worked over by somebody premortem. I would venture a supposition that the damage was done with a blackjack and brass knuckles."

"Was the beating done before or after she was hung on the beam?" Rourke asked.

The Ghoul thought a moment, then shrugged. "I could not say. It was not the first time, though, that she had been so brutally pummeled with bone-crunching objects. During the preliminary inventory of the body, I noticed an unnatural bend in the left ulna and so I had her X-rayed. I discovered multiple healed fractures: three ribs, the clavicle, both arms, the left leg. It was hard to tell the age of the breaks, except to say that they were not recent, and they all appear to have been incurred within the same relative span of time."

"Sweet Jesus. It sounds like she nearly got beaten to death."

"Indeed, from the extent and degree of her injuries, I would say it must have been a close run thing . . . She was also suicidal during an earlier time in her life." The Ghoul picked up the corpse's hand, turning it so that the inner wrist and forearm were exposed. "The wound left by the crucifixion nail makes it difficult to make them out, but these small scars here . . . they are old hesitant marks. The little cuts a suicide makes while summoning up the courage for the big cut."

The scars, like scraps of white string, went across the priest's wrist. You couldn't, Rourke knew, kill yourself that way. You had to take the razor or knife or piece of glass, or whatever you were going to use, and slash up the forearm. Up and deep.

So either she hadn't known how to do it right. Or she hadn't, deep down inside, really wanted to die.

Rourke looked at the raw-boned wrist, thinking about the scars, the hesitant marks, and the hole left by a seven-inch spike, thick as a man's thumb. "The killer chose to put the nails through her wrists, instead of her hands," he said aloud, "but by doing it that way, couldn't he have also ended up killing her quicker? I guess I'm wondering if he could have hit an artery."

The Ghoul lifted the sheet, laying it back over the corpse with care. "Indeed he could have. Either the radial and ulnar arteries could have been punctured, although the radial lies in the more vulnerable place within the wrist. An injury to either can be fatal if followed by traumatic aneurysm or acute hemorrhaging. In layman's terms: one may bleed to death."

He looked up at Rourke, his small eyes blinking. "Only no such thing happened in this case. Which rather suggests, does it not, that the killer knew what he was doing."

"Or maybe," Rourke said, "the killer just had beginner's luck, and all my fine theories don't mean diddly."

"No, no," the Ghoul said, producing one of his rare smiles. "Theories are only useless when they have no basis in fact. It is a fact that crucifixion is a slow, painful death. It is also a symbolic one. There are countless quicker, easier ways to end the life of a fellow human being, yet the killer chose that particular one. He does have a fascinating mind, your killer. I rather hope I get an opportunity to meet him."

"You're going to have to get in line."

The coroner had tacked the crime scene photos up on his corkboard. They went over them together, but could come up with nothing new, but as Rourke was about to call it quits for the evening, the Ghoul stopped him at the door.

"I almost forgot to tell you that I was able to analyze that paper you gave to me. I am fortunate to have in my possession a book called the *International Ink Library,* which contains the chemical composition and formulation of over six thousand types of ink. I went through four thousand and seventy-six of them before a thought occurred to me, and you might have told me at the onset," he said, at the look that crossed Rourke's face, "that the same thought had already occurred to you."

"Jesus . . ." Rourke lifted his hat to push his fingers through his hair. "So it was blood, then."

"Indeed. Human blood, type O. I performed the latest precipitin test, whereby I placed a sample of the element in question on a glass slide treated with gelatin next to a second sample of a biological reagent. When I passed an electrode through the glass, the protein molecules in the two samples filtered outward through the gelatin toward each other and a precipitin line formed where the antigens and the antibodies met, indicating that the first sample was human blood . . . But I am getting carried away with myself, Lieutenant. You are not interested in method, only results."

"I'm interested in both," Rourke said. "Truly," he added with a sudden smile. "And thanks."

"You are welcome." The Ghoul hesitated, frowning.

"What?" Rourke said.

"You did not tell me what this is about, and I shall not ask. But I took the liberty of reading the contents—well, how could I not?

And if I might venture an opinion: I have done some reading in the new science of psychoanalysis and it is my thought that the individual who could write such words in human blood . . . I believe his mental faculties are most disturbed. He might be someone with whom Miss Lelourie was once intimate, or he could be fantasizing an intimacy that was never there, but one nevertheless that he believes is most real."

"You think Remy might actually know this guy?" Rourke said. "I kind've had him pegged as some crazed fan just looking to get her attention."

"A crazed fan, perhaps, but crazed in a particular way. This man—he has formed an obsession with Miss Lelourie. She has become an object to him, and he is driven to possess the object. He might even have himself convinced that he already does possess her . . ."

The Ghoul had been staring off into space while he gathered and recited his thoughts, but now he brought his gaze back to Rourke and in the small eyes lost in their rolls of fat there was an urgency that Rourke had never seen before.

"If he were to have his illusions shattered," the Ghoul said, "this obsessed individual . . . If he were to come to realize that not only does he not possess Miss Lelourie, but that he is unlikely ever to possess her, then I fear he will not be able to bear the thought of another possessing the object of his desire, either. And then, Lieutenant, the most logical step in his diseased mind will be—"

"To kill her," Rourke said.

"Or to kill the man who does possess her."

The sour, cheesy stink of the morgue lingered in Rourke's nose and on his hair and in his clothes, but then he figured time in a jail cell wasn't going to help him smell any better.

He didn't take the connecting hall that ran from the City Courts Building to the abutting Parish Prison, but instead went outside to where he'd parked the Bearcat and got out the fiddle that he'd been carrying around in the trunk for two days. It was a Louisiana country fiddle—made of cypress slats from some old barn, and with bones for pegs and strings from a window screen—but it had soul.

The guard in the block where they housed Titus Dupre had gnarled teeth stained with nicotine, and bushy eyebrows arched over small eyes. The eyes looked at the fiddle in Rourke's hand with hard suspicion.

"You got a piece of paper that says you can bring that thing in here?" he said through the tobacco plug he had stuffed in his lower lip.

Rourke took out his money clip and peeled off five dollars. The guard's eyes didn't change expression, so Rourke peeled off another five.

"I gotta take a good look at it, though," the guard said. "The scut going 'round is that you're a nigger lover, so could be you're smugglin' a tommy gun inside, or sumthin'. That's why I gotta look."

The guard took the fiddle gingerly, as if he feared it would metamorphose at any moment into a machine gun and spray bullets around the room.

He shook it, rapped on the soundboard, peered with one eye into the F-hole, and then gave it back to Rourke. "Gonna fry that darkie's ass tonight, uh-huh," he said. "And not before time."

Titus Dupre's cell was at the end of the block and all the cells around him had been left empty. Their footsteps echoed on the stone slab floor. The heavy key rattled in the lock, and the cell door opened with a clatter of iron bars.

The cell was a six-by-six stone box. A rust-streaked sink and toilet hung from the wall in one corner. An iron cot with no mattress was chained against the back wall beneath a high, small window that showed only scraps of a darkening sky. The cell smelled of the toilet and boiled collard greens and sweat.

The guard locked Rourke inside and then left him alone with Titus Dupre.

The warden of the Louisiana State Prison farm up in Angola had told Rourke once that as an inmate got deep into a stretch of long, hard time his needs got whittled down to only two: something to hope for and absolution for his sins. Rourke wasn't sure if the warden had it right, but he had no hope to offer Titus Dupre this evening, and the boy was too proud to ask for absolution, even from himself.

Rourke suspected, anyway, that the one thing Titus Dupre wanted most right now was simply more time.

He had been lying on the cot, but he stood up when the door clanged open. Tall and slender and ebony black, he had cut a fine figure in the clothes of his profession as a chimney sweep: the swallow-tailed coat and silk stovepipe hat. Chimney sweeps worked in pairs and he had walked the streets of the city with his younger brother, Cornelius, singing *"R-r-ramoner la cheminée!"* Since almost all the houses in New Orleans were heated by charcoal burned in a fire grate, they'd made a good, steady living.

Nina Duboche, the murdered girl, had had hair like dark honey and dimples in her cheeks the size of dimes. She'd been good at algebra and knew the steps to all the latest dances. She'd volunteered at Charity Hospital and had told her friends she was thinking about becoming a nurse when she graduated from high school.

The evening she'd disappeared she had been on her way to a school mixer, wearing her school uniform, but she'd been naked when they'd found her. Naked and a corpse.

Only a few men had the real killer lust, and Rourke kept finding it hard to believe that Titus Dupre was one of them. He thought, sometimes, that it had probably all begun with an accident. That the first girl to disappear, Mercedes Bloom, had teased him, maybe she'd even gone so far as to offer sex, and then had tried to back out of it at the last minute and things had gotten rough and she had ended up dead.

And then something must have broken loose inside of Titus Dupre. The trip wire that's in your head and acts as a brake on all your worst impulses and desires. He might have killed that first time in a frenzy of frustrated sexual passion, but he had discovered that he liked it.

Titus Dupre waited now until the guard's footsteps had echoed away down the hall and then he pointed his chin at the fiddle in Rourke's hand. "You been to see my gran'mon? Did she get you to bring me that?"

Rourke shook his head. "It was all my own idea. Your grandmama won't let me do anything for her." He didn't think the boy would take the instrument from his hand, so he crossed the cell and laid it down on the iron cot. "I just figured you for a fiddle player, when I noticed how the tips of your fingers were callused."

Titus stared at the fiddle, his face set hard. Then he leaned over and picked up the bow first and then the instrument, cradling it softly in his hands. "You got a real mean streak in you," he said, "even for a cop."

He looked up at Rourke, and in the permanent blue dusk of the cell, his eyes were like marbles. He braced the fiddle against his chest and played a few licks, and then set it back down. The cell was hot and he had the sleeves of his prison shirt rolled up to his elbows. His muscled arms were like flats of dark steel, but when he put down the fiddle they were shaking.

"It don't got no tune no more," he said. "Been too long without anyone to play it."

In the six months that Titus Dupre had been in this cell awaiting execution, Rourke had come to see him a couple of times a week and yet in all that time he'd never gotten a real sense of the boy. Titus Dupre possessed a reserved dignity beyond his seventeen years, but then he was a black Creole and like their white Creole counterparts they held themselves proud and aloof from others of their own race. In New Orleans where family was everything, Titus Dupre could trace his roots back two hundred years, to when his ancestors had come over from Haiti. The Dupres had never been owned by any man. They'd been *gens de couleur libres,* free people of color.

At his trial, Titus Dupre heard all the evidence against him but had spoken not one word in his own defense. He'd preserved a haughty-faced silence about the fate of both girls—the one whose strangled and ravaged body had condemned him to the electric chair, and the one girl still missing.

Since the conviction, Rourke had spent maybe fifty hours in this cell with Titus Dupre and in the end he'd gotten nothing of substance and precious little, even, of understanding. Maybe, he thought, the boy just wanted to be able to say that he'd both lived and died without ever crawling to the white man. Whatever the reason, Rourke had figured out long ago that he wasn't going to be able to trick or seduce or force the truth out of Titus Dupre. The boy would either tell him what he wanted to know of his own impetus and will, or not.

Still Rourke kept coming back and sometimes he found himself liking the kid. Until he remembered the dead girl's bulging eyes and the savage bite marks he'd seen between her thighs.

They stared at each other now, the cop and the boy, and unspoken between them was the knowledge that they'd come to the end of their strange road together.

"Is there anything you'd like me to see if I can get for you?" Rourke asked, putting it out there—that tonight Titus Dupre would die. "They're supposed to give you what you want for your last meal, but . . . I don't know. Cigarettes? A bucket of beer?"

A smile full of white, even teeth flashed in the boy's face. "Me, I don't want for nothin' but tomorrows. But you, you be lookin' tired this evenin'. Why don't you have a sit?"

Rourke moved the fiddle over and sat down on the iron cot. To his surprise Titus joined him. They both sat bent over, elbows resting on thighs, like two old men sharing a park bench.

Rourke figured it would be an insult to the both of them if he wasted time by sidling up to what he had to say. He took the photograph of Mercedes Bloom out of his pocket and held it to where Titus Dupre would have to turn his head away if he didn't want to look at it.

"Her parents came to see me a while ago," he said. "They say they'll have no peace in their life if you go tonight without telling them what happened to their daughter. They'll have no peace anyway, but they're begging you."

Titus Dupre didn't look away. He stared down at the photograph, not blinking. Rourke was sitting close to him, though, and he thought that somewhere, deep inside, the boy had flinched.

"And how 'bout you, Mr. Po-liceman?" he said. "Are you beggin' me?"

Rourke let a little bite show in his smile. "I don't ever beg."

"Hunh. You got your pride, but so does I." He took the photograph from Rourke's hands, looked at it closer, then gave it back to him. "My gran'mon would say we both of us're caught 'tween the sour pickle and the sour juice. If I dint kill that girl and stuff her body somewheres, then I can't never be tellin' you what I don't know. An' if I did do that thing, then I wouldn't be givin' a damn 'bout any sufferin' that was to come from it. I'm already in jail and fixin' to be 'lectrocuted, what more can you do to me?"

"There's what folk will think about you after you're gone. You have a chance to do a little good here, to weigh against all the bad."

"Let people think what they big enough to think." He pushed himself to his feet and took a turn around the small cell, and then again, and then stopped to stand over Rourke. "I know what you thinking, though."

"Yeah? What's that?"

"That I don't got a heart. Uh-huh, uh-huh . . ." His head bobbed and he rocked up and down on the balls of his feet. "Well, what if I was to say the only thing a heart does is pump blood and nothin' else? You can stop it, but you can't break it."

"Will you be saying that to your grandmama tonight, before they strap you in that chair? That her heart isn't really breaking?"

In a place like this you learn how to cry without showing a thing or making a sound, but something in his eyes gave him away, and

Rourke realized that for a long time now Titus Dupre had been weeping inside, down deep in the place where he lived.

Rourke looked down at the cement floor between his spread knees, but not before he'd betrayed his knowledge. The boy whirled away from him and crossed the cell in two strides. He leaned his shoulders against the bars, his face averted now from Rourke's gaze.

"She goin' to be there?" he asked after a moment.

"Yes," Rourke said. "And your baby brother, too."

He tried for a smile, but didn't make it. "At least somebody'll be cryin' at my funeral."

Rourke straightened up and reached over to pluck a couple of strings on the fiddle. They made a sound like drops of water falling down a gutter spout. "She keeps fretting about the funeral arrangements, your grandmama. But I don't think it's hit home to her yet, what all's going to happen tonight."

Rourke plucked at the fiddle strings again and then let the cell fall into a heavy silence.

The boy's next words came rough out of his throat, costing him. "This new-fangled 'lectric chair—does it hurt?"

"They say it doesn't," Rourke said. He didn't believe it.

"Doesn't matter if it does, anyway, since I'll probly only be getting a head start on one long eternity of sufferin' and pain." He turned his head, meeting Rourke's eyes, and he smiled. "I been thinking, though, that hell's goin' to be a mighty dull place without you there to rag on my ass."

"Yeah, I'm going to miss you, too," Rourke said, smiling back, and then they laughed together, but the laughter sounded too raw in the cell and they both cut it off. Only now the silence that followed was worse.

Again, the boy was the first one to break it. "You goin' be there when they do it?"

"If you want me to be."

"You be there, then."

Rourke got to his feet and went to the barred door. He called for the guard.

"You come in here with my fiddle," Titus Dupre said suddenly, the words coming fast and desperate and harsh. "You come in here talkin' with me like you think I'm a man, comin' in here to talk 'bout havin' a heart. If I had a truth that you would believe, I still wouldn't give it to you, 'cause you white and a cop, and she was white, and what you all done to me can't never be forgiven."

His big hand slammed against the bars next to Rourke's face, as if the door was about to open and he had to hold it closed to keep Rourke inside until he was done.

"Man," he said, and Rourke could hear the cold hatred in his breathing, "you can't even be bothered to ask what it is you all done."

"I know."

He shook his head slowly back and forth, breathing hard. "Maybe you do. But I'm goin' to say it anyways, 'cause they murderin' me tonight and I mean for them to be my last words. An' I mean for you to be the one who hears 'em."

He leaned close so that Rourke could look into his eyes and see the rage that lived in him. "You made me hate what I am."

CHAPTER FIFTEEN

This time, laughter and loud honky-tonk were bursting out the seams of the speakeasy on the corner, and darkness had settled in deep beneath the balconies and in the alleyways of the Faubourg Tremé by the time Rourke walked back through the carriageway of his house on Conti Street.

He pushed open the kitchen door, calling out, "Evenin', Mrs. O'Reilly," to his daughter's latest nanny, who was at the sink adding soap chips to the running water.

"I'm sorry for missing supper, I—" He stopped and did a slow take around the room. Frogs leaped from the table, to the floor, to the icebox, to the dish safe, to the butcher block, to the coal scuttle. Dozens of frogs. Dozens of wet frogs, fresh out of the bayou, and leaving behind trails of brown slime. They croaked and their splayed feet made little sucking pops every time they jumped.

"There are frogs," Rourke said, "in the kitchen."

"Frogs?" Mrs. O'Reilly said cheerfully. She dried her hands off on the towel that was tucked into her apron and turned around, her mouth falling open with mock surprise. "God save us, so there are."

Mary Margaret Kelly O'Reilly was a widow in her forties with a pillowy bosom and a tongue on her that was frank and furred with Irish brogue. Her hair was her best feature, thick and of a color that on a horse was called blood bay. Normally, her two eyes were a deep peat brown, except tonight one of them was purple-red and swollen shut.

"Oh, Christ," Rourke said. "What'd she do to your eye?"

"She shot me with this, the wee holy terror," Mrs. O'Reilly said, pulling a popgun out of her apron pocket. The gun was made with a piece of bamboo and a wooden plunger whittled to fit the hollow of the bamboo. An empty spool was the top of the plunger, and the ammo—Rourke knew from the experience of having beaned a nun with one once during Sunday school—would have been a cherry from a chinaberry tree.

Frogs in the kitchen and an assault with a popgun. His daughter, Katie, was apparently waging all-out war now in her effort to drive Mrs. O'Reilly back to County Kerry.

"Well, to be fair," Mrs. O'Reilly was saying, "she was aiming for my bum, but I spun 'round when I felt her coming up behind me and got a smack in the eye for being so smart."

A frog leaped out of the sink at Rourke, landed on his shoulder with a webbed grip and clung there, burping in his ear. He plucked the amphibian off him and looked around for something to put it in. Mrs. O'Reilly handed him an empty water bucket.

Rourke dropped the frog in the bucket, only to watch it jump back out again. "Where is the little demon-possessed brat, anyway?" he asked.

"Where else would herself be but upstairs in her bed at this time of night? You were thinking, maybe, that she'd run away from home to join a circus and put the devil of a proper fright in you for a change?"

Rourke's smile was evil. "She's going to be wishing the thought had crossed her mind."

He made his way through the bayou-slimed kitchen, dodging frogs, and went up the back stairs. The door to Katie's room was ajar and he paused within the light of the hall to look in on her. He was used to seeing her thick braids wrapped around her head on the pillow; it was still a shock to see what was left of her hair looking like ragged patches of saw grass. She slept with one hand curled beneath her cheek, though, like an angel on a Valentine card, her lips puffing little soft snores that were like sighs. The room smelled of her, of Katie.

She was our little girl. Our baby . . .

Sweet Jesus, the look on Otis Bloom's face, in his eyes. The howling desperation in his eyes that was like a man starving for food and water and air, for all the things that give you life. How many times over the years must Otis Bloom have done what he was doing now, standing in the muted light of a hushed hallway, watching his daughter sleep.

Rourke pushed the door open and walked up to the bed on quiet feet. He leaned over and kissed his daughter's forehead, soft so that she wouldn't waken.

Back in the kitchen, Mrs. O'Reilly had found a big milk can with a lid and she was putting the frogs in there as she caught them.

Rourke plucked a fat, warty toad off the top of the dish safe and put it in the can. He saved another from leaping onto the stove and snatched another out of the air as it shot out of the coal scuttle. He could feel the Irishwoman's eyes on him, but she wasn't saying anything, and so after a while he said, "She was asleep."

"I thought as much since I didn't hear any bellowing."

"I don't bellow."

"You do."

"I don't— Ah, shit!" Rourke had grabbed a frog that was hopscotching across the kitchen table, but it squirted out of his hands as he was heading for the milk can.

It landed with a squelchy plop on top of Mrs. O'Reilly's head and she squealed "Jesus, Mary, and Joseph," and then she laughed. Her laughter sounded like water spilling into a fountain, and Rourke thought he might be a little in love.

He pried the frog out of her hair. "I'll have a talk with Katie in the morning, Mrs. O'Reilly," he said. "A serious one."

She made a noise that sounded like a cat hacking up a hairball. "Och, to be sure you will. 'Tis why she's naughty. 'Cause she knows you'll be having a talk with her over it and so she'll be having her da with her for a wee bit at least, whilst he's bellowing at her. And the devil of a good it'll ever be doing the pair of you."

"A homicide cop can't keep banker's hours. She knows that."

"No doubt she does, for it's smart, she is, and she can play you easy as a pennywhistle."

Mrs. O'Reilly had climbed up on a stool, going after a frog dangling from the tin-shaded lamp that hung from the kitchen ceiling. Rourke held the milk can up to her so she could drop it inside.

"That appears to be the last of them," she said, as together they screwed the lid down tight. "The silly, slimy creatures that they are."

"Mrs. O'Reilly," Rourke said, grinning up at her. "You are a gem, a peach, a rare prize. If I do the mopping up, will you promise not to quit on us?"

"Hunh." She tried too hard not to laugh, so that when it spilled out she snorted and that made her laugh all over again. "Will you be listening to yourself, you fool of a man?" she said. "Blathering on about fruit an' such. And it's Miss Katie herself who should be down on her hands and knees in the mornin', doing the scrubbing."

"Faith, now, you may have the right of it," Rourke drawled, teasing her for her oh-so-very Irishness. "I'll make sure her little web-footed partners in crime find their way back home tonight, though."

He carried the milk can full of frogs out to the stoop and set it there. He stood within the open door, looking out at the night-shrouded courtyard. A brisk wind sent leaves scurrying along the paving stones, and wispy scarves of clouds floated above the trees and rooftops. The water in the iron fountain tinkled, sounding like chimes made of ice, and he felt a sudden chill.

He was both tired enough to sleep for a week and wound up like the spring on a mousetrap. In a moment he would walk the couple of blocks down to Congo Square and let Katie's frogs loose. Then he'd come back to his *garçonnière*—the outbuilding at the back end of the courtyard that had once been slave quarters and was now a place where he slept and washed up sometimes, especially when he was working on a case and in and out at all hours.

He would shower and change clothes before he went back down to the Parish Prison where he would watch tonight's execution, but he wouldn't sleep. He thought maybe he would take out his saxophone and play a little blues and then he wondered if Titus Dupre was playing his fiddle now, pulling one last tune out of that lonely, hurting place where the music lived.

Titus Dupre, no fool, had called it right, had seen clean through him. It had been mean what Rourke had done, a mean and deliberate thing, bringing that boy his fiddle on the last night of his life, because music had a way of breaking a body in two and Rourke had wanted him broken. He'd wanted to win.

Somewhere on the edge of his consciousness, he caught the sound of Mrs. O'Reilly's voice saying his name and he turned, and was surprised to find that she was right behind him.

Her steady brown gaze searched his face, a little too closely for comfort. "I said, won't you be wanting some supper, then? I've some red beans and rice I could heat right up."

"Thank you for offering, but I've got to go back out in a bit. I'll get something later."

Her gaze narrowed a little, but then she smiled, letting him off the hook. "I've a mind to deliver you a scolding myself," she said, "but I'll hold my tongue for now. You can be setting your mind to rest about the one thing, though. She can do her worst, your Katie, but I'll not be leaving the poor wee motherless thing."

Rourke smiled and reached out to take the Irishwoman's hand and bring it up almost to his lips, as if he would kiss it. "God bless you, Mrs. O'Reilly."

She pulled her hand from his, looking flustered. "Och, Mr. Rourke. Better you should be saying, God help me."

The saxophone bled blue into an indigo night.

Remy Lelourie stopped within the shadows of the banana trees and the sagging courtyard walls to listen. It was music that sliced down to the bone, sharp as a surgeon's scalpel, cutting and healing both at the same time.

The horn went crying up a note, and then segued into the wild and wicked growls of "I Wanna Hot Dog for My Roll." She laughed and came out of black pools, past the fountain with its water music, and climbed the old porch steps that sagged and groaned beneath her feet as if weighted with memories.

He stood with one leg bent at the knee and his foot braced against the wall of the *garçonnière* at his back. He stopped playing and leaned his head against the weathered cypress boards and watched her come.

"Hey, Remy," he said softly, and she smiled, for she loved to hear him say her name.

She thought that the world might have hurt him today. Shadows lay beneath his cheekbones. His eyes, startlingly blue even in the moonlight, were bright and tired. For all the years that she'd known him, he'd had those fearless but wounded eyes. He had a need to believe in a world that should be, rather than in the world that was, and sometimes he had too hard a time bearing up under the reality.

He tried, though; he always tried. He was the most grandly heroic man she'd ever known.

She came into his arms, up against his chest, laying her palms there and tucking her chin into his neck, pushing the saxophone aside as if she was jealous of it, and in a way she was.

"You seem tired and lonesome tonight," she said.

He rubbed his open mouth against the top of her head. "Not anymore."

He set the sax down and took her in his arms, and then his hands were all over her, urgent and a little rough. He turned her around and pushed her against the wall, bracketing her head with his hands. He pressed his pelvis against her stomach, grinding it against her. He was hot and hard for her and he wanted her to know it.

She could match his passion, but she knew that his heart was already dancing out there on some edge only he could see. He loved the way he lived, and she couldn't keep up with him sometimes; it was too close to pain.

They were in bed, still breathing hard, his face hot against her naked belly. He moved up to kiss her breasts, sucking a nipple between his lips. When he started to pull away, she brought her hands up and held his head to her chest, held tight, keeping him there. As if she could press hard enough, then he'd be able to slide inside her skin and live there.

He lay on her until his breath quieted, and then he broke the embrace again and this time she let him.

He switched on the goose-necked lamp on the bedside table. She watched him get up naked from the big brass bed and go to a marble-topped commode, where he poured them both a scotch-and-rye. She knew every plane and hollow of his body, the marrow of his bones and all the crevices of his heart and it wasn't enough. It would never be enough.

She'd fallen in love with him one sweet summer when they were both wild and crazy kids and sex was everything and they were going to live forever. Oh, Lord, she had been purely mad for him in those days. He'd worked on an oyster lugger that summer, hard and rough work, and while he was out on the water she would go into the room where he slept just to touch the towel he'd used to dry his face with that morning, to bury her own face in the rough cloth and smell his scent. She'd been jealous of everything that was close to him then, even that old towel. Sometimes she couldn't even bear to think of him walking down a city street where just anyone could see him, maybe touch him. He was hers.

That was then, though, and this was now, and the years passed and life changed things. And she had learned the hard way that the only thing you can really own is yourself.

He came back to bed and lay down alongside her, giving her one of the glasses of booze and resting the other on his belly. He slipped his arm beneath her shoulders, cradling her against him. He played with her hair, then brushed the rounded curve of her breast with the backs of his knuckles. He liked to touch, and over the years other women besides herself had taught him how to do it well.

"How did you know it was me out there in the courtyard?" she said.

"I do got me a lot of dames," he said, drawling the words like an Irish Channel gangster, "comin' over all the time in the dead of night to jump on my bones, this is true."

She aimed a mock punch at his chest, but he grabbed her by the wrist and kissed her fist. "I didn't hear a car pull up, though," he said a moment later. "How did you get here?"

"By taxicab. I had him let me off at the corner because it was easier."

"Aw, baby . . ." He lay his head back against the bed's brass bars and blew a deep breath at the ceiling. "The studio gave you a car and chauffeur, why didn't you use them?"

"Because the poor man had fetched me to and fro all day, and I thought he might want to go home for a while and see his wife and babies."

"Tomorrow I'm going to call that director—what's his name? Kohl?—and ask him to put a bodyguard on you, 'round the clock."

"All right."

He rolled onto his side, bracing his elbow into the mattress and leaning his head on his fist to stare at her face. "That was way too easy," he said after a moment. "So something more must have happened today. What was it?"

"That's the reason why I came . . . well, one of the reasons. To tell you. Only now I got a feeling we're going to get in a big ol' fight over it."

"Only if you don't follow orders and say, 'Yessir, boss' . . . What happened?"

As she told him what she'd found in her dressing room after the shoot, he set his drink on the nightstand and got back up, shimmying into his pants. He took a couple of turns around the room, and there was a tension inside him that seemed to give off a pulse, like a blinking neon light.

"I just wish you'd called me soon as it happened," he said when she was done. "I could've come down and taken a look. Questioned the people who were around then."

She'd expected him to bellow, but instead he was being so reasonable that she made a face at him. "I thought we'd decided that he was just some fan trying to get my attention, and the best thing I could do would be not to give it to him. And besides, I did call you. You weren't in."

He stopped in front of the window, looking out at the night, thinking, and she watched him. She loved the way his mind worked. Most people looked at the world head-on and full of awe, like it was a master's painting enclosed in a gilded frame. He came at it from angles no one else ever thought of, and then he made intuitive leaps until suddenly he was *inside* the frame and looking out.

"I asked the Ghoul to take a look at that letter you gave me this mornin'," he finally said, coming back to the bed.

She sat up and wrapped her arms around her bent legs and he lay down beside her, on his belly this time, touching her again, running his fingers down the length of her spinal cord as if he was counting the bones, and she thought suddenly and for no good reason that she wanted this moment to last forever.

"This guy is certifiably nuts," he was saying. "He wrote the damn thing in human blood, and you can wipe that look right off your face. This isn't some movie where life goes back to normal after the organ stops playing and the lights go up."

"I just find it interesting, is all. I wonder how he got the blood . . . Oh, all right." She tried to hide her face from him by resting her forehead on her bent knees. "What else?"

"The Ghoul thinks he might be an old lover who never got over you. Anybody meeting that description been hanging around you lately?"

"Well, there is this one homicide detective . . ."

He didn't smile at her feeble joke, and when she twisted around to look at him better she couldn't tell a thing about what he was thinking or feeling. He had his cop's face on. "There haven't been that many men, Day," she said.

"Sure . . . Let's start with Alfredo Ramon, though, just for the fun of it. That reporter for *The Movies* said y'all had once had an affair, and after you ended it Freddy-boy tried to slit his wrists."

"Oh, that's an old story and it mostly isn't even true."

"I know. They're all lies and damn lies . . . Tell me about Freddy."

It had been the first movie for both of them, *The Glass Slipper,* and Alfredo Ramon had been Prince Charming to her Cinderella. It had been a dark, erotic version of the classic fairy tale and their intense onscreen lovemaking had spilled over into their real lives, but their affair had ended with the picture's wrap party. And with the coming of director Peter Kohl into her life.

She'd met Peter at another party the week after the wrap and they had become lovers that first night. He was there when *The Glass Slipper* was released and she had gone from a nobody to a star in what had seemed like a single, blinding instant. The Cinderella Girl. He was there when the money and the offers started coming in, and her face was suddenly everywhere. When for the whole of her life she had felt like a gangly, ugly thing and now they were calling her the most beautiful woman in the world and she was only twenty-two, and Peter had made her feel safe.

They were together for four years, until he got on an ocean liner and went home, to make his movies in Germany. On the morning he left her, he had said, "He's a lucky bastard." And when she didn't ask him who, he had told her anyway: "The man who finally figures out what it is you want and can give it to you."

Until that moment she hadn't realized that she was the one sending him away, and she still didn't know what she had done wrong.

"Freddy Ramon was just a six-week fling. Peter was . . . He told me once that love can be the single most selfish act of a person's life. I took Peter's love and gave back only what was easy, and he was the one who left me." She stretched out beside him, close, so that they shared the pillow and she could feel his breath on her cheek. "I admit it gives me a little thrill to know you're jealous, Day, but you have no reason to be."

"I'm not jealous. I only hate their guts and want to kill them on principle." She couldn't tell if he was serious or not. He still had his cop's face on. "Could either one of these assholes be behind this?" he said.

She shook her head quickly, because she'd already given it some serious thought. "I don't think either one of them have that much craziness in them, but more than that they both need this picture. I don't mean to sound all full of myself, but they can't afford to scare me into such a tizzy that I can't work. Freddy's been on the verge of being a big star for years and if he doesn't break out soon, he's never going to. *Cutlass* could do that for him. And Peter needs one of his projects to make money or he's finished in the business."

"You're being logical, though, and I'm not sure logic has any part in this."

She pushed herself up a little so that she could see him better. "This is scaring you," she said.

"Yeah." He brushed the hair back from her forehead. "Yeah, baby, it's scaring me."

She didn't like hearing that. He wasn't supposed to have any doubts or fears, only certainties. And even though she'd never really liked being careful, when it came to reckless behavior he was just as bad and maybe worse. In that way they had never been good for each other.

"Promise me you won't take any chances," he said.

"I promise," she said, and in that moment she meant it.

He lowered his head to kiss her and then he stopped. "Jesus, I forgot . . . Did Katie see that mess in your dressing room?"

"No, she turned my invitation to come along to the shoot down flat, thank the Lord in hindsight. She said that since she couldn't fly the kite with her daddy, she was going to stay in her room all day and sulk . . . What? What's so funny?"

He'd buried his face in the pillow and was muffling something about frogs.

She punched him lightly on the shoulder. "What?"

He raised his head to look at her. His smile was a wicked thing. "Come here," he said.

She must have fallen asleep after they made love the second time, because when she awakened the moon had risen and filled the room with its light and the bed beside her was empty.

She sat up abruptly, and then she saw him silhouetted before the half-open slatted blinds that covered the window. He was fully dressed. He even had his hat on.

She thought that he was looking out at the courtyard, until he took a step toward her and the moonlight fell on his face. The violent intensity of feeling in his eyes startled her, then he turned away and she felt almost bereft.

"Where are you going?" she said.

"They're executing Titus Dupre in an hour. I promised him I'd be there."

She pushed away some thick emotion she couldn't name and didn't want to. We all live, she thought, by an act of faith: that happiness can be defined and for every *I* there is a *you,* and that every time the sun sets it will be coming back up again in the morning.

And we could all be wrong.

He came all the way up to the bed, but he didn't touch her. "Will you be here when I get back?" he said.

She nodded. She pulled the sheet up tight under her chin, as if she could hide beneath it, as if it could protect her from what she was feeling, which mostly came from inside herself. "I'm scared for us, Day," she said. "I feel like we're about to lose something. Maybe forever."

"If you—" She thought he'd been about to say that if she would only marry him then they could be together forever, but then he held it back. "You won't lose me," he said.

"At least believe that I love you," he went on, when she didn't say anything.

She knew he loved her. He wore his love in his eyes, all over his face, and he made no effort to hide it.

"I do," she said. She wanted to reach up and take his face in her hands. Maybe feeling her hands on his face would make him understand what she was trying to say to him. "I do," she said again. "But only if you believe that I love you."

He leaned over and kissed her goodbye, and then he left her. She didn't go to the window to watch him on his way, but she did lie down on the bed, not moving, barely breathing, while she listened to his footsteps cross the courtyard and fade away.

CHAPTER SIXTEEN

Even with the big oak chair sitting up there on the platform, the room that night had the atmosphere of a Fourth of July picnic. City dignitaries were using the waiting time for politicking and glad-handing. The gentlemen of the press were chasing sources and cracking wise. The state executioner and the electrician, who'd both come along with the chair, were laughing about something over by the generator and sharing cracklings out of a greasy paper bag.

"Hey," one of the reporters called out. "You juice that hot seat up yet to see if it's working?"

"You volunteering to sit in it and find out?" the electrician shot back, and the reporter laughed and shook his head. Rumor had it, though, that when they'd run through the rehearsal earlier this evening, they'd had to use a tailor's dummy because they couldn't find anybody willing to sit in the chair even for pretend.

Daman Rourke looked at the chair with its thick legs and wide arms and the restraint straps and the wires running to the generator, and he felt a chill. You don't see the bullet that comes flying through the air to pierce your heart, or the flu germ that settles in your lungs and drowns you. But this chair—to have to walk up to it and sit in it and die . . .

A couple of other people had laughed with the reporter, but like

Rourke they were drawn to look at the chair and the mood settled into a heavy silence then, broken only by the hollow, plinking sound of dripping water from the Negro toilet next door.

The room they were in had been used for storage before its conversion into a death chamber, and the bare light bulbs hanging from the ceiling barely penetrated into the corners filled with file boxes, reams of paper, and a couple of broken typewriters. About twenty wooden folding chairs were lined up in rows facing the makeshift platform. Nobody was sitting down yet.

The victims' families had formed a somber little knot, though, at one end of the front row. As Rourke came up to them, Otis Bloom looked a question at him and Rourke shook his head. The cab driver looked away and his throat worked hard as he tried to swallow.

Ethel Bloom started to reach for her husband, but then she let her hand fall without touching him. She swayed so violently that Rourke had to grab her by the arm or she would have fallen flat on her face. The gin was rising off her in fumes, and her eyes wouldn't focus.

Nina Duboche's father was doing all the talking, telling the others everything he knew about the instrument of execution that would soon end the life of his daughter's killer. Clive Duboche had bootblack hair that grew into a widow's peak halfway down his forehead, and his nose and the hollows in his cheeks were sprayed with tiny acne scars. He had the slick, good ol' boy air of a politician about him, although he was in fact a fisherman of a sort. He had begun by selling catfish and frog legs off the back of his pickup truck, and now he supplied fish to most of the city's restaurants.

"A wave of one jolt will hit the murderin' bastard for about one minute and that'll be it," he was saying, his voice a little too loud. "Two thousand volts, and they say his blood's going to literally be boilin'. Still, if you ask me, it's too easy a way of dying for what he done."

The others all nodded but they didn't really seem to be listening. Rourke doubted even the man himself was hearing what he was saying. He was only trying to control the moment with words, filling any silent spaces that might otherwise allow someone to ask the wrong questions. Like how any of them had come to be in this place, in this moment of time.

It had been coming on to a spring evening when Rourke had first gone to the Duboche house to tell them that their daughter's nude and ravished body had been found on the riverbank with a rope around her neck. The Mister and Missus, along with their two older girls and their husbands, had all been out in the backyard hosting a crab boil for the Old Regulars, the Democratic Party machine that ran the city and provided the jobs and doled out the operating licenses for things like fish markets and restaurants.

The trees had been strung with Japanese lanterns, the air had smelled of jasmine and roses and freshly watered dirt, and Rourke had been surprised and suspicious to find the Duboche family enjoying themselves at a party when their youngest daughter hadn't come home the night before. When he'd told them the bad news, though, Nina's mother had broken clean in two like a piece of flawed china.

Clara Louise Duboche held herself now as if she were still broken. Her ash blond hair was meticulously coiffed and the expensive black silk suit she had on was offset with a perfect strand of pearls, but Rourke got the impression that keeping up appearances was the only thing keeping her together.

She must have felt Rourke watching her, for she turned her head and met his gaze and her own eyes were as empty as the husk of a corpse. "Is this so-called electric chair painful?" she asked.

"It's not supposed to be," Rourke said, and in the next instant realized that that was not the answer she wanted.

"That's an awful shame," she said with a little rictus of a smile. "Because I want him to *hurt.*"

Her husband patted her arm. "Two thousand volts, honey. Of course it'll hurt."

* * *

Rourke found Titus Dupre's grandmother at the far back end of the room, one gnarled hand leaning on a bamboo walking stick, the other on the arm of a short colored man with hardly any teeth and yellowing Geneva bands around his neck.

Rourke held out his hand and the man introduced himself as the Reverend Roland Wright. "Is it all right if we be back here, boss?" he asked. His gaze skittered away from Rourke's, and his palm had been damp with sweat. "We won't be sittin' in them chairs or nothin'."

"You're fine." Rourke wanted to tell them that they could go ahead and use the chairs if they wanted, but the fact was they probably couldn't.

Titus Dupre's younger brother, Cornelius, stood off to one side. His face was flat as glass, but the eyes that glared back at Rourke were dark with rage.

His grandmother's eyes were scaled over and frosted with cataracts. Her deep brown skin was soft and crinkled like fine old kid gloves. "Mrs. Dupre," Rourke said. "They let y'all visit some with Titus this evening?"

"Yessuh. An' they let me bring 'im some of my shrimps *étouffée* for his supper."

"That's good. He told me you make the best *étouffée* in all New Orleans," Rourke said. He knew he was being patronizing, but he had no real words of comfort to give to this woman, and even if he'd had them to give, he would have had no right to offer them.

Yet she managed a smile of gratitude for him anyway, although it trembled around the edges. "I'ma worried 'bout what they goin' to do with Titus afterward. I tried to tell that man, the warden, that I got the burial insurance for my boy, but I don't think he listenin'."

The Negro burial insurance would have cost her fifty cents a week. She would have scrimped and saved and done without for years for a cheap plywood casket and a piece of cheesecloth dyed black to wrap the corpse in, but the funeral she was buying on time was supposed to have been for herself.

"I'll make sure the arrangements are all taken care of," Rourke said.

"God bless you," Gran'mon Dupre said, and Rourke felt ashamed because he knew she'd meant it.

There was a little commotion over by the door just then and they all turned. A man in a dark suit came in carrying a black bag: the prison doctor who would be the one to pronounce Titus Dupre officially dead.

A raw grating sound erupted out of Gran'mon Dupre's chest. "Oh, Lordy, Lordy. Why they doin' this? Why they killin' my gran'baby? You can say he was alla time angry over the stuff he cain't do and the stuff he cain't have, but he couldn't do what they say he done to that white girl. He come from good stock, my boy. Good stock."

"Hush, now, Gran'mon," the Reverend Wright said. He gripped her arm tighter, as if she needed support, but she wasn't swooning. If anything she had drawn herself up taller. "You got to be takin' comfort that your boy be goin' home to Jesus."

Cornelius Dupre took a jolting step forward, his fists clenched, and for a moment Rourke thought he was going to take a swing at the old man. "You think Titus takin' any comfort, ol' fool?" the boy said. "When they goin' to strap his ass to that chair and fry him till he's like cracklin's."

Gran'mon Dupre moaned again, so loudly this time that she quieted the rest of the room.

Rourke gave the boy his cop look, but he spoke to the reverend, whose face had gone gray. "Sir, why don't you take Mrs. Dupre out in the hall for some air?"

The old man's lips pulled back from his few teeth in what was supposed to be a smile and he nodded vigorously. "Yessuh, boss. We can do that. Uh-huh. Get us some air."

"Don't you think you could have spared her that?" Rourke said to the boy once his grandmother was out of earshot.

Cornelius Dupre could produce a sneer better than anyone

Rourke had ever seen. "What you goin' to do 'bout that, Mr. Policeman? Arrest me now just for tellin' the God's ugly truth?"

Rourke surprised them both by smiling. A smile that wasn't mean. "Man, Cornelius, you got some brass in you," he said.

Cornelius's eyes narrowed, as if he didn't know whether to smile himself or use up another of his sneers. "What you about?" he said.

"I would just like," Rourke said suddenly and with feeling, "to keep you alive and out of jail."

"Hunh." Cornelius started to push past him, but then he stopped, and his throat worked hard to dredge up the words. "Titus is my brother," he finally said, and though it came out a whisper, it might as well have been a shout. "You killin' my *brother.*"

Rourke said nothing, because there was nothing he could say—certainly not, *I'm sorry.*

It didn't matter anyway, because a reporter came running into the room, hollering, "They're bringing him down now. Titus Dupre is walking down."

Titus Dupre wasn't walking, he was shuffling. What with the shackles and chains on his ankles, which were linked to the shackles and chains around his waist and on his wrists.

His freshly shaved head shone beneath the bare light bulbs and the skin of his face was stretched tight with fear. His shirt was so drenched with sweat, you could see skin through it. Rourke thought he looked much younger than he had earlier this evening. Too young for this.

They didn't waste any time getting him in the chair.

The guard with the gnarly teeth and another whose large round head rested on broad shoulders without visible assistance of a neck, buckled the leather straps around the boy's chest and arms and legs. The state executioner knelt on the floor of the platform and fixed an electrode, along with a brown sponge dripping with saline, to the calf of his right leg.

Then the prison warden stepped toward the chair. "You got somethin' you want to say, boy? Might be you want to ask forgiveness from the folks of those girls you raped and killed."

"Won't get no beggin' words out of me," Titus Dupre said, but his eyes looked wildly around the room, and it seemed to Rourke that his gaze passed over his grandmother and brother and fastened hard onto Rourke's face and there was real terror in those eyes, and an accusation.

"So be it," the warden said and he stepped back, and the guard with the gnarly teeth took a black silk hood from off a brass hook on the back of the chair and rolled it down over the boy's face, shutting off those staring eyes.

The hood had a hole in its top, and the executioner took a leather cap and strapped it onto Titus Dupre's head. A second electrode and saline-soaked sponge had been fastened into the leather cap and they came in contact now with the boy's bald scalp, so that the two thousand volts could shoot between that electrode and the one on his calf. It was why his head had been shaved—so that his hair wouldn't catch on fire.

The executioner stepped away from the chair, and Titus Dupre was left alone. A seventeen-year-old boy, hooded and strapped to a chair and trailing electrical wires. All you could see of his flesh were his hands, and when the electrician turned the knob that goosed the generator, a steady low humming started up and the bones of his knuckles pushed white against the skin.

"Titus Dupre," the warden said. "You have been tried by a jury of your peers and found guilty of the rape and murder of Nina Duboche. You have been sentenced to death for those crimes by a judge in good standing in New Orleans Parish of the State of Louisiana. That sentence will now be carried out."

The warden for the New Orleans Parish Prison gave the thumbs-up signal, and the executioner for the State of Louisiana counted down: "Three, two, one—the execution is now in progress . . ." And he pulled the switch.

Clara Louise Duboche screamed and then laughed and then

sobbed, and her husband shouted, "Die hard, you murdering bastard!"

Titus Dupre died hard. The leather cap on his head hummed and his hands spasmed into fists. A split second later his body convulsed and surged against the straps, so violently the chair rocked. He seemed to be trying to lurch to his feet to get away from what was happening to him, and then his bowels and bladder let loose.

Electricity coursed through the body of Titus Dupre for one full minute, and Rourke heard a sound like frying bacon, and the sickly sweet smell of burning flesh filled the room, and the smell of hot electricity.

The executioner shut off the juice, and after a long moment when everybody just stood there, the doctor—who had been pressed against the wall with his black bag cradled against his chest—stumbled on stiff legs over to the body in the chair.

He took out his stethoscope and listened for a heartbeat, and then he whirled toward the warden so fast he nearly fell. He shook his head, and his eyes were wide and horrified.

"Shee-it," the warden said, panic making him forget that he was in mixed company and putting a squeal into his voice. "God almighty, good God almighty, the fucker ain't dead yet. Give 'im another jolt."

The executioner, looking a little panicked himself, gave the chair another jolt, and the body of Titus Dupre jumped and twitched in the grip of the current for another full minute and it didn't seem like it could be real at first, but then it couldn't be denied. Wisps of smoke were feathering from the cap on Titus Dupre's head.

"Stop!" Ethel Bloom screamed, pushing to her feet with such force the wooden folding chair toppled over. She tried to climb onto the platform, still screaming at them to stop.

Her husband got to her first. He wrapped his arms around her and pulled her back, and she twisted around, trying to push free of him with her balled-up fists, and she was crying, great, gulping sobs. "Oh God, oh God, oh God, he's on fire. He's on fire."

* * *

The family of Titus Dupre stayed in the back of the room while it emptied out, because colored people couldn't go through any door of any room until all the white people there who wanted to leave had already done so.

As two reporters passed by the old woman, the one said, "Man, that nigger had some cold in him," and the other laughed and said, "Got fried in the end, though."

Up on the platform the guard with the gnarly teeth was taking the hood off the dead boy. Titus Dupre's eyeballs had popped out onto his cheeks, and as dark as his skin had been, it looked boiled red now, and stretched to the point of bursting. There were burns on his head, black and blistered, and so deep you could see the skull bone.

The burns were still smoking.

It seemed to Rourke that the boy had to have screamed when they shot the two thousand volts through him. His rational mind told him that hadn't happened, but it seemed to him the boy's scream had ripped through his own ears because he could hear no sound.

Someone told Rourke later that the crowd outside the Parish Prison had cheered and celebrated for hours upon the official announcement of Titus Dupre's death, but when Rourke stood on the prison steps afterward he couldn't hear a thing. He could see black mouths open wide, and he watched as some Klansman swung his "Burn, nigger, burn" sign against a lamppost and it shattered into kindling, but it did so silently, as if Rourke was seeing it enacted on a movie screen. The man from this morning with the yellow shirt and purple suspenders played an accordion for a white man in blackface, who was dancing a jig and slapping out make-believe flames on his head and arms and legs, but Rourke could hear no sound.

He watched as one laughing woman tossed a gin bottle to another, only it fell short and the smash of glass on the pavement was like a slap against Rourke's ears, breaking through the shroud of silence.

He heard the shouts then, and the laughter and the accordion and car horns. He smelled car exhaust, and the New Orleans smell of swamp and must. The wind bit at his flayed skin and he could feel sweat in eyes, and his own heart beating in his chest.

He breathed, and sucked life deep into his lungs.

After the execution, Romeo had hung around with the crowd in front of the Parish Prison, drawn into it in spite of himself. Some jackass in a yellow shirt and purple suspenders and teeth like a beaver's was talking about how Titus Dupre's head had caught on fire when they'd pulled the switch, talking as if he'd actually been in the room when it happened and describing the moment in all its gory detail. He talked a good game, but Romeo knew the man had no real conception of what fire could do to human flesh: the way the flames could melt skin and tissue and boil the blood, and how fat crackled and popped when it burned, and smelled like the back end of a greasy diner.

Romeo had joined in the laughter, though, because the whole thing had amused him even if he really didn't give a holy fuck if the State of Louisiana had fried that colored boy's ass tonight, or fried his head. It didn't change things. Not what had come before, and it sure didn't change what was coming after.

It wasn't long before he had grown bored with the man in the purple suspenders and so he'd ducked into a nearby speakeasy for a drink, but the gin they served had tasted sour and he'd never taken much pleasure from drinking alone. He'd left the glass on the bar still mostly full and went back into the night. He prowled the empty neighborhoods for a while, which were deserted except for near the prison where the party looked to be lasting until dawn, and when the first brush of daylight was painting the river water gray and washing out the neon lights on Canal Street, he went on home to bed.

To bed and into the arms of Remy Lelourie.

* * *

Romeo loved Remy Lelourie to death, but she wore him out at times. She could be wild and wicked one night, soft and loving the next. Some nights she could be cruel. She'd tease him until he'd almost be coming and then she'd pull back, again and again, until his balls were blue and his cock was raw, and then she would threaten to leave him in that state, making him whimper and beg. Sometimes she would go on and leave him anyway, and he'd hate her to death then.

He wasn't feeling particularly charitable with her tonight, in any event. The notes that he'd written her, in his blood, in her lipstick—they were supposed to make her see that she had to change her ways if there was to be any hope for them. All those lies of hers, all those betrayals and broken promises . . . Why couldn't she see that they had to *stop?*

"Don't make me do it, Remy," he shouted at her. "Don't make me do it." And then that little voice deep in his head, the one he couldn't shut up now no matter how much dope he shot in his veins, began to chant:

> *"For never was a story of more woe*
> *Than this of Juliet and her Romeo."*

The voice made him so mad he swung at her face with his balled-up fist. Only he caught himself up at the last minute, shifting his weight so that he punched the wall instead. Punched a big hole through the plaster.

He fucked the hell out of her after that. Pounded into her until the bed shook and more pieces of plaster crumbled out of the wall. Pounded into her so hard his butt lifted off the bed, and when he came he hooted like a loon.

Romeo lay on the bed, running with sweat, his chest heaving, his cock twitching and slowly dying.

When he could catch enough of a breath, he got up. He wiped off his belly and hands with a ragged towel and then tossed the towel on top of the pile of dirty clothes in the corner. As he tucked his wet, limp penis back into his trousers, for some reason an image came into his head of that colored boy they'd fried tonight. When two thousand volts of electricity shoot through your body, do you get a hard-on?

Hey, he should've asked that know-it-all asshole with the purple suspenders, Romeo thought, and then laughed at himself.

"Jesus, you're one sick bastard," he said, and then the laughter fell off his face. Melted off his face, as if it had been burned off. "Fuck it," he said to that, and then he shouted it, nice and loud, drawing out the vowels. "Fuuuck iiiiit!"

He made a halfhearted attempt to straighten the bed. The sheets were gray and reeked of sex, and the bottom one was starting to rip at one corner. He hadn't noticed that before and he felt suddenly ashamed. She was used to better, used to the best, and yet she hadn't complained. He'd pick up some new sheets tomorrow and maybe some of those nice, sweet-smelling soaps they sold in drugstores.

"I'll do right by you, darlin'," he told her. "But you also got to do right by me."

He picked up her photograph and put it back on the bedside table, but not before kissing her first.

"Soon, Remy," he said. *Soon.*

But not yet.

In the meantime, though, a new day was dawning and he had places to go.

Someone to see.

Chapter Seventeen

Early every Sunday morning for the last fifty-seven years, Tornado Jones had gotten up with the sun and gone on down to the river to catch himself a mess of catfish to fry up for breakfast. It had gotten harder lately; what with the way the rheumatism was twisting up his old bones into sailor's knots, it had gotten hard just dragging his sorry ol' ass out of bed. He kept on doing it, though, even on the Sundays when he wasn't much hungry for fish. Habits made a man dependable and Tornado Jones prided himself on being a man of habit. Tornado Jones liked to say that come Sunday mornings, you could *depend* on finding him down at the riverbank cleaning up a string of fresh-caught mudcats.

Tornado's mama hadn't given him such a name when he was born, of course. Tornado liked to tell folk he couldn't remember what his given name was—he'd been called Tornado for so long. He'd been a champion prizefighter in his younger days, and the newspapers had taken to calling him Tornado because of the way he windmilled his punches and danced around his opponent in the ring. Hunh. He hadn't been dancing, he'd been ducking, only he'd never told anybody that. Lord Gawd, he'd been fast in those days, though. Everything about him had been fast, including his patter. He'd had a patter that could charm the peaches off the trees, in those days.

Not so quick anymore, though, uh-uh, he thought, as he picked through a web of dried algae and river trash on his way across the mud flat to the river. Certainly wasn't moving like any tornado this morning. Done lost his patter, and his ducking and dancing, and his windmill punches, too. He was going on eighty-three now, and it had been a long time since he'd swatted at anything bigger than a mosquito.

His old bones creaked and his old joints cracked as he squatted on the bank and dipped a tin pan into the water. He pulled a mudcat off the string and slit its belly, enjoying the heat of the morning sun on his back. It had been cool lately, but today it looked like it was fixing to be hot. The sky was white as bone.

He paused in his fish cleaning for a moment to take in the morning. He watched the mud daubers fly around and the crawfish peep above their mud holes. Around a bend upriver it looked like there was a dead garfish lying on the gray mud beach, adding to the stink. The Mississippi, he thought, was one big mess of smelly mud.

He went on with his chore, but his gaze kept going back to that dead garfish upriver. Finally, he creaked and cracked back to his feet, wiping the drying fish scales off his hands on the seat of his britches. He walked along the bank, toward the bend in the river, squinting against the sun.

Wasn't no dead garfish, after all, thought Tornado Jones as he got closer. Not unless garfish had figured out a way to grow hair.

Daman Rourke found a parking place two blocks from Our Lady of the Holy Rosary, just as the bell began to toll for the eight o'clock Mass. He shut off the Bearcat's engine and turned to look at his daughter, who was in the passenger seat next to him.

She didn't look as if she could ever cause her daddy a day of misery, sitting there in a yellow dress all frilled up with ruffles and lace, little white cotton gloves on her hands and her First Communion missal in her lap. Her straw hat covered most of her massacred hair, but she still smelled strongly of lye soap, thanks to Mrs. O'Reilly, who'd had her on her hands and knees in the kitchen earlier this morning, scrubbing up frog slime.

She turned just then and looked up at him, and Rourke had to work hard to keep from melting beneath the power of her smile.

He cleared his throat and tried to look as a responsible daddy ought. "And while we're sitting there in church, young lady," he said, "I want you to be thinking about nothing but frogs and the wages of sin."

She heaved such an exasperated sigh that the brim of her hat flapped. "Sweet Jesus," she said, in a dead-on imitation of Rourke himself. "I just don't know why you're making such a big fuss over a few frogs in the kitchen. I bet you did lots worse when you were my age."

"Watch your mouth, and my sins are not under discussion here. Besides, boys are allowed to do worse. It's part of the grand scheme of things."

"Sweet . . ." She caught his eye and changed her mind. ". . . mercy. Who made up that rule? I bet it was a boy."

"Hunh." Rourke tried to sell her an I-got-your-number look, but she wasn't buying.

Instead, she tried to sell him a little-miss-innocent look in return. "It's supposed to be a really big sin, isn't it, Daddy? To miss Mass on Sunday?"

"You'd better not be going with this where I think you're going . . ."

"I'm only saying that, shouldn't Mrs. O'Reilly be setting a good example for me? If she's going to be my nanny, and all?"

"Mrs. O'Reilly's relationship with God and the Holy Catholic Church is her own business. And you might as well give it up, Miss Katherine Elizabeth Rourke, because she's not only staying, she's going to end up reforming us both."

Bells rang and incense drifted in a heady cloud above an altar draped in white silk. From his knees, Daman Rourke watched his brother raise the golden chalice above his head for all to see and adore. *"His est enim calix sanguinis mei . . ."*

If you were a Catholic who still believed, then what you were witnessing was a miracle: where bread and wine *became* the body and blood of Christ, and if you partook of Him, then your salvation was possible.

His est enim calix sanguinis mei . . . Take this, all of you, and drink from it: this is the cup of my blood, the blood of the new and everlasting covenant.

If you still believed . . . If you were who you were, though, and always thinking of yourself as so damn tough, doing what you had to do and relying only on yourself, then you would long ago have turned away from the faith of your childhood and gone looking for your own brand of salvation in the arms of a woman or the bottom of a bottle, or in a betting slip or a *bourré* pot, and you would have learned not to pray for favors or forgiveness until eventually there came that day when you realized that you had forgotten how.

Only if you were a priest . . .

If you were a priest, you not only must believe in miracles, it is you who must make them happen. *I am a priest.* Father Pat had written those words in his notebook. Written them emphatically, pressing the lead hard into the paper, digging three deep lines under the words. Father Pat. He. She. Even as he wrote those words, she had to have seen the lie in them. The woman who called herself Father Patrick Walsh could never be a priest in the eyes of the church he had vowed to serve. But if so, then had all her miracles been false ones?

And what about Paulie? As he performed his miracle on this Sunday morning, as he changed the wine and bread into the living blood and flesh of Jesus Christ who died on the cross so that all God's children could know eternal life—what lies was Father Paul Rourke living even now?

We are each of us two people, Rourke thought, the one you see and the one nobody sees. And it is often those we love the most and should know the best, who most elude us. He did know, though, that in order to unmask Father Pat's killer, he was going to have to rip the masks off the souls of the priests in this parish. *All* of their souls, including his brother's, and if Paulie broke under the exposure, then so be it.

A man relied only on himself, and he did what he had to do.

Agnus Dei, qui tollis peccata mundi: misere nobis. Lamb of God, who taketh away the sins of the world: have mercy on us.

One by one the communicants knelt at the chancel rail and took the body of Christ into their mouths and they were saved. At least until they sinned again.

Domine, non sum dignus, ut intres sub tectum meum, sed tanum dic verbo, et sanabitur anima mea. Lord, I am not worthy that You should enter under my roof, but only say the word and my soul shall be healed.

Katie went, but Rourke did not, because he had sinned plenty since his last confession. Too many sins, he thought with a smile that should've been ashamed of itself, but wasn't—the most recent being last night, when he'd made love to a sex goddess three times, out of wedlock.

Rourke watched, though, as Floriane de Lassus Layton and her own daughter knelt and received the Host. The woman teetered on her high-heeled shoes a little as she stood up, and the man who'd preceded her turned back to take her arm, and it seemed to Rourke for a flash of an instant that she'd cringed beneath his touch, and Rourke thought, *hunh.*

As if he felt Rourke watching him, the man looked up just then and met Rourke's gaze, and he smiled. A challenge there, perhaps, and Rourke thought, *hunh,* again.

Father Paul Rourke ended the Mass by bending over and kissing the altar, and as he turned, Rourke searched his brother's face for signs of joy or even of wonder, but he didn't see any.

The closing hymn had a dying fall in it, a musical swoon, and as the last notes floated up to the vaulted ceiling, Rourke turned to his daughter and said, "Sit here and wait for me, honey. And think about frogs."

Katie made a face at him, but then she laughed. He kissed the top of her straw hat and then made it out of the pew in time to intercept the Laytons as they were coming down the aisle.

Flo Layton looked pretty in a yellow linen cloche hat with a white silk rose, but she still had that shame going on deep in her eyes. "Mornin', Lieutenant," she said softly, and then looked over at her husband as if she were drowning and she thought him more likely to push her under than save her.

Albert Payne Layton had light red hair, the color of orange peel, and a smooth, heavily freckled face. He toyed with a Phi Beta Kappa key dangling from the thin gold chain that stretched across his brown and yellow checked wool vest, and Rourke saw that he even had freckles on the backs of his fingers.

"A terrible thing, Detective," he was saying. "What was done to Father Pat. I trust you all are close to apprehending the murderer. Otherwise, one shudders to think that simply no one is safe and we could all be slaughtered in our beds."

"I shouldn't worry if I were you," Rourke said. "It seems to have been a selective killing."

"A personal vendetta, then, you think? And not the act of a madman?" A secretive little smile seemed to be playing around the corners of the man's full mouth. "All the more reason then, surely, to hope that everyone . . ." And he paused to give his wife a look that served to underline the word. "That *everyone* has been cooperating fully with the police in their investigation. I'm willing to oblige, too, of course, but I don't know what I can tell you. As Holy Rosary's accountant, I had some dealings with the Father, but we weren't particularly close. My wife, on the other hand . . ." He turned to her again and touched her arm, and this time Rourke was sure he saw her flinch. "Y'all were especially fond of each other, weren't you, darling? You and your precious Father Pat."

"Bertie, don't. He was our priest."

"I'm sorry. Was I being flippant? I didn't mean to be."

Rourke smiled at him and said, "I'd like to know where you were, Mr. Layton, during the late hours of Friday night. Say, between midnight and three."

It happened sometimes when you were interviewing a suspect or witness. You saw it deep in the back of their eyes—a little *click,* like the shutter on a camera. A revealing flash that told you that here was someone with something to hide.

And Albert Payne Layton appeared to be a man who relished his secrets, sucking on them and savoring them like they were hard rock candy. "Must we go into that here, Detective?" he was saying, lowering his voice and looking around the emptying nave. "We are, after all, in the presence of the Holy Eucharist."

"We can go into it downtown in the squad room," Rourke said, still smiling. "Where I keep a sockful of nickels in my desk drawer."

Layton laughed and gave a little shudder. "Dear me. I've heard about the methods you cops use to beat the truth out of your suspects." He paused and then made his eyes go wide, as if suddenly shocked. "Am I a suspect? Good heavens, I rather hope not, since I grow queasy at the merest sight of blood, especially my own . . ." Another pause, followed by a little sigh of surrender and a chagrined glance at Mrs. Layton. "If you must know, I spent the night, the whole night, with a woman other than my wife, but one who can and will support my alibi, and in public if necessary. Should that be necessary."

"We can be discreet, but we will need to talk to her," Rourke said, thinking: That, Mr. Albert Payne Layton, was smoothly, if a bit too obviously, done. And all the while there had been laughter in those pale eyes. Laughter and something else.

That little *click.*

Rourke found his brother with the two altar boys back in Holy Rosary's oak-paneled vestry. One boy was helping the priest take off his chasuble, the vestment worn to celebrate the Mass. It was a heavy satin and brocade cloak, green for this time of the liturgical season, and thickly embroidered with silver and gold thread.

The other boy was putting the holy oils away in a mother-of-pearl cabinet and laughing about something. Laughter that cut off abruptly when he glanced up and saw Rourke in the doorway.

"Give me a few minutes alone with Father, would you please?" Rourke said.

The two boys looked to their priest, who nodded.

"Well, Day," Paulie said, when they were alone. "I wish I could believe it was devotion that brought you to Mass this morning, but I am thankful nonetheless."

Rourke said nothing. He looked at his brother and saw that since yesterday morning the fear had found its way into the cast of his eyes and the set of his mouth. Their mother's mouth, Rourke realized suddenly, and for the first time. Paulie had their mother's mouth, and the thought made him feel sick.

Paulie turned his back to him, going to the big walnut armoire that housed the priests' vestments. "What've you done with your Katie?"

Rourke waited another beat and then said, "I parked her in your Sunday school and told her to think about frogs. Maybe it'll do her some good, although I doubt it."

"Never did you any good. In fact, the way I remember it, you used to terrorize the poor nuns who taught Sunday school at St. Alphonsus." He took off his cincture and stole and hung them in the wardrobe. "So how come Katie has to think about frogs?"

Rourke recounted Katie's latest campaign to rid the Conti Street house of Mrs. O'Reilly, telling it in such a way that he soon had his brother laughing. In a street brawl, it always helped if you distracted your opponent before you nailed him with your sucker punch.

"You reap what you sow, little brother," Paulie said, when he was done. "Remember how we used to go out and catch crawfish in the ditch after it rained and that one time when you found a baby alligator? You tried to make a pet out of him. You used to take him for a walk on a leash just for the pleasure of seeing all the neighbor ladies run off screaming into the night."

"Yeah, yeah. I remember," Rourke said. "But don't you ever go telling Katie that story. Not if you care at all about my peace of mind."

Paulie laughed again, but he was still being careful most of the time to avoid Rourke's eyes. He untied the amice from around his neck, took it off and folded it, making a slow and careful production out of it.

"Who's the woman?" Rourke said.

Paulie's head snapped up. He blinked and his mouth actually fell open, just like a character's in a comic strip.

"What woman?" he finally said, having waited way too long to go into his innocent act. "I don't know what—"

Rourke had closed the distance between them in two strides. He grabbed his brother's shoulders and slammed him up against the wall, so hard he heard Paulie's teeth knock together.

He asked it again, punctuating each word with a slam, so that his brother's head was smacking a tattoo against the plaster. "Who is the woman?"

"God," Paulie said, the word exploding out of him. "Will you look at yourself? You're just like—" He cut it off, stopped by the pure, unadulterated fury on Rourke's face.

Rourke held his brother hard up against the wall, his fists crushing the fine linen of his priestly alb, held him until he felt the flesh beneath his hands begin to tremble, and then he let him go.

He started to turn away, then spun back around and pointed his finger between Paulie's eyes. "I can help you. But you got to stop fuckin' lying to me."

Paulie stayed flattened against the wall, as if he'd been hung there, and then all the air seemed to collapse out of him. He tried for a smile, failing badly. "I suppose it's useful to have a cop for a brother, but I haven't committed any crime, Day. Not even spitting on the sidewalk, as God is my witness."

He groped his way along the wall until he found a chair and eased into it. His hands clutched his thighs and he looked at the floor.

"What," Rourke said, "was the bargain that you made with Father Pat?"

Slowly, Paulie lifted his head. A tic had started up at one corner of his mouth. Their mother's mouth. In his eyes was the reckless desperation that you often saw in the eyes of the man sitting across the *bourré* table from you, when he suddenly realizes he might have to cover a pot he can't afford.

"My God," Paulie said again. "How do you find out these things?"

Rourke didn't tell him it was a simple matter of reading the dead priest's notebook. He tried pushing the anger out of himself, coming down off the balls of his feet and putting his hands in his pockets. "Is there any wine in here that hasn't been made into a miracle?"

A set of cupboards bracketed the locked showcase that displayed Holy Rosary's treasure: gold-plated patens and a pearl-encrusted pyx, and a tabernacle fashioned of beaten silver. Rourke looked in the right cupboard first and found a bottle of bourbon and a glass in the bottom drawer.

He poured the bourbon in the glass up to the rim and put it in Paulie's shaking hands. Paulie drank it down fast, in two swallows, and with some apparent experience, and Rourke thought of how often they'd both heard their father say that all a man needed to get through the day was a little booze and God's good grace.

Rourke refilled the glass, and his brother drank some more, slower this time. "Let's start with her name," Rourke said.

Paulie shook his head, and the rim of the whiskey glass clicked against his teeth. "If I tell you everything else, can we leave her name out of it? She's in a . . . difficult marriage, and they have children. They could all be hurt."

"Go on then for now," Rourke said. "Maybe we'll get back to her name later after I hear what you have to say." He'd know the woman's identity before long anyway. Since yesterday evening, they'd had a tail on all the priests of Our Lady of the Holy Rosary. Sooner or later, Paulie would lead them right to her.

"It happened last spring," Paulie said to the floor, "when I was still over at Immaculate Conception. You can't imagine how lonely I've . . ." He stopped, laughing harshly. "No, of course you can't. Not my little brother, who just happens to be sleeping with the most beautiful woman in the world."

"Sometimes," Rourke said, "a bedroom can be the loneliest place on God's earth."

Paulie was quiet for a moment, and then he sighed. "Forget I said that. I'm probably only jealous because, priest or not, I wouldn't have the confidence even to say hey to your kind of woman." He waved an impatient hand. "It's not about sex, or celibacy and the Church, anyway—not only about that."

He went silent again, but this time Rourke waited him out, knowing that his brother had come to that place where he had to unload at least part of the burden because carrying it had become unendurable.

"It's as if," Paulie finally said, "I spend my life caught inside some kind of giant soap bubble. I can see things, but they're all blurry. I can hear, but the sounds are muted. Worst of all, I can't touch anybody and nobody can touch me. People come to me—they come to *me*, and they confess how lonely they are, and I tell them to look to God, that God will give them a friendship more glorious than any they can ever imagine, and all the while I'm thinking that I don't even know where God is anymore. Then one Sunday I mount the pulpit to give my homily and I look out over the congregation and I see her, and it was as if someone had come along and whitewashed the world."

Paulie raised his head. He had been crying again. "I thought all I wanted was the closeness, you know? To be able to put my arms around her and feel her head on my shoulder. To sit across from her at the kitchen table and wait for her to look up at me and smile. But then after a while the holding and smiling weren't enough and I realized that I was lusting after her in my heart, and now you're laughing at me."

"I'm not laughing at you," Rourke said, lying a little. "It just sounded so quaint and old-fashioned, to be lusting in your heart."

"Yeah, well I'm a priest, remember? And that's pretty much all the lusting that God wants me to do."

Most people, thought Rourke, subscribed to a hierarchy of wrong: there was dead wrong, there was wrong but not bad, and there was wrong but everybody does it. Not the Rourke brothers, though. Uh-uh. For them there was always only wrong and right. Even their daddy had had that uncompromising and unaccommodating view of the world; it was, in fact, what had destroyed him. Becoming a cop and a priest was probably the last thing the two sons of Mike Rourke should ever have done.

"It would have been bad enough," Paulie was saying, "if I was her next-door neighbor wanting to . . . to lie with her, a married woman. But I'm her priest and so for me to touch her in that way, that would be like God doing it. Like Jesus doing it. I was putting both our immortal souls in danger, and so I confessed my sin to the archbishop. He sent me here to Holy Rosary, and as part of my penance I had to swear a solemn vow never to go near her again."

He let go of his knees and rubbed his face, pushed his face hard into his hands, as if he wanted to rip off his flesh. Then he let his hands fall back into his lap.

"I managed to stay away from her for a while," he said, "but it was too . . . I just couldn't bear not seeing her. So I did see her."

"And Father Pat found out about it," Rourke said.

Paulie squeezed his eyes shut and nodded, swallowing hard. "He felt it was his duty to inform the archbishop of my disobedience and he was right. Only I pleaded with him—God, I'm telling you, Day, I literally got down on my knees and begged him not to tell. He shouldn't have given in to me, but he did. And I swore again on the altar that I would stay away from her."

"Only you couldn't."

"God help me, but I did try."

His brother was also, Rourke thought, one of those who needed to be caught telling a lie while he was telling it. Father Paul, the priest, might have started out to bare his soul with the truth, but Rourke was almost certain that he was lying about something now.

"So you went over to her house Friday night for supper," Rourke said. "The night Father Pat was killed."

Paulie nodded, then said on a gasp, "Yes."

"Did you stay there with her the whole night?"

He nodded again, swallowed. "Her husband works a night shift. And when he comes home to her in the morning, he smells like a parlor chippy and he's already half in the bag. He's still drinking when he . . . claims his conjugal rights of her, and when he's done he passes out drooling a river of spit, and as she's telling me this, she's sitting across from me with a split lip and her eye all puffed up, and I'm thinking that what this man is, Day, what her husband is, is our own daddy come back to life."

A fury, seeming to come out of nowhere, surged through Rourke, balling his hands into fists. He took a step toward his brother, with some thought of slamming him up against the wall some more, of hitting him, maybe, only the other man's tormented face stopped him.

That didn't stop him from unloading the words, though. "You don't know a fucking thing about it, since you made sure you got your ass out of there before it got bad. So the old man liked his booze and he had a temper—he wasn't either the first or the only one. And you're forgetting how he took us fishing up at the lake every summer, and showed us how to strip a car's engine and pitch a sinker ball. He could tell a fine story and laugh at himself, and he was a good cop—"

Paulie came off the chair so hard and fast that for a moment

Rourke thought his brother was going to take a swing at him. "My God, how can you stand there and defend him?" Paulie cried. "He was our enemy. He waged *war* on us."

"Then you should've stayed and fought back, damn you. When I think of all the times that I—"

"That you what? Got in his face for my sake? I never asked you to be my whipping boy."

He had, as a matter of fact, but Rourke didn't want to go down that road. Suddenly he and his brother were face-to-face and seeing in each other's eyes the kind of secret and shared knowledge that makes you ashamed of your own thoughts. Ashamed of the memories of what went on in that house in the Irish Channel.

"Does this woman's husband know she's fucking her priest?" Rourke said.

His brother stared at him, breathing hard, and looking as if he hadn't been able to keep up with the abrupt change of subject. "God, no!" he finally blurted. "I mean, I'm not . . . I never said I was doing that with her. I thought you understood. We're friends, intimate friends, she and I. But we've never been intimate in bed."

"Uh-huh," Rourke said.

Paulie looked around the vestry wildly, as if in search of someone who would come to his defense. On a table, close to where he stood, was the gold-plated ciborium that he'd used during the Mass, the vessel that had held the consecrated Hosts. He seized it and held it out to Rourke, his arms shaking.

"I will swear on the body of Christ—"

"Don't." Rourke took the ciborium and set it back on the table. There were apparently still enough shreds of his childhood faith left clinging to him, for him to fear such a blasphemy. "Don't do that," he said again.

The air in the vestry felt violated. Paulie stepped back to lean against the wall, still breathing hard, but Lieutenant Daman Rourke wasn't really seeing his brother anymore. He was thinking suddenly that maybe somebody had screwed up—the woman's husband, or

Tony the Rat, or maybe the killer himself. Maybe Paulie was the priest who was supposed to have been found crucified on a beam in an abandoned macaroni factory.

Paulie's head moved, looking toward the door, and Rourke realized that for the last few seconds heavy feet moving in a hurry had been pounding outside the vestry.

Fiorello Prankowski knocked and pushed the door open, both at the same time. "What is it?" Rourke said at the look on his partner's face. "Another crucified priest?"

"Another girl. Raped and strangled with a chimney sweep's weighted rope."

CHAPTER EIGHTEEN

Rourke spotted Fio waiting for him at the top of the levee, beneath the green plumed shade of a willow tree.

He'd had to take a detour on the way to the crime scene to drop Katie off at her grandparents' house, where she often spent a couple of hours on a Sunday afternoon after Mass anyway. Now he parked his Bearcat behind the Ghoul's chauffeured green Packard and got out.

Before he climbed the levee, Rourke paused to look across the street. He saw a trucking garage with signs advertising that it was for sale, a small iron foundry, a rag and bottle warehouse, and an old stable. On Sunday morning, this seedy wharf area was mostly empty, but any other day of the week it was a bustling part of the waterfront.

He turned and sprinted up the grassy slope. A wind smelling of musky Mississippi River mud pushed against his face. In the distance, he could hear a ship's horn blowing across the water. A white crane took flight from the top of the levee, into a sky the color of souring cream.

The batture—the low-lying land on the river side of the levee—was littered with a squatters' colony of flotsam houses, whose occupants scratched out a living by fishing, gathering driftwood, keeping pigs and chickens, and making wicker furniture out of the batture's willow trees. A wrecked tugboat lay among the ramshackle houses on its side in the mud, leaking rust and green slime.

The river was a lazy swell of brown water this morning, and the body lay sprawled at the edge of the tide, with the Ghoul looming over it like a vulture.

"It appears to be a dump job," Fio said.

For a moment the dead girl on the muddy riverbank went out of focus for Rourke, as if he were trying to peer at her through water. He widened his eyes and made himself breathe. "He's thumbing his nose at us, the killer. He did her last night while Titus Dupre was being executed, and then he made sure he put her where she'd be found first thing this mornin'."

Fio took a notebook out his pocket and flipped through the pages. "A . . . Mrs. Trescher telephoned the Second Precinct last night around nine to say that her daughter, Mary Lou Trescher, had gone missing. The body matches the girl's description, down to the little mole between her eyebrows."

They scrambled down the levee, the ground giving like a wet sponge beneath their feet. Nate Carroll and his partner were interviewing an old Negro downriver, a fisherman from the look of his scale-splattered dungaree overalls.

"He's the one found the body," Fio said.

The man had a rag tied around his coiled gray hair to keep the sweat out of his eyes, and his old man's arms were webbed with veins. He was doing a lot of talking and whatever he was saying had the two cops laughing.

The girl was naked and she'd been brutally raped. The rope the killer had strangled her with was still wrapped around her neck. Her mouth was open wide, as if in a scream that would be forever caught in her throat. Savage bite marks ripped the flesh high up between her thighs.

"It makes you feel so fuckin' helpless," Fio said.

Rourke turned and walked away, going downriver. He felt the

skin of his face tighten and flex, and something popped in his head, cutting off all sound. Like last night, after they'd executed Titus Dupre.

He could see the branches of the batture willows dancing in the wind and a pair of seagulls squabbling over a mess of fish guts. A paddle-wheeled ferryboat churned across the river, but they all made no sound.

And then he caught an echo . . . no, not so much an echo as an *impression* of Fio saying, "Could be a copycat."

Rourke shook his head, and the movement made his ears pop, and he could hear again. His throat, though, burned now as if he'd been swallowing sand. "The bites never made it into the papers or any of the court testimony," he said.

"Yeah but, you know . . . Cops talk."

Nate Carroll and his partner, finished with the witness, had drifted back over to the body.

"Hey, Day," Nate called out. "You know this girl? She looks a little like Remy Lelourie."

Rourke walked back over to take another look. "I don't know. Maybe . . ."

The grass in the front yard was thick with mockingbirds, and Al Jolson singing "Swanee" was coming out the open window. The house, half of a double shotgun, had seen better days. The porch stairs were spongy, and the scrollwork was badly in need of a new coat of paint.

The woman who answered the doorbell was shaped and colored like a brown hen. The precinct report had said she was a widow who worked the last shift in a Piggly Wiggly grocerteria. She was wearing her salesclerk's uniform of black skirt and white blouse, but they were stained and wrinkled, as if she'd slept in them. Her face was raw and puffy from crying.

At some time, though, during the long hours of last night, while she'd waited for her daughter to come home, she'd put her hair up in tight pin curls and pulled a pink hair net over her head. So when she opened the door and saw the two cops standing on her front porch, her hand shot to her head in embarrassment that any stranger would see her in such a state.

"Mrs. Trescher?" Rourke said.

Mrs. Letitia Trescher's idea of interior decorating was to mount a massive attack on all exposed surfaces with vases, figurines, and what-nots. A surfeit of pillows crowded the sofa and chairs in the small parlor, and numerous prints vied for attention with the gold-flocked wallpaper.

She led them with leaden feet into the parlor, and then went to the radio and turned off Jolson in mid-croon. "I just couldn't stand the silence anymore," she said.

A vigil light flickered on the fireplace mantel before a photograph of a man in a military uniform. On a nearby pier table was another pair of photographs in matching frames: of a young man standing next to an oil rig and of the dead girl taken a few years back, on the occasion of her confirmation.

Mrs. Trescher twisted her hands in her skirt, watching Rourke while he studied the girl in the photograph, and when he looked up at her, he knew she would be able to see the horrible and unbearable truth on his face.

A sound like the cheep of a dying bird erupted from her throat. She swayed on her feet, and Fio, who was closer, wrapped his arms around her and led her to a puce mohair sofa. She clung to him, sobbing noises that were barely human. Fio looked over her head at Rourke, his face craggy and bleak.

"May I take a look at your daughter's bedroom?" Rourke said, when he couldn't bear it anymore. She lifted her tear-sodden face and nodded, but he wasn't sure she'd really heard him.

The girl's bedroom was off a kitchen that smelled of burning coal and souring milk. A bowl of soggy corn flakes sat on the table. He could hear Fio talking in the parlor now, telling the woman some of how her daughter had died.

The bedroom was only large enough for a small white iron bedstead and a maple wardrobe with matching dresser. It was cheerful, though, with yellow chintz curtains and rose-sprigged wallpaper.

Rourke hadn't known exactly what he'd come in here looking for, but he found it within minutes—propped up against a ballerina music box on the dresser. A photograph of nine young, smiling flappers in short dresses and cloche hats, standing in front of a movie theater. Mary Lou Trescher had one arm wrapped around Nina Duboche's waist and the other around Mercedes Bloom, and if his gut hadn't already been certain, this confirmed it.

The same killer had done all three of them.

"They called themselves the Fantastics," Mrs. Trescher said from the doorway. Her face was flushed and spotted as though she had a fever, and she jerked slightly each time she breathed. "It was just a silly little club in honor of the movie star Remy Lelourie, but the girls had such fun with it."

From behind her, Fio looked a question at Rourke, and Rourke nodded. "May I keep this?" he said to the girl's mother, already slipping the photograph into his coat pocket.

"Oh, please. Please take whatever you need to . . ." She finished the sentence with a wave of her hand, and then she stopped, her eyes widening and filling with fresh tears. "Oh, dear God. She isn't coming home, is she? She's gone. She's gone . . ."

"Mrs. Trescher," Rourke said gently. "When was the last time you or anyone saw your daughter?"

"She, uh . . ." She swallowed and her throat made a sound like a bubble popping. "My sister-in-law's son, Reggie, is an electrician for Bright Lights Studios and he invited her to come watch the filming yesterday. They were doing a sword fight, and Mary Lou was just so excited that she was going to meet Remy Lelourie in person. Reggie said Miss Lelourie was ever so nice to them both, so gracious, and Mary Lou had the time of her life. The last time he saw her, she was standing right out front of that warehouse where they're making Miss Lelourie's movie. She told him she was going to catch the streetcar home."

Hundreds of rose petals and words scrawled with lipstick . . . Are you scared yet, Remy?

Rourke caught Fio's eye, telling him with a little flick of his head to go back into the kitchen.

"Ma'am," Rourke said to dead girl's mother. "Do you have anybody who can come stay with you?"

She'd gone to her daughter's bed and was staring down at it, as if she still couldn't quite envision a world in which it hadn't been slept in last night. "My sister's at Mass now," she said, "but she'll be coming to the house soon as it's over."

Rourke followed Fio out of the bedroom. Mrs. Trescher had sat on the bed and was cradling the pillow up against her face. Her daughter's smell would be clinging to the linen, Rourke thought, as he looked back at her on his way out the door. Slowly, though, it would fade over the days, until it, too, was gone forever.

"The sick bastard who left that letter for Remy I was telling you about yesterday?" Rourke said to Fio once they were out of the woman's earshot. "He wrote the same thing on the mirror in her dressing caravan during the shoot, which puts him at the studio around the time the Trescher girl disappeared. We could be talking about the same guy here."

"Aw, man," Fio said. "Where's Miss Lelourie at now? Is somebody with her?"

"Christ, I don't know. She was supposed to be doing an exploitation stunt for the studio this morning, some dance marathon in City Park."

"You better go to her," Fio said.

"Yeah, I gotta go . . ." Rourke headed for the door at a near run, then stopped and spun back around. "Shit, Fio, we aren't thinking straight here. We need to get the names of all the Fantastics from Mrs. Trescher and have the captain give their parents a call. Make sure they know they gotta stick close to home until we catch this guy, and above all not to go off with anybody they don't know."

"You go to Miss Lelourie," Fio said. "Make sure she's all right. I'll get the other girls' names and cover for you with the boss."

"Yowsah, yowsah, yowsah!" the master of ceremonies bellowed into the WDSU microphone. "The marathon dance is about to begin."

The crowd hooted and hollered and stamped their feet, until Johnny Dedroit, who had played in the Cave at the Grunewald Hotel, tooted on his trumpet to get them to quiet down long enough for the radio announcer to go on with his patter.

People in New Orleans loved to dance, and on a nice evening there was always a crowd at the City Park bandstand, with its permanent octagon-shaped dancing platform and pyramid roof that offered shade from the sun. This Sunday morning's dance marathon was a first, though. A Bright Lights flack had come up with the idea of sponsoring the contest as an exploitation stunt to promote the studio's movies and its stars. And the best thing was the stunt wouldn't cost Bright Lights a cent. The press agent had talked a local soda pop company into co-sponsoring the event and footing the entire bill.

The winning dancers would get as their prize a lifetime's supply of Zip Cola and the opportunity to appear as extras in *Cutlass*'s grand finale ballroom scene. They'd had to cut off the contest entries at fifty couples, for there certainly had been no lack of crazy kids who saw themselves as potential screen material. After all, if Greta Garbo could be discovered as a shop girl in Stockholm, then anything could happen.

Every girl and boy saw themselves as just one lucky break away from being the next Remy Lelourie and Alfredo Ramon.

"Well, fuck this," Freddy Ramon said, his Bronx accent twanging through his handsome Latin nose. "I wish they'd hurry up and get this show on the road."

Remy Lelourie used an advertising flyer as a fan to blow a wind on her face. "Stop your complainin', Freddy," she said. "At least we'll only be dancing through the first tune. The other couples are going to have to keep on flapping until they all either quit or drop dead of heart attacks."

As if on cue, the radio announcer told the spectators on hand, and those listening in their homes, that one time a dance marathon in Chicago had lasted one hundred and nineteen days. "There you go," Remy said. "I give them a day and these kids'll be dragging their poor, aching feet across a floor that's going to feel like it's coated with glue."

Freddy blew a snort out of his handsome Latin nose. "They're all idiots, and just because they're idiots doesn't mean we got to be idiots along with them."

In a way, Remy knew how he felt. She didn't know why she'd agreed to do this; she couldn't remember agreeing to it. The studio must have agreed for her.

She'd never minded this kind of thing before, though; it came with the fur coats and diamond jewelry and her name in lights on the marquee and above the title. Only she didn't want to be here today. She wanted to go back to the Conti Street house, to the *garçonnière,* and wait for Day to come home. Lately, it seemed that her life was just an interlude between when she'd last seen him and when she would see him again.

Still, it was a bright, beautiful morning, and in spite of missing her lover and not really wanting to be here, she felt happy. They'd decorated the jigsaw balusters of the dancing platform with bunting in the Mardi Gras colors of yellow, green, and purple, and with balloons that bobbed in a gentle breeze that was scented with popcorn and cotton candy.

The band looked jazzy, too, in their white silk shirts and white hats. Their instruments caught and bounced the sunlight like mirrors. The radio announcer was telling the crowd and his listeners at home that they would probably go through a dozen bands before the dance marathon was over.

Waitresses in short black skirts and starched white aprons were passing out free paper cups of Zip Cola. The soda pop company had erected a huge billboard next to the bandstand with a ten-times-life-size image of Remy herself jigging the Charleston on top of a piano, a bottle of Zip in her hand and what was surely one of her sillier smiles on her face. And above her bobbed head in bright red script: "Put a little Zip into your life."

"So how much did they pay you to do that testimonial?" Freddy asked.

Remy felt her face go hot because he'd caught her looking at the billboard. He probably thought she'd been admiring herself.

As it happened, they'd paid her five thousand dollars, but if she told him he'd fall into a jealous funk. He was only getting five hundred dollars a week to her ten thousand for making *Cutlass,* and he groused about it constantly. Freddy had never been able to live with the Hollywood axiom that there was always somebody out there better looking, richer, or more famous than you were.

"A gentleman never talks about money, Freddy. It's vulgar."

"Who says I'm a gentleman?"

"You're an actor. Pretend."

Freddy had always been able to laugh at himself and he did so now. He threw back his head and the bright sunlight etched the crow's-feet deeper into the edges of his eyes and exposed the creping skin beneath his chin, and she felt a sudden pity for him. And fear for herself. Their business was all about looks and Freddy was losing his, and every time he grew a year older, so did she.

His laughter cut off abruptly, but not because he'd caught her staring at him. His gaze had focused on something behind her, and he said, "Hey, I'll be right back. I got to go see a man about a dog."

* * *

"Ten minutes," the radio announcer said. "Ten minutes and Miss Remy Lelourie is goin' to be showin' y'all how they do the shimmy out there in Hollywood."

The reporters, picking up their own cue, all turned their cameras her way, and dozens of shutters snapped in volleys, sounding like a fieldful of crickets.

Garrison Hughes of *The Movies* caught Remy's eye and wagged his flash lamp at her in a sardonic greeting. She smiled and waved back and blew him a kiss, playing the part of the movie star while he took his shot. She figured it was the least she could do for the poor man after Day had broken first his camera and then his wooden leg.

It was growing hotter, and she thought about going to stand under the shade of the billboard, but then she saw that Freddy was there, talking to a shaggy-haired man who was all wrapped up in a coat in this heat. The man was selling Freddy something, all right, but it wasn't any dog.

Freddy and his friend weren't the only ones enjoying the shade provided by the giant billboard. Peter Kohl lounged with one hand braced up against one of the board's supporting struts, looking very much the moving picture director in his jodhpurs and tall boots and open-necked shirt. The man he was facing looked like he'd just rolled out of a skid row dive: with his cheap, wrinkled suit, his big, knobby bald head and round, thick shoulders, and his long gorilla-like arms. Far from being a bum, though, Max Leeland was the head of Bright Lights Studios, and one of the richest and most powerful men in Hollywood.

At the moment, the studio boss and his director were arguing about something, and from the way Max kept throwing black scowls in her direction, she didn't need to strain her pretty little movie star head to guess that the something was her.

Max Leeland had ridden over here to City Park with her earlier this morning, in the studio's chauffeured car. The studio boss was still trying to sweet-talk her into accepting his contract, but she could tell all that effort to be nice was starting to wear on him.

When she'd told him for the umpteenth time that she was still thinking it over, the black hairs that sprouted from his ears had started to quiver.

Now he punctuated whatever he was saying to Peter by thumping the director in the chest with a stiff finger and stalking off. Peter stared after the man a moment, then turned, crossing the expanse of green lawn that surrounded the bandstand, threading through the throng of spectators and expectant dancers, and heading her way.

"Five minutes," the radio announcer's voice crackled over the microphone. "And once she starts, my friends, she won't end until only one lucky couple is left alive and standing."

"Don't you even start, Peter."

The director brushed his star's cheek with a phantom kiss. "You're breaking my heart over this, Remy . . . And a good morning to you, too, by the way."

"I don't really break hearts," she said. "It is all only an illusion. An optical effect."

She had looked away from him, but she could still feel him staring at her profile. "It always astonishes me," he said, "how you continually underestimate the amount of wreckage you are capable of leaving in your wake."

"It's my fame and fortune to walk away from if I want to."

"It isn't only your fortune, and you know it. If you don't want to give up your cop, then bring him back out to California with you."

Remy had to smile at the idea of her tough, swaggering lover who was addicted to risk, getting his kicks from such tepid things as champagne baths and tango dancing and petting parties in the purple dawn.

Peter curled his fingers under her chin and turned her head around so that she was facing him and looking him in the eyes. "I want you to listen to me very carefully, Remy darling. Listen and believe: Max Leeland is not going to take no for an answer."

She knew he was serious and she believed him. She'd heard the rumors about Max Leeland being "connected," and that Bright Lights Studios got a lot of the financing for its movies by laundering money for the Chicago Mafia.

She laughed, though, and pulled away from his touch. "Lord, Peter, you sounded like you were reading those lines off a title card." She twirled a mock mustache and growled in a fake German accent. "I vill not take no for an answer."

His head came up and his pointed beard jutted forward, but she caught the burn of pain in his eyes, and she was suddenly sorry for having teased him just because he cared for her.

"Peter . . ." She lifted her hand to touch him, but he stepped out of her reach.

"Men don't fall out of love with you once they've had you and lost you, Remy," he said. "And I'm no exception."

He turned and walked away from her, and she watched him go around to the other side of the bandstand. He stood there a moment, as if undecided about where to go next, but then she realized he'd only been waiting there for the dark, good-looking man in natty plus fours and a polo sweater to join him.

The man was Max Leeland's baby brother, Eli. Eli Leeland served as the casting director for most of Bright Lights's pictures and he was notorious throughout Hollywood for holding auditions for both male and female roles on the blue velvet couch in his office. She wondered what he was doing here in New Orleans, though, since he rarely came to a set once the picture went into production.

Eli seemed to have picked up in the argument with the director where his brother had left off, pointing a finger in Peter's face this time, instead of poking him in the chest with it. Peter listened for a moment, his eyes on the ground, and then he looked around at her, and even from this distance—because she knew him so well—she could see the desperation on his face.

It isn't only your fortune . . . Lord, she must have seemed particularly dense a moment ago, but she understood it all now. Bright Lights had made Peter Kohl personally responsible for getting her signature on that contract, and if she knew the Leeland brothers, they hadn't asked him nicely.

Peter stood motionless now, looking at her across the empty dance floor, then he wrapped his hands around his neck, and stuck out his tongue and bulged his eyes in the way of a man dangling on the end of the hangman's rope. She laughed at his antics, but she also felt the burn of tears in her eyes.

Oh, Peter . . . She didn't love him anymore in the way that she had when she was twenty-two, but she still cared for him deeply. In a way he was the father she'd never had, and she owed him, owed him plenty.

For he had rescued her at a time in her life when she'd badly needed rescuing, and he'd given her back something she hadn't even known she'd lost—her courage and her self-respect.

A movie star is rarely left alone. *Cutlass*'s lead cameraman, Jeremy Doyle, had been hovering in the background while she talked to Peter, and he now came up beside her. She turned to him, blinking to keep the tears that threatened from spilling over.

"I'm sorry, Jere. Did you need me for something?"

The cameraman's ruined face rarely showed emotion, but his gaze was soft with concern as he looked her over. "Are you all right?"

She forced a smile. "I'm only tired is all. Of being Remy Lelourie . . . Oh, Lord, that must've sounded terribly conceited." She brushed at her cheeks. The tears had fallen after all, and they were ruining her makeup.

"It sounded honest," he said. "Which is a rare thing in our world."

She looked up at him, and this time her smile was real. "You're a sweet man, Jere."

He smiled back at her, the scars creasing and buckling like stiff paper. "That's me. Sweet . . . Still, I'm going to need you to be Remy Lelourie for just a little longer this morning. The studio's rapacious publicity machine needs stills of this little shindig we're having. So I'll be over there," he said, pointing at the Zip Cola billboard, "and while you and Freddy are dancing, I want you to look my way and do that little baby doll pouty thing you do with your bee-stung lips."

"Baby doll pouty thing? Oh, God . . ." Remy said, and laughed.

"One minute till showtime," the radio announcer said.

Alfredo Ramon took her hand, and they walked out into the middle of the platform—a Hollywood dream come true. He in a white tie and top hat, and she in a drop-waisted flapper dress decorated with hundreds of pearls, crystal beads, and tiny mirrors.

The crowd of spectators and contestants fell into an expectant hush that was disturbed only by the snapping shutters of dozens of cameras. "Hey, Remy!" someone shouted, and then they all were chanting her name, "Re-my, Re-my, Re-my Le-lourie."

She turned in a circle, smiling, laughing, waving, feeding off them. She was being Remy Lelourie and loving it now. Touched by the magic.

Johnny Dedroit put his trumpet to his lips and began to belt out "Runnin' Wild," and Freddy swung her out across the dance floor in a frantic shimmy.

They danced alone in the middle of the platform, while the crowd screamed and whistled and threw flowers at them, and old Mardi Gras beads.

Runnin' wild, lost control
Runnin' wild, mighty bold
Feelin' gay, reckless too . . .

The master of ceremonies fired a pistol into the air and the contestants poured onto the platform. The band segued into "Heebie Jeebies," and the flappers and their sheiks shimmied and shook until the wooden floor began to quake beneath their feet.

Remy and Freddy had stopped dancing to watch them, laughing

together. He still had her by the hand and his palm was icy wet with sweat, his whole body jittering with a heroin high. She could feel the pulse in her own palm beating against his flesh, and then from out of nowhere she thought of the man who called himself Romeo, and it struck her that he could be out there now, watching her. The man who had written to her in human blood.

She felt vulnerable suddenly, with the dancers jostling her and pressing against her, and just then—as if her fears had conjured the threat into a reality—a hand reached out and snatched one of the tiny mirrors off her dress.

She turned toward Freddy, to tell him that he had to get her off the floor.

Her mouth opened on his name, just as an explosion ripped through the bandstand in a billowing cloud of smoke, shredding the bunting and popping the balloons. A string of smaller explosions followed, rat-tat-a-tatting through the panicking crowd. The dancers on the platform simultaneously all had the same thought—to get off.

Freddy kept hold of her hand as they were buffeted and pushed. He dragged her toward one of the gaps in the balustrade, but then a shrieking girl in a red-fringed dress knocked Remy to her knees, tearing her loose from Freddy's grasp. A man kicked her in the side, and she would have been trampled if another man hadn't grabbed her arm and hauled her back to her feet.

She was carried along with the press of people, the way a twig is pulled downstream by rushing rapids, and then somehow she was off the platform and out on the lawn.

She stumbled toward the Zip Cola billboard, where the crowd was thinner. She had to lean up against one of its supporting struts, her legs were shaking so. The terror that had jolted through her when she'd been caught in that panicked mass had left her exhausted and her head feeling mushy. It surprised her how scared she'd been. She usually didn't scare so easily.

The smoke was starting to clear now, and the screams had died down. She looked for Freddy, for someone from the studio, but everyone around her was a stranger.

Nearby, a little girl in a pink dress was turning in circles, crying for her mama. Remy had just taken the first step toward the child, when rough hands wrapped around her throat, and a harsh voice grated in her ear:

"Are you good and scared now, Remy?"

CHAPTER NINETEEN

Daman Rourke's heart stopped when he drove through the City Park gate and saw the squad cars and the ambulance parked by the bandstand.

He sent the Bearcat hurtling off the road and up across the green lawn. He slewed to a stop and jumped out, flashing his shield at the uniform cop who started toward him.

"What happened?"

"Don't know yet for sure," the cop said. "Looks like some kids set off a cannon cracker and then a string of little crackers, and folk reacted like it was frigging Armageddon."

Two men carrying a stretcher approached a small knot of people who'd gathered around something lying at the bottom of the steps to the bandstand. "Somebody get hurt?" Rourke said.

The cop turned to see what Rourke was looking at. "Somebody got dead."

The body lay on the ground beneath a blanket, and all he could see of her was the one hand that lay flung out from her side. He'd done this twice before, walked toward women he loved, who were lying dead on the ground.

Once, it had happened on a sunny day in October, when white

cottontail clouds tumbled across a sun-washed sky, and she had been laughing. Once, it had happened on a night when the moon was new and sharp as a sickle, and she had been screaming. Each time it had been nearly more than he could bear.

He knelt and turned back the edge of the blanket, uncovering her head, and saw a plump, middle-aged face with graying red hair.

"Must've been a heart attack," he heard someone say.

He got slowly back to his feet, his legs feeling rubbery, his throat thick.

It was the sun sparkling off her dress that caught his eye. She knelt in the grass beneath a giant billboard of herself dancing on a piano. She was hugging a small bawling child to her chest, stroking the child's hair.

She looked up when he got close to her, and when she saw him, she smiled and said, "See, honey. Here's a big strong policeman come to help us find your mama."

"Hey, Remy," he said, and then he saw the blood on her neck.

He tilted her chin up so that he could get a better look. Her attacker's fingernails had left bloody gouges as she'd twisted away from the grasp he'd had on her throat. The man's thumbs had left dark red blotches on the soft flesh beneath her chin. They'd be turning into bruises later.

Rourke's hands eased down onto her shoulders, and he pulled her against him until he could smell the sun's heat in her hair.

"Are you sure you're okay?"

Her hair brushed his cheek as she nodded. "I just feel so stupid now, for behaving like such a hysterical little ninny."

"Jesus, baby. He tried to strangle you."

"I don't think he was going to choke me dead, Day. He's still trying to scare me, and he was just upping the stakes." She laughed, pushing a little away from him, and then coming right back into his arms. "I gave him a good ol' jab in the belly with my elbow, though. I hope it's aching now."

"Jesus." She was trying to sound so tough, but he'd heard the little catch in her voice. She'd been more frightened than she would ever let on.

After Rourke had reunited the lost little girl with her frantic mama, he had taken Remy to the Bearcat and driven deeper into the park, away from the bandstand and the dance marathon that had turned out to be more of an exploitation stunt than either of its sponsors had ever wanted. He'd pulled off the road again and parked beneath a couple of oaks, where once, almost a hundred years ago, Creole men had fought duels of honor in the dawn mist over women and cards.

Yellow light was splashing now through the moss-draped branches and onto her face. He smoothed a damp wisp of hair off her forehead with the backs of his knuckles. He, too, had been more frightened than he was letting on.

"You sure you didn't get any feel at all for who it was? Did you notice anybody familiar hanging around you right before it happened?"

She started to daub at the scratches on her neck with her fingers, and he gave her his handkerchief. "There were a lot of people, most of them running around like headless chickens," she said. "But they were all strangers to me. And after I fought loose from him and turned around, I would swear there wasn't a soul behind me either. It was as if he'd just disappeared into the air."

She made a sudden, jerky movement and turned into him, pressed into him hard, and as awkward as it was, with the gearshift sticking up between them, he pulled her even tighter to him, as if he would never let go. As if he were trying to disappear into her, or she would disappear into him.

He turned his head to rub his mouth in her hair.

"My big, strong policeman," she said. "I'm sure not complaining that you're here, Day, but I don't think you came to watch me dance. It's something bad, isn't it?"

He told her about the girls. About Mary Lou Trescher and Nina Duboche and Mercedes Bloom, and what they all had in common.

By the time he was done, she was back in her own seat. The fitful wind, gone for most of the morning, had come back up. It lifted the moss on the branches of the oaks and ruffled the short shingled locks of her hair.

"I met her at the studio yesterday," she said. "Mary Lou Trescher. She—" She pushed her fist against her lips and shut her eyes. "I was going to say she reminded me of myself . . . Oh, God, Day. I feel like it's all my fault. Do you think it's Romeo doing it? That he's warming up to killing me by killing them?"

"I don't know what to think. Except that whoever the killer is, he sure as hell isn't picking them at random."

He took the photograph of the Fantastics out of his coat pocket and held it cupped in his hand. He rubbed his thumb over their faces, but he was seeing them dead.

And he was seeing someone else dead, too.

She stilled his restless hand with her own. "Titus Dupre," she said, reading his thoughts.

"Yeah."

"Day, it wasn't your—"

"Yes, it was."

Rourke started up the car and pulled out from beneath the oaks and back onto the road. He drove in silence to his father-in-law's house and found Katie out by the swimming pool, sailing paper boats with her cousins. He told her he had to work a while longer and that she was going to be having Sunday supper with her nana and paw-paw. He hugged her tight, and she must have felt his need for comforting, because she hugged him back and said, "I love you, Daddy," her breath soft and warm against his neck.

He crossed the Mississippi River by car ferry and drove, with Remy in the passenger seat next to him, through the wetlands and along the sugar country of the Bayou Lafourche. Getting away from New

Orleans, away from himself and the image of Titus Dupre on fire and the guilt he felt over that. The guilt that was like a fist squeezing his heart.

Out here, the land and water were at war with each other, with the water mostly winning. Rows of sugarcane would lay claim for a while, only to give way to the swamp and cypress and saw grass.

It was the harvest season, but at some farms the cane was still uncut, growing thick and gold and purple in the fields. At others, they were already burning the stubble. The hundreds of small fires sent up plumes of gray-brown smoke to dirty the sky. Rourke sent the 'Cat's speedometer up well past eighty, until the needle was flirting with the red zone. The wind that pushed against their faces smelled of burnt sugar.

His gaze kept cutting back and forth between the oiled dirt road and the love of his life. She was watching the miles click away, not saying anything. It was Remy Lelourie all over, though, to go driving off into the wild blue yonder without the least idea or care of where they were going.

Since he knew her enough to know she would never ask, he told her. "Paris," he said, only he pronounced it the way the little town's natives did: *Pa-ree,* like the song.

Her gaze remained on the road ahead, but a smile played over her mouth. "It's always been my heart's desire to go to Paris."

They drove on in silence for a few more miles, and then from out of the corner of his eye, he saw her hand move. An instant later, he felt her touch his thigh. Felt her stroking his thigh, up and then down, up and then down, and with each upward stroke she got closer and closer to his cock, and his cock, having enough of a mind of its own to know what was coming, got hard.

"Uh-oh," he said. "We got trouble."

Her hand stroked up and down some more, stroked up again and then stayed there, her fingernails lightly grazing his erection through the soft gray flannel of his trousers, and he felt huge now against her hand.

"Big trouble," she said.

"We, uh . . . we gotta . . ."

"Go to Paris."

". . . take care of something here."

She gripped him, gave him a little squeeze.

"Jesus." He groaned, shifting in his seat.

She took her hand away.

He looked over at her. She looked out the window and began to whistle.

"You tell her," he drawled in his Irish Channel gangster accent. "You tell her that no dame plays Daman Rourke for a chump and gets away wid it."

She laughed, and then her eyes went wide. "Day, watch out!"

Rourke slammed on the brakes and swerved, swinging wide into the oncoming lane, reacting before he was even sure what it was that he was trying to avoid hitting at eighty miles an hour with the Bearcat's precious chrome grille.

He had the impression of a big knobby head with bulging eyes and a lot of teeth, and he thought, 'Gator, out for a stroll across the goddamn road, just as a truck full of cows rounded a bend, heading right at them.

He whipped the wheel back again and floored the accelerator. The Bearcat's back end fishtailed violently, and then the front end hit gravel and the whole car slid sideways toward the deep ditch that lined the road and was filled with dust-coated four-o'clocks and stagnant water left over from last week's rain.

Rourke turned into the skid and for half an instant, he felt the right rear tire spin through air, and then the other three tires bit at the packed, oiled dirt, and the Bearcat pulled out of it and settled right down, going at a reasonable speed now, and on her own side of the road just as the truck rattled past them, its horn blowing, the cows mooing.

Remy, being Remy, had been laughing wildly the whole time, and when she got it back under control, she said, "Well, I guess that's one way of taking care of your big trouble without stopping the car."

"Hell, baby," Rourke said. "Who said it got taken care of? I'm still stiff as a pole down there," and then he began to sing, "How ya gonna keep 'em down on the farm after they've seen Paree? . . . "

When they quieted back down again, he looked over at her, feeling wildly and hopelessly in love, and without thinking about it, just letting it happen, and for the second time that morning, he broke one of his cardinal rules: the rule that said he never talked about the job to anybody not on the job.

"That crucifixion killing that I'm working on," he said. "The priest is supposed to have grown up in an orphanage in Paris, on the Bayou Lafourche." And then he told her everything else that he knew about the case and Father Patrick Walsh—including that he was a she.

It was hard sometimes to get Remy to take things seriously. She carried her scars on the inside, buried deep, and then played at life to show the bastards how much she didn't care. So as he told her about the case, what surprised him, what he never expected, was how closely she listened, and the kind of questions she asked, and how she right off saw angles that he hadn't thought of yet.

"Something earth-shattering must have happened to Father Pat," Rourke said, after they'd been working through it together for a while, sifting and hashing it out. "Something that sent him off down the road that eventually ended in that macaroni factory Friday night. Maybe whatever it was, happened, or at least got its start, in Paris, Louisiana."

"Or maybe," she said, "it happened in New Orleans an hour before he was crucified."

Rourke grunted. "Yeah. Dammit . . . Still, you don't just wake up one day and decide you're going to cut your hair and bind your breasts and become a priest. You got to be *driven* into something like that. Or be pulled into it. And whatever is doing the driving or the pulling has to be powerful enough to make you willing to live every moment with that secret in your heart, and the fear that someday you could be found out."

He hadn't been thinking of her when he'd said it, until the moment the words left his mouth. She went quiet beside him, and when he looked at her, he saw that her head was turned way from him, toward the burning cane fields.

"Remy . . ."

"You don't need to go to Paris to find out what it was like for her, Day; I can tell you. There were whole hours at a time when she forgot what she really was, but then something would happen, or somebody would say something, and the truth would come crashing in on her, making her feel afraid and sick clean through her soul and all the way down to the bone. Afraid and sick and ashamed, and hating herself so much for her shame—*especially* for her shame—that even the consequences of the truth coming out would seem preferable to the lie she was living."

"I love you," he said.

"I know."

"And I'm never going to leave you. No matter what you do; no matter what is done to you, or to me for loving you, I'm not leaving."

"I know that, too."

So don't you leave me. He wanted to say that, but he didn't. Because sometimes, even with all your good intentions, life is neither fair nor gentle.

"I wonder," he said to her half an hour later, knowing she would have followed his thoughts because she always did, "if he was ever in love."

"Or if she was."

Paris, Louisiana, had grown up back when sugar was king, but she was like an aging Southern belle now. Still showy on the outside, but afflicted with a melancholy that life was passing her by.

The Bayou Lafourche divided Paris in the same way railroad

tracks divided other towns. On the east side ran Napoleon Boulevard, lined with cottonwoods, stately Victorian houses, and shops with false fronts and narrow spooled rail galleries. West of the bayou was the back side of town, where a dime was a fortune, and sugar mills belched smelly smoke over honky-tonks, whorehouses, and ramshackle homes.

A couple of colored boys with straw hats were fishing for bream from the drawbridge that crossed the bayou onto Napoleon Boulevard. Rourke pulled up and asked them where the orphanage was, but they said they hadn't heard of any orphanage in Paris.

"The *Times-Picayune* article said he grew up in a St. Joseph's Home for Children," Rourke said to Remy. "So if there ever was such a place, it was probably near the church."

They found St. Joseph's easily enough because its steeple could be seen from any part of town. They didn't find anything nearby that looked remotely like it could have been an orphanage, but on the other side of the church rectory was a field choked with jimsonweed and cattails, and in the middle of the field was a tall, narrow chimney of blackened, crumbling brick that pointed like a finger into the sky. The field was enclosed by a rusting iron fence, and the scrolled gate was chained shut and posted with a faded NO TRESPASSING sign.

Rourke gave the gate's chain a yank for the hell of it, but it held fast. "If it was here, then it burned down a long while ago."

"There might've been records," Remy said. "If they didn't go up in flames with the building."

"Yeah. Maybe the local law would know."

The courthouse, they discovered, was back across the bayou, but they could get there by taking a nearby footbridge. As they crossed the bridge, Rourke looked over the wrought iron railing and down into the brown water where dead leaves floated and bream fed among cattails that had long since gone to seed, and the low sweeping branches of a willow tree blew in the wind like a woman's hair.

Winter's coming . . . He must have caught some of the town's air of melancholy, because the thought made him feel lost and lonely.

Then he felt Remy slip her hand into his. She didn't say anything, just held his hand, and they finished crossing the bridge together.

Built out of thick gray stone and with crenellated balconies and a pair of turreted towers on either end, the courthouse looked ready to withstand the siege of any army.

They found the parish sheriff alone, seated at his desk in his office, wrapping blue luminescent thread around a fishing hook, making a fly. "It's Sunday," he said as they came through the open door. "If you're here to confess to the crime of the century, you can damn well wait until tomorrow."

He cast a sideways glance up, saw Remy, and lurched to his feet, his enormous belly banging so hard into his desk he nearly tipped it over. "Lord-a-mercy," he said.

Sheriff Pascal Drake had hangdog yellow eyes and was the kind of fat man who was fat all over, even his little fingers and ears were fat. His tan wash-and-wear Sears suit looked in danger of splitting open every time he breathed.

His droopy eyes had fastened onto Remy and stayed there, all the while Rourke showed his credentials and gave an edited version of what they were after. He went on staring in a kind of gaping silence after Rourke was done, then he sighed loudly and shrugged, lifting shoulders that were as round as melons.

"I don't think I'm going to be much help," he said. "But why don't y'all go ahead and have yourselves a seat?"

The courthouse might have looked like a fantasy fortress on the outside, but the sheriff's office was furnished the same as squad rooms everywhere. Rourke set his fedora down on a metal desk and pulled up a couple of cheap pine ladder-backed chairs, while Pascal Drake took a cob pipe out of his shirt pocket, stuck it in his mouth unlit, and watched Remy Lelourie's every breath.

"The Home, as folks called it," he began, once they'd all settled, "burned down . . . oh, we're talking maybe thirty years ago. I got hired on here five years back myself, from over in East Texas, but I've heard some talk about what happened, and it was bad. Seventeen children and three nuns were inside, asleep in their beds, and none of them made it out alive. It was an old Creole raised plantation house, with two centuries' worth of varnish on its walls and floors, and it went up like a torch. By the time the fire was put out, there wasn't anything left but charcoal and ash, and that one lone chimney that still stands to this day."

"What we're trying to find out," Rourke said, "is if our murder victim, Father Patrick Walsh, ever lived in the Home, and if anybody around these parts would've known him."

"Or known his family, maybe," Remy said. "Before he got orphaned."

The sheriff looked startled that Remy could talk. He stared at her mouth, scrutinized the rest of her some more, then came back to her mouth.

"Yeah, I can see where y'all are going," he finally said. "But I can't think of who could help you. Your best bet would've been them nuns who ran the place, but they died in the fire and whatever they knew about any Patrick Walsh would've died with 'em. I can ask around for you, though. There's a bunch of real old-timers who park themselves on the benches outside the Parker Hotel billiard hall every afternoon—if there's anybody left in Paris who might've known your victim, it'd be one of them."

Rourke took a card out of his pocket, laid it on the desk, picked up his hat in turn, and stood up, holding out his hand. "If you find out anything, I'd appreciate it if you gave me a call."

The sheriff started to lumber to his feet and knocked into his desk with such force that the laws of physics sat him back down again. He shook Rourke's hand, but his gaze was still on Remy.

"Ma'am," he said, "I just have to come out and say it—otherwise I'm going to be stewing about it the rest of the evening. It's the goldarndest thing, but if you're not the spitting image of Remy

Lelourie . . ." He laughed, a big booming laugh that shook his belly like a bowlful of clabber. "Lord-a-mercy. As if Remy Lelourie would come waltzing into the Paris courthouse on a Sunday afternoon. You sure do have the look of her about you, though, even if you do got a few years on her."

Rourke bit the inside of his cheek.

"Why, Sheriff," Remy said. She did a Southern belle thing, managing to pout and smile both at the same time. "I do believe that's the nicest thing anybody's said to me in all of my considerable years." She looked over at Rourke, her dark eyes fairly shimmering with pent-up laughter. "Honey, before we go, don't you think we ought to ask this gentleman if he knows who did for the orphanage before it burned down."

"Gol-darnit!" Drake exclaimed with a snap of his sausage fingers. "I don't know why I didn't think of him . . . Louis Toussaint. He did the odd job around the place, and the reason why I know that is because he was one of the first ones they suspected of setting the fire. Turned out he was somewhere else where a good dozen people saw him, and all of 'em white, so he was let off the hook. But some folk even all these years later still hold to the notion that he did it."

Remy gave him the smile that had lit up the covers of a thousand magazines. "See there, Sheriff. Your astute powers of observation have led us to a clue, after all."

Pascal Drake's chest swelled, bringing his belly with it, and the desk levitated. "Always happy to oblige, ma'am. And I expect ol' Louis Toussaint'll be obligin', as well. He's probably pushing a hundred now if he's a day—fact is, he's probably Paris's oldest citizen. But his memory's better at recollecting something that happened fifty years ago than what he ate for breakfast this mornin', and there's nothin' he likes more than to engage in a good jawin'. So if there was anything to be told about the Home, he could probably tell you more about it than you'd ever want to hear."

Rourke put on his hat, gave the crown a tap, and smiled at Remy. "So where can we find the guy?"

The sheriff twisted around in his chair to look at the clock above his head. "What's it now? About three? Then he'd be down at T'Boys, halfway through his third jarful of white lightning."

Chapter Twenty

T'Boys sat at the edge of the bayou, at the end of a rutted, gravel road. To get there, though, you had to park in an empty field next to an old general store that was attached to a filling station, whose pumps were rusting to their blocks, and then follow a path through a stand of cypress down to the water.

A half dozen Negro men were sitting on crates on the store's sagging gallery, playing checkers and chewing on jimsonweed and their memories. When the shiny yellow Bearcat roadster pulled up in a cloud of dust, and a white man and woman got out and started down the path to the colored honky-tonk, the gallery turned so quiet you could hear the old wood settling. It was hard to tell, though, whether they recognized Remy Lelourie or they were just in awe of a white woman passing through the neighborhood, wearing a dress made out of glass and mirrors that shone like a bucketful of stars.

Rourke took Remy's arm to help her around a puddle of stagnant water coated with mosquitoes. They crossed the field, past a big old chinaberry tree, beneath whose shade a farmer was selling fruit off the back end of his truck. The mingling odors of gasoline and overripe blackberries made Rourke nostalgic for those summer days of endless possibilities out at the lake when he was kid.

T'Boys was built long and narrow, like a railroad car. Its corrugated tin roof was rusting through in patches and it had been whitewashed once, maybe back when Louis Toussaint was a boy, but time and the sun had browned it to match the bayou at its back. Nevertheless, its purpose in life was obvious, and it hadn't done anything to change its appearance since Prohibition except to take down its front sign.

The tonk was crowded for a Sunday, but their entrance was met with the same awed silence they'd gotten from the grocery's gallery. It got so quiet you could hear the floorboards, warped from years of spilled booze, creaking beneath their feet and the groan of catgut when the fiddler laid down his fiddle. The place smelled of Saratoga chips fried in chicken fat and the juniper berries that were used to make the gin in the still out back.

A pair of alligator skins, complete with snouts and teeth, were tacked to the knotty pine wall above a bar that was little more than plank boards resting on old ale barrels. Behind the bar and framed by the alligators stood a man who looked tough as jerked meat, and who had eyes that had been around enough blocks to be able to pick out the cop on the corner.

His gaze left Rourke for a half second to take in Remy, widened a little, then came back to Rourke. He put down his glass-polishing rag and crossed his arms over his chest. "Who you lookin' for?" He waited a beat, then added, "Suh."

Rourke put some bite into his smile, as a way of laying the ground rules: all he wanted was a conversation, not trouble, but what he wanted he would get. "Louis Toussaint," he said.

The bartender nodded toward the back end of the long room where an ancient mulatto the color of a copper penny sat alone at a table, his gnarled hands wrapped around a jelly jar full of juniper gin.

"Thank you for your help," Rourke tossed over his shoulder, as he guided Remy with a hand in the small of her back around the rickety chairs and water-ringed tables.

"What's the ol' fool done?" the bartender called after them, but Rourke didn't answer.

Louis Toussaint looked up from under a straw hat stained with age and sweat and watched them come with turquoise eyes set deep in a face as wrinkled as dried snakeskin.

"Lord Gawd," he said, in a voice that sounded surprisingly robust to be coming out of that face. "I'ma too old to be goin' to jail. What I done, anyways?"

"Nothing, as far as I know," Rourke said, keeping the edge on his smile for the moment. "We'd just like to ask you a few questions about the old orphanage that burned down. The St. Joseph's Home for Children."

The old man's lips stretched open to reveal gray gums and a scattering of teeth that were brown and worn to the nub. "So y'all back to thinking this nigger done it, huh?"

"I'm a New Orleans cop, Mr. Toussaint. I don't have jurisdiction here. How about if I fetch some more 'shine from the bar and some food, and my woman and I sit down and we talk?"

The lips stretched open again. "S'long as you buyin', this chile is easy." His gaze shifted over to Remy. "You Remy Lelourie?"

This time her smile was the one she shared with friends. "That I am, Mr. Toussaint." She shook the old man's hand and then sat down in the chair Rourke held out for her. "I don't believe I've ever met anyone who's lived a century before."

Louis Toussaint looked both embarrassed and pleased. "Aw, shucks. It ain't no great accomplishment. I reckon with me, livin's just got to be a habit I can't seem to break."

Rourke went up to the bar, bought a jug of moonshine, and brought it back to the table along with two more jelly jar glasses. He went back to the bar for the food: plates of alligator smothered with *sauce piquant* and three slices of *tarte a la bouille.* By the time he'd brought it all back to the table, Remy was filling up her jar again with more moonshine, and Louis Toussaint was looking considerably more blurred around the edges.

"It's only fair that I warn you, sir," Rourke said as he pulled out his own chair and sat down, "that as experienced as you no doubt are, there isn't a man alive who can claim to have matched Miss Lelourie jar for jar and lived to tell of it. She's getting on in years now, but in her younger days, she could outdrink a hillbilly at a rooster fight."

Louis Toussaint looked Remy over carefully, then he sucked on his gums and nodded slowly. "I had me a lil' gal like that once. A high-yeller gal from over in New Iberia, and, man, was she prime. She ate me up like I was a peach—meat, skin, and juice. Ever'thing but the pit. Lord, I loved that lil' gal more than life an' pride an' everlastin' glory . . . What can I do for y'all?"

"We want to know about a Patrick Walsh who might've been in the orphanage sometime during the nineties, give or take a few years."

"You talkin' about right befo' the fire. I could name you ever' chile livin' in the Home then, and not one of 'em was called Patrick Walsh."

"How about a girl called Patricia, and with a different last name?" Remy said. "And she might have had a brother."

Rourke, growing mellow from the moonshine, alligator, and custard pie, looked over at his woman and decided that she was prime.

"No'm. No Patricia," the old man said. "Was a Miss Patrice, though. Patrice LaPage, and she had a brother, sure 'nuff. Swamp chillens, they was, from out in the Lafourche Basin. Their mama died young and for a time they lived alone in the wetlands, in an old log shack, they and their daddy. I don't know what-all their daddy done to get on the bad side of the law, 'sides poachin' a few 'gators, but he got himself shot and killed stone dead. No kin would take them chillens in, so they ended up being brought to the Home. That poor lil' gal, Miss Patrice, she was no more'n thirteen if she was a day, but she was carryin' a chile of her own. Ever'one thought it was her own daddy knocked her up, but I'd of put my money on her brother. That Mister Henri, he always had a *look* 'bout him. You a po-liceman, so you'd know that look."

Rourke filled up the old man's glass with more lightning, then took care of Remy's and his own. "Like he'd enjoy sticking a pin through a fly just to watch it squirm."

"Mmmm-huh. Mean down to the bone." The old man drank the booze down, smacking his lips with the pleasure of it. "That lil' gal of mine that I was tellin' you about . . . ?"

"The one that spit you out like a pit?" Remy said.

"Mmmm-huh. That the one . . . She did some midwifin', my Sally Blue, mostly for colored folk, but they called her up to the Home the night Miss Patrice had her baby, and she told me afterward there were things goin' to stick forever in her mind after that night. She said that Mister Henri came in after the baby was borned, and the snake-eyed look that passed 'tween the two of them, brother and sister, woulda made the hair roach up on the back of a peeled egg. But that wasn't the oddest of it . . ."

The old man paused to eye the bottom of his glass as if surprised to find it empty.

"More lightning, Mr. Toussaint?" Rourke said.

"Is she havin' more? . . . Then, don't mind if I do."

"Fill them up, Day," Remy said, pushing her empty jar up to the jug, to join the old man's. "And don't be parsimonious about it."

"There you see, Mr. Toussaint," Rourke said. "Most people couldn't say that word sober without twisting their tongue into knots."

For a moment Rourke thought Louis Toussaint was having a heart attack, the way he was choking and shaking, but then he realized the old man was laughing.

Rourke waited until Louis Toussaint had calmed himself down and applied himself to the lightning again before he said, "What was the oddest of it?"

"The oddest of it," Louis Toussaint said, "happened during the birthing. That Miss Patrice, she sweated blood . . . Man, I'ma tellin' you no lie," he protested, even though no one had suggested that he was. "They drops popped out on that lil' gal's forehead, like they was sweat, only they was red and my Sally Blue said they had the blood smell to 'em, like rustin' nails. My Sally Blue said . . ."

His voice drifted off and his gaze turned inward, and Rourke thought he was probably back in the moment, listening to his woman tell the tale of a girl who sweated blood, listening and being with his woman, whom he'd loved more than life and pride and everlasting glory.

Louis Toussaint blinked the wetness out of his eyes and cleared the lump out of his throat. "My Sally Blue said that lil' gal's palms sweated, too, and worse'n her head. They'd tied ol' twisted-up pieces of sheets to the bedposts for her to hold on to while she was laborin', and my Sally Blue said they sheets were soaked bloody by the time she was through. Uh-huh. Sweated blood, and you can believe me or not. That's yo' privilege."

"We believe you, Mr. Toussaint," Remy said, as she leaned forward, reaching for the jug of moonshine. She had a shine of her own on from the liquor, but it was also excitement. "Tell us about the baby. Did it survive its birth?"

Louis Toussaint looked at Remy's empty jar and compared it to his nearly full one. He girded his loins, drank his down, shuddered, and wiped his mouth. He looked at Remy cross-eyed and grinned.

"Eh? Oh, Miss Patrice, she had herself a fine, healthy baby boy. Couple nights after the birthing, that Mister Henri, he lit off for God alone knows where. And a couple of nights after he left, the Home burned down from a fire that was set. Now they some folk always goin' to have to believe it was me done it, but they others talked 'bout how that Mister Henri must've snuck in from wherever he run off to and got his own back out of pure meanness and spite. But nobody could never prove nothin', and neither hide nor hair of 'im has ever been heard of or seen again. As for Miss Patrice and her baby—they died in the fire."

"Is that a certainty, though, Mr. Toussaint? Maybe they weren't in the house when it burned down."

"I was there when they carried out the bodies, Miss Remy. Or what was left of 'em, and they wasn't a body short. They was all so black and twisted up you wouldn't've recognized 'em for human bein's if you didn't know 'em for what they was. But when we laid them out on the lawn, they was three of them growed-up and seventeen chillens, just like they was s'posed to be. And one of they chillens had a babe in her arms."

Cockleburs and tar-vine leaves stuck to their clothes as they picked their way through the overgrown cemetery on the outskirts of town. A smoky light had gathered in the tops of the trees from the lowering sun and the burning cane.

The tomb they were looking for was smothered with honeysuckle vines. Rourke had to rip whole branches off it, before they could read the names etched in the stone. She was there, third up from the bottom: PATRICE LAPAGE AND INFANT LUCAS.

He let the vines fall to cover it up again and stepped back, dusting off his hands.

Remy slipped her arm around his waist and leaned into him. Rourke was surprised after all the moonshine she'd consumed that she was still reasonably functioning. Louis Toussaint wasn't. They'd had to carry him back to the room he rented in a boardinghouse not far from where the Home used to stand. Rourke thought the old man would live through the night, but the hangover he was going to suffer in the morning would probably have him wishing he hadn't.

Remy stirred against him, holding him tighter. "Do you think Father Pat was ever really here in Paris?"

"Yeah, I do." It felt right, like twisting the viewfinder on a camera until the image sharpened into focus. Father Patrick Walsh and Patrice LaPage were the same person, or at least they had been at one time.

He worked a scenario out in his mind of how it could have happened. Henri LaPage had run away from the Home, but then he came back the night of the fire, came back for his baby sister and their child of incest. Only she'd wanted nothing to do with a brother who, along with her father, had been beating and raping her for years. What she had wanted was to be shed of it all, shed of her brother and the baby, and of all the ugly memories of that house in the swamp and what had been done to her there.

Whether she had set fire to the Home that night, or Henri had, or it had gotten set by accident—Patrice LaPage had used it as a way to get free.

"She didn't die in the fire like everybody thought," Remy was saying, echoing his thoughts. "But Mr. Toussaint said they laid the bodies out on the ground afterward and they weren't a body short. Three nuns and seventeen children. So the body holding the baby must have been her brother, Henri."

"Yeah. Probably," Rourke said, and that, too, felt right. "If the bodies were burned badly enough, they might not've been able to tell male from female all that easily, especially if the coroner wasn't a medical man. And people see what they're expecting to see."

"You don't expect to see someone sweat blood."

"No . . . You remember that salvation show we went to that summer when we were kids, how that preacher could bend spoons and send books flying through the air?"

"That was probably just a magician's trick, though. Are you saying you think Patrice LaPage faked her blood-sweating episode?"

"Hell, I don't know what I'm saying . . . except, I think there exists in the human mind and heart whole rooms behind locked doors that we haven't opened yet."

They stood arm in arm in a silence of rasping locusts and of the wind pushing through the branches of the cypress and willow trees. A blue jay sat on top of the cemetery's scrolled iron gate and preened. Cloud shadows moved over the tombs.

"Maybe," Remy said, "they should never be opened."

They walked back, arm in arm, through the cemetery to the car. The drive out here to Paris had been just an excuse to get away, to burn up the hours like fallen leaves, but because he had come, he thought now that he had a better understanding of the paths taken in Father Pat's life, the choices made. And understanding her, he still believed, was the only way he was ever going to find her killer. His killer . . .

They stopped at the cemetery gate and looked back. They stood on a small rise, a veritable mountain for south Louisiana. From here you could look back at the town and see St. Joseph's steeple and the courthouse towers, and you could follow the lazy curve of the brown bayou as it cut through the burning sugarcane fields. He wondered if Patrice LaPage had stood here on the night of the orphanage fire and looked back at the conflagration of her old life. If that had been the moment when she had become he.

What she'd probably been too young to know then, though, was that you can run from your past, but you can't escape it. What you've done and what's been done to you, the choices you've made—it all gets carried along with you, like stones you've piled on your back. After a while the stones begin to weigh on you, they slow you down, until one way or the other and somewhere down the line, your past catches up with you.

Rourke drove back down through town, crossed the bayou, and picked up the highway heading home.

He drove lead-footed and reckless for about twenty miles and then turned off onto an unmarked lane and lurched and bumped through some farmer's fields until he couldn't see the road anymore. He braked and cut off the engine, and the wind stopped blowing through him and the world grew still and warm.

Remy got out of the car and walked down the lane some more to where it met the bayou. Purple and gold four-o'clocks grew wild along the untilled patch of dirt between the lane and the rows of sugarcane. Green dragonflies danced and darted over the cattails along the water.

Rourke sat in the car for a moment longer, then he, too, got out. The cane leaves were edged with the sun's last red lights, and clouds were piling up purple on the horizon, bringing rain with them for tomorrow morning.

He tilted his head back and shut his eyes. The sun was sinking out of sight behind the clouds, but he could still feel the heat it had left in its passing. It wasn't enough heat, though, to heal the hurt he felt for the world.

He heard her footsteps and he opened his eyes. She'd stopped while she was still several feet away from him. Her eyes went deep into his, and he stared back until her face blurred soft at the edges.

He understood that a part of the reason why he loved her, what rooted him to her, was because he saw in her a reflection of himself, of his own paths to both perdition and salvation. She had a hard shell of hurt and loneliness, and a gambler's need to test the limits. Of fate and of herself.

"Titus Dupre," he said, "got framed for a killing he didn't do. And last night we killed him in turn, and I'm not going to tell you what a bad death it was."

"I know," she said. "But all you were ever trying to do was be a good cop. Intentions do matter, Day."

In another moment he thought he would go to her. He would touch her and run his hand down the curve of her breast. He would bury his face in her hair, and breathe in the smell of her.

"Except that I never for a moment thought that boy wasn't guilty," he said. "Sure, we had evidence all over the place, and it all pointed right at him, but I should have seen the frame. It was my *job* to see the frame."

Her eyes had not left his face. She took a step toward him, but he said, "No, wait. Let me finish . . . The murdered ones, they need someone to speak for them, you see? To tell the world who killed them and why. Only this guy, this monster who's still out there, still raping and strangling girls—he suckered me good. And what the world got told about Nina Duboche and Mercedes Bloom was a lie and an innocent boy is dead."

"So catch the right man this time," she said, "and then you can speak the truth, not only for the girls he's murdered, but for Titus Dupre. What you shouldn't do, though, is go making that poor boy into your cross."

"Well, hell," he said, almost laughing because the two things you could always count on never getting from Remy were platitudes and useless sympathy.

Her words about not making Titus Dupre into his cross had sent a thought flitting through the compartments of his mind, though, only in the next instant it was gone. He could have chased after it, but he let it go, because while she'd been talking she'd been closing the distance between them and he was really touching her now instead of just thinking about it. He caught the back of her head with his hand and pulled her face to his. They kissed, locked together and turning in a circle, swaying, until they knocked into the Bearcat's front fender.

He let go of her mouth, long enough to groan. "I've been wanting to do this all day, wanting you all day."

He had her braced up against the hood of the car and he was wrestling, tugging, bunching her dress up around her waist, and scratching the hell out of his hands. "Christ, what is this thing made out of—tiny knives?"

"Careful with it, Day. It belongs to the studio and cost a fortune."

"I only want to . . ."

Her knees fell apart and he came between them. He worked two fingers into the open leg of her silky French panties, found the soft nest of hair, and slid his fingers inside of her. She was wet, quivering, ready for him. Her hands clutched his shoulders, and she arched her spine and her head fell back, her mouth open.

He worked her with one hand while he undid his trousers with the other, and he entered her as she was coming, and she was so hot, so tight, so incredibly fine. It was as if God had made her just for him. He knew it was irrational, but it seemed that no other woman had ever *fit* him the way Remy did.

He let himself go, let himself be held by her, until he was drunk with her and drunk with loving her, more than life and pride and everlasting glory.

CHAPTER TWENTY-ONE

As soon as he walked in the joint, Fiorello Prankowski felt an uncomfortable itch between his shoulder blades. It took a moment for him to realize that the feeling came from being the only white man in a speakeasy full of colored folk.

It wasn't that he was the object of stares; rather the opposite, since everyone was taking care not to meet his eyes. He could feel their fear, though, because he was white and a cop, and with white cops the Negro was always only a word or a look or a bad moon rising away from jail or the lynching tree.

And he could feel their hate, which came from having the white man's boot on their necks for all their lives and their daddies' lives and *their* daddies' lives and so on back, so that the hate got bred into the blood. At least that, thought Fio, was how his partner had put it to him once, but then Day Rourke had this thing about the Negro race that Fio didn't understand. Although he had, after a fashion, learned to live with it.

The speak was just one big old room with a bandstand at one end. The air was thick with the smell of muscatel, cheap perfume, hot grease, reefer, and years worth of God-knew-what-all that had been soaked and ground into the rubber tile floor. Feathery smoke curled in and out of the open rafters and seeped through the cracks in the knotty-pine walls.

Fio looked for Daman Rourke among the men standing hipshot at the bar and the couples dancing in front of the bandstand, pressed closed together, doing that slow dip and drag. Some whores were plying their trade among the joint's few tables, wearing not much but big bolo knives strapped around their waists to keep their johns in line.

Fio was beginning to think the beat cops had steered him wrong, when he finally spotted his partner up among the Negro musicians on the bandstand. They wore John B. Stetson hats, purple silk shirts, and the pointed high-button shoes called Edwin Clapps; all but Rourke, who was still in the suit he'd had on that morning. At the moment only a tall, skinny guy was doing any playing, blowing a deep, moaning bass on a harmonica. Rourke stood next to him in utter stillness, his saxophone idle in his hands, lost to the music and probably high on more than just booze.

Still, Fio felt the ache in his chest ease out in a breath of relief. He'd expected to find his partner on a path of self-destruction, but this was mild compared to what the man could be doing. What he'd been known to do. When Daman Rourke got one of his moods on him, he craved and fed off danger and edgy excitement, and if it didn't come his way naturally, he went out looking for artificial stimulation.

Now, as Fio watched, Rourke lifted the sax to his mouth, licked his lips, took a tight breath, and then he hit a note that would have left an impression on bone.

Fio knew his partner played a jazz horn, but this was the first time he'd ever heard him. What he played on this night was dark music, and deep, like the ocean, and you felt it in your liver as well as your heart. You heard things in it you'd never heard before, things you weren't sure you wanted to go near.

Fio didn't want to imagine what a man had to be feeling to play like that. You let music like that take hold of your guts, he thought, and you could end up at two in the morning putting your gun in your mouth.

Fio watched his partner wend his way across the smoky room, carrying a tin lard bucket full of beer, two glasses, and a bottle of something that would probably leave them paralyzed and blinded if they were only lucky, and dead if they were not.

"Hey, partner," Rourke said. He hooked a chair away from the table with his foot and set down the booze and glasses.

Fio watched Rourke sit and dip beer out of the bucket and into the glasses, then pour a jigger of whiskey into each glass of beer. On the bandstand the drummer had gone into a solo riff, making the floor vibrate beneath their feet.

"That tune you were playing," Fio said. "What's it called?"

A smile touched the corners of Rourke's mouth, but his eyes were like two cigarettes burning in the night. "'Black Snake Blues.'"

"Yeah, well, that snake sure did bite me," Fio said and then wished he hadn't. He had meant it for a joke, but it had come out sounding too close to a confession.

Rourke was the one to look away. "It's not the music, Fio," he said after a moment. "It's the memories the music evokes that makes it such a killing thing."

There was an ache going on in Fio's chest that he didn't like. "What in hell are we talking about anyway?" he said.

Rourke laughed. "Damned if I know." He nodded at Fio's boilermaker. "Better drink that up before it grows hair on the glass," he said, even though his own was still untouched.

The band shifted tempo, from jazz back to the blues. A young woman joined them up by the piano. She was startlingly beautiful: soft caramel skin, long hair in tight coils with a lot of bronze in it, and a body that looked poured into the red Chinese silk wrapper she was wearing instead of a dress. She looked familiar to Fio, although he couldn't place her.

It seemed that she was looking right at him, and with such an intensity of feeling that Fio felt hot color flood his face. And then he realized that burning look was not meant for him, but for the man sitting at the table with him. Fio glanced at Rourke's face in time to see him answer her look with one of his own, and then she smiled and blew him a kiss.

"I reckon she knows you," Fio said, a bit sourly.

"She's my sister."

The woman was singing now, all about the men who had done her wrong, and in a voice that was as hurting and hurtful as the saxophone had been.

Sister, hunh.

It was possible, of course. White men in New Orleans had taken up colored mistresses since back in the days of slavery. Miscegenation was supposed to be against the law, but human appetites didn't always recognize the civil code, and from what he'd heard of Rourke's daddy, the man had lived by few rules anyway.

So sister, maybe, but still Fio doubted it.

The woman was lost now in her song, her eyes seeing, maybe, all the men of her own she had loved and discarded along the way. In the muted light they glinted gold like a cat's eyes, and again Fio felt that twinge of familiarity.

"A girl that pretty shouldn't be singing such a sad song," he said, hoping, probably in vain, to get Rourke to tell him more about her.

Rourke only laughed. "That's why they call them blues, partner. They're sad and you get to make them up as you go along."

Or maybe, Fio suddenly thought, when he called her his sister, he'd been speaking metaphorically. Fio knew that the closest friend in Rourke's life had been a colored man. Fio had watched that man die from a hail of bullets in an Angola Prison cane field and he'd thought that something of Rourke might also have died on that day. Once Fio had dared to ask him why he had made such a good friend of a Negro, and Rourke had answered, "Why do you make any man your friend? Your, I don't know . . . souls are in tune, I guess."

The truth was, Fio thought, the truth was he was jealous of a dead man, maybe even jealous of that colored gal who was leaning against the piano and singing about heartbreak, jealous of her even if she really was his sister. The truth was Daman Rourke let few people get close to him and Fiorello Prankowski wasn't one of them.

And such was the man's charm that you forgave him even that.

Like he was forgiving him now . . . Rourke was pushing his boilermaker around in circles, drawing wet rings on the scarred table and looking like a man whose soul was being consumed by itself, and what Fio most wanted to do was take him home with him and have his wife feed him some of her special pot roast, and maybe even, Fio thought with a sudden inward laugh at both himself and Rourke, tuck the poor boy into bed and read him a bedtime story.

"Where you been at all day?" Fio said instead.

"Paris." Rourke stopped his fiddling with the glass and looked up. "The one here in Louisiana. I found out our murdered priest was probably born Patrice LaPage, who died in an orphanage fire thirty some years ago, along with her baby boy, and then got reborn again as Patrick Walsh. It's only a feeling, but I think she set that fire, and if she did then she murdered twenty-one souls, including her baby."

"Man," Fio said, "that *is* something: A lot of motive for a revenge killing there."

He tried to think of what that did to the case. They'd just gone from having priests and the whole damn Catholic Church as suspects, to the whole town of Paris, Louisiana. It made his head hurt.

His head had been hurting all day, anyway, what with the way they now had serious, political hot-potato murder cases coming out of their ears.

"Meanwhile, back at the ranch," he said, "we got shit-all on the Trescher girl's murder. There's a loading dock, a greasy spoon, a sailor's speakeasy, a Chinese laundry, and a sugar refinery all around that warehouse where Bright Lights Studios is doing their filming. But nobody saw her get snatched, even though it happened in the middle of the day, which suggests she knew this guy enough to go off with him willingly."

"He knows all the Fantastics, and they must all have a passing acquaintance with him," Rourke said. "And he's been killing them off one by one."

"Yeah, well, I talked to the captain like you said, and the other girls' parents have been warned. What's left of them."

"He had to know that once he did Mary Lou Trescher, we'd right off make the connection between her and the other two girls," Rourke said. "I can't see him going after another Fantastic now unless he wants to get caught. Or unless . . ."

"Unless what?"

"Unless it's about more than just the sex and the killing."

"Scaring Miss Lelourie, you mean?"

Rourke didn't say anything. His thoughts had turned inward, but Fio was relieved to see the wild light had left his eyes.

"If I had any money and was a betting man like you," Fio said, "I'd put it on someone connected with the movie studio. We talked to most everyone who was at that warehouse yesterday, and a lot of them remember seeing Mary Lou around during the filming, a couple even remember talking to her, but nobody saw her go off with anyone. Of course, it must've been like a goddamn Chinese fire drill there, what with smoke bombs and wind machines and people called grips and gaffers and extras all running around the place. And even though you're supposed to have a pass to get on the set, they had people off the street coming and going and delivering food and booze and stuff all morning. So the upshot of it is: anybody and nobody could've done it."

The band and the singer—who might or might not be Rourke's sister—were taking a break now, passing a reefer around among themselves and drinking sour mash out of tin cups. A door, which Fio hadn't even noticed was there, opened in the wall behind him. He heard the crack of billiard balls and the rattle of dice in a cup, but by the time he turned to look, the door had closed again.

When Fio looked back around he found his partner studying him, laughter now in his eyes. "What are you doing here anyway?" Rourke said.

Fio rolled his shoulders in a shrug. "Aw, I thought I'd come try to stick a finger in your eye. That way you'd be hurting somewheres different for a change, and you'd have someone else to blame for your misery besides yourself."

"Remy already told me not to make Titus Dupre into my cross. So I'm not."

"Yeah, well you do have a tendency to think you're the fuckin' Second Coming, come down to earth to save us all. So when you do mess up, you— What?"

Rourke suddenly had that look on his face that he got when doors started opening for him you didn't even know were there. "What?" Fio said again.

"Nothing . . . It's just . . . Why did they crucify Christ?"

"What is this—catechism class?"

"Think about it though. It was supposed to be about taxes and treason, but mostly it was to prove to Him and to the world that He wasn't the son of God."

"If you say so. And what does this have to do with anything?"

"I don't know."

"Well, fuck me," Fio said. "How about another drink?"

Rourke pushed abruptly to his feet and slid his untasted boilermaker across the table to Fio. "Here, have one on me. I'll catch you in the morning."

"You going on home then?"

"The night's still young. I think I'll go to the Pink Zebra and see if they got a game of *bourré* going on."

"Aw, jeez, Day. Do you got any idea what you're doing?"

He flashed that smile. That brilliant smile that made it so you just had to love him. "It's like the blues. I'm making it up as I go along."

* * *

The Pink Zebra on Bourbon Street was the kind of speakeasy patronized by college kids who wanted to show they were hep, and by tourists who were under the mistaken impression that they were slumming.

The speak went for the exotic look, starting with the zebra skin on the wall, with its white stripes painted a cotton candy pink. The zebra shared space on the gold-flocked paper with gilded mirrors and a sign that said, NO SPITTING ON THE FLOOR PLEASE. The bar was solid mahogany with a brass railing, and the man behind it sold Manhattan cocktails and gin fizzes, and maybe a little marihuana or cocaine, but only if he knew you.

He also sold whisky from Scotland that went for twenty-five dollars a fifth. It came uncut in a bottle with a genuine label and it was so smooth it brought tears of joy to Lieutenant Daman Rourke's eyes.

The speak's main attraction, though, was the drag queen who owned the place. She was also a bootlegger and dope dealer, and one of the best informants Rourke had. He always had to pay her first, though, for what she would give up to him later, by playing her a game of *bourré.* The games were brutal, with sums of up to ten thousand dollars having been known to change hands, but it was never about the money anyway.

It was all about the game.

At the moment Miss Fleurie was looking Rourke over with amusement in her deep, slanted eyes, as she took a carved jade case from her pocket, extracted a rolled joint and lit it. It wasn't her first of the night. In the bright flare of the match, Rourke had seen that the whites of her eyes were tinged blood-red with too many reefer hits.

She drew deeply on the current joint and held the smoke down for a good thirty seconds before she let it out. The smoke curled in a stream between her thin, quivering nostrils and her pursed and very red lips.

"My," she said, as she gave Rourke another look-over. "You sure do look wrapped up in some misery tonight, honey. Which for you is saying something."

Rourke was standing at her bar with one foot on the rail and his elbows on the polished wood, and the warm, smooth taste of her whisky still tingling on his tongue, and he had to laugh. "I'm just tired is all."

She held the joint out to him pinched between nails she'd painted pink to match the zebra. "Here, honey. Smoke a little dope and let that bad ol' day float away in the wind."

He wanted it, but he shook his head.

She shrugged and took another toke on it herself. "Since you wouldn't be coming to Miss Fleurie with jelly roll on your mind, it must be about murder and *bourré.*"

Rourke gave her the smile he sometimes used in the bedroom.

Miss Fleurie tossed back her head and laughed, and her long, straight black hair flowed over her shoulders like liquid silk. "Oooh, daddy-o, let's get it on."

Four hours later Miss Fleurie stood up from the *bourré* table and stretched her tall, sensual body. She lifted the heavy fall of her hair off the back of her neck and worked the kinks out. The skin of her throat was the color of butter cream, but when she swallowed you could see her Adam's apple. That and her big hands were what gave away her sex, but she was still beautiful.

She'd already sent the other players away, who'd been invited into the game to enliven the pot. It was just the two of them now.

The Pink Zebra's *bourré* parlor didn't have the chichi class of the saloon up front, but then you shouldn't be looking around at the decor when you played the game, unless you enjoyed the pain of losing. The green felt-covered table was lit by a tin-shaded lamp that swung from an old anchor chain, lost in floating layers of cigarette smoke. The walls were bare except for a sign that said there'd be a five-dollar pot with a fifty-cent limit, but that was meant for the amateurs. They'd just been playing for stakes forty times that much.

The game bore some resemblance to poker, except that the loser of a hand got *bourréd* and had to fill the pot with the ante for all the players' next hand. It seemed to Rourke that he'd been stuffing the pot all night. He'd lost a lot, lost too much. He'd always gambled for the risk, though, and risk had no bite to it, and no joy, if you only played with what you could afford to lose.

Miss Fleurie had produced another cigarette case from somewhere—this one silver, encrusted with rhinestones. She flicked it open, took out a pinch of white powder, put it on her wrist, and sniffed it up her nose. She shuddered and Rourke almost shuddered with her; he almost thought he could taste the cold, white bite of the cocaine on his tongue.

When she came back from the rush, she looked at Rourke and made a little tsking sound in the back of her throat. "That was no game when Miss Fleurie ends up feelin' like she just picked your pocket."

"I warned you that I was tired."

"You didn't play tired. You played like your heart wasn't in it. Miss Fleurie doesn't like that. It makes her cranky."

Rourke felt a flash of anger that he deliberately let show on his face. "Now you're making me cranky, and trust me when I tell you that you don't want that."

She pushed her red mouth into a perfect pout. "Hunh. Be like that then. But since you paid, after a fashion, I'll go ahead and say. Ask me what you want to know."

"Father Patrick Walsh. Tell me what you've heard about him."

She batted her lashes at him, and they swept her high cheekbones like feather dusters. "Miss Fleurie is a pagan, not a Catholic. She does, however, read the newspapers. How else would she know which are the latest boring fads and fashions to avoid?" She swept her hand down the length of herself, and then posed, showing off her gown of silver lamé and purple sequin swirls. "I mean, really, darling . . . that dreary black cassock *alone* would stop one from taking holy vows. One priest, however, is not just like any other."

Rourke sat in silence a moment, digesting that last bit, trying to divine how much she really knew. He framed his next question carefully. "Do you know a reason someone might have had for killing this particular priest?"

Miss Fleurie always played *bourré* with an open bottle of champagne icing in a silver bucket and a crystal flute close at hand. She went to it now and poured herself a glass of the sparkling wine, while Rourke studied her face, trying to read if she was really thinking over the question, or only sifting through the pieces of the truth in order to choose which ones she would tell.

She turned and met his gaze over the rim of her champagne glass and said, "It could be he found out about the club."

"The Catholic Ladies Social?"

She made a soft hooting noise deep in her throat. "Honey, that was just a front. The club I'm talking about is way, way deep underground. Kind of like what that underground railroad was, only instead of taking slaves up north to freedom, this little choo-choo is for women who want to get away from their men. You know how some men would sooner kill their woman or go on using her face for a punching bag, than let her walk out the door? So sometimes the only way for a woman to get away from a man like that is to go somewhere he can never find her. Somehow these women would hear about Father Pat and they would come to him, and he and his little club would arrange for them to disappear."

A frisson of excitement had curled up Rourke's spine like a chill. His cop instincts were telling him that this, at last, was the tip of the lever that was going to break the case wide open.

An organization like what Miss Fleurie was talking about would of necessity be small, he thought, but it would eat up a lot of operating expenses. It was also something one man, or woman, couldn't run alone.

Rourke got up and went to where she stood on the other side of the table, putting himself into the kind of close space with her that lovers shared. "Who are the other conductors on this railroad?"

Her gaze slid away from his, and she forced a laugh. "Honey, we're not talking about the Orleans Club here, where you want to go around bragging about your membership."

"Give me some names. Honey."

She took a step back, but he stayed with her. Her gaze came back to him, then cut away again. "I only know the one name, anyway . . . Cassandra Poule."

It made beautiful sense. Cassandra Poule had been born the only and genteel child of a wealthy old Creole family, only to grow up to make a notorious name for herself in New Orleans as a rabid champion of the suffragette movement. She'd led marches for the vote at the state capitol in Baton Rouge and in Washington, where she'd been sent to jail for burning President Wilson in effigy. While in jail she'd gone on a fast and been force-fed, and got her picture in the paper for it. From time to time she'd lived in her townhouse in the Quarter with other ladies, whom polite society always insisted on referring to as her companions, and whom she always insisted on referring to as her lovers.

Once the vote had finally been achieved seven years ago, she'd taken up the cause of free love. "I do not," she had written in a letter to the editor of the *Times-Picayune,* "mean that women, any more than men, should hop from bed to bed like rabbits. I only mean that, married or not, a woman's body is her own, to give to a lover or not, when she so chooses and as she so chooses."

Just the words *lover* and *bed* together in the same newspaper had been enough for many New Orleans matrons to feel faint over their café au lait.

"Were they lovers?" Rourke asked now. "She and Father Pat?"

Miss Fleurie raised her plucked and penciled eyebrows in exaggerated shock. "A priest and a muff diver, my heavens. What have *you* been smoking?" She breathed a laugh, then caught it suddenly, and Rourke saw the realization dawn in her eyes. "Oh, my heavens . . ."

Rourke smiled. "Miss Fleurie has a vivid imagination. The man was a priest." He reached around her to pluck his hat off the coat tree and got a whiff of her perfume, and the musky smell of reefer smoke.

"You ought to go home and get some sleep," she said. "You keep on like you're going, and you'll be dead before your time."

"I'm touched that you care," Rourke said and smiled again. A different smile this time. "But if you were suddenly going to develop a tenderness for me, I wish you'd done it before you made me broke before my time."

She laughed and he started to leave, but then she stopped him by laying her hand lightly on his arm. "Mr. Day . . . Don't judge him, don't judge us."

"I wasn't aware that I was."

"You say that, and you probably believe you mean it. But when I touched you just then, you stiffened all up as if you could catch what I got like you can catch a dose of the clap." The smile playing around her mouth deepened, became self-derisive. "You shouldn't assume, Detective, that a man dressed as a woman wants to fuck only men."

"Then why . . . ?" Rourke began, but then he didn't know how to frame the question.

"Why am I the way I am?" She lifted her shoulders in a shrug that was pure female. "If I believed in God then I might say that I am how He made me. But since I don't believe in God . . . I only know that when I stand naked before a mirror the body I see isn't mine, and my own body feels like a voodoo doll with pins stuck all over in it. So one day, long ago, I figured out that those pins don't hurt as much when they got to go through a dress."

She laughed and cupped his cheek with her hand, and Rourke smiled because she had expected him to stiffen again and he had, a little. "Now yours, on the other hand," she said, "is one naked body I wouldn't mind seeing. So now you know, Mr. Day, that sometimes your assumptions just might be right."

Her head came forward slowly, and Rourke had time to take a step back, but he didn't. She kissed him full on the mouth and to his shock, and her amusement, a little jolt of desire passed between them.

Rourke only half took Miss Fleurie's advice to go home and get some sleep. He caught a two-hour nap sitting in the Bearcat in front of Cassandra Poule's porte-cochere townhouse on Royal Street near the cathedral. When arabesques of light splashed through the iron lace balcony above his head and onto his face, he awoke with a crick in his neck and a taste like swamp water in his mouth.

He watched the house while a dog wagon rolled by, picking up strays. A coal vendor came next, the load in his creaking, mule-drawn wagon glittering like black diamonds beneath the morning sun.

"Stone coal, laaaa-dy. A nickel a water bucket."

He watched the bakery open up for business across the way, spilling smells of fresh-baked French bread into the street. A newspaper boy claimed the corner and began hawking the *Morning Call*: "Police no closer to apprehending killer-rapist! Read all about it in the *Call*!"

When the jalousie shutters on the front parlor window of the Poule house opened with the flash of a white, slender hand and arm, Rourke got out of the car, crossed the brick banquette, and mounted the townhouse's front steps.

The woman who answered his knock had skin so pale it was almost blue, like skimmed milk, and a plain, flat-nosed face that had probably never been pretty, not even at the peak of her youth. She wore her contrasting ink-black hair unfashionably long and rolled up into a pouf on top of her head. Yet she was dressed flamboyantly in green lounging pajamas embroidered with orange and red parrots, and there was something compelling about her small, dark eyes. They glowed like two lit matches, from within.

"Yes?" she said.

Rourke was about to reach for his badge when another woman

called out from the parlor, "Cassie, is that her already? I thought she wasn't due for another hour yet."

That woman stepped into the hall, wearing matching lounging pajamas with purple parrots, and looking sleep-tousled and well pleasured.

"Mornin', Mrs. Layton," Rourke said.

CHAPTER TWENTY-TWO

The only desire I've ever felt," said Floriane de Lassus Layton, "was for another woman."

They sat in a courtyard ablaze with purple wisteria and climbing yellow tea roses. Coffee sweetened with sugar and cream sat on the green wrought iron table between them. Inside the house, Flo's lover began to play "Rhapsody in Blue" on the phonograph.

Cassandra Poule's response—when Rourke had told her he wanted to ask some questions about "the club"—had been to suggest that he take a long walk off a short pier, and then she'd given him the name and telephone number of her lawyer. She seemed to treat her lover's need to confess, though, as her lover's own business.

"The first time it happened," Flo said, "was two years after I married Mr. Layton, right after the birth of our daughter. He caught us, my . . . friend and I, he caught us together one day and he was . . . furious. Of course, the Church forbids divorce, but I think his pride would have forbade it in any event. And I, of course, promised that I would never indulge in such shameful acts ever again."

When they had first sat down, Rourke had positioned his chair so close to hers that their knees were almost brushing. Now he leaned closer as if he would touch her or hold her in comfort, although he did neither. "The heart has a will of its own, though," he said, "and it guards itself well."

She smiled a little. "That sounds like something Father Pat would say."

"It was something he wrote. Or close to it anyway."

She smiled again, then looked away, toward a pair of mockingbirds who were squabbling among the fallen crushed husks of a pecan tree. "I kept my promise, though, Lieutenant Rourke. For many years."

She had not been able, though, to stop her thoughts, or the little flashes of desire she would feel for a shop girl or the mama of her daughter's playmate. She confessed these sins to her priest, Father Pat.

"They were sins against the Holy Catholic Church—he never said they weren't. But somehow when we talked about it, I stopped feeling so ugly inside. He showed me how God loves each of us just as we are. That He wouldn't have made it possible for us to be a certain way and then despise us for it."

The morning light was gentle on her mahogany hair and the round, smooth paleness of her face. It was easy, Rourke thought, to imagine God creating such a creature and being pleased with and forgiving of his creation. And then you remembered that He had also made the creature who had nailed one of His priests to a crossbeam.

"I think for a time I even found contentment," she was saying. "I thought, This life is what you have, Flo, and there is no point in grasping for something other."

"And then you joined Father Pat's club and met Miss Poule."

"Oh, yes . . ." The face she turned to him held both wonder and sadness, as if a mystery she'd carried inside was finally working its painful way out. "It happened in an instant. And it was then that I realized I had not been holding true to a promise, I'd only been waiting, and one look at her dear face and the waiting was over."

Inside the house the telephone rang, and Flo's hands, which had been making little pleats in the lap of her lounging pajamas, spasmed into a fist.

"Tell me about the club," Rourke said.

"One day a few weeks back . . ." She paused to smear the tears off her cheeks, then looked at her fingers as if surprised to find them wet. "One day Father Pat came over to the house to fetch back the Charities' yearly accounts book and he saw . . . Mr. Layton can be mean sometimes, and Father Pat saw the evidence of that on my arm. He told me about the club then and asked me if I wanted to help out with it. I think he was hoping that I'd make use of it myself someday, but that was never to be." She tried to laugh, but the sound she made popped like a wet bubble. "I've never been a particularly courageous person."

"It must have taken some courage, surely, to work with Father Pat and his club." He leaned into her again and this time he took her hand. "That was what y'all were doing the night he was killed, wasn't it?" he said, holding her hand but putting just the hint of the cop in his voice. "Helping some woman to escape her man."

She started to pull her hand free of his and then stopped. "I didn't exactly lie to you, sir. Father did leave my house at ten that night, but I was with him. We met a woman with a baby under the clock at D. H. Holmes's and we brought her here for a while, before we put her on a train for . . . put her on a train, and then we went our separate ways. The last I saw of Father Pat, he'd just crossed the street to catch the streetcar back to the rectory."

"Who was the woman you put on a train?"

"I can't tell you."

Rourke leaned into her, closer still, intimidating her a little with his size. "Mrs. Layton, you are going to have to. The woman's husband may be Father Pat's killer."

"No, I truly mean I cannot tell you. We volunteers are never told their names, or where they're going. We just help them with changing clothes and feeding them and calming their nerves. Cassie . . . Miss Poule knows what their final destination will be, because she makes all the arrangements—getting them jobs and places to live, coming up with their new names, and getting things like the made-up birth and baptismal certificates. But only Father Pat ever knew *who* they were." She tried for another laugh. "He was always calling them all by the same name. Mary. He would say, 'Don't be afraid, Mary. This is the first day of the rest of your life.'"

While they'd been sitting in the courtyard the morning sky had started to cloud over. A breeze had come up, smelling of the coming rain and of omelets and cush-cush cooking in the kitchen. Rourke gave her hand a final squeeze, then let it go. He leaned back into his chair, putting space between them again.

"What will become of us now?" she said.

"You'll be all right," he lied.

What would happen, he thought, was that they would get a warrant for Father Pat's club, even though there probably weren't any records anyway, except for what had been in the priest's head. So they would try to compel Flo's lover to tell what she knew, but Cassandra Poule would probably go to jail rather than betray the new identities and whereabouts of the women who'd been given a ride on her railroad. The club, though, whose existence had been dependent on its secrecy, would cease to exist.

And the world would find out about Cassandra Poule's latest "companion," and Floriane de Lassus Layton would be destroyed. Father Pat might not have intended for it to happen, but he had given his Flo the strength and self-knowledge to come to this house, and then he had left her to face the consequences alone.

Father Pat. Rourke wondered if he . . . if she . . . had felt desire for either of these women, and if either one or both had felt desire in return. He had asked Flo Layton once if she and Father Pat had been lovers; to ask it of her again now would be a revelation he wasn't prepared to make to her just yet.

It was a road he might have to go down eventually, though, with both Mrs. Layton and Cassandra Poule, but Rourke had had another thought that he wanted to pursue first. Something that had almost come to him while he'd been talking to that doddering old priest, Father Delaney, on the rose-framed kitchen stoop of the rectory on Saturday. Something that had just come back to him now while Flo had been talking about the club and her role in it.

"The Catholic Charities yearly accounts book that Father Pat came to collect from your husband that day—what's it like?"

She'd picked up her coffee, cold by now, but she wasn't drinking it anyway. She was staring down into the cup as if it contained her salvation, and at his question she looked up at him, blinking in confusion. "What? Oh . . . why, it's bound with expensive green leather and has these pretty gilded pages. Father Ghilotti gave it as a gift to the Charities last Christmas."

Old Father Delaney had talked about devil's bargains and he'd kept asking Rourke if he'd come for the book. But it wasn't Father Pat's appointment book he'd been talking about; it was the accounts book for the Catholic Charities.

It helps to know where the bodies are buried, Father Ghilotti had said. Somehow he had found out about the club, and it would have been his duty as Holy Rosary's pastor to shut it down. The Church could never countenance an organization that was for all intents and purposes fostering the dissolution of the blessed sacrament of marriage. But Father Pat had discovered a buried body in turn, something in the Catholic Charities' accounts. And so they had made a trade, he and his pastor, a body for a body.

Only Father Pat had been the one to turn up on a slab in the morgue.

Out in the street a woman strolled by, singing the delicious praises of her banana fritters just as the cathedral's bell began to toll, calling the faithful to the daily morning Mass. And as if the bell had been a tocsin for all her coming pain, Flo Layton uttered a little cry and bent over, clutching at her belly while harsh sobs racked through her, for a minute, two, then she seemed to grab hold of herself from within.

She straightened slowly, rubbing the tears from her eyes with her fists like a child. "Heavens," she said. "What you must think of me, Detective. Every time we are in each other's company, I end up falling into utter pieces. It's just . . . I shall miss him so. He had this way of listening that was a gift, like a beautiful singing voice, or an artist's eye. He could make you believe that not only did he forgive you all your trespasses, but that he loved your soul. And the way he loved you, it made you feel chosen and sheltered."

She turned to Rourke. Her face was soft in the morning light. "You are a lot like he was, Detective. In the way you have of prying open the human heart. It must make you good at what you do."

It was sometimes what solved the toughest cases, Rourke thought, when you started prying open the secrets of the guilty and you found the heart of a murderer. Sometimes, though, on the way to catching your killer, you had to rip open the hearts of innocent bystanders along the way. And because everyone lives behind a tissue of lies and secrets and illusions, and even though you don't want it to happen, you sometimes can end up destroying the innocent simply through your own ruthless efficiency.

Sometimes, Rourke thought, truth can kill just as effectively as a bullet or a knife.

It was an image he didn't like remembering, but he deliberately called it to mind now: the priest hanging by the spikes through his wrists, the beaten face, the burned feet. Usually when a killer killed he was being driven by a need or a compulsion to wipe his victim's existence off the face of the earth. Father Pat's killer, though, hadn't only been after ending Father Pat's life. He'd been trying to break the priest open, to get at his secrets.

The damn, persistent, and crazy-making question, though, was still: which secrets?

Romeo watched his own true love emerge from a chauffeured Peerless touring car the color of a midnight sea. Her bodyguard got out of the car's front seat and walked with her to a scrolled iron gate. She went through the gate alone, though, and the guard took up a wide-legged stance next to a fence that was all a-tangle with overgrown honeysuckle vines.

The bodyguard was fucking hysterical. An ex-prizefighter with chewed-up ears wasn't going to save her. Only Romeo could do that. Of course the press agents would milk the bodyguard angle for all it was worth once they got hold of it. *Remy Lelourie's life threatened by mystery Romeo . . .* Yeah, he liked that. Mystery Romeo. Maybe he ought to write the copy himself.

The Peerless was hysterical, too. A movie star's perk, courtesy of Bright Lights Studios. Romeo had taken a look inside the . . . hell, you really couldn't call it a car. It was an English country estate on wheels. All mahogany and leather and quadruple-plated silver trim. It even had Axminster carpeting on the floor, and cushions of Italian brocade with silk-tinseled velvet borders.

Romeo laughed. He had fucked her on the leather and Italian brocade back seat of that car once, and he'd often wondered what Hebert the chauffeur thought when he'd found the evidence of the dirty deed later.

Romeo stood now behind the concealing leaves of a banana tree, watching while the love of his life followed a path from the gate to a dilapidated raised cottage with flaking paint and cardboard in some of the windows. Watching her stop and turn her face up to the sky, enjoying the cool pause before the first raindrops fell.

Her gray coat matched the sky, and he thought it made her look . . . He'd been about to think *drab,* but Remy Lelourie wouldn't look drab in sackcloth and ashes. She was looking . . . well, subdued. Yeah, that was the word. But then Remy always looked subdued when she visited her mother and sister.

Romeo had to take it on faith that Remy's mother and sister lived in the house, since he'd never actually laid eyes on the women. Their neighbors up and down Esplanade Avenue claimed they were honest-to-God recluses and had been for forever, ever since old Mr. Lelourie had deserted the wife and kiddies for another woman. This trauma was always spoken about in whispers, but as if it were also possessed of capital letters. The Scandal.

Because of The Scandal, the Lelourie women—mama Heloise and baby sister Belle—had entombed themselves alive in typical Southern blueblood fashion. Just the two of them in that ramshackle old house, alone with themselves and with all their bitter gripes and sour grapes, going on twenty-eight years.

Just then the front door to the ramshackle old house opened beneath a mysterious hand, and Romeo strained to get a look before Remy disappeared inside, but all he saw were shadows.

Romeo grunted with satisfaction, though. They were home—hunh, as if they fuckin' wouldn't be—but he could count on her to be staying for at least an hour now. It was probably some Creole etiquette thing going back umpteen generations, that whenever you visited *la famille* you stayed for at least an hour.

Romeo smiled. He had to leave her now, but he liked knowing where she was and what she was up to when he wasn't around.

Mama was the one to answer the door this morning, to fuss with Remy's hat and gloves and umbrella, and talk about the weather. "I was just telling Belle, it's going to be one of those long, cold, silent rains . . . Why don't you do the honors with the *café,* Remy dear? Belle's ankles are all swollen up today."

They took up their usual places in the parlor. Mama on the red-velvet chair next to the empty fire grate, sitting slender and straight-backed in her high-necked bodice and long black skirts from another era. Her blond hair and gray eyes fading some now, but her face still high-bred and timeless.

Belle on the black horsehair settee beneath a window enshrouded in lace panels that were tattered and yellow with age, knitting a little yellow cap and resting the cap on a belly that was five months full of baby.

Remy poured the thick black chicory coffee and hot milk together in two steady streams into the cups. She handed one to her sister, along with a smile. "You look tired today, honey. Are you sure you're getting enough rest?"

Belle had been given her nickname as a child because of her prettiness, but in the last few months her face had turned sallow and drawn, as if the baby were sucking all the life out of her. Her hair, once the color of summer apricots, now looked so orange that Remy wondered if she was tinting it.

"You hardly need to ask," Mama said, answering for her. "Like all the Lelourie women, your sister is delicate down below. You mark my words if this baby doesn't kill her."

"Oh, surely not, Mama," Remy said. "You're a Lelourie and yet you've managed to survive the experience twice. That we know of."

"Don't get cute, missy. Cute does not become you."

Remy busied herself putting sugar in her coffee so that Mama wouldn't catch her smiling. If she ever got to thinking too much of herself as the glamorous movie star, she could always trust her mama to put her back in her place.

Mama and Belle had wandered into a discussion of all the hazards of childbirth, on top of being delicate down below. Babies strangled by their umbilical cords, Siamese twins, breached deliveries, and the infamous 'Gator Baby, who had come into life with a cracked, leathery hide and a snout. They'd covered all this ground before and yet they never seemed to tire of it

"You remember Maggie, Matilda Dayries's girl?" Belle was saying. "She's the one who always had to be sitting right up in the front pew so Father could see her, and she thought she was God's gift all right, up until she had those twins. One came out white, like it should've, but the other came out black as a coal scuttle. Well, *something* had obviously being goin' on in that family's woodpile."

"Belle," Remy said a little too loudly. "What are you still wearing that ol' blue dress for? It looks fit to burst at the seams. Didn't you like any of those new maternity dresses I had sent over from D. H. Holmes?"

"I liked them fine. I'm only saving them, is all."

What for? Remy wanted to say, but she already knew they'd been added to the bulging cedar hope chest that lay at the foot of her sister's bed. Everything that had ever come Belle's way, she had put aside in her hope chest, saving it for a future that had passed her by long ago when she hadn't been looking.

Remy heard her name and realized she must have drifted into a reverie while Mama had launched herself into one of her scolds.

". . . making a spectacle of yourself in City Park. You do these things without a single thought for *la famille.*"

"Mama's right," Belle said. "You're going to be sorry if you keep on in this way, Remy. Everybody knows no nice boy will marry a girl who's gone and made a spectacle of herself."

Remy lifted her shoulders in a small shrug, pretending that they still didn't have this power to hurt her. Knowing that they would always have the power to hurt her. *La famille.* "I doubt I'll ever marry again, anyway. No good seems to come of it."

No good can ever come from it.

It was a Southern expression that ought to be adopted as the motto of this family, she thought. We go through the motions, we tell our white lies, we touch each other's hands and tender each other promises, and no good ever comes from it.

"I brought something for you all," she said, taking a sheaf of brochures out of her handbag. "Information on some agencies for y'all to look at later."

Belle took the brochures from her hand, then immediately dropped them onto the threadbare carpet and burst into loud sobs, as if she'd been saving her tears up all morning, just waiting for the right moment to let fly with them.

"You are just the cruelest thing," she cried. "Why, all the while growing up you've always wanted what I had, and things haven't changed just because you're a movie star now with your picture in the papers all the time. You're jealous 'cause I'm having a baby and you're not."

Mama got up and gathered up the brochures. She brought them

back to her chair and sat down. She made a neat pile of the brochures in her lap, and then began to tear them up, one by one. "I'll not have the word 'adoption' mentioned in this house ever again," she said.

Remy had not used the word; in fact, she had made it a point not to use the word.

"After all, there's no true shame attached to Belle's condition," Mama went on, "for the baby's daddy would surely have done the honorable thing and married her, if not for the tragic accident that claimed his life. He was a St. Claire and blood would have told. Blood always tells."

Remy had to turn her head aside and press her lips together to keep from either laughing or screaming, she wasn't sure which. The baby's daddy would never have done the honorable thing. Aside from the fact that Charles St. Claire hadn't had an honorable bone in his body, he happened to have already been married to another woman, namely herself. And the tragic accident that had removed him from their lives had been his murder with a cane knife out in the old slave shack in back of Sans Souci one night last July.

Belle's sobbing had stopped with the same abruptness with which it had started. The parlor fell back into its customary silence, except for the clink of Mama's spoon against her cup and Belle's knitting needles clicking in tempo with the rain against the windows.

"Belle, you ought to take one of those pralines," Mama said, the soft French accent from her youth more pronounced now, as it always was when she became agitated. "You must remember you eat for two."

"I don't know, Mama," Belle said. "It seems anymore my tummy just rebels at the thought of sweets, as if they were Yankees." Then she laughed softly, the storm not only over now but already forgotten, and in a strange way, forgiven.

Even though no good had come from it.

And it seemed to Remy then that this house and the women in it had become enclosed in one of those bell jars that you shake to make it snow. The tableau so frozen in place that you could change nothing about it except the weather.

Romeo had stripped naked and fucked her on her bed and now he prowled through her bedroom, touching her things, smelling her clothes. He lifted her peignoir from off a brass hook on the door and buried his face in it. The silky material snagged on his callused fingers, the feather boa around its neck tickled his nose. So fine . . . all of her was just so fine . . .

He gave a little start, shaking his head. Had he drifted off somewhere? He checked his watch . . . No, only a minute gone, maybe two. The horse he'd shot up was galloping through him, stringing him out, but he had it under control. Yeah, under control.

He looked for the letter he'd sent her, but he didn't see it. He yanked her dresses out of the wardrobe, emptied brassieres and panties and camisoles and stockings out of her drawers and onto the floor. Sent his arm sweeping through all the bottles and feminine things that littered her dressing table. *Bitch.* She'd thrown it away, the fucking bitch. Didn't she get it? Couldn't she see that he was trying to warn her? And she should've known the very *act* of reading the letter—the letter he had fucking *bled* over—meant that she now belonged to him.

He prowled the bedroom some more, muttering bitch, bitch, bitch under his breath, looking for the letter, looking—

Jesus fucking Christ. Pain stabbed up through his foot, pain so bad it brought tears to his eyes. What? . . . He looked down and saw that he'd stepped on a piece of glass. Christ, he was bleeding like a . . . like a . . .

Bleeding all over her was what he was doing. The studio had sent over some new publicity stills and she'd been going through them. He remembered that they'd been on her desk, but now they were scattered all over the floor and he'd gotten blood on one of them. The one where her head was thrown back, and she was laughing, pushing her fingers though her hair. God, how he loved her when she did that thing with her hair . . .

Something startled him, someone in the house, in the kitchen banging pans. His foot hurt and he looked down, and saw the broken glass and the blood. He turned in a slow circle, looking around him.

"Whoa," he said, shocked at the mess he'd made, and then he laughed. *How do you like them apples, Remy?*

Car tires crunched on the shell drive below. Romeo limped to the window and looked out in time to see her emerge from the Peerless, along with her bodyguard. She turned around and stuck her head back inside the car and said something to Hebert the chauffeur that made him and the bodyguard laugh.

Romeo wanted to kill them.

He watched her walk out of sight and then he heard her footsteps on the downstairs gallery, going around back to the kitchen.

Time to get outta Dodge, he thought. Or . . .

Or he could stay and fuck her again, there on her bed, on her pink satin sheets that smelled of jasmine and sex. Fuck her good and then give her the only salvation that ever truly lasted.

> *"For never was a story of more woe*
> *Than this of Juliet and her Romeo."*

* * *

Remy opened the kitchen door to the sizzle of chicken frying in a pan on the old-fashioned black iron stove. "Mornin', Miss Beulah," she said. "My, it sure does smell good in here."

The housekeeper was sitting at the round oak table, shelling pecans into a pan, and she looked up smiling. "Don't you know it," she said. "I just got that chicken fresh at the Poydras Market, plucked and cut up already it was, and wrapped up in waxed paper—land, what will they think of next? All's I had to do was walk in the door with it and plop it right in the fry pan . . . Did you have yourself a nice visit with your mama and Miss Belle?"

Remy made a face. "I need to fix me a julep and the sun isn't even over the yardarm yet. So what does that tell you?"

"Mmmm-huh," Miss Beulah said, laughing. She was an ample woman with a shelf for a bosom, but she had a fairy's tinkling laugh. "Like that, was it? Families, they are a trial sometimes. But you got to love 'em."

"Do we? Yes, I suppose we do." Remy took a block of ice out of the box and began to scrape it with the shaver. "Shall I make you one?"

"Why, I don't mind if I do."

Remy made a pitcher's worth of the cocktail: bourbon, sugar, a splash of water, and finally some crushed mint. She put shaved ice into two tumblers and poured the julep over it.

"Have a taste and tell me if it needs more sugar," she said, handing one of the glasses to Beulah.

"Don't need no taste to know it's just right, honey. You make juleps like you were born to it."

"I was," Remy said, laughing. "I'm going upstairs for a bath. I've got that wretched ball to go to later on this evening."

"The studio done sent over your costume. I hung it up in your wardrobe in the bedroom . . . You want I should bring up a tray when that chicken's done fryin'?"

Remy went back out onto the gallery, carrying her julep and waving at Beulah over her shoulder. "I'll come back down and eat with you later."

Sans Souci had been built in the French Colonial plantation house style, and so to get from the kitchen to the upstairs, where the parlors and bedrooms were, Remy had to go outside onto the lower gallery and climb the stairs. As soon as she set foot on the upper gallery and saw the open doors, she knew he'd been in her bedroom.

Was maybe still in her bedroom.

Once, she had been so proud of her nerve that she would fashion deliberate tests for it, just to show off her own courage to herself. She hated that he could do this to her now, that he could make her feel vulnerable and polluted with fear. That he could make her so aware of the beat of her own heart, the pumping of air through her lungs, aware of all the veins and organs, the muscles and bones of her body and how they could all, in an instant, be reduced to a piece of meat on a slab in the morgue.

"Go to hell, you bastard," she said, loud enough for him to hear, and then she strode through the doors.

It was as if a whirlwind had gone through her things. Or a ravaging beast. Clothes, papers, cosmetics strewn everywhere, figurines and perfume bottles shattered into pieces. Bloody smears glistened on the cypress floor. God, the blood was still wet. While she'd been down in the kitchen, he'd been up here with her things, touching her things, bleeding . . .

The worst, though, was what he'd done to her bed. He'd ejaculated all over her bed.

Rage, terror, disgust—they all imploded inside her at once and with such force that she swayed on her feet.

Lord, Remy. Will you for God's sakes get ahold of yourself.

The bell box for the telephone rang, and she jumped as if a live wire had been touched to her chest.

The box rang again, jangling on her exposed nerves as she waded through the mess on the floor to her desk. She snatched up the phone and spoke before he could: "I think you're the one who's scared, Romeo."

She heard his surprise, a little hiccup of a caught breath in the crackling static on the line.

"Remy," he said, and she felt again that little flash of familiarity at the way he said her name. There was something, something . . . an accent maybe. "I've been trying to warn you, but you just aren't paying attention. Anytime, anywhere I want to take you, I can."

"Only in your dreams, Romeo."

He laughed, a little stuttering *heh-heh-heh* that sounded even more familiar to her than his voice had. The open line crackled with a strained silence, but she could hear his breathing. She thought he was about to hang up and then he laughed again, *heh-heh-heh.*

"Did you kiss your cop goodbye this morning, Remy?"

CHAPTER TWENTY-THREE

Lieutenant Daman Rourke had been invited by the Ghoul to take another look at the body of Mary Lou Trescher where she lay on a slab in the morgue, and so he stuffed his hands in his pockets, set his jaw, and made himself look.

The chimney sweep's rope had left a deep furrow around the girl's neck. Finger marks from open-handed slaps had left bruises on both cheeks. Her nose had bled, and the blood was caked black now around her nostrils.

Christ, he thought, but she'd been so young.

"The rapes were multiple and particularly violent," came the Ghoul's voice from behind a cloud of cigarette smoke. "There is evidence of petechiae on the face and blood hemorrhaging at the corners of the eyes, and the cricoid cartilage in the neck was fractured in two places—all consistent with death by strangulation, as was to be expected."

The coroner paused in his dry recitation and looked down, shuffling his feet through the cigarette butts on the stained tile floor. His face was sallow and shiny with sweat. "The bites on the thighs were made postmortem," he went on. "It is the same killer, Lieutenant. Or rather, I believe so. I am sorry."

"So am I," Rourke said after a moment. "Unfortunately we can't make our apologies known to Titus Dupre."

"Physical evidence does not lie," the Ghoul said, "but it can mislead."

This time Rourke said nothing.

The Ghoul stuck his cigarette back in his mouth and used both hands to gently lift the girl's wrist. "The bruises here show impressions of heavy links and there are flakes of rust on the skin. Her hair smells faintly of gasoline, and I found a smear of grease on her right buttock and small pieces of grit embedded in her back and shoulders."

He laid the girl's wrist with care back onto the slab and squinted up at Rourke through the smoke. "My assessment is he kept her chained in an automobile garage somewhere while he was raping her and then killing her. And perhaps for a while afterward—lividity was consistent with the body having been moved some time after death."

Rourke let out a deep breath as if he'd been holding it. "Thanks, Moses."

"The bites," the Ghoul said. "I took the trouble of examining them more closely this time. Among the more savage tearing I found small, what you might call, love nips. As if he regretted killing her and so he began by kissing her there, where he'd hurt her before, perhaps to make her better, but then the kisses turned to nibbles and then something snapped inside of him, and he quite literally tried to consume her. He hated her, but he also—I cannot say *loved* . . ." The Ghoul shrugged, for once at a loss for words.

"Urge colliding with resistance," Rourke said.

A steady rain dripped from weighted clouds and the temperature felt like it had dropped twenty degrees by the time Rourke left the morgue in the Criminal Courts Building. He'd arranged to meet Fio at his car at eleven o'clock, so they could catch up on their cases before he headed out to the Girod Street Cemetery for Titus Dupre's funeral.

He walked through the rain down to Canal, where he had parked the Bearcat near the Saenger Theatre. The theater was all gussied up with banners and bunting and balloons in honor of its grand opening this evening. A work crew was out front erecting a flagpole for the world-renowned flagpole sitter Shipwreck Kelly.

Shipwreck Kelly was just a publicity stunt, though, arranged as entertainment for those not fortunate enough to have been invited to the masquerade ball that would follow the theater's first screening later this evening. The film they were showing was a first-run print of Remy Lelourie's *Lost Souls,* and because she was so fortuitously in town, she'd been invited to assist the mayor with the ribbon-cutting ceremony.

Shipwreck Kelly wasn't due to start his flagpole sitting for hours yet, and so Rourke wondered why there were so many people hanging around outside the theater, hunched under their umbrellas and raincoats and huddling under the shelter of the marquee. Then it occurred to him that they were already lining up just to watch Remy Lelourie take a ten-second walk down a red carpet. The encroaching enormity of her fame, and the burden of it, still kept surprising him.

Rourke stood at the curb, studying the fans gathered in front of the theater and wondering if one of them might be Romeo. He was waiting, also, for a break in the traffic, and breathing deep to get the stench of the morgue out of his nose and throat.

A taxicab rolled up to a stop alongside him, the Model T's fresh wax job beading in the wet. Otis Bloom rolled down the window and leaned his head out into the rain. His bald pate was as shiny as the Ford's hood. "Are you waiting for a taxi, Detective Rourke?"

"No, thanks. I've got my car."

Bloom looked down the street, then back at Rourke. He put on his hat and got out of the cab, buttoning up his black duster against the rain. He stared at Rourke, his throat working to dredge up his words. Rourke knew what was on the man's mind; he just didn't want to hear it.

"You'll never believe who I gave a ride to the other night," Bloom said. He was trying to sound normal, even cheerful, but it just wasn't in him anymore, if it ever had been. "Your Remy Lelourie was actually in my cab. Look here . . ." He bent over and reached inside the car, rummaged around for something on the front seat, and came up with one of the cab company's advertisement flyers that they tacked onto telephone poles. "Look at this. She was kind enough to give me her autograph, and as soon as she did I thought of my Mercedes, of how thrilled she's going to be when she hears how I'd given Miss Lelourie a lift in my cab, because she's such a fan of the lady, and then I remembered . . ." He looked away, swallowing hard, choking the words back down now.

Rourke didn't want to be rude, but he wished the man would just go away. "Mr. Bloom—"

"I saw the papers this mornin'. The monster who took my daughter is still out there."

"We'll get him, Mr. Bloom."

"You thought you had him before."

A young woman, who had been waiting for the streetcar, gave up as it began raining harder and hailed Bloom's cab. He acknowledged the woman with a wave of his hand and then looked an apology at Rourke. "I do know that you're trying your best."

"Yeah," Rourke said, a little bitterness showing.

"And I know that she's dead," Bloom said. "In my heart I know it. I just want to bring her home, Detective. I just want to know she's resting in peace."

"I'm sorry," Rourke said, because that, although inadequate, was all he could say.

Otis Bloom nodded and made an odd gesture with his hand, raising it as if in absolution. He turned away, opening the car door, and the wind caught at the skirt of his black duster, slapping it against his legs. The rain came down harder.

Rourke started to cross the street, but the light had changed again, and then he saw Fio anyway, trotting toward him up Canal.

Fio slowed when he spotted Rourke, tugging the hat with the bullet hole lower over his forehead and hunching his shoulders to keep the wet from running down the back of his neck. He looked like he had a golf ball tucked in his right cheek.

"What happened to your face?" Rourke said, as Fio joined him at the corner.

Fio gingerly touched his jaw with his fingertips. "Aw, I woke up this morning with a toothache. Son of a bitch hurts like holy hell."

"You ought to see a dentist."

"Why? So he can poke and drill and pull at it, and it'll hurt even worse."

"Baby," Rourke said.

They grinned at each other, feeling good because at least one of their cases was finally breaking. It had only been two days since Father Patrick Walsh had been found crucified in a macaroni factory, and Rourke was still running high on the adrenaline that always surged through him at the beginning of a case, so that he sometimes forgot to eat and sleep.

Rourke had called his partner earlier this morning, as soon as he was done with Floriane Layton, catching him as he was leaving the house, and telling him about Father Pat's secret club and the Catholic Charities' accounts book. As soon as the banks had opened, Fio had paid a call on his contact at the Hibernia National Bank, where Our Lady of the Holy Rosary and her priests kept their money.

Fio sniffed now at the air, then leaned into Rourke, sniffing some more, his broad nose quivering like a hound dog's. "You smell like the Ghoul," he said.

"I was in the morgue, talking to him about the Trescher girl and killing time while I was waiting for my hot date with you."

"Man, I don't know why you keep hanging out in that place. It gives me the fucking heebie-jeebies."

"Yeah, well, to each his own. Looking at those green ledgers and all those columns of numbers gives me the heebie-jeebies . . . Did you get anything?"

"Uh-huh." Fio touched his jaw again, wincing. "If Father Pat was blackmailing anybody, it wasn't for money. His deposits were all salary, which he withdrew periodically—probably to help finance his underground railroad for runaway wives. Something hinky, though, was definitely going on with the Catholic Charities. Only Father Ghilotti's and Mr. Albert Layton's names are on the accounts; Father Pat's wasn't. And, man, were those guys ever moving money around all over the place. Most of it was too fancy and complicated for me to follow, but some checks were drawn on the Charities' funds in thousand-dollar chunks supposedly for bond purchases, which makes sense. I mean you want to make money on your money, right? Except that the day after Father Pat was murdered, those debits were reimbursed to the penny by a cash deposit. Looks like somebody got busy covering his ass."

"More than one somebody, maybe," Rourke said, working through it. "So Father Ghilotti finds out that Father Pat has been helping some Catholic wives to run away from their husbands and he tells him that he's crossing the line as far as the Church is concerned and that he's got to cut it out. Meanwhile, though, Father Ghilotti and Mr. Albert Payne Layton are playing patty-cake with the Charities' money. One day Father Pat gets a look at the accounts book, and something in it tips him off. So he goes to Father Ghilotti and offers to make a deal: he'll keep quiet about the financial shenanigans as long as he gets to keep his railroad going. Father Ghilotti caved, but maybe Albert Payne Layton didn't."

"Sounds good in theory," Fio said, distracted because he was digging in the inner pocket of his wrinkled pongee suit coat for something. "Only to prove that's how it went down we're going to need to get a look at the Charities' accounts book."

"Yeah, but if we go for a warrant, we'll give the archbishop fair warning and whatever's been going on there will get buried so deep nobody will ever find it."

It might not be quite as bad as having the world learn that one of his priests was really a woman, Rourke thought, but neither was the wily Archbishop Hannity going to want it exposed that one of his priests had been embezzling charity money.

"I can think of a way we can get a look at that book without a warrant, though," Rourke said. He saw that Fio had found what he'd been looking for. A Baby Ruth candy bar. "If the chairwoman of the board invites us to have a look-see of her own volition."

They thought about it, trying to see if they were missing any angles. Fio thought about it while trying to tear open the wrapper on his candy bar. His thick blunt fingers weren't doing the job, so he used his teeth.

"I'll give Mrs. Layton a call and set it up for sometime tomorrow morning," Rourke said. "It's going to take some careful thought to figure out how we're going to finesse this."

And there was also Remy's theater opening to go to later this evening. What Rourke would rather have done was go home and spend a few hours with Katie, eat Mrs. O'Reilly's home cooking, and catch up on some much needed sleep, but he had a really strong hunch that Romeo was going to pull another stunt at the masquerade ball, just like he'd done at the dance marathon, and he wanted to be there when it happened.

"You know, if you think about it," Fio was saying, "maybe Father Ghilotti was only pretending to go along to get along for the meanwhile. A guy whose daddy is in the racketeering business wouldn't cave to a little blackmail . . . So, want to make a bet on which one of them did it? I'll give you ten to one it was Father Frank Ghilotti."

"Five bucks to your one it wasn't," Rourke said.

Fio grinned. "You're on."

"Because I'm leaning toward the third possibility," Rourke said.

"Aw, man, two possibilities are more than enough. Don't go messin' with any third possibility."

"That a husband of one of those Marys Father Pat made disappear was trying to pay him back for it, or make him talk about it."

"You see? That's what happens when you get involved with a third possibility. All of a sudden you got suspects coming back out your ears again."

"And we also shouldn't lose sight of the fourth possibility."

"Aw, man."

"That there was some kind of love triangle going on with Father Pat and our ladies of the club."

Fio gave Rourke his long-suffering look. "Gee, let's make sure now that we don't leave the lesbians off our list. We'll put them down right between the archbishop and the town of Paris. Other detectives, they go out detecting and the possible who-done-its are all nicely whittled down until there's only the one left. But you, you gotta go digging and poking and turning up rocks until the whole damn world's a suspect and only then are you happy."

Fio glared at the end of his candy bar a moment, thinking about all their suspects, then he bit it off.

"You really are eating that thing with your aching tooth," Rourke said, wonder in his voice.

"I'm hungry . . . Want some?"

Rourke laughed and shook his head.

Fio said something else, but he was drowned out by the streetcar rattling down the tracks in the neutral ground. The streetcar braked with a screech and a smell of scorched metal, and then Rourke heard someone calling his name and he turned.

The kid who sold newspapers on the corner and was in love with Rourke's Bearcat came running up to him so fast he had to hold on to his cap.

"Hey, Lieutenant," the kid said half out of breath, as he skidded to a stop. "You comin' for the 'Cat? Why don't I drive it around for you. That way you won't have to cross the street in the rain."

Rourke's car was parked on the uptown side of Canal Street, and he and Fio were standing on the downtown side, with the neutral ground between them and the car. For the kid to bring the Bearcat to Rourke, he would have to drive it all the way around the block.

"It's raining on this side of the street, too," Rourke said.

"Yeah, well . . ."

Rourke laughed and tossed the kid the keys.

"He'll hit somebody," Fio said through a mouthful of candy bar, "and they'll sue you and take you for your last dime."

"That's what I like about you, partner. You're a man who looks into the future and sees it bright with endless possibilities."

Rourke's mama had told him once that he'd been born with a caul over his face. It was a New Orleans old wives' tale, that a caul over a baby's face endowed it with the ability to find lost objects, and to get what were called "funny feelings" that presaged a change in the future, for both good and ill. Rourke thought his funny feelings had more to do with walking a beat and learning the hard way to anticipate trouble, so that you could get at it before it got at you.

Whether it was the caul, though, or his cop instincts, or Fio's bad thoughts at work—but suddenly Rourke didn't want the boy getting in his car.

He ran out into the street, dodging a beer truck, and hollering at the kid to stop, just as the kid punched up the ignition and the Bearcat's engine blew so high it peppered bolts and screws and pieces of metal onto the Saenger Theatre's giant new billboard with its one hundred-times-life-size movie poster of Remy Lelourie.

Rourke could see Fio's mouth moving, but no sound was coming out. Then his ears did that popping thing and he heard the whoop of sirens and horns honking, and the drum of the rain on the Saenger Theatre's marquee. A squad car careened around the corner with a screech of tires. Cops were walking around the mangled

Bearcat, crunching glass and scraps of metal underfoot. A woman was sobbing, and Fio was saying, "You got to let go of him, Day."

"She's dead," Rourke said. "Bridey's dead." And it seemed to be the most terrible thing in his life, too terrible to bear.

When he looked down, though, he saw that the body in his arms wasn't a woman, but a boy. The boy was very dead. The top of his head seemed to be missing. Rourke seemed to be sitting on a street curb with his feet in a puddle that he prayed was rain and not blood.

The cop part of Rourke's brain knew that his own body was going into a state of shock. He had to clench his teeth together to keep them from chattering, and his limbs felt numb and floppy, the way they got when you were falling down drunk. His mouth tasted like he'd been sucking on copper pennies.

He knew he was sitting on the curb on Canal Street with the dead newspaper boy in his arms and with his car having just been exploded into scrap metal by some kind of a bomb. He knew that, but time kept segueing to a night last summer when he'd sat on another curb in another street and held in his arms the body of a woman he had loved, who had died by a grenade meant for him.

The Chicago Mafia had killed Bridey Kinsella, but that business had been settled, and he couldn't imagine why they'd be coming back after him now.

"Why is this happening?" he said aloud, asking nobody in particular, except maybe God, who seemed to have gone missing.

Fio squatted on his haunches in front of him. "Day? You got to let go of him. The ambulance is here to take him away."

"Okay," he said, but his fingers seemed to be locked in a death grip on the boy's blood-soaked corduroy jacket.

Fio reached down and gently pried his fingers free one by one, then other hands took the boy and carried him way. Rourke pushed up onto his feet, but his legs still weren't working so good and Fio had to grab his arm to steady him. The rain ran out of his hair and into his eyes.

Fio was peering at him from beneath the brim of his battered, shot-up hat. Rourke felt his mouth smile. He knew it was a bad smile, and he tried to stop it but he couldn't. "It was me all along. I got you shot at, partner. I'm sorry."

" 'S okay. Day, why don't we—"

"So maybe you shouldn't get too close to me for a while, huh? I'm lethal to people who get close to me."

Fio's smile wasn't a very good one either. "You need to go to the hospital?" he said. "You look kinda wobbly there."

Rourke shook his head; it felt as if he had water sloshing around in there. "I'm all right."

"Maybe we should go back to the squad room. Put our feet up and talk this through, figure out who's doing this. We're gonna need to file a report anyway, and the captain, he's gonna want to chew some on our asses."

Rourke shook his head, and the water sloshed again. "You go on, Fio. I got a funeral I got to go to."

"Aw, man . . ."

Rourke was aware that his partner was giving him that craggy-faced worried look, and so he tried to act as normal as possible. He straightened his jacket and dusted off his pants. He looked for his hat and found it on the sidewalk, next to a fire hydrant. He put it on, then he looked around for his car, and then he remembered that the 'Cat was dead, and so he started walking.

Fio borrowed a squad car and picked Rourke up before he'd gone two blocks, which was a good thing since he couldn't feel his legs all that well and the water was still sloshing around in his head.

The Girod Street Cemetery was often where you ended up if you died poor and Protestant. A tenement for the dead. Over two thousand vaults had been dug out of the cemetery's whitewashed brick walls, stacked one above the other like ovens in a bakery, and the wooden coffins were sealed up inside them.

By the time Fio parked the squad car across the corner from the cemetery, the wooden coffin that contained the earthly remains of Titus Dupre had already been slipped into its oven and the door bolted shut. The band had tightened up the snares on their drums, they'd pulled the slide out on their trombones and lifted their trumpets to their lips, and swung into "Didn't He Ramble."

The mourners followed the band, dancing through the scrolled gate, their umbrellas bobbing to the beat, and sending Titus Dupre's soul off to glory and Jesus.

Rourke got out and stood by the squad car until Cornelius Dupre saw him. For a moment the boy looked set to keep on dancing, but then he stopped, rigid and vibrating in his rage, letting the parade pass him by and waiting for Rourke to come to him.

Rourke took the boy by the upper arm and led him over to the dubious shelter of the cemetery's crumbling whitewashed walls. Cornelius didn't drag his feet, but he wasn't bothering either to hide the hate in his eyes.

Rourke looked back toward the squad car idling at the corner with Fio at the wheel. He caught Fio's eye, telling him with a shake of his head that he could stay where he was.

"I want to talk with you," he said to the boy.

Cornelius smiled a wide, phony smile. His teeth were pure white in the ebony of his face. Raindrops sparkled in his long matted hair. "Where you been at, Mr. Po-liceman? You been busy this mornin' killing somebody else's brother?"

Rourke looked down at his chest because that was where Cornelius Dupre was looking. Blood caked the whole front of his gray flannel suit and white shirt, and for a moment he couldn't imagine where it all had come from, and then he remembered that he'd lifted the boy's body out of the car.

Cornelius made an uh-huh sound in the back of his throat. "So what you goin' to say to me? That you fried the wrong nigger and now you're sorry. Lord, my brother never so much as kicked a dog in his life, but that didn't stop the white law from takin' care of bidness as usual."

"Don't," Rourke said.

The funeral had drawn a crowd of curiosity seekers and a big part of that crowd was white. They were hanging around outside the grilled doors of a neighborhood speakeasy and they were starting to shuffle their feet and murmur among themselves as Cornelius's angry words carried to them on the heavy, rain-sodden air. Already letters to the editor had shown up in the morning newspapers, pointing out that Mary Lou Trescher had been strangled with a chimney sweep's weighted rope. Saying that white girls were being "preyed" on by black boys, and that the police ought to be taking a long, hard look at Titus Dupre's little brother.

Cornelius, though, either wasn't listening or was beyond caring. "A negro's wife is a white man's jelly roll, and nobody gives a hoot," he said, raising his voice even louder. "But Lord help the nigger who dares to turn it 'round back on the white man. What it's all about, what it's only *ever* been about, is the white man protecting his white woman from the big bad black buck."

"Shut up." Rourke grabbed him by the scruff of the neck and slammed him up against the cemetery wall, hard enough to make the crowd think he was rousting the kid, so that they'd lay off him later, once he and Fio were gone.

He held the boy up against the wall a moment longer, then let him down slowly. "Just . . . shut up with that," he said, gentle now. "Before you give your gran'mon something else to cry about."

The boy glared hate and fury at him a moment longer, then his gaze went to the restless crowd of white men in front of the speakeasy and all the air seemed to leave him.

"Your brother got framed for the murder of those girls," Rourke said. "I want you to tell me how you think that happened."

"You the detective, so what you askin' me for?"

"Because I don't believe it was just bad luck."

Cornelius stared at Rourke, his mouth and the skin around his eyes trembling, then he nodded. "If you hired my brother, Titus, to clean your chimley, you got your money's worth. He played a mean fiddle and he could whip any man alive at dominoes, but he liked his glass or two of white lightnin' on a Saturday night, liked to brag on himself, too, when he had a snootful. And, man, that boy believed that he was some *special* nigger."

Tears were mixing with the rain on the boy's face, but Rourke doubted he even knew that he was crying. "He believed," Cornelius said, his voice breaking, "that havin' a white girl in his bed made him less colored. The fool."

"Ah, Christ," Rourke said.

So Titus Dupre really had been with the Bloom girl the evening she'd disappeared, but there'd been no rape, no tease and rejection. She'd gone to him willingly. Only when the boy got liquored up, he liked to brag about his exploits in the Negro smoke joints. He just had to talk about the sweet loving he had gotten from a white girl, and that was what had made it so easy for the real killer of both girls to frame him.

"They were lovers," Rourke said. "Your brother and Mercedes Bloom were lovers."

Cornelius shook his head. "Man, you still don't know nothin', do you? It wasn't her, it was that other one. It was that Duboche bitch from the starting. And he wasn't fuckin' her, it was the other way around—she was fuckin' him. Only it don't make a straw's bit of difference anyways, he would've still hung for what he was doin'—a nigger puttin' it to white pussy, even if she'd been beggin' for it."

"Jesus. Why in hell have you all waited so long to tell me this?" Anger surged through Rourke with such force he wanted to put his fist through the crumbling wall. Then right on the heels of the anger came a sadness. He despaired at times that he was never going to understand human nature. "Your brother sat in that courtroom and heard himself called her rapist, all those months afterward sitting in that cell, waiting to die, and he never once said he was innocent."

Cornelius's laugh was like the noise of a hickory stick breaking.

"Innocent's a word for the white man. Ain't you heard? We were born in sin. Uppity niggers like my brother get lynched all the time just for looking at a white woman. If you think the truth woulda set him free, you a fool."

He was a fool. The chimney sweep's rope, the girls' hats under his bed, his bragging down at the local tonk—Titus Dupre would have been arrested anyway, and no amount of proof that Nina Duboche had been a willing partner in his bed would have calmed the irrational fears of the jury's twelve white men that their own women weren't safe.

Rourke had been staring at the ground while he thought, his hands in his pockets and his shoulders hunched against the rain, but now he raised his head and faced the pinched angry light in Cornelius Dupre's eyes.

"I should have seen it, though," Rourke said. "I'm—"

"Don't," the boy said, snarling the word. "Don't you tell me you're sorry for what you all done to my brother. You can leave me and him both a little pride by not tellin' us you're sorry."

Rourke nodded, saying nothing more.

"And I'll tell you something else, too, Mr. Po-liceman. Nina Duboche was a bitch, but my fool of a brother loved her. He knew what the world would think of a white girl who'd been with a Negro. He figured he was going down for it no matter what, and she might've been dead, but he still had a care for her."

A wind kicked up, driving the rain and carrying the smell of mud from the river and of rotting husks from the cemetery's pecan trees. The parade of mourners was long gone, the crowd around the speakeasy was dwindling. Fio had gotten out of the car and was trying to light a Castle Morro without much help from the wind and rain.

"Your brother paid for a crime he didn't own," Rourke said to Cornelius Dupre, "while the man who does own it is still out there, still killing. If I stop him it won't be an apology, it'll be evening up the score."

The boy cuffed the tears and rain off his face with the back of his hand. "Why? So's you can sleep at night? Why should I care, if he does more? He's killin' white girls. I hope he goes on killin' y'all till they none of you left."

CHAPTER TWENTY-FOUR

Remy Lelourie used her little finger to rub the lipstick off her fangs. "My lord, at this rate the sun'll be coming up on a new day before we get there," she said, as the Peerless touring car rolled forward a couple more feet and then stopped. "And we all know what the sun does to vampire bats."

She looked over at Rourke to see if he was smiling at her little joke, but she might as well have been talking to herself. The car rolled forward another couple of feet and stopped again.

They were following along behind a parade of floats and marching bands, and as soon as the parade passed by the Saenger Theatre, Remy Lelourie's car was supposed to pull up out front, and she would make her grand entrance down the red carpet. Canal Street was jam-packed with spectators, many in costume themselves even through they wouldn't be going to the party. People in New Orleans loved playing dress-ups, though, and parades were practically a religion.

Remy sucked on her bat teeth and then wiggled them with her tongue—they were driving her crazy. They'd been fashioned out of celluloid to fit over her own teeth, but they kept scraping the inside of her cheeks and lips. She'd forgotten how much they'd done that all during the filming of *Lost Souls* last winter. By the wrap party the whole inside of her mouth had been raw.

Along with the fangs, she was wearing the tattered white shroud and black winglike cape that she'd been buried in in *Lost Souls.* The Saenger Theatre people had wanted her escort to be a complementary vampire bat, but nothing was going to get Daman Rourke into a costume of any sort, not even the promise of sex with a sex goddess. He was looking good, though, in tails and white tie and a topper.

Remy reached across the expanse of Peerless maroon leather seat that separated them and brushed his freshly shaven cheek with the back of her hand. "You clean up well," she said.

The moment it was out of her mouth she wanted it back. It was only a flapper girl's way of telling her date that he was looking handsome, but from the way he'd pulled back from her touch, he must have thought she'd been talking about washing off the newspaper boy's blood.

Did you kiss your cop goodbye this morning, Remy?

Even with him sitting there safe beside her, Remy thought she still hadn't gotten over the belly-clenching fear she'd felt on hearing those words. She hadn't even bothered to hang up the phone. She'd just dropped it on the floor and walked right out of the house and asked Hebert to drive her to the Criminal Courts Building, praying that Lieutenant Daman Rourke would be at his desk, knowing that he was hardly ever at his desk, getting furious with him that he was never at his desk, and all the while thinking that if she didn't see him this very minute, in the very next second, she wouldn't be able to bear it, she would surely die from it.

She had just about decided she was maybe overreacting a little when they turned off North Rampart onto Canal and saw a truck dragging away the mangled wreckage of Rourke's fancy yellow Bearcat roadster. Police and firemen were all over the street, talking about a bomb, but Rourke was nowhere in sight and nobody had any idea where he was.

She had waited for him in the detective's squad room and if she'd been writing this as a movie scenario it would have said: *Miss Lelourie cannot sit still, she paces the floor, back and forth, back and forth, as if to stay still in any one place too long is to die. She has trouble getting a deep enough breath and the look on her face is of a woman who is about to fly apart into a million pieces.* Only this wasn't a movie and she hadn't been acting, and when he'd finally come through the door all covered head to foot in blood, she would have fainted if she'd been the type. She'd been so furious with him for making her so scared that she might have shouted at him just a little.

Did you kiss your cop goodbye this morning, Remy?

She turned her head to look at him. The shades were down over the back seat windows, but Hebert had turned the Peerless's recessed electric lamps on for them, and the soft yellow light limned the curve of her cop's cheekbone, the straight line of his nose, the arch of his upper lip. It was the dark side of ecstasy, she thought, to love another this much.

"Day . . ."

He turned to her, and even though she rarely cried for real, her eyes filled with tears.

"Hey." He hooked his hand around her neck and pulled her to him. He brushed the tears off her cheeks with the pad of his thumb. "What're these for?"

"That was a stupid thing I just said. I'm sorry."

He smiled and shook his head. "You know . . ." His thumb kept brushing her cheek, even though the tears were gone. "I keep going over it in my head, over what happened, and I feel sick about the boy, but I guess I was also sitting here feeling sorry for myself. Damn it, I loved that car."

"You used to call her 'baby.'"

They shared a smile, and then even though she had a perfectly good window on her side of the Peerless, she leaned across his lap to look out his side, pressing her palm on his thigh to brace her weight, fooling around . . .

"A couple of inches to the right and higher," he said.

She laughed and raised the green silk taffeta window shade a couple of inches. They were almost at the theater, finally. She could see the red carpet, and Mayor O'Keefe standing next to a blue ribbon with a giant pair of scissors in his hand. The crowd lining the curb and sidewalk all had their heads craned way back, peering at something high into an evening sky that was being swept with giant violet spotlights.

"Good heavens, Day. I'm not sure my vanity can stand it, but there appears to be something going on out there that's more interesting than me." She sprawled further across his lap trying to peer sideways out the window and up into the drizzle coming out of clouds the color of soot. "What are they all looking at?"

"Some fool . . ." His breath hitched as she wriggled some more, pretending that she was trying to get a better look. "Some fool who hasn't got the sense to get down off his pole and come in out of the rain."

They laughed together and then couldn't stop, and because, Remy thought, you couldn't live on the knife edge every second, they were able to let some of it go.

She pulled apart from him to touch his face with her fingertips, tracing the planes and angles as if she would sculpt him again later from memory. "I guess I'm not so tough. When I saw what he'd done to the 'Cat, when I thought I'd lost you . . ."

"Sssh. I'm here, baby."

He cradled her face in his hands, but before he could kiss her the car door opened to the chant of Re-my, Re-my, Re-my Le-lourie and the explosions of dozens of flash lamps.

Rourke got out first and turned to give her his hand. Remy Lelourie gathered her cape around her shroud and emerged from the Peerless. She paused at the end of the red carpet, turning in a slow half circle to let the cameras get their shots, and she could feel the acceptance, the admiration, the worship coming at her from the screaming crowd in pulsing waves, like blood pumping through a heart.

And then she smiled, showing her fangs.

The Saenger Theatre was being hailed by those who'd built it as the "Florentine Palace of Splendor," but Remy had been a guest in a real Florentine palace once, and it had nothing on this. This was like walking into a fairy-tale piazza at night. Statues lined the tops of the loges that were decorated with friezes and columns. Water cascaded from marble fountains, and above their heads the azure ceiling twinkled with stars.

The owner of the theater made a speech up on the apron of the stage and Remy made a speech. Then, just as she was about to push the button that opened the thick red-velvet curtain, another vampire bat emerged from behind it and swooped Remy up, wrapping her in his black satin cape. He bent her over his arm and sank his fangs into her neck, and the audience erupted into sighs and screams.

"Lord, I can't believe it's you," Remy said as they ran off stage right on a thunderous wave of applause. "You about stopped my heart, you wretch."

Once in the wings, the vampire bat whirled to face her, his cape flaring. "Remy, love," he said. "I forgot how deliciously fun it is to suck you."

Laughing, Remy took a mock swing at his head. "You are worse than a wretch. You're a vulgar . . ." She couldn't think of a word. "Wretch."

Hugh Granger spat his celluloid bat teeth out into his hands and rubbed the mouth that had set the hearts throbbing of thousands of women across America. "Dammit. I forgot how much these bloody things hurt."

"So what are you doing in New Orleans?" Remy said. "I thought you were in Mexico making a Western."

"No, I finished with that three weeks ago, and when the studio asked me to make an appearance at this tedious affair . . ." He lifted his shoulders in an elegant shrug. "I decided to be obliging for a change." He gave a sudden start, widening his eyes. "Good God, do you think I've turned over a new leaf?"

"Fat chance," Remy said, laughing again.

She took his hands in hers, squeezing them, then leaned back to look him over. The expression "tall, dark, and handsome" seemed coined for Hugh Granger. His looks were so classically aristocratic—the high forehead and pronounced cheekbones, the wide mouth and thin nose—that he was almost always cast in the "bloody duke roles," as he called them. His haughty demeanor with the press and his fans had only added to that image.

It had taken Remy the first month of making *Lost Souls* to get to know him, but once she did she realized that what had seemed to be vanity and aloofness was really a deep reserve, and after he warmed up to you he could be charming and funny and sweet. Still, Remy had sensed—perhaps because she had one herself—that there was an opaque barrier he'd put up between himself and the world, and beyond which even the closest of his friends were never allowed to penetrate.

"Oh, Hugh," she said now. "It's so *good* to see you. When this 'tedious affair' is over, I'm bringing you home with me and we can catch up on old times over some of my world-famous mint juleps."

"Well, I, uh . . ."

"Got a hot date tonight?"

"Yes," he said, and to Remy's secret delight he actually blushed a little. "Sort of a date, anyway."

Remy smiled and leaned into him, standing on tiptoe to kiss him lightly on the cheek. "Never mind. We'll do it later," she said, whispering now, because the lights were dimming and such a hush of anticipation had fallen over the house that you could hear the leader film clicking through the projector.

Then the organist struck the first chord of the eerie cemetery music that had been composed especially for *Lost Souls,* just as the first title card appeared on the screen:

In a castle deep in Transylvania . . .

After the screening they went out into a lobby that was all gilt and mirrors, where a jazz band was playing "Dixie." Waiters carried around trays of fruit punch, and within seconds flasks had emerged from pockets, sashes, garters, even hats, to spike it with. Buffet tables groaned beneath the weight of spiced baked beans, fried chicken, Saratoga chips, and coconut cake.

Almost everyone was in costume: harem girls and their sheiks, cowboys and Indian maidens, matadors and flamenco dancers. Once Remy saw a Romeo arm in arm with a Juliet, and her stomach clenched with a residual of that morning's fear, but this Romeo seemed too young to be the owner of the voice on the telephone, and he was making puppy-love eyes at the girl on his arm.

She waved at Freddy Ramon, who was dressed as a harlequin, and then she saw a Bright Lights cameraman, a sound technician, and an assistant director all in harlequin costumes as well—black and white diamond-patterned shirts and fat-legged pantaloons, floppy shoes, and silly pointed hats with red pompoms on top. Apparently the studio's press agents had decreed that everyone involved with *Cutlass* except herself was to have come as a harlequin.

"What do harlequins have to do with Louisiana pirates, though?" she wondered aloud, but her lover hadn't heard her. Daman Rourke's gaze searched through the crowded lobby, as if he would know Romeo right off when he found him, and there was almost a *heat* radiating off of him, of violence barely held in check.

He stuck to her side like a cocklebur while she signed autographs and made nice to all the dignitaries and distinguished guests. Yet she, too, could still sense Romeo's presence nearby, in the way that she could feel the air on her bare skin.

Then a man's hand clasped her arm beneath her elbow from behind, and she nearly jumped out of her skin.

"Why so nervous, darling?" Peter Kohl said as he slipped around in front of her.

"Peter . . ." She smiled to hide the hitch in her breathing. She thought she could actually feel her pulse beating in her neck. "You shouldn't sneak up on a girl like that. Especially one with such long, sharp teeth to bite you with."

She held out her hand to the director, palm side down. With his jutting beard and monocle, he looked just a little ridiculous in his harlequin costume.

He took her hand, turned it over and kissed the palm. "Remy, darling. You look like the living dead."

"Why, Peter. Darling. Your words are like a stake in my heart," she said back at him. From beside her, she thought she heard her cop snort under his breath.

Her director nodded at her cop. "Rourke."

Her cop nodded at her director. "Kohl."

The first time she'd introduced them, they'd circled each other like curs in an ally after the same bone, and they would probably be doing that here again, she thought, if there had been room to perform the maneuver.

The band was playing "Runnin' Wild" and quite a few couples were trying to dance the Charleston among the press of people. Her name was being shouted at her from all directions. *Hey, Remy . . . Smile, Remy . . . Over here, Remy . . .* And flash lamps were popping with her every breath. The theater lobby was awhirl in flashes of color, light, and sound, like a merry-go-round spinning wildly out of control.

Her director was feeling in the pocket of his harlequin suit for his cigarette case, all the while keeping his eyes on her cop. He had his cigarette lit and smoking by the time he turned back to her. "Have you talked to Max yet tonight?" he asked, then went on without waiting for her answer. "He's got the perfect vehicle for you, Remy.

A gangster flick about a beautiful moll who falls for the G-man who's hunting her brother. And if *The Jazz Singer* isn't laughed out of the theaters this month, he was saying we might even use the Vitaphone process for a few feet of film. Maybe have you sing a number draped over a piano or something."

"God, Peter," Remy said on a laugh. "You know I'm practically tone deaf."

"Nonsense, darling. There isn't a scenario written that you can't pull off beautifully." He turned as another harlequin came up to them, too perfectly timed not to have been arranged. "Isn't that right, Max?"

Remy had never seen Max Leeland in anything other than a cheap suit bought off the rack, but the harlequin costume he had on tonight looked as if it could have been worn to a fancy dress ball at Versailles by the Sun King. The black and white diamonds were fashioned of jacquard silk and embroidered with gilt thread. The buttons that ran down the front were the size of plums, and they looked like they'd been carved out of black jade and then studded with real pearls.

It must have been by Max's orders, then, that everyone from Bright Lights had come to the party dressed as harlequins, and she wondered what point he was trying to make with it. That the world was full of clowns? That the movies he made were entertainment, not art? That he had the power to make an entire film crew dress to his whim?

The studio boss stared at Remy from beneath the thick shelf of his eyebrows. He didn't have any natural charm, and as long as she'd known him he'd never tried to fake it. "You know where I'm staying, Miss Lelourie. The Roosevelt Hotel. I'll be there until the end of the week. I trust you'll be bringing me the signed contract before I leave. A word, Kohl," he said and walked away without even a "so long" or "good evening."

The director looked at Remy and lifted his shoulders in a very European shrug, then he followed in Max Leeland's wake.

Rourke had gone perfectly still beside her, as if he'd suddenly been emptied of air. She was afraid to look at his face, so she grabbed a glass of punch off a floating tray. The band was doing a drum solo now, and the dancers had formed a conga line. It was wending its way through the knots of conversation and the buffet tables, getting longer and longer as it went along.

Remy flapped her hand in front of her face like a fan and laughed. "My, it smells like a bull ring in here, what with all the snorting and pawing at the ground that was going on between you and Peter."

"What contract?"

"There isn't one, Day. I'm not going to sign it."

She took a drink of the punch; it was so sweet she almost choked. When he didn't say anything more, she turned to look at him and got his cop face.

"You think I didn't feel a little of what you were feeling out there on that red carpet?" he said. "There isn't another rush like what you get from being on top of the world. You can't stop being Remy Lelourie because of me. You can't put that kind of burden on me, but more importantly, you can't put it on yourself."

She looked away, blinking, swallowing down the tears that had been threatening on and off all night. "Do we have to talk about this here and now?"

"Well, hell," he said, smiling a little. "Did you expect me to wait until after you were gone to show off to you how noble I can be?"

She tried to smile back at him, but she couldn't manage it. He was telling her he understood and had already accepted that it was inevitable she would leave him someday soon, and she wanted to throw up words of denial in the same way you would cross your fingers against a voodoo curse.

"I'm not—" she said, but she got no further. The line of dancers snaked between them, separating them as Rourke took a step back. A man in a pirate's costume jostled Remy, spilling spiked punch down the front of her shroud. Then a hand grabbed her arm from behind, and she thought the person was only trying to steady himself in the crush until she felt a sharp, stabbing pain lance into the crook of her elbow.

She cried out loud, as much from the pain—it *hurt*—as the shock.

Rourke broke through the line of dancers and was at her side in an instant. "My arm," she paid, holding it up to see what was causing the pain—a short, deep gash near the bend in her elbow that was almost *pulsing* blood.

"Jesus . . ." He whipped a white silk handkerchief out of his pocket, folded it into a pad and pressed it against the bleeding cut. He held it there for about a minute, pressing hard, although after that first shock of sharp pain, the cut was only throbbing now.

He took her other hand by the wrist and put it in place of his own. "Hold that there and bend your arm up tight against your chest. That's it . . ." He searched her face, and she wondered what he saw. She felt oddly detached, as if she were watching herself in a film she'd made years ago. "I think you'd better breathe, darlin'," he said.

She breathed and felt so light-headed she swayed a little on her feet, and that made her angry. She was *not* the fainting type.

He brushed the hair back off her face and then trailed his fingers down her cheek and along the line of her jaw. "Remy. Jesus, baby . . . I hate to ask this, but can you tell me what-all you saw while it was happening?"

She closed her eyes to replay it in her mind. "It happened so fast, it was like getting a glimpse of a room by a lightning flash on a dark night. It was some kind of knife, but a strange one. It had a hooked point on it, like a can opener. And his sleeve . . . I got an impression of black and white." She opened her eyes, a little surprised to realize how much it hurt to think that someone she knew could have attacked her in that way. "I think he could be one of the harlequins, Day."

"The damn place is half full of harlequins."

Although, oddly, as they looked around the press of people closest to them, those dancing and the others chatting and drinking in their little groups, there wasn't a single harlequin. She did see

Garrison Hughes of *The Movies,* though. The reporter waved and lifted his camera for a shot, and her cop went right for him.

"Hey . . ." he said, retreating a couple of steps, but Rourke kept coming.

"Hey . . ." Hughes turned and ran, pushing his way roughly through the crowded lobby, with Rourke on his heels and Remy following close behind.

Hughes disappeared into the men's toilet facilities, and Rourke went in after him. Remy stopped outside the door, hesitating, and then she heard the reporter's voice, high-pitched and cracking on the edges. "I got a right to be here. I'm with the press. They *want* me here taking pictures, for crissakes."

She pushed the swinging door open and went in. "Don't hurt him, Day."

"I wasn't going to," he said, looking wounded that she'd even think it. He was leaning up against the sink, his hands braced on the porcelain behind him. Garrison Hughes was standing across the room, by the urinals. Her cop was smiling, though, and his smile could be scary.

"I want you to take pictures, too, Hughes," he said. "In fact I'll pay you a hundred bucks if you take some pictures for me tonight."

The reporter's mouth opened as if he'd been punched, and even Remy was surprised. To pay a guy a hundred dollars for a couple of hours work was a lot of money, even for Rourke, who supplemented his detective's salary by playing the cards and the ponies and being good at it.

Garrison Hughes stared at Rourke a moment longer, then his head snapped around to Remy as his reporter's instinct kicked in. His eyes widened a fraction as he took in the way she was holding her arm and the drops of blood splattered on the white tile floor. "Holy cow . . ."

Rourke pushed himself off the sink and took a couple of steps toward the reporter, moving like a boxer dancing up to his opponent. "You could be a world of help to Miss Lelourie and the police if you would go around the lobby this evenin' and take a picture of everybody you see wearing a harlequin costume and then get their names, if you can."

The reporter's gaze clicked back and forth between them, then he nodded. "Yeah, I can do that. Everybody and his brother wants their picture in *The Movies* and their names spelled right. I also want the story, though. Exclusive. And on top of the hundred bucks."

"Sure," Rourke said, and he smiled again. "Only I decide when you get it." He cocked his head toward the door. "Now, beat it."

Remy could almost see the gears and wheels turning in the reporter's head. He could trust that they were playing square with him and maybe get the scoop of a lifetime. But with every moment he held back what little story he already did have, he risked getting scooped by someone else.

He finally nodded, a bit reluctantly. "Okay. But how and when do I—"

"I'll find you," Rourke said.

He waited until the door swung shut behind the reporter's back before he went to her. "Let me look at that again," he said, taking her arm and gently turning it so that the cut was exposed to the hanging glass globe lights. "It's pretty deep. Maybe a doctor should be taking care of it."

Now that the wound wasn't welling so much blood, Remy could see that she'd been punctured, not slashed, by the odd little knife. It looked like it should be hurting worse than it was now. "I don't know," she said. "It's almost stopped bleeding and the minute I walk into a hospital somebody'll recognize me and there'll be a fuss kicked up and it'll get in the papers."

"Yeah, okay. You'll be okay," he said, but his hands were touching her all over, her neck, her waist, her upper arms, before settling on her shoulders.

"He's winning, Day. I'm scared now."

"Jesus . . ." His arms tightened their grip on her shoulders, then he leaned forward until their foreheads touched. "Let's get out of here. I'm taking you home with me and you're moving into the Conti Street house until this is over."

They left the Saenger Theatre by a back service door onto Rampart Street. The street lamps and shop signs and awnings all dripped with the wet, but a moon haloed with rings was trying to shine through the clouds. The air, clean and sweet-smelling from the rain, was a little cool and Remy huddled under her bat cape.

Here, around the corner from the red carpet, hardly anyone was on the street. A pair of squad cars was pulled up to the curb, their engines idling, and three uniforms were standing alongside, drinking coffee they were spiking with something illegal out of a flask.

Hebert wasn't due to bring the Peerless back for another couple of hours, but Rourke's Conti Street house was only three blocks away, so he took Remy's hand and they began walking.

They heard a shout behind them and turned to see another patrolman come running around the corner from Canal, holding his nightstick down at his waist to keep it from slapping his legs.

The patrolmen yelled something and then followed it up with, "Go, go, go!" Two of the cops standing by the cars hopped into one and it peeled away within seconds, lights flashing, siren blaring.

Rourke let go of Remy's hand and reached into his coat pocket as he started toward the two remaining cops, and Remy saw the strap of his gun's shoulder holster.

"Evenin', Detective Rourke," one of the patrolmen said, recognizing him before he could produce his shield. "Miss Lelourie," the cop added, a flush staining his already ruddy cheeks. "How's the party?"

"Swinging," Rourke said. "So what's going on?"

"Aw, a bunch of the Klan boys took it into their heads to go nigger-knocking over in the Dryades neighborhood. The foot patrol over there called in on the box, said they'd been mixing it up with some colored boy in a Felicity Street speakeasy and things were starting to get out of hand."

"Goddammit. Okay . . . this your car? 'Cause I'm taking it, but I want y'all riding along with me," Rourke said. He took a half step toward the remaining squad car, then turned back to her. "Listen, I got to . . . The Dupre house is on Felicity."

He stared at her, not really seeing her, but playing scenes through in his head. She knew he wouldn't want to leave her behind with Romeo maybe still on the loose inside the theater, but he wouldn't want to be taking her with him into an unruly mob of Klansmen either.

Before he could make up his mind, Remy went around him, opened the door to the squad car, and got in.

CHAPTER TWENTY-FIVE

Rourke drove, punching up the siren as he turned onto Canal Street and headed toward the river with the gas pedal pushed to the floor. The beams of the squad car's headlamps cut through a drizzly rain that glistened like spun glass. The city's neon lights looked like ghosts in the mist.

The Dryades neighborhood was mostly Victorian-era houses full of working-class Jewish and Italian and colored families. The area for a couple of blocks on Felicity Street between St. Charles and Baronne was where the Negro wives and mamas came to do their shopping and the men did their drinking.

They saw the trouble the minute they turned onto Felicity from St. Charles. A loud, tough knot of about twenty men flexed and bulged like a muscle in front of a wisteria-covered brick building that had been a school in its glory years but was a low-down smoke joint now. The smoke joint was between a colored theater and a shuttered hardware store, and as soon as Rourke pulled the squad car up to the curb, siren wailing and tires screaming, the lights on the movie marquee went out.

Rourke slammed the gearshift into neutral and was jumping out of the car while it was still moving. The other two cops were only a couple of seconds behind him and pulling their nightsticks out of their belts.

The knot of men in front of the smoke joint, if they were Klansmen, weren't wearing their white hoods and robes. A couple were armed with fence slats and one guy looked like he had a baling hook, but most just had green quart bottles of beer in their hands. They hadn't scattered, though, when the squad car pulled up, and the beat cops who'd called in the disturbance and the first squad car were all strangely nowhere in sight. Trouble was hanging in the air like a bad smell.

Rourke took a couple of steps toward the trouble, then he came back to the car and stuck his head in the rear window. He had seen Remy Lelourie stare death in the face and laugh, so he shouldn't have been surprised now to find her staring into one of those little round mirrors that women carried around with them everywhere and putting on lipstick. She had, he saw, removed her fangs.

"Remy—"

"Don't worry, Day," she said, running the pad of her little finger along her lower lip. "My timing is impeccable, I never miss my marks, and I certainly do know how to steal a scene."

"Right," he said, straightening and backing away a couple of steps, and wondering what in hell she was talking about.

The knot of men in front of the smoke joint let out a collective noise that sounded like a growl. Rourke unsnapped his holster and took out his gun, but he carried it with his arm hanging down at his side, the gun's muzzle pointed toward the ground.

The two patrolmen walked a pace or so behind him and he said to them low and soft, out the corner of his mouth, "I'm probably going to have to run a bluff you could drive a truck through, so don't y'all go shooting or swinging your sticks at anybody. Not unless I'm hollering and going down."

As they got closer to the smoke joint, Rourke saw that a chimney sweep's paraphernalia was scattered along the gutter: brooms, brushes, weights, coils of rope, and bundles of twigs. The black silk top hat was crushed flat and smelling like it had been peed on.

Rourke passed by a street lamp and his shadow leaped forward ahead of him, onto the sidewalk. The men on the back end of the knot saw him, or felt him, coming and they melted out of his way without resistance.

Cornelius Dupre was in the middle of the knot. He had put up a fight, by the looks of him, and he was still fighting. He bucked and heaved and kicked out against the two men who had him by each arm. One was a big old redneck-looking guy with a pot gut, jowls hanging down to his chin, and eyes the color and sheen of wet mud. The other man had one eye that was dead and receded into the socket, and dried spittle whitened the corners of his mouth.

Cornelius Dupre had a rope around his neck, and the eyes he turned to Rourke were feral, like those of a cornered cat. "You comin' to join the lynching party, Mr. Po-liceman? This your way of evenin' up the—"

The rest of it was stopped by the redneck burying his fist in the boy's belly.

"Let him go now," Rourke said gently. "Y'all don't want to be doing this."

He'd expected the defiance to come from the two men holding Cornelius. Instead, it came from behind him, in a voice that was big and booze-roughened.

"You burnt the wrong nigger."

Rourke didn't turn his back on the men holding the boy, just shifted his weight a little so he could take in the owner of the voice. It was the damn buck-toothed man in the yellow shirt and purple suspenders.

The man took a menacing step toward Rourke. He wasn't armed with anything more than his fists, but he was big and mean and full of too much hate to stop. "We're done with having our women kilt and defiled by these chimney sweep niggers," he said. "Tonight we're doin' what needs doin'."

Rourke raised his gun and pointed it between the man's eyes. He didn't say anything, just pulled back on the hammer with his thumb, and the sound of the gun cocking was loud in the sudden silence.

The buck-toothed man spit out the corner of his mouth, then cuffed it dry. "You can't shoot all of us."

Rourke smiled. "I don't have to. Just you."

The silence now was like after a bell has stopped tolling. Rourke could smell the sweat on the other man's skin, hear the suck and grate of the man's sawing breaths. From out of the corner of his eye, he saw one of the patrolmen take a tighter grip of his stick.

Somebody kicked over an empty beer bottle on the ground, sending it rolling down the street, and the noise let some of the tension out of the moment. They weren't going to jump him and tear him limb from limb, Rourke thought, but he still wasn't getting the rope off Cornelius Dupre's neck without a struggle.

The wail of sirens that had been hovering in the distance grew louder. The buck-toothed man made a small movement, more a coiling of his muscles, and Rourke saw in his eyes that he was going to make a play for the gun. And then his head jerked and he looked beyond Rourke, and never in his life had Rourke seen a man look more surprised.

Remy Lelourie floated toward them from out of the mist, like something out of a graveyard in the black flowing cape and tattered white shroud. The face, though, this was unmistakably one that they'd all seen larger than life on the silver screen.

She walked right into the middle of the trouble with wonder on that face and an aura about her of impish excitement and a shared secret. As if she were Cinderella who'd suddenly been transported by magical pumpkin to the ball.

"Gentlemen, I declare that I am fascinated," she said, her words more heavily spiced than usual with the Creole accent she'd grown up with. "Positively overwhelmed, I am, for if this isn't just like a scenario from right out of one of my movies."

"Jesus God," someone said on an exhaled breath, then grunted as the man standing next to him thumped him in the belly hard with of all things a baseball mitt. As if he'd been out playing catch with his boy, Rourke thought, when he'd gotten the call to go lynching.

"Pardon his profanity, ma'am," the man with the mitt said. "It's just . . . are you really Remy Lelourie?"

She focused her tilted, catlike eyes on the man with the mitt until he began to squirm, and then her wide mouth broke into a smile that was pure Remy. "Oh, you're only funnin' with me, and you can just cut it out."

Rourke watched her turn on the power of Remy Lelourie. Her gaze went from man to man, sucking them in, before it came to rest finally on the buck-toothed man in the yellow shirt and purple suspenders.

"*Oh, Susannah!* is the movie I was talking about," she said. "Did you see that one, sir?"

And the man—who a moment before had been facing down the muzzle of a .38 Policeman's Special—shuffled his feet and mumbled, "No'm," to his shoes.

"Well, never you mind," she said, laughing. "I'll tell you the plot, shall I? Susannah is this dance hall girl, you see? But one with a heart of gold, of course. And in the town where she's living there's about to be a gunfight between the wild and handsome outlaw she's in love with and this mean ol' corrupt sheriff and his six deputies, when suddenly an idea comes to her of how she can get everybody to put up their guns and thus escape disaster."

The men looked as if they weren't sure if they were supposed to be identifying with the handsome outlaw or the corrupt sheriff and his deputies, but it didn't matter anyway for she owned them.

She was also, Rourke saw, slowly unraveling the knot of men and separating them from Cornelius Dupre. Rourke took a couple of slow and quiet steps closer to the boy.

"What Susannah does," said Remy Lelourie, "is she tells the men that she's going to auction off a dance with herself to the highest bidder . . . You, sir? Why don't you play the part of the auctioneer?" She linked arms briefly with the redneck with the jowls and pot and when she stepped away again, he went with her, mesmerized, and letting go of the boy Cornelius without an apparent thought.

"And any money we make can go to Miss Mary Lou Trescher's mama. So why don't you"—and she held her hand out to the man with the dead eye—"start the bidding out at a nickel."

The man let go of Cornelius's other arm and took a couple of spastic steps toward Remy. He stuck out his head and twisted up his mouth and started stuttering so hard he was spitting.

"Aw, jeez," said the redneck. "You don't want him bidding anyway. He dances just like he talks." He waved his arms in the air and hollered, "Hey, y'all. Who'll give me five cents for a dance with the beauteous Miss Remy Lelourie?"

"Heck, I'll give you a dime," came an old man's voice from the back.

As soon as the two men had let go of Cornelius Dupre, the boy had whirled to run, but Rourke grabbed him by the arm and forced him down the street toward the patrol car. The two patrolmen followed, covering their backs.

Rourke heard the redneck say, "Hey, wait a minute. What'll we do for music?" And the man with the baseball mitt answered him, "I got me a harmonica."

Cornelius twisted against the grip Rourke had on him, and Rourke gave him a little shake. "Don't you be giving me any more grief tonight, kid."

"Where you takin' me?"

"To jail." One of the patrolmen had run up ahead now and started up the car. Rourke opened the door to the back seat and thrust Cornelius inside. "Until we rid the world of the man who's killing those girls, jail is the safest place for you."

Cornelius flung himself against the far window and crossed his arms over his belly. "Hunh. Tell that to my brother."

Two squad cars peeled around the corner from St. Charles, sirens whimpering down to moans. The men, who'd been about to lynch a fifteen-year-old boy, were all laughing and whooping and clapping now in time to a harmonica wailing "Oh, Susannah!" Stars of their own scenario. The moment when it could have turned ugly had already come and then gone when Remy Lelourie, with impeccable timing, had hit her mark and stolen the scene.

Rourke asked the patrolmen to take their "material witness" and stow him out of sight in the Mid-City Precinct.

He shut the door, and the squad car pulled out into the street. Cornelius Dupre turned to stare back at him through the rear window, and Rourke had to laugh, because the boy sure didn't look grateful that the police had just saved his ass.

When Floriane de Lassus Layton heard the wail of the police sirens from a block away on St. Charles, she felt a moment's panic that they were coming for her.

It wasn't as if she'd committed any crime, unless you counted the love she'd made with another woman . . . Other women. But when guilt is so much a part of you that you're breathing it in and out through the pores of your skin, then you have long ago stopped needing a reason for your fear.

The sirens faded away, though, after a few minutes and she smiled at her own foolishness. Yet as she walked around the parlor, plumping pillows, straightening a book here, a painting there, she imagined she could still feel her heart thudding against her rib bones.

When the grandfather clock struck the hour, she started so violently she almost knocked over the milk glass vase of American Beauty roses that she'd been rearranging on the mantel. Then, even though she was looking right at the face of the clock and could see the time, she counted the deep bongs, counted them out loud like a ritual. He'd told her that he'd be coming home from his club by nine o'clock, but he could be late. He often was.

Still, when he came through the door, he would want his bourbon poured and the fire going in the grate because the night was cool.

She knew better than to disappoint him.

She sat on the green and cream silk sofa to wait for him, arranged herself there like a proper young lady expecting a gentleman caller. She waited while the grandfather clock bonged ten times, then eleven, then twelve. And when he finally came, his bourbon wasn't poured and the fire had died in the grate, and she sat as if the waiting had petrified her, turned her into stone.

Hating his confidence, fearing it, she watched her husband walk to the bourbon decanter and pour his own drink.

He turned to her, smiling, and lifted his glass in a toast. "Why, Flo, darling. What a sweet and loving wife you are. You've waited up for me."

"I'm not, Bertie," she said.

His smile tightened a little. "Not what?"

"A loving wife."

His mouth relaxed again, but his eyes had a hard sheen on them. "I know, darling. That much has been obvious for quite some time."

She'd been remembering things, while sitting on the sofa and waiting for him to come. Remembering the time she'd first seen him running across a lawn with a tennis racket in his hand. The sky had been a hard, sun-washed blue behind his smiling face and a salt breeze had riffled through his bright hair, and it seemed that since he was everything she was supposed to want, she had wanted him.

And she had remembered, too, going back to that same house only a month after they'd been married, walking across that lawn beneath another sun-washed blue sky, and wondering already to herself how they could be walking arm and arm, and still not be touching.

"Bertie, do you know what the word obscene means?"

He'd gone to the window, drink in his hand, to look out at a night dark and full of rain. When she'd spoken, after such a length of silence, he cast a look at her over his shoulder, then turned back to the window again. "You are behaving strangely tonight."

"I looked it up in the dictionary this afternoon so that I would be sure to get it right. It means disgusting to the senses, because of some filthy, grotesque, or unnatural quality. You are obscene, Bertie. You revolt me."

She'd been rehearsing that little speech all day, and it had sounded that way, stilted, overexposed. Still, she was proud of it. It was the second bravest thing she'd ever done in her life.

She hadn't quite been brave enough to say it to his face, though, and she saw his back go rigid before he turned to look at her. His face wore his slightly cruel, smiling mask. What Albert Payne Layton really felt, he had always kept inside, showing nothing to anyone except polished manners or a balled-up fist.

"Flo, darling. I do believe you have finally gone and lost your mind," he said, and only by the careful way he pronounced the words did she know that he was starting to boil inside.

Good, she thought. She wanted him boiling.

"You murdered Father Pat," she said.

His mouth fell open a little and then he laughed.

"You nailed him to a piece of wood and watched him die."

She watched her husband cross the room from the window back to the whiskey decanter and she saw his guilt in his step and the set of his shoulder, in the stiff way he held his head. She heard his guilt in his calculated and carefully articulated words.

"I don't know whether I should feel astonished that you would think so," he said, "or complimented."

"You were stealing money from the Church and Father Pat found out about it and so you killed him."

He was staring down at the bourbon in his glass, but she saw the flash of fear cross his face and she relished it. He waited just a little too long before he raised his head and met her eyes and laughed again, shaking his head. "Flo, Flo, Flo . . ."

He went to the cherry wood secretary where they kept the telephone. He hesitated a moment when he saw the Catholic Charities' green leather accounts book that she had taken from his desk and so carefully placed there, but then he lifted the phone's handset and held it out to her.

"Here, dear wife. Call up the police and tell them you've solved the case. Only, why don't we just tell them *all* our dirty secrets while we're about it, huh? Mine . . . and yours."

Once when she was a young girl, a friend had taken her for a sail on the lake and a terrible squall had come up. The little sailboat had groaned like a thing in agony as it bucked and climbed the waves. And as the rain lashed the deck and the wind howled and shrieked through the rigging, she, Floriane de Lassus, had believed that she was looking death in the face and as scared as she'd been in that moment, she had also been laughing with an odd and savage excitement.

She hadn't experienced that feeling again in her life, until now.

"What secrets of mine are you talking about, Bertie?" she said, pushing him hard now, baiting him. "Is it the one where I arise from my lover's bed flush with pleasure, wet between the legs and with my nipples still tingling. If that's your secret, darling, then you're too late because Lieutenant Rourke already knows."

There they are, she thought, and she felt nearly faint now with fear and that sick excitement. The first fissures in the crust covering the boiling geyser that lived inside Albert Payne Layton. His mouth turned white at the corners and a blood vessel throbbed in his temple. His freckles had darkened to the color of dried blood.

"The whole world's going to know the truth about me soon," she said. "About *us,* Bertie. Do you even need to imagine what they'll be saying in your clubs, on the exchange and the golf course, about a man who is such a poor lover that his wife turned to other women for satisfaction?"

He set his bourbon glass carefully down on the secretary, next to the Charities' accounts book. "This time," he said, coming at her, "this time I am going to make you sorry, bitch, that you were ever born."

She shrank back onto the sofa and brought her arms up to her chest like a shield, as she had learned to do over the years. He wouldn't hit her face, he never hit her face. And it seemed that she was counting the steps it took him to get to her, one, two, three, four, counting until the whole world and her place in it was reduced to one last second.

A second is a long time. In a second you have time to regret the lies you've lived and the truths you've told. A second is long enough to see your daughter standing in the doorway and to wish it didn't have to be this way. In a second you can watch Bertie cock his fist and send it flying—for the first time in eighteen years of marriage—toward your face.

And in a second you, Floriane de Lassus Layton, can pull out the Colt revolver that you have hidden behind the pillow on the sofa, the one that your grandfather on your mama's side took with him when he marched off to fight in the War of Southern Independence.

In a second you can pull your grandfather's gun out from behind the pillow and shoot your husband in the heart.

CHAPTER TWENTY-SIX

Lieutenant Daman Rourke went first to the man lying sprawled on the rose and green Oriental carpet with a bullet hole in his chest. He pressed his fingers to the man's throat, where the pulse would be if there was one, but the flesh was already cooling.

He went next to the girl. She was folded up against the wall in a corner between a secretary and a potted palm, her arms wrapped around her chest, her thin batiste nightgown pulled down tight over her bent legs to cover her toes. There was, he saw, a smear of blood on the hem.

Rourke had just been falling into the unconsciousness of sheer exhaustion when the telephone jarred him awake. His head was so thick with sleep he felt drunk with it, and it took him a while to make sense of Della Layton's hysterical sobbing that Mama had shot Daddy. She was beyond that hysteria now, though; her body had shut down into shock.

He picked her up and carried her out into the hall, set her down on a padded bench, found a raccoon fur coat hanging in a closet and wrapped her up in it.

He went back into the parlor and covered the body with a throw he found laid over the back of a chair. And only then did he go to the woman sitting on the green and cream silk sofa that was splattered now with tiny droplets of her husband's blood.

He crouched in front of her. "Mrs. Layton."

"He was going to kill me this time. I saw it in his eyes."

Rourke thought that was probably true. Only for the sake of the trial that was coming, he wished that she had waited to fire the gun until after her man had hit her.

She still held the gun in her hand. He covered her hand with his own and tried to take it carefully away from her. "Let go now," he said softly. "You'll be all right, but you're going to have to let go of the gun."

Her rigid fingers relaxed. He kept hold of her hand while he took the weapon away from her with his other hand and slipped it into his coat pocket. "He laughed," she said. "When I told him what he'd done, he didn't even bother to deny it. He laughed."

"Mrs. Layton. Flo . . . listen to me." He gave her hand a little squeeze. "You have the right not to say anything that may incriminate you. I don't want you to tell me anything more until I've taken you downtown, and you've called your lawyer and talked with him first."

She waved her free hand as if she were brushing away a bothersome mosquito. "No, no. I've shot my husband dead and now I must pay for it. Deeds have consequences, as my mama, may God bless her soul, was fond of saying."

She straightened her spine, pulling herself up tall and lifting her head. She looked dressed for tea at the Roosevelt Hotel in a soft gray wool suit and pearls. He didn't see any blood on the suit, but there were tiny droplets of it on the peaches-and-cream skin of her face.

"Family is everything," she was saying. "My mama always used to tell me, 'Flo, *la famille* is what matters most in this life. You have obligations and to disgrace yourself is to disgrace *la famille.*'"

Rourke pushed himself to his feet and looked around for the telephone. He found it on the secretary, along with the Catholic

Charities' accounts book. He called the precinct and asked for a patrol car, an ambulance, and the coroner.

He picked up the accounts book and ran his hands over the expensive green leather, but he didn't open it. He looked up and caught Floriane Layton watching him, caught an expression on her face he didn't trust. Under any other circumstances he would have thought it was suppressed exultation.

"I'm almost as smart as you are, Lieutenant," she said, and this time he was sure he heard the exultation in her voice. "When you asked about the accounts book, it took me only moments to figure out what Bertie had been doing, and to guess that Father Pat had somehow found out about it."

He came back to her, where she sat on the green and cream silk sofa splattered with her husband's blood.

"But did he kill him for it, Flo?" Rourke asked putting a little steel into his own voice. "Did your husband really confess to you that he'd killed Father Pat?"

"He laughed," she said. Her face had sharpened, wary now. "You need to know him, to know what he was like. He'd been caught in an act of embezzlement, and exposure would have ruined his perfect, New Orleans society life. If you knew him at all, then you would know that he would do anything to prevent that from happening."

"And that's all there was to it?"

She was looking up at him, but he didn't think she was seeing him. She was deep in that place where lived the Flo Layton who could point a gun at her husband's heart and pull the trigger.

"Does the *why* of it really matter anyway, Lieutenant? Father Pat became my salvation and for that reason alone, Bertie would have felt he had to crucify . . . him."

It was possible that he'd imagined it, but Rourke didn't think so. That little instant's hesitation when the mind filters out the truth while going for the lie.

Floriane de Lassus Layton had been about to call her priest *her.*

* * *

Father Frank Ghilotti opened the door to Rourke's knock even though it was four o'clock in the morning. The pastor was already dressed in slacks and sweater, and he didn't comment on the ungodly hour as he led Rourke into the rectory's comfortable parlor, where a fire burned against the chilly damp.

An open breviary lay on the seat of a brown leather winged chair, and a half-empty glass of milk sat on a scalloped-edged maple table nearby. Father Ghilotti picked up the breviary and sat down. He marked his place in his reading with a cigarette wrapper, and then lay the breviary down on the maple table.

Rourke had brought the Catholic Charities' accounts book with him, and he laid it down on the table so that it and the breviary were side by side. He took a seat in a matching brown leather wing-backed chair on the other side of the fire. He hadn't realized he was cold until he felt the fire's heat.

A piece of coal hissed in the grate, and a clock ticked on the mantel. An orange cat jumped on the priest's lap and began purring loudly beneath his kneading fingers. Rourke had decided to let the silence stretch until Father Ghilotti chose to break it.

"Has another priest been crucified?" the other man finally said.

"Why would you think that?"

Lamplight flashed off the lenses of his eyeglasses as he leaned his head back and smiled. "I don't know. Maybe because you've come here at four in the morning, and presumably it was to see me, since you haven't asked after your brother. Who is, by the way, upstairs and sound asleep in bed. Unless he snuck out through the window in the middle of last night when I wasn't looking."

"It's been a bad night," Rourke said. "A colored boy was almost lynched from a lamppost outside a Felicity Street smoke joint. And now I've just come from putting Mrs. Floriane de Lassus Layton in jail for shooting her husband point-blank in the chest."

Father Ghilotti sat in stunned silence a moment, and then his own chest collapsed in upon itself with a soft *ahhh.* He closed his eyes, praying, and hiding maybe any thoughts that might be revealed in them.

Rourke waited him out, and when the priest opened his eyes again, Rourke said, "She'll probably end up doing some jail time."

"God," Father Ghilotti said on a sharp expulsion of breath. "I can't help thinking about their poor kid. We all knew that marriage was in trouble, despite appearances, but there seemed to be so little we could do. There was a devil in Albert Payne Layton . . . I don't suppose you brought the accounts book here to save me the trouble of fetching it?"

Rourke had to laugh. "No. In fact, I'm going to have to take it with me when I leave. It's evidence."

A small smile pulled at the corners of the priest's mouth. He turned his head and looked out the parlor's bay window, at a new day untouched yet by the sun. "You probably aren't going to believe this," he said, "but on the morning of my ordination, when I lay prostrate before the altar and received the Holy Spirit, I truly believed that I would spend my life serving the poor, the elderly, the abandoned, the unloved. That I would help lead people back to the loving God and bring hope to the hopeless. Most of the time I still believe I can do those things."

He pulled his gaze away from the window and looked at the fire now, and Rourke saw that the skin around his eyes and nostrils was white. "Father Delaney had been going senile for a long time before I took over here as pastor. He'd run the parish into a couple hundred thousand dollars' worth of debt. The archbishop sent me to Our Lady of the Holy Rosary expecting a miracle, and so I tried to produce one."

"By playing the stock market with the Charities' money," Rourke said. "And with Albert Payne Layton as your broker and partner in crime."

Father Ghilotti made a sound that was halfway between a laugh and a groan. "We did pretty well at first, but then a couple of months ago we made some bad buys on margin. When those stocks slumped, we had to put up more margin, and we could only do that by selling off our other shares. It was like flushing a toilet and watching it all go down the drain . . ."

He paused, buying himself some time by removing his eyeglasses and polishing them with the linen handkerchief he took out of his pocket. The movement disturbed the cat, who jumped from his lap and fled the room.

"I'd just about decided to cut my losses and get out," he went on, hooking the glasses back over his ears, "when Father Pat found my sin out, so to speak, and so we traded a body for a body."

Rourke didn't ask what the bodies were, since he already knew: Father Pat's secret club for Father Ghilotti's little bit of embezzlement. That a couple of Fathers had been up to that kind of dealing didn't surprise him either. In the Irish Channel some of the wildest boys he knew had grown up to be priests.

"Also, I think—" Father Ghilotti had to stop and clear his throat. "I think we were seeking absolution from each other."

"In my experience, Father," Rourke said, standing up because he was done now, "when one sinner turns to another, it isn't forgiveness he wants, so much as companionship in guilt."

"Yeah," the priest said, with a sudden, grim smile. "But in the Catholic Church, guilt and forgiveness are a married couple, joined together until death do them part."

He pushed slowly to his feet. He picked up the accounts book from off the maple table and handed it to Rourke, and then the way he stood there, stiff, with his head up and his arms hanging down straight at his sides, he looked, to Rourke's amusement, like he was bravely facing a firing squad.

"What will happen now?" he said.

"Well, if you weren't pastor of Our Lady of the Holy Rosary, you'd probably pull a ten-year jolt for what you did. As it is—"

"The archbishop—"

"Will protect your ass."

"Will protect my ass."

They laughed together, and it loosened up some the sour knot of disappointment in Rourke's gut. Despite everything, he still liked the man.

"I'll be given a scold," Father Ghilotti said, "and maybe a demotion and transfer." He flashed another sudden smile, but this one only underscored the toughness in his eyes. "Or maybe not—I know where too many of His Grace's bodies are buried, too. I still intend to be archbishop myself someday."

The smile Rourke gave back at him had an edge in it as well. "I wouldn't bet against you."

Father Ghilotti led the way into the hall. Rain was spitting against the fan light above the door. From the direction of the kitchen, they could hear a plaintive meow. "He wants milk," the priest said, and then, "You haven't asked me if I killed him. Killed Father Pat."

"I asked you that early Saturday morning," Rourke said. "You told me you didn't do it."

"Saturday morning. Jesus . . ." Father Ghilotti pinched his nose and rubbed his forehead. "What day is it today? Tuesday? It's hard to believe it's only been three days." He dropped his hand, uncovering his face, and met Rourke's eyes. "What I told you then was the truth. That hasn't changed."

Rourke believed him, as much as he believed anybody.

At the front door Father Ghilotti stopped and turned around, and said to Rourke, "It wasn't about greed, you know. I did it for Holy Rosary. Although I will admit to the sin of ambition."

"And you got high off of playing the game."

"You know the feeling."

"Yeah, but the difference between you and me is I don't risk what isn't mine."

It had been a low blow, and Rourke saw that it had hurt. The priest's mouth opened on a denial or an explanation, but then he shut it and turned back to the door.

"Yesterday morning," Rourke said, "you tried to cover your ass by returning what you'd taken from the Charities' accounts. Where did that money come from?"

Father Ghilotti's back jerked as if he'd been punched, but he said, "You know where. From my father, of course. It seems I am his son after all." He reached for the doorknob, but he still didn't open it. "Your brother told me once, Detective, that you like to think of yourself as so cynical and tough, but what you really are is the most idealistic man he's ever known."

Rourke shook his head, not wanting to believe it, because in a bit of irony that wasn't entirely lost on him, he thought it made him seem weak. "Paulie doesn't know me. He left home to enter the seminary when I was thirteen, and we've maybe seen each other only two or three times a year since then."

"That's a pity," Father Ghilotti said, "because y'all are more alike than you realize. Deep in your hearts you both wish that God still made burning bushes."

Rourke went home and woke up Remy and they made soft, early morning love. Then he slept around the clock and when the telephone rang again it was just past seven on Wednesday morning and her side of the bed was empty.

He fumbled the telephone to his face and croaked, "Yeah?" His head this time feeling fuzzy because he'd gotten too much sleep.

The phone crackled in his ear. "O'Brien here, Loo. I'm calling from the Carrollton–City Park box. He's finally led us to the woman. Only there's been some trouble."

Rourke shucked into his clothes, unshaven and unwashed, and tore out of the *garçonnière* at a half run, heading for the Rampart Street garage. He got as far as the corner before he remembered with a bite of melancholy what had happened to the 'Cat.

He went back home through the carriageway and got his old Indian Chief motorcycle from where he kept it in a shed at the back end of the courtyard. Ten minutes later, he was driving the Indian up onto the lawn of a double shotgun on Carrollton Avenue.

* * *

Two uniform cops stood with their hands on their hips, jawing with each other beneath a lone, straggly palm that grew in the middle of the scraggly yard. One was the man who'd been put on the surveillance of Rourke's brother, and the other was Jack Murphy, whom Rourke had first met four nights ago, standing next to the crucified body of a priest.

Paulie, dressed in his black cassock, sat on the running board of a shiny new Lincoln with his head in his hands.

It was the woman, though, that Rourke went to first. She sat on the stoop—a woman in a rose-printed housedress, and with wheat-colored hair and a heart-shaped face. Her left eye was swollen into a purple knot and a cut on her mouth trickled blood. Two little girls stood on either side of her, at her shoulders. One was a toddler and the other was around Katie's age.

Rourke took a deep breath of sour air. "Who hit you?" he said.

The woman's gaze flashed to the men under the palm tree. "He didn't mean to," she said.

For some reason that made no sense now that he thought about it, Rourke had assumed that Jack Murphy was here at this house on this morning as part of the job. Now he realized, with a sudden hard twist in his gut, that the woman and the kids on the stoop were his.

"Do you want to press charges of assault?" Rourke said to the woman, but the question came out harsh because of the anger he was holding back.

The woman looked up at him, weary, defeated, having been through this too many times before. "He's a cop. Just like y'all."

"Press charges and I promise I'll see it through."

She looked back at her man where he stood under the palm tree. He and the other cop were laughing about something now. He was rocking back and forth on the balls of his feet and the laughter shone on his face, and the woman's face softened as she watched him.

"I don't want him going to jail," she said. "I love him."

Rourke turned away, but then he made the mistake of looking

back. The little girl who was about Katie's age was watching him leave with drowning eyes. Eyes that said, *Make it stop. Please, you got to make it stop.*

Rourke didn't go near Jack Murphy under the palm tree because he was afraid for the moment of what he might do to the guy.

He went to his brother instead, not feeling particularly charitable toward him either. Paulie heard him coming and dropped his hands from his face, looking up.

"You've been having me followed like I'm some sort of criminal," he said.

"Is this your car?" Rourke said.

"It's Father Frank's. I borrowed it."

"Give me the key and get in," Rourke said.

"But—"

"Get in the goddamn car."

"What is the penalty for impersonating a priest?" Paulie said.

For a moment Rourke thought with a jolt that he was talking about Father Pat, and then he understood that his brother was only talking about himself.

"Eternal damnation probably."

Paulie had been looking at the ground between his feet, but now his head jerked up and the eyes he turned to Rourke were bloodshot and wide. "You aren't happy, are you, Day, without an excuse to be mean?"

"Jesus."

They were sitting on the bottom row of the small grandstand that overlooked the baseball diamond in City Park, where they'd played some good pickup games with the other neighborhood teams when they were kids. The outfield grass looked smooth as green velvet beneath the low-lying clouds, but Rourke knew that if you walked out into it you'd find the gopher holes and dandelion weeds.

"When I was in the seminary," Paulie said, "we had this priest who always answered our questions on Catholic morality with one of his own. He would say, 'What would Jesus do?' You saw her, Day. You saw what he's always doing to her. What do you think Jesus would do?"

"Lord, brother. That's one question I surely don't go around asking myself."

"Maybe you should."

"Hey." Rourke pushed to his feet and walked off a couple of steps before he put his fist through something, then he swung back around. "I'm not the one here banging some other guy's wife."

"I told you, I'm not . . . doing that with her."

Rourke flung his arms out from his sides. "Sweet Jesus. What do you want from me?"

"How about some simple, brotherly advice?"

Rourke strode away again, came back. "Fine. My first piece of advice is to walk away from her now and stay away. She's married, she's Catholic, and you're a priest. My second piece of advice would be to go find a nice, clean bordello and visit the place once a month, except that you're too priggish and righteous and you're probably still a fuckin' virgin and, oh, did I mention that you're a priest?"

"God help me," Paulie said. "I'm in love with her."

There probably wasn't a man in the world who didn't know how much it goddamn broke your heart when the woman you wanted above all others belonged to somebody else, and Rourke thought of the look on the woman's face and her saying, *I love him,* only she'd been talking about her husband, about Jack Murphy, and not Paulie, and Rourke ached now for his brother. There was going to be no happily-ever-after ending to this scenario.

"Also, I think . . ." he began, and then decided maybe Paulie had been slapped in the face with enough truths on this morning.

Paulie stared at him out of bleak eyes. "What?"

"I think that some things are worth the sacrifices you've got to make to have them. And that's all the soul-searching you're going to be getting out of me today."

Paulie's throat worked, trying to swallow, and Rourke thought that what kept getting stuck there was that same knot of hopelessness and desperation that he'd seen in the little girl's eyes. *You got to make it stop.* It doesn't ever go away, that feeling, not even after *it* has stopped and you've grown up and your daddy's dead.

"He shouldn't be allowed to beat the snot out of her like that," Paulie said.

"No, he shouldn't."

"But . . ."

"What?"

"You were about to give me a 'but,'" Paulie said.

"Okay. Jack Murphy is a cop, and cops don't arrest other cops if they can help it, unless it's for capital murder and even then the guy's got to practically be caught with the smoking gun in his hand. And the DA's office tends to shy away from prosecuting wife beaters unless or until the woman ends up dead, mostly because the woman usually backs out before it gets to trial. The lawyers, the judge, the jury—they're all men, and hell, I don't know . . . maybe most of them figure that if he popped her one, she probably deserved it. You and I know that isn't right, the whole fucking world knows it isn't right, but that's how it is."

"Fuck how it is," Paulie said, but the vulgarity had sounded strained, as if he was trying it on for size and it wasn't fitting.

He looked away from Rourke, out over the baseball diamond. His lips were taut and gray, and he kept swallowing as if he had a fishbone in his throat. He was fighting his way back from the edge, Rourke thought, and so he left him alone.

"Field of dreams," Paulie finally said. "It always broke my heart that I was never any good at that game."

Rourke kept his mouth shut on all the things he could have said to that, like: *You never even tried to play the game, big brother. You never really swung the bat like you were going for the fences.*

"I heard," Paulie said, "that there was another terrible tragedy last night. That Mrs. Layton shot her husband dead."

Now that, on the other hand, was worthy of a comment or two. "Yeah, and now it's come to light," Rourke said, putting some cop into his voice, "that you weren't the only priest at Holy Rosary making devil's bargains with Father Pat."

"I don't know what you're talking about," Paulie said. "I told you there was never any bargain. I begged him for a second chance and he gave it to me."

"You're lying through your teeth again," Rourke said mildly. "You remember the Sunday the *Times-Picayune* reporter came to do a story on Holy Rosary's famous and popular priest? He photographed Father Pat celebrating a Mass, and because it was such a big deal, y'all didn't use the regular altar boys. No, a special Mass like that, it wouldn't at all have been unusual for one priest to serve another. You served Father Pat at his Mass the day the reporter came, didn't you, Paulie? I know because you were in the photograph. So tell me what happened at the end of it."

Paulie's face had gone gray all over and there was a tick in his cheek. "Nothing happened," he said.

"Father Pat was sweating blood that day, wasn't he? From his head and his hands."

The breath exploded out of his brother as if he'd been punched. "God. How do you find out these things?"

"It was just simple detective work, not hoodoo. The photographer caught it, but he didn't know what he had; he probably thought the film was defective. I put it together when I learned that Father Pat had sweated blood at least once before."

Paulie leaned over and braced his elbows on his thighs so that he could rub his face with his hands, then he gripped his head as if he were literally trying to pull himself back together.

"It must have happened right at the end," he said, "because no one noticed it until we were back in the vestry." He straightened again and tried to laugh, but it broke coming out. "I mean, you tell yourself you believe in God's miracles, but when you're actually face-to-face with one . . . His palms were *bleeding,* Day. Just like Christ's wounds."

"If it had been just like Christ's wounds, he'd have been bleeding at the wrists."

"What?"

"Never mind. Go on."

"There isn't much more to it. He tried to convince me it wasn't really happening, but I could see it with my own eyes. So then he begged me not to tell anyone. I told you that I got down on my knees before him, but it was the other way around. Only I thought I *had* to tell, you know? For the Church's sake. And that was when he said he knew that I'd been seeing Colleen again while her husband was on the night trick, and that he'd tell on me if I told on him. God, you should've heard us. We sounded like a couple of kids, bargaining away our souls to try to get out of a spanking. Only what was at stake seemed like everything at the time, and I suppose you think that I got the better end of it."

Rourke didn't suppose any such thing, but then when it came to secrets, he had a few up on his brother.

"But you would be wrong," Paulie went on. "Because the archbishop would've cared plenty to know that Father Pat had finished up a Mass with bleeding hands, and as his obedient priest I should have told him. I don't know what Father Pat would have done, though, if I hadn't agreed to just pretend like it had never happened. If you could have seen him, Day . . . He was pure terrified of anyone who mattered in the Church knowing about this bleeding thing . . . this stigmata, I guess you could call it that, I don't know. I don't think I want to know . . ."

Rourke could well imagine the horror Father Pat must have felt when he looked down at his hands at the end of the Mass and saw them sweating blood. A politically sensitive and expedient archbishop like Peter Hannity would have reacted with both greed and wariness at the discovery that he had a possible moneymaking miracle going on in his archdiocese. He would've insisted that Father

Pat be looked at by a whole bevy of doctors, to expose any fakery going on, and the medical examination would have ended up exposing Patrice LaPage instead.

"It all doesn't matter anymore, anyway," Paulie said. "Now that Father Pat's dead."

"No. It doesn't matter anymore."

Yet the images in the photograph stayed in Rourke's mind. Father Pat with his hand raised in a blessing, just starting to bleed. Paulie standing behind him and off to the side, swinging a censer. And another man, wearing a server's alb, too, but almost cut out of the photographer's frame so that all you can see of him is his arm and a bit of his shoulder.

"Who served Father Pat along with you at the Mass that day?"

Paulie, who'd been holding his head in his hands again, looked up. "What?"

"There's usually at least two altar boys."

Paulie shrugged and spread out his hands. "How should I remember? It wasn't Father Frank, I know. So it must've been some layman, I suppose. Whoever it was, he probably didn't see the bleeding, because he would've said something surely. And only Father Pat and I were in the vestry when it got bad."

They fell into a silence then while neither brother looked at the other, and they might each have been alone there, sitting in the bleachers and looking at an empty baseball field, and then Rourke said, "You got to leave her alone, Paulie. Otherwise no good is going to come of it."

"I know," Paulie said.

Rourke listened while his brother talked about the temptation of Christ and the power of prayer, and about how he was going to give up his love for Colleen Murphy and dedicate his life to being a good priest, and Rourke didn't believe a word of it.

He looked toward the stand of cypress in right field, where Paulie had hit the one and only home run of his life that had won it for them in the bottom of the ninth. Growing up, they had been taught the hard way that when things got tough you looked to yourself to get yourself out of trouble. And so they had grown into men, and he had been drawn into their father's violent and aberrant world, while Paulie had fled from it.

And so, too, they had been avoiding each other all these years, each afraid of what he would see in the other. They were too alike in their deepest places, after all—the sons of Mike Rourke. They both hid from the world their need for help, and the need they had to refuse any help that was offered to them.

Chapter Twenty-Seven

Fiorello Prankowski's cheek now looked like it had a baseball tucked away inside it. He was sipping a milk shake through a straw and looking at Rourke's fried oyster sandwich with greedy eyes.

"If you did something about that tooth," Rourke said, "you could eat chewable things."

They were sitting in a booth with cracked red-leather seats, in the greasy spoon across from the Bright Lights warehouse where Mary Lou Trescher had last been seen alive. The studio was out filming in the swamp somewhere today, so they'd walked all over the surrounding waterfront, searching for somebody who had seen something. Nobody had.

"I did do something about my tooth," Fio said. Or at least that was what Rourke thought he'd said. He was also talking like he had a baseball tucked in his cheek. "I went to this sadist who calls himself a dentist. The guy said he was gonna pull it, so I said I'd catch him later."

Rourke made chicken noises and flapped his arms.

"Fuck you and your mama, too," Fio said.

Fio took his bankroll out of his pocket, peeled off five ten-spots and pushed them across the table's gold-speckled oilcloth toward Rourke.

"What's this?" Rourke said.

"The fifty bucks I owe you. We bet on Father Ghilotti being the killer. You said he wasn't, and it turns out he wasn't."

"We don't know that yet for sure."

Outside an organ grinder was churning out Italian opera, and inside there was a sizzle from the steak the cook had just tossed on the grill. The red leather sighed as Fio shifted his weight. He sucked on his tooth, making a slurping sound, then shifted some more. "You gonna hit me if I say something?"

"Depends."

"You can't start leaving case files open because you're afraid you're going to make another mistake like what got made with Titus Dupre."

"I know. I'm not. This one just doesn't feel finished to me, is all."

"Okay, let's talk about why Albert Payne Layton probably did it." Fio held up a finger the size of a sausage. "One: he'd been embezzling money from the Catholic Charities, and Father Pat knew that, and so Father Pat had to be shut up."

"Why crucify him for it, though? A bullet to the head would've been a lot more efficient and a lot less risky. I can see Layton playing with his victim, wanting to make him suffer. But I can't see the man sticking his neck out to do it."

"Maybe," Fio conceded. "So let's go with number two then. You said you thought Floriane Layton might've known the truth about Father Pat, about he being a she. So how would she've known that unless they'd ended up in the sack together at least once? Maybe Layton walked in on his old lady when they were doing the dirty deed."

Rourke shook his head. "The killer crucified Father Pat with his cassock on."

Fio snatched his napkin out from the neck of his shirt and threw it on the table. "Fuck me. I knew you'd bring up that stuff about him not being naked."

"Sorry," Rourke said, meaning it.

Fio lit a Castle Morro and dropped the burnt match into his empty milk shake glass. He sulked during the rest of the meal and when they went back outside, the weather was weeping again, too.

They stood on the sidewalk in the rain, trying to decide what they should be doing next. The Fantastics killings case had gone flat, but hanging on to the edge of their every thought and word, like the distant wail of a siren, was the fear that if they didn't catch him soon another girl would get snatched up off the street, raped, and strangled, and then dumped somewhere easy for them to find.

"Well, hell," Fio said, echoing Rourke's morbid thoughts. He shook his head like a dog, tossing raindrops off the brim of his battered, bullet-riddled hat.

"You ever going to get a new hat?" Rourke said.

"What's wrong with this one?"

"Well, for one thing, it leaks now that it's been shot. What good's a hat that lets your head get wet?"

"I ain't gonna melt." Fio grinned, and then his eyes opened so wide their whites showed. "Goddammit. It's like somebody's driving a nail in there, you know?"

"So go to the fucking dentist."

"I already got a perfectly good mama up in Des Moines. I don't need another one for a partner, telling me all the time what I should or shouldn't be doing."

"Fine. Then come along with me while I have a heart-to-heart with someone. You can cover my back."

Fio gave his partner a long, careful look. "Aw, jeez, Day, you're breaking my balls here. What're you gonna do, and who are you gonna do it to?"

Rourke didn't tell him. He started across the street toward the patrol car they were borrowing for the day, and he was thinking that he was going to have to get over the 'Cat's loss soon, so he could go shopping for a new set of wheels.

Fio was following on his heels, off on one of his riffs. "You're gonna get us fired. Only you won't be fired 'cause you got angels in high places and you're banging a movie star. So they'll fire me instead, and my wife'll have me sleeping on the couch for what's left of my miserable life."

Rourke stopped so suddenly that Fio almost walked up his back. "You don't have to come if you don't want to," Rourke said.

Fio gave him a look that would have curdled cream and held out his pie plate of a hand. "I'm driving, so shut up and gimme the keys."

Rourke gave him the keys and they got in the car. Fio turned over the engine and put it in gear, but he didn't pull out.

"This guy we're going to have the heart-to-heart with," he said. "Are you gonna kill him?"

Rourke smiled. "Odds are I won't."

The speakeasy hadn't changed any since they'd been here the afternoon following Father Pat's murder. Damp, rotting sawdust on the floor and the stink of cheap booze and bad food. The same man with the flattened face was there tending the bar, and he still wouldn't meet their eyes, but instead occupied himself with polishing a glass on the hem of his flannel shirt.

Even Rourke's snitch, Dirty Eddie the house creep, was at the same table against the wall. He spotted Rourke and scurried off into the back toilet, and Rourke wondered why Dirty Eddie always ran away from him, because when he wanted to catch the kid he always could.

The one difference between this time and last was that the exotic dancers were dancing, and they were pretty deep into their routine, down to the pasties on their nipples and a string. The one wasn't bad, but the other had thighs and a bottom that looked like clabber.

Rourke saw the man he had come for, sitting at the far end of the bar, but turned around so that he could watch the dancers. He was smoking a cigarette and drinking a boilermaker that was sure to have been on the house.

Before coming inside Rourke had taken his .38 Policeman's Special out of its shoulder holster and put it in his coat pocket, and now he put his right hand in the pocket, wrapping it around the gun's grip.

Jack Murphy saw them coming and he grinned, breathing smoke out through his teeth. "Evenin', Dee-tectives. What brings y'all down here slummin'?"

Rourke took the gun out of his pocket and pressed the barrel into Murphy's side. "Let's go see the dogs."

The dog fighting pit was through a back door and into an attached building made out of plywood and tin.

Rourke took his gun out of Jack Murphy's side as soon as they were through the door. The door had a heavy iron bar that could be laid down across it, and Fio used it. Then he leaned his back up against it, his hands hanging loose and ready at his sides.

Without the gun barrel poking him in the ribs, Jack Murphy's mouth had recovered its perpetual smirk. "I got nothin' I want to say to y'all," he said.

"Good," Rourke said. " 'Cause I've been listening to one confession after another for the last two days now and I'm sick and tired of it."

The building smelled of dog shit, wet fur, and old blood. One end of it was taken up with the pit and crude bleachers. At the other end were the dog pens, fashioned out of rusting cyclone fencing. The dogs had started barking as soon as the door had opened and the racket they made was nerve jangling. They were snarling and snapping at air and throwing themselves at the walls of their cages. When they fought in the pit, they tried to rip each other's throats out.

Rourke left Murphy standing by Fio and the door and walked

down a short aisle between the bleachers for a closer look at the pit. It was rectangular in shape, with a dirt floor and enclosed by wooden slats. The slats were stained and splattered with blood. The cement floor between the bleachers was littered with empty Red Man pouches and decaying chicken bones.

"Hey, Rourke," Murphy called out to him, stirring the dogs to an even greater frenzy. "You tell your cocksucking brother to stay away from my Colleen."

Rourke went back to him, getting in close, close enough that he could have kissed the other man on the cheek if they had been lovers, and he smiled.

"What we got here, partner," he said, "is the guy who was fool enough to put Tony the Rat up to soliciting a beating for the priest who was getting a little too friendly with his wife."

"Man," Fio said, shaking his head and clicking his tongue. "He must've just about shit a brick then, when a priest turns up crucified in that old abandoned macaroni factory."

"I had nothing to do with that," Murphy said.

"Yeah, well, you knew that," Rourke said, "and Tony the Rat knew that, but that didn't stop good ol' Tony from trying to blackmail you over it. He wanted coke and so you gave it to him, laced with cyanide, and poor ol' Tony took a ride to the moon."

"So who gives a fuck? The guy was swamp scum."

Rourke took out his gun, and Murphy said, "Hey," and took a step back, but then he relaxed again when he saw Rourke break open the loading gate and empty the cartridges into his hand. He put five of the cartridges into his pocket, keeping back the sixth one.

"Are you feeling like a lucky man today, Jack?" he said.

Murphy took another step back and then he looked over at Fio by the door. "What's he doing?"

"He's kinda unpredictable," Fio said, his face deadpan.

Rourke loaded the single bullet, closed the gate, and spun the cylinder, once, twice, three times. He looked up at Murphy and smiled, and then he slammed the man into the wall so hard he knocked the breath out of them both and rattled the tin.

Rourke had his forearm braced up against the other man's throat, and when his lips parted, to breathe or to shout, Rourke rammed two of the .38's four inches of barrel into Jack Murphy's open mouth.

For some reason, the dogs had suddenly gone silent. In the dim light, the bluing of the gun shone with a thin layer of oil. The grip was hard and round and cool against the palm of Rourke's hand, and the hammer made a loud snap under his thumb as he cocked it.

"Five empty chambers and one live round. How do you like those odds, Jack?"

Rourke waited, though, doing nothing, letting the man's fear build until you could smell it, a gray smell. Until you could hear the breath ripping through the man's nostrils, and sweat ran down his cheeks and dripped onto Rourke's hand.

"Want to see how they'll play?" Rourke said, and Murphy's eyes bulged and crossed, watching as Rourke's finger tensed and squeezed the trigger.

The *snick* of the hammer falling on the empty chamber might as well have been as loud as a thunderclap. Murphy's eyes flinched shut and he made a gagging sound in the back of his throat.

"Four empty chambers left and one live round. Are you going to leave my brother alone, Jack?"

Murphy tried to talk, but Rourke pushed the gun barrel deeper into his throat and cocked the hammer again . . . waited a beat and pulled the trigger.

And the hammer fell on another empty chamber.

"Three empties left now and a live one. Are you going to stay away from him, Jack?"

Murphy sobbed as his mouth stretched wider around the barrel of the gun, trying to stretch away from it. He made a gargling noise deep in his throat, and snot blew out his nose.

"What do you think, Fio? Was that a yes?"

"Sounded like a yes to me, partner."

Rourke cocked the hammer slowly, so that Murphy could watch the cylinder rotate, could see maybe his death coming, only the man's eyes had rolled back in his head and something like a scream was whining in his nose.

Rourke squeezed the trigger, the hammer *snicked* on an empty chamber, and then all was quiet again except for the tinkle of urine running down Murphy's legs and hitting the cement floor.

Jack Murphy was a broken man, but because he was also the kind of man who would bring his broken pieces home with him and take them out on his wife, Rourke knew that he would have to break him even more.

He pulled the gun out of Murphy's mouth and lowered it to his side, taking a step back. Murphy sagged against the wall, breathing hard, retching, and rubbing the snot and tears and sweat off his face with the back of his wrist.

"Jack," Rourke said.

Murphy looked up at him out of eyes that were wet and bloodshot and pleading. Rourke swung the gun back up again, hard, with his feet set solidly, throwing his weight into the movement, swinging and smashing the .38's two pounds' worth of metal into the man's face. Murphy's head snapped back, and Rourke felt his front teeth and the bone in his nose go like sticks.

Murphy's legs fell out from underneath him and he slid onto his knees on the cement floor. The dogs had started barking again and the din they made hit against the tin walls and was deafening. Murphy flinched even though Rourke hadn't moved again, covering his smashed and bleeding face with his arms. "Stop, please . . ."

"Now that you know what it feels like to get hit, you're never going to hit your wife again, are you, Jack?"

He shook his head, splattering blood and spittle, and he was crying now like a child.

"No, you got to say it. I want to hear you say it."

He made him say it twice before they left him.

* * *

They left the speakeasy and walked down the crib-lined alley toward Chartres, where they'd parked the car. The whores were in their front windows and on their stoops, showing off their wares, but neither man was looking.

"Tomorrow," Rourke said, breaking the silence, "I'm sending the wagon down here for those dogs."

"Yeah," Fio said, after another moment of silence passed. "I think maybe I'll go back to that dentist now, have him take out this tooth."

"It won't hurt," Rourke said. He looked down and saw to his surprise that he still had the gun in his hand, and that both the gun and his hand were wet with Murphy's blood. "He'll give you some kind of gas before he pulls it."

A cat leaped off a windowsill onto a trash can, and the noise sent a rat scurrying along the gutter.

"Partner?" Fio said.

"Yeah?"

"Please tell me that was a blank cartridge you put in your gun."

Rourke's smile felt like ice cracking across his face. He raised the gun, pointed it at the rat, cocked it, and pulled the trigger.

The explosion of the gunshot slammed down the alley, and the rat dropped dead in its tracks.

Fio kept casting sideways glances at his partner as he drove down Chartres toward Canal Street, paying less and less attention to the traffic in front of him until he almost sent the patrol car up onto the back of a beer wagon. He swerved, almost wiping out an old lady with a cane who was crossing the street, then he leaned on the horn and told the driver of the beer wagon to watch where the fuck he was going.

"That was all your fault," Fio said to his partner, once the ruckus was over. "Because you are a crazy man. I have a crazy man in the car with me and that's making me crazy and that's why that accident we almost had was all your fault."

Rourke looked out the rain-smeared window. His blood still felt like it was popping and boiling, but the violence had been some kind of cathartic, like a drug, and he thought that was probably not a good thing, but he also didn't want to think too much about that right now.

"I need to have Jack Murphy believe I'm crazy," he said. "Otherwise he was going to do something to Paulie and I'd've had to kill him for it."

"Christ, you nearly *did* kill him . . . I still don't get why you didn't use a blank cartridge."

"Because I didn't think of it."

They laughed and then after another moment, Rourke said, "And, besides, it wouldn't have been nearly as much fun without the real thing."

"I am stuck in a car," Fio said, "with a crazy man and a tooth that's gonna be the death of me."

Rourke checked his watch. "If you're really going to get that thing taken care of today, you'd better do it now because it's almost closing time."

Fio grunted. "I don't know whether I dare leave you to your own devices, though. The City that Care Forgot hasn't had a crime spree for at least thirty minutes now, and I'd like to keep it that way."

"Actually, I was thinking of paying a visit to the dead," Rourke said, serious now. "Miss Della Layton was going to be waking her daddy today."

Rourke had driven his motorcycle to work that morning, and so Fio dropped him off where he'd parked it in the alley in back of the Criminal Courts Building.

The wake was still in the preparation stages when he arrived at the Laytons' handsome Greek Revival raised villa on Prytania Street.

A wreath of white magnolias and a black satin ribbon hung on the front door, and inside all the lintels and mirrors were draped with black crepe. Vigil lights flickered in the front parlor, where the body lay in view in an open black-lacquered casket.

Albert Payne Layton's older sister had met Rourke at the door, but it was the girl Della who led him into a room in back of the house where they could talk alone. The music room, she had called it, and Rourke saw that a harp did sit next to the marble fireplace, and a piano with duet seats stood in a bay full of windows draped in thick gold velvet.

It was a pretty room, and he wondered if Flo and Bertie Layton had ever once come here of an evening to play and sing duets on the piano. Somehow he didn't think so.

Miss Della Layton was not the baby vamp today. No hibiscus red lipstick or greased eyelids, no rouged knees. She invited him to have a seat, but instead he took both her hands in his and studied her face. It was drawn and pale with shock and grief, but he saw strength there, too. The kind of strength a girl acquires fast when she suddenly finds herself handling alone the arrangements and etiquette for her daddy's wake because her mama is in the Parish Prison for having killed him.

"You're going to survive this, Miss Della," Rourke said.

"Thank you." Her smile was fleeting, but he could see that she'd understood the compliment and had felt pride in it.

"I was wondering if you would help me by answering a few questions. Not about what happened with your daddy, but about the Fantastics. You and Mary Lou and Mercedes and Nina, and the other girls."

Pain darkened her eyes some more, but she nodded solemnly. As if it weren't enough that her family had just been destroyed, in the past year she'd also lost three of her good friends.

Mary Lou Trescher, she told him, was the one most involved with the fan club. She'd always been writing letters to Remy Lelourie and sending off to the studio for their giveaways. She'd devoured the fan magazines for photographs so that she could have her hair bobbed just like Remy's. She'd read all the articles to find out things like what Remy Lelourie's favorite lipstick color was, so that she'd know the exact shade to get when they next went shopping at D. H. Holmes. For the rest of them the daydream was just for fun, but for her it had been real. She'd talked all the time about going to Hollywood when she graduated from high school.

Nina Duboche had apparently thought of herself as a "hot number." Once she'd even had a lingerie party at her house, and she was always pushing it with the nuns over the length of her skirts and the rouge on her cheeks. Right before she'd been killed, she'd started acting like she had a big secret, and the other girls had all decided that she'd finally done "it" with a boy, instead of just talking about doing it.

"Boys were always making a play for Nina," Della said a bit wistfully. "But she liked stringing them, you know?"

Mercedes Bloom was something of an odd girl. "She was a jane," Della said. "But with her it was more than just not being especially pretty. She dressed so old-fashioned all the time. She even wore her hair long and in finger waves. Everybody was always teasin' her about them."

Mercedes hadn't been all sweet and innocent and old-fashioned underneath like she had seemed, though. The time they'd all tried cigarettes, she'd smoked like she'd done it before, and Della had once caught a glimpse of a whiskey flask in the other girl's handbag.

"At the lingerie party," Della said, blushing to be talking about such a thing to a policeman, but also, Rourke thought, feeling maybe a little proud of herself for being able to do so, "we got to talking about s-e-x and what it feels like when you do it with a boy, and Mercedes said the French called it *le petit mort,* the little death. She said sometimes you could have a *petit mort* whether you wanted to or not . . . And the way she said it, it was like she really *knew.*"

And Rourke, a little surprised, thought, *hunh.*

He took the photograph that had come from Mary Lou's room out of his coat pocket and showed it to her. "Do you remember when this picture was taken?"

"Oh, I have that one, too," Della said. "We all do. It was Mercy Bloom's birthday that day and her folks had given her a Kodak for a present. Instead of having a party, she took us all to the movies and our picture got taken with her new camera."

"Do you remember who took it?"

Della wrinkled her nose, thinking. "No . . . Mercedes was about to since it was her camera, but then this man came walking down the street and he offered to do it so that she could be in the picture, too."

"Do you remember anything at all about the man? Had you ever seen him before?"

"No, I don't think so." She shrugged. "He was about my . . . daddy's age, I think. And he might've had brown hair. He seemed nice."

He couldn't get much more out of her about what the Good Samaritan photographer had looked like, but she promised to come down to the squad room tomorrow and take a look through the Rogues' Gallery cards.

Rourke smiled at her as he put the photograph back in his pocket. "You've been a really big help, Miss Della. And, listen . . . if there's anything I can do . . ."

She looked up at him out of eyes that had lost the kind of innocence a girl should still have at sixteen. "She's going to go to prison, isn't she?"

"I hope not, but yes. Probably."

"He was going to hit her. That's why she shot him."

"When the attorneys talk to you about what happened, you can tell them that," Rourke said, but he was thinking now that she'd seen more that night than she was letting on—like maybe how the gun had happened to come into Floriane Layton's hand.

She had averted her gaze from him, and he could see her struggling with the need to pass along a terrible secret in the hope that he might then take it away with him. "He told me . . ." She swallowed hard, choking back the tears that were now crowding her eyes. "A while back, Daddy told me that she'd once done this really sick, disgusting thing. He said that she had . . . that she'd done it with another woman."

The tears were falling freely now, and she looked back around to Rourke, wanting the kind of answers you hardly ever got. "She's doing it again now, isn't she? Please . . . I don't understand how could she *do* something like that."

This time what Rourke took out of his breast pocket was a small, folded piece of paper. "Here. I brought this with me on the chance that you might want it."

"What is it?" she said, taking the paper from his hand.

"It's the name and address of her lover. If you go see her, you can talk with her about your mama. And maybe she can help you to understand."

Rourke stood on the Laytons' front gallery, going over what the girl had said about the Fantastics, thinking about Nina and her secret, daring love affair with a colored boy, and Mary Lou dreaming of becoming the next Remy Lelourie. Both of them ending up raped and strangled and their bodies dumped by the river. And Mercedes Bloom, the "jane" with her old-fashioned finger waves, missing now for over six months and probably raped and strangled, too, her body thrown away somewhere to be found a year from now, or ten.

Something, though, wasn't quite adding up right. And there was something, too, that Della had said when they'd been talking about the photograph . . .

A patrol car was pulling up in front of the house. Rourke waited on the gallery while Fio got out, and as his partner started up the walk, Rourke saw that his cheek was still all swollen up. He was about to make some wisecrack about it, but by then Fio had gotten close enough for him to get a better look at his face.

"Ah, Jesus. No . . ." Rourke said.

Fio stopped at the bottom of the gallery steps and looked up at him with bleak eyes. "Another girl's gone missing."

CHAPTER TWENTY-EIGHT

"She was supposed to be meeting my sister under the clock at D. H. Holmes at one."

Sean Daly stood before the mullioned bay window, staring unseeing at the green lawn bordered by a hedge of hydrangea and azalea bushes. In one hand, he had a whiskey that was not his first, and the hand was shaking.

"I drove her down there myself," he said in a voice that was thick as wet sand, and in an accent that was blue-collar, Irish Channel. "But I had a meeting at the union hall and I was running late, and I thought, Hell, it's the middle of the day on a sidewalk crowded with people and Judith will be coming any minute now, and I . . . ah, Jesus."

He looked down at the booze in his glass as if he wanted to drown in it, a big man with broad shoulders and a thick neck from a youth spent loading and unloading freight on the docks.

He turned from the window and looked at the two cops standing in his front parlor, and on his face was the dawning horror that he'd made a mistake whose consequences were going to be beyond bearing. "I should have waited there with her," he said. "I should have waited."

"How long afterward was it before your sister showed up?" Fio asked.

The room fell into a thick silence while Daly couldn't answer, then he cleared his throat and said, "About a half an hour. The damn fool woman had a coffee klatch at her club that ended up running late."

An oil painting of the missing girl hung above the limestone mantel. Gillian, her name was—his partner had told Rourke on the short drive to the imitation Tudor house on St. Charles Avenue. Her mother, Fio said, had died during the flu epidemic when she was seven and her father had never remarried, and so she was an only child.

Her father, Sean Daly, was the head of the local stevedores' union, and a certain portion of the money in any union's war chest was always automatically earmarked for the police department's pad. So he had, as Fio had said, "a lotta juice."

In the snapshot of the Fantastics that Rourke had been carrying around in his pocket for the last three days, Gillian Daly was the fourth in line and the tallest of the nine girls. He had already thought she was the prettiest, even though in the black and white photograph you couldn't tell that her hair was the red-gold of a sunset and her eyes were an unusual jade green.

"What else do y'all need to know?" Daly was saying. "She was wearing her school uniform—the St. Francis of Assisi Academy for Girls. They only had a half day today, because of some senior pageant they were supposed to be getting ready for. That's why she was going shopping."

A tall colored woman with beautiful bones and dark, liquid eyes came into the room bearing a massive silver tray loaded with a steaming *cafetière,* milk, and three sets of cups and saucers. "I told that chile," she said, as she set the tray down on a chrome and glass coffee table. "I told her be sure to take your umbrella, Miss Gilly, 'cause it's been threatenin' rain off and on out there all mornin'."

Sean Daly looked at the woman as if it couldn't be possible that just a few hours before their world had been so normal, so sane, and then he said, "Thank you for thinking to make us some coffee, Mrs. Jousett," and she straightened from arranging the cups and saucers and looked at him with such tenderness in those liquid eyes that Rourke thought, *hunh.*

They all watched in silence while Mrs. Jousett poured the café au lait and left the room. Then Daly sat down on the modern white-leather sofa and looked at the coffee as if he ought to be doing something with it, but he didn't know what. "What can I do?" he said "There's gotta be something I can do."

Rourke had gone back to the painting, thinking out loud now, "She's standing there under the clock," he said, and Daly looked up, surprised, because it was the first time Rourke had spoken since their introduction. "And her aunt is late, and she knows what's been going on with the other Fantastics, so she gets scared, or maybe she just gets smart, and decides she wants to go home . . ." He turned and crossed the room, coming to Daly where he sat on his expensive art deco sofa. "What you can do is make a list of everybody she trusts well enough to go off with in those circumstances."

The two men stared at each other, assessing and challenging. The labor leader had penetrating gray eyes and a tough-looking face, the kind of toughness it took to control a union of several thousand strong. Sean Daly had the power to bring the city to its knees and he'd been known to use it.

"Gilly's a tough little fighter," he said. "She would've made it hard for some stranger to come along and snatch her off a Canal Street sidewalk in broad daylight. So, yeah, I can do that list." He stood and went back to the window. "I was just thinking . . ."

"It could be a cop," Fio finished for him.

And then Rourke said, "Or a priest."

He went back again for one last look at the painting. There was something about her smile, he thought, that on any other day would have made you want to smile, too, just looking at it. "Do you mind if I take a look at her bedroom?" he said.

Daly spun around, sweeping out his hand in a welcoming gesture. "Christ, no. Do whatever you got to do . . ."

Sean Daly took Rourke up to his daughter's bedroom while Fio went back in the kitchen to talk some more with the housekeeper.

He'd been in too many bedrooms like this one lately, he thought. Gilly's was pink and yellow satin and white lace. She had a collection of teddy bears sitting on a wooden shelf that ran along three walls, but one, a polar bear, lay snuggled up against the pillows on her bed: one-eyed, mangy white fur, well loved.

"That missing eye got eaten by her collie dog when he was a pup," Daly said. He was in the doorway, one shoulder braced against the jamb, holding himself up. He wore an expensive gray flannel lounge suit, but he had his tie and coat off and had rolled his sleeves up, and Rourke could see the faded tattoo of an anchor under the black hair on his right forearm. The gold watch on his wrist gleamed in the light. "This year for her birthday her girlfriends gave her a new polar bear, but she couldn't bear to part with the old one . . . You got kids?"

"A daughter. She's seven."

"Then you've got all the real scary stuff still ahead of you."

Rourke grunted a half laugh. "I've had a few hairy moments already."

They started to share a smile, then both lost it at the same time as the horrible truth of what had just been casual, polite, space-filling conversation struck home.

Rourke saw where she had tucked snapshots around the mirror on her dressing table. She had the one of the Fantastics in front of the movie theater. And there was a picture of herself in her school uniform, standing on the steps of St. Francis of Assisi Academy for Girls, and several of her with her daddy. Riding the flying horses in the park, at a shrimp boil, sailing on the lake.

Among the snapshots was a postcard with a teddy bear on it. He turned it over to read the back. *Happy Birthday,* someone had written in a schoolgirl's hand, and then beneath the salutation, eight signatures, one for each of the other Fantastics.

Rourke turned, holding up the card so Daly could see it. "Can I keep this for a while?"

"Yeah, yeah. Whatever you need."

Daly pushed off the jamb and took a step into his daughter's bedroom, and Rourke saw the terror in his eyes break through like water splitting through the bottom of a paper bag. "Jesus Christ, God almighty, save me. What should I have done?" he said. "Kept her locked in here for the whole of her life?"

"The last girl he took," Rourke said. "Mary Lou Trescher . . . She stayed alive for a while after he took her."

"He'll be raping her." Daly had said the words flat out, but his eyes said he was dying inside.

"You told us she was a fighter," Rourke said.

Daly nodded, his face like stone. "Just find the son of a bitch before he kills her."

They stood on Sean Daly's lawn in the drizzle and looked back at the house that was imitation Tudor on the outside and all expensive modern art deco on the inside.

"Poor bastard," Fio said.

"Yeah," Rourke said, and thought of how Daly had looked like he'd been hit with a fist in the heart.

They had every squad car and foot patrol out looking for the girl, because they had to try. Rourke had let Daly think there was a chance they'd get her back alive, but he didn't believe it.

"I got all this shit buzzing around in my head," he said. "I gotta go somewhere quiet where I can think. Maybe go through the file, see if I can make some connections by reading papers that we haven't been able to do chasing our tails around in circles out here on the street."

Rourke looked over at his partner's swollen face; the big guy had perpetual tears in his eyes from the pain. "And you got to get that tooth out before your head explodes," he said.

"Yeah," Fio said, morosely. Then, "Shit."

Rourke had Fio drop him off at the Criminal Courts Building. He went up to the squad room, debriefed the captain, flipped through his telephone messages and made some return calls, and then picked up the case file on what the detectives had started calling the Fantastics killings, putting a label on the horror so that they could distance themselves from it.

On a whim he dug out all the paper on the crucifixion killing, too, and threw it all in a cardboard carton. He was back out on the street with the box in his arms, when he remembered that he'd left his motorcycle at the Layton house, and he had to go all the way back inside and upstairs to get a key for a squad car from the desk sergeant and arrange to have a patrolman pick up his bike, drive it to his house, and bring back the car.

Remy was waiting for him when he got home. The day's shooting on *Cutlass* had ended early because of the weather, and she told him she'd been trying to improve her mind by reading Anatole France's *Revolt of the Angels.* She was wearing one of his white shirts and a pair of denim overalls that looked like something a boy would wear fishing, only on her they looked sexy as all get-out.

He told her about Gillian Daly while she brewed a pot of coffee, and as he watched her move about his kitchen, he thought how much he loved that she was living with him now, and how he shouldn't let himself start thinking about them making it permanent.

They could hear Katie in the parlor laughing with Mrs. O'Reilly, while they listened to the amateur hour on Professor Shramm's radio show. It was a sweet moment, he thought. The sound of his daughter's laughter floating down the hall, the sight of his woman's bottom cupped by a pair of denim overalls and filling him with lust. The smell of hot coffee brewing on a rainy afternoon. It was the kind of moment you take for granted until something evil comes along and snatches it away from you.

"The guy had this look," he told Remy, talking about Sean Daly. "Like inside he's shattering into a million pieces and nothing is ever gonna put him back together again. Otis Bloom and his wife—they've got that same look. You don't survive it, losing a kid. Every breath you take afterward, you're just marking time."

She came to him where he sat at the kitchen table. She linked her hands behind his neck and pulled his head up against her so that his face was buried in the hollow beneath her breasts, and he could hear her heart beating and smell her smell. She had no words of comfort to give him, though, because they didn't exist.

When the coffee was done they took it into the dining room, along with the case files, and spread the paper on the Fantastics killings out on the walnut table that Mrs. O'Reilly had polished until it glowed like a pool of water under the sun.

"What are we looking for?" Remy asked.

"Connections. A thread. Something that's in here that shouldn't be, or something that's missing. A miracle . . ."

Remy spent a long time looking at the photograph of the Fantastics and when she looked back up at him, her face was drawn with pain. "In the movie business it's easy to start thinking that everything is all about you. But the biggest connection that I'm seeing between these girls is the fan club. Day, what if this *is* my fault?"

"Jesus, baby. If you are the connection, then it's all in this sick bastard's mind. You can't go blaming yourself for that."

Rourke saw that Nate Carroll had done up extensive lists on the friends, family members, and acquaintances that the Fantastics all had in common. He looked through them carefully, but nothing clicked so he passed them over to Remy. "Look through these names and see if anything strikes you."

She took the lists and began reading, and a few minutes later she said, "They certainly knew a lot of the same people."

"Yeah, well, they all lived in the same neighborhood, went to the same school and the same church, ate at the same restaurants, and shopped at the same stores."

"They came from different rungs on the social ladder, though," she said. "The Laytons are old money, and Mrs. Trescher works at the Piggly Wiggly. Mr. Daly is a powerful union boss, while Mr. Bloom drives a taxi."

"I guess that stuff is just not so important with kids. To hear Della Layton talk, the Fantastics shared practically everything. Lingerie, favorite lipstick colors, secret knowledge about s-e-x . . ."

"Boys don't share secret knowledge about s-e-x?"

"Nah. We don't have any knowledge. We just make it up as we go along and then brag about it to each other afterward."

He was staring at her face, at the small smile that was playing over her mouth with the bantering, at the way her hair brushed the tops of her ears that were like small translucent shells, and the way the curve of her breasts pressed against his shirt. He wanted desperately to make love to her now, and he knew a good part of that want came from a need to thumb his nose at all the bad things God could do to him.

She colored a little at the intensity of his staring and looked back down at the precinct's first incident reports that she'd been reading earlier.

"This might be something here," she said, "although I don't how important it is. The last anyone saw of Mercedes Bloom, she was leaving a beauty parlor on Canal. It had just started to rain and she was running for the streetcar, afraid that her new bob was going to get all messed up. And then here it was raining the evening Nina Duboche disappeared while walking the six blocks to her school hop. Gillian Daly disappears today and it's raining. It was sunny, though, last Saturday, when Mary Lou got taken. Drat it."

Rourke sat up straighter in his chair, reaching for the incident reports. He felt something push against his face, like a wind had come up in the room.

"Still, we've been figuring this guy is able to approach these girls because they know him. So it's raining and he comes along and offers them a ride, they get in his car, and that's it—he's got them."

He was picturing a girl walking down the street, it's raining now so she picks up the pace a little, she's got somewhere she needs to be, and then a car pulls up to the curb alongside her, and the guy calls out her name, and she slows down now, because this guy, he knows her, and she looks over at him and she sees . . .

"Sweet Jesus. Remy, what you just said about Mercedes, how she'd just gotten a new bob . . ."

He rifled through the stuff on the table until he found what he was looking for: the framed photograph of her daughter that Ethel Bloom had given him the evening of Titus Dupre's execution. Rourke wasn't sure exactly what finger waves were, but they sounded like what Mercedes Bloom had on her head in this picture.

So on the day she'd disappeared Mercedes Bloom had changed herself, the old-fashioned, odd "jane," with the dark knowledge in her eyes had bobbed away her old-fashioned finger waves. Mercedes Bloom, the first girl the killer had chosen, and the one they'd never found.

Remy had gotten up and come to look at the photograph over his shoulder. "She looks sad," she said. "Her eyes are like what you see on those marble angels they put on top of the tombs in the St. Louis Cemeteries."

The eyes, Rourke thought, of a girl who knows too young all about s-e-x and *le petit mort.*

Then he saw it, like a flash lamp exploding in his head. He saw the killer, saw all that the killer had done, saw *all* of it. And why.

"Mercy," Rourke said aloud.

He jumped to his feet and went out into the hall, to the hook where he'd hung his suit coat when he'd first come home. He started to turn around, to go back to Remy in the dining room, but she had followed him into the hall.

"When I say 'mercy' what do you think of?" he said.

"That you're calling on God, or whoever, to spare you any more suffering."

"Right, that's what I thought, too. It was what we all thought Father Pat was saying right before he died." Rourke handed her the postcard that up until a couple of hours ago had been tucked into the mirror of Gillian Daly's dressing table. "But now look at this and tell me what you see."

"A teddy bear."

"No, I mean on the back. Look at the signatures on the back. She must have gone by a nickname, sometimes, with her closest friends. I heard Della Layton use it just this evenin'."

Remy turned the postcard over and looked, and he saw the flash lamp go off in her head as she, too, made the leap. "Oh, God . . ."

Rourke went back into the dining room and rummaged through the carton that had all the papers on the crucifixion killing, because he had, on a whim, thank God, thank God, tossed it in there.

He dug out Father Pat's notebook and turned to the end page where the priest had written the telephone number that he was now cursing himself for not tracking down sooner. And all the while the blood was humming through him and he was thinking, *I've got you, you sadistic, murdering, cocksucking bastard. I've got you.*

He went into the parlor where Katie and Mrs. O. were now playing what looked like a cutthroat game of poker with real pennies, and where the telephone sat on a small ormolu-mounted desk.

He rang up the operator, gave her the number, and asked her to find out what city the exchange belonged to and to get the address of the establishment. Then he and Remy went over it all again while they waited for the operator to call back, looking for the flaws in their theory and all the while their ears were straining for the telephone's bell box to ring, so that when it did finally jangle, they both jumped.

"It's a boardinghouse in Galveston, Texas," he said to Remy, who was hovering by his side, grabbing a piece of paper to write the address on.

He had the operator then connect him to the squad room and got his captain on the phone. He went through the whole thing with him now, hoping it didn't sound as far-fetched and flimsy to Malone as it was beginning to sound to him.

"I'm gonna fly to Galveston now," he said, "and make sure this isn't just something I'm pulling outta my ass out of desperation. We can't know anything for a certainty until I get there, but in the meantime the Daly girl could still be alive, so we need to pick this murdering prick up now and start sweating him hard—if we break him, we just might get to her in time. Also, make sure whoever goes out to his house, that they check the garage."

They spent a few more precious minutes ironing out logistics, before Rourke hung up and turned to Remy, who was looking tired now. "That poor girl," she said.

He hooked his arm around her waist and pulled her to him, kissing her forehead. "Listen, don't go out again today, okay? Stay here with Katie and Mrs. O. I need to know all my guys are safe."

She snuggled into him, ducking her head so that it fit into the crook of his neck. "You be safe, too."

Rourke changed into his flying clothes: the whipcord britches, knee-high boots, and brown leather jacket that would keep him somewhat warm five thousand feet up in the open cockpit of a biplane made of wood and wire and fabric.

Then he jumped on his motorcycle and drove it at a tearing speed out of town and down the St. Bernard Highway, to a small airfield that had been converted from an old dairy barn.

When Remy Lelourie had left him the first time, the summer he was nineteen, Rourke had—in the time-honored tradition of brokenhearted men everywhere—gone off to war to show her good. In his case it was the Great War, and he had joined a French flying squadron of American volunteers, the Lafayette Escadrille, where he'd learned how to pilot a SPAD mounted with a pair of machine guns that fired eight hundred rounds a minute, and then he'd learned how to hunt his enemy down with it and shoot him out of the sky.

He'd loved the flying too much to give it up after the war, and so when one of his bets at the track had paid off big, he'd bought a surplus SPAD—without the machine guns.

The rain had stopped and a weak sun was trying to push through the clouds by the time Rourke turned off the highway, onto the track that cut through a pasture toward the dairy barn. He checked the sock that hung from a pole at the end of the field and saw that the wind was picking up.

He rolled the SPAD out of the hangar, which had once housed milking cows. He had plenty of daylight left to get there, but he'd be coming back in the dark, and so he made himself take the time to do an extra careful preflight check, even though he was so jazzed he could have flown to Galveston without the plane.

As he ran his hands over the struts and tested the tension of the flying wires, he was thinking that it was a good thing he'd done an overhaul of the engine only a couple of weekends ago: replacing a cracked cylinder, cleaning valves and piston rings that were starting to stick a bit, tightening bolts, and mending any tiny rents that he'd found in the fabric.

He finished the preflight check, topped off the fuel tank, and five minutes later he was airborne. He banked high on the turn and headed west, following the soft shine of the struggling sun on the water of the Bayou Lafourche.

The faltering and sinking sun was etching the Gulf's rolling breakers silver and turning Galveston's sandy beaches a rosy orange when he set the SPAD down at a barnstormers' airfield on the north end of town. He borrowed an old jalopy from the owner of the field and asked directions on how to get to the address the telephone operator had given him.

He found the boardinghouse—an aging three-story Victorian

fronted by a deep wooden porch—with little trouble and good timing, for a girl in the black skirt and white blouse of a grocerteria clerk was walking down the sidewalk from the streetcar stop, coming his way. He waited until she was abreast of him, and then he got out of the jalopy and stepped into her path.

"Evenin', Miss Mercy Bloom."

CHAPTER TWENTY-NINE

Gillian Daly lay naked in the dark with the rats.

She would go away for a while, off to a soft white nothingness, where she was alone and nothing could hurt her, and she would stay there for as long as she could. She would stay there until something jerked her back: a cramp, thirst, hunger, a bite of pain, the click of rat claws on brick. A bad memory.

Once, she had come back to the sounds of screaming and she thought there was another girl in here with her, being hurt along with her, and then she realized the screams were hers and they were coming from inside her head, because she couldn't scream out loud, not with the rag stuffed in her mouth. She could barely breathe with it there, and so she lay in the dark, her lungs straining for air and her ears straining, straining, listening for the little squeak the bay doors made in the darkness when they slid open on their tracks, and for the crunch of shoes on the oiled gravel floor.

She'd gotten scared, standing under the clock, when too much time passed and Aunt Judy hadn't come. It had started to rain harder and there was less traffic on the sidewalk. A streetcar had rattled by, but she was afraid to get on it, to sit among a bunch of strangers, any one of whom could be . . . But her mind had shied away from that thought, and just then the taxicab had pulled up to the curb, and Mercy Bloom's daddy had rolled down the window and called out her name, telling her that he'd give her a ride home, that it wasn't safe for her to be standing there alone, not even under the clock at D. H. Holmes.

It had hurt really bad when he'd raped her, and when she'd fought him he'd hit her, slapping her dizzy. Her face felt raw and swollen, and she thought she might be bleeding down there, between her legs. As bad as that was, though, it wasn't the worst. The worst was knowing that he would be back, and that he would rape her some more and then he would kill her.

Daddy, she screamed behind the gag. Tears burned her eyes, and she squeezed them shut, choking down sobs. *Daddy, save me from this. Please, Daddy, I'll be good, Daddy, please, please, only you got to come get me now. Please come get me now, Daddy, please . . .*

Oh, God. She opened her eyes, blinking, and then she realized that it must be growing darker outside, because she couldn't see the motes of spangled dust floating through the air anymore, or the open rafters of the ceiling. Only a faint glow was coming through the row of frosted windows high on the wall.

She tried to move just a little and, oh God, it hurt, it hurt so bad.

He'd chained her with her arms stretched above her head to a radiator, that was in turn fastened to a brick wall. The chain was black iron and heavy, the links thick, and he'd wrapped it around her left wrist and then her right wrist, and then he'd pulled the chain taut and padlocked it to the clawed feet of the radiator. The chain had bruised her flesh so badly, it looked pulpy. Like rotting fruit.

She tilted her head back and twisted onto her shoulder, whimpering behind the gag, trying to get a better look at the chain. She tried pulling hard against it with her arms, but it was a hopeless thought that she could break any one of those big links.

She'd made a lot of noise, though, clattering and banging the iron chain against the iron radiator, and she felt a sudden, sweet surge of hope that maybe somebody had heard. So she rattled and banged some more, until it hurt too much to bear and she fell back exhausted.

At least the noise had scared the rats away.

She didn't know this place, where she was. When it was lighter and she had been able to see better, she thought it looked like an old garage. She'd seen a pile of rotting tires in one corner and a couple of crumpled bumpers leaning against the wall, stacks of empty oil cans, a funnel, greasy rags. Most of the space was taken up with one of those hydraulic lifts used for working under cars. And there'd been tools spilling out of a box on a nearby workbench.

Tools . . .

She'd seen a wrench lying on the floor, close to the lift.

She looked for it again, peering into the enveloping darkness. The wrench was black iron like the chain, and rusted at the grip, but its jaws looked big and strong. Maybe strong enough to twist it like a lever around the chain and pry open one of the links. Maybe she could use the wrench to break the chain, if only she could reach it.

Gillian Daly shifted her battered and bleeding body over bit by bit, her chest bucking as she struggled to breathe, her mouth open around the gag in a scream, shifted until the chain was stretched out its full length, straining, stretching, reaching with her fingers as far as they would go, reaching with her fingers . . .

And they were still about four inches too short.

Remy Lelourie poured some rose oil into the flowing water and then turned off the taps. She slipped out of a red silk kimono and stepped into the tub, gingerly, for she'd made the bath extra hot.

Too hot, she thought as she sucked in her breath. She went on inching down into the water slowly, though, and by the time she was lying down flat with her neck resting on the back rim of the tub she was used to it.

She could hear Mrs. O'Reilly downstairs in the kitchen, whipping egg whites in a metal bowl. The rain had finally let up, and through a crack in the window that she'd made to let out the steam, she could hear rainwater dripping off the eaves and the banana trees, and Katie out in the courtyard, jumping rope. The rope slapping on the wet stones and Katie chanting, "I had a little puppy. His name was Tiny Tim . . ."

The homey sounds and the hot, perfumed water ought to be soothing her frayed and knotted nerves, but she kept thinking about that poor girl, chained up in a garage somewhere, suffering God knew what, and then when her mind would leap away from that horror, it would go right to Day. For no really good reason, she was scared for him.

She'd watched him fly plenty of stunts in the SPAD before. Loop the loops, barrel rolls, chandelles, tailspins, and one particularly spectacular and daredevil maneuver called the Immelmann turn. So a little ol' two-hour jaunt along the Gulf Coast should be nothing, but still she was scared for him. And it wasn't as if anything bad could happen to him in Galveston. Mercedes Bloom couldn't do anything to him but hurt him with words. Otis Bloom was back here in New Orleans and he didn't even know they were on to him. He might even, she hoped, be locked up tight in the Parish Prison by now.

She told herself all that, but it wasn't stopping this feeling she kept getting. It was like waking up from a deep sleep in the middle of the night, to think you've just heard the menacing footstep of someone creeping through your house.

Remy shuddered. She was suddenly feeling vulnerable, lying naked in a tub of water. She'd stood up, splashing, and reached out for the towel she'd laid on a nearby stool, when her eyes caught a flash of movement in the mirror above the sink.

She froze, staring at her own wide eyes staring back at herself, and staring behind her, where the door was half opened into the bedroom, showing just the end of the big tester bed. She held her breath, listening, and heard something—a soft *whish,* like cloth brushing against cloth, and a creak of the old cypress floorboards.

And then she saw him in the mirror . . . a hulking shadow rising up out of the bed.

Remy Lelourie had never thought of herself as the screaming type, but this time she opened her mouth wide and hit a high note worthy of an opera diva.

And the intruder ran.

He pounded out the bedroom and down the hall and front stairs, banging through the front door, while Mrs. O'Reilly and Katie came running up the back stairs to see why she had screamed. Remy snatched her kimono off the hook on the back of the bathroom door and threw it on before running out into the bedroom, slipping a little on the wet tile floor, and then screaming again, maybe just a little, when she saw what he'd written on the wall over the bed. In blood.

Not his usual message this time, though; something different, something worse:

Anytime. Anywhere.

Daman Rourke listened while Mercedes Bloom talked, and what she didn't or couldn't tell him, he filled in for himself with intuition, supposition, and his years of seeing so much of the dark and ugly side of life.

The girl had been sleeping in her daddy's bed since she was eleven. Her mama had known about it; her mama, in fact, had moved out of her marriage bed and into her daughter's old room and left Mercy to her daddy's mercy.

Otis Bloom knew what he was doing was a sin, and so once a year, on Good Friday, he would go to a confessional and cleanse his soul of it. He went to different priests each time, though, different churches and once even to a different town.

Some of the priests had been more disturbed by the deeds he spoke of in the confessional box than others, but they'd all, once he had shown them how sorry he was, been willing to perform the sacrament of absolution and let go of it. They would tell him, though, how it wasn't enough to repent of what had gone on with his daughter, he had to resolve never to go near the sin again. He had to do penance, and when he was confronted in the future with temptation he had to pray to Christ Jesus for the strength to resist.

And perhaps in that moment in the confessional box, when the priest raised his hand for the absolution and, as God's emissary on earth, washed his soul clean, Otis Bloom might truly have believed he would change. For Otis Bloom, repenting had never been hard, and he needed his absolution. What he didn't want to do, in his heart of hearts, was to go and sin no more.

Mercedes's father had made her go with him to those Good Friday confessions, he'd sent her into the box right after him, because as he had explained to her, the sin they'd made was as much hers as his. It took two to fuck, he said. Two to experience *le petit mort.*

And then on this last Good Friday, out of carelessness maybe, or a growing arrogance, Otis Bloom had chosen for the first time to make their confession close to home, at Holy Rosary. But Father Pat, Rourke thought, had been in the box that day, and *she* was one priest who had not let go of it.

Rourke had been leaning against the rail on the boardinghouse porch while he listened to the horror that had been the life of Mercedes Bloom and watched more rain clouds build thick and black over the Gulf water.

The girl sat on a wicker swing rocker with blue-flowered cushions, and as she spoke she pushed on the floor with the ball of one foot and the accompanying creak of the swing rocking in its joints was the only inflection in her voice.

The crucifixion killing and the Fantastics murders were too

sensational not to have made it into the Galveston press, but Mercedes Bloom seemed oblivious to their happening, and when he'd told her, she'd shown no horror. And as she described in their prurient and graphic detail all the things that had been done to her over the years, Rourke thought that she was indeed a marble angel, all her heart and feeling having been petrified by her father's perversion.

Yet somehow Father Pat had managed to touch this stone child and then she'd tried to save her.

"Father told me that it was all my daddy's sin," Mercedes said, "and none of it was mine, and he made me see how I could stop it."

Rourke thought of Mercedes Bloom changing herself, bobbing away her finger waves, and getting on a streetcar that took her, not home, but to the train station. To a new name, a new town, a job and a fresh life—all provided for by Father Pat's special club.

And she'd done it all just as Father Pat had told her she should, except for one thing.

"Father said I wasn't to tell anyone where I'd be going, not even Nina or any of the other Fantastics, but I kept fretting about poor Mama, about how she'd worry so that something bad had happened to me. So one night, a couple of weeks after I got here, when I knew Daddy would be out driving his taxi, I called up Mama and I told her—I just said it really fast and hung right up, I didn't say anything about *where* I was—I just said, Father Pat had figured out how to get me away from Daddy and that I'm okay now."

And Ethel Bloom, out of some dark motive that Rourke didn't want to fathom, had turned around and shared that telephone call with her husband.

Rourke thought of the priest as he'd first seen her that night, crucified on a crossbeam in an abandoned macaroni factory. The brass-knuckled beating to her face, the votive candles burning the soles of her feet, the nails through her wrists—they'd all been done to Father Pat to make her give up the whereabouts of Mercy Bloom.

And now the girl Father Pat had died protecting looked at Rourke out of those marble angel eyes and said, "Do you think now that Father Pat's dead that I could go home? I don't like checking groceries, and the lady who runs this house, she's a niggardly old thing. She only lets us take a bath once a week and she counts everything, even down to the lumps of sugar you put in your coffee."

Rourke left her question unanswered because he couldn't have managed words for the life of him at this moment. The porch fell silent except for the creak of the swing and the rushing of the rising wind through the big elm tree in the yard, and then she said, "I think Father Pat was wrong about Daddy, anyway. Daddy never really meant to hurt me. He always told me it would feel good and sometimes it did."

Rourke borrowed the boardinghouse's telephone and put a call in to the squad room, pacing the tiny, cramped parlor impatiently while he waited for the operator to call back with the connection.

It was Fio on the other end of the line.

"It's her all right," Rourke told him. "Miss Mercedes Bloom, alive and well, if you can call it that, and living in Galveston . . . Y'all pick him up yet?"

Fio's voice seemed to be coming at him from outer space, breaking into hiccups as it crackled over the wire. "He wasn't at home, and he doesn't have a garage, just an old shed, but it was full of nothing but junk. The wife was passed out cold in bed. Nate Carroll got her sobered up enough for us to figure she doesn't know squat where Bloom is. Although . . . Nate says he thinks she knew what her old man had been doing to her daughter."

"She knew."

"Yeah. Anyway, we've got every man on the force out stopping taxis, but the captain doesn't think he's on the streets. He thinks he's probably with the Daly girl."

"Goddammit. Okay, I'm coming back now. It looks like some rough weather's brewing, but I'm going to try to outrun it."

The line popped and hissed and then Fio's voice faded in long enough for Rourke to hear, ". . . Miss Lelourie and your Katie had some . . ." before it broke apart completely.

"What?" Rourke shouted, but the line crackled again and went dead.

He rattled the cradle and dialed O, but he couldn't reach the operator. The wind must have taken the wires down somewhere. He paced once around the room, telling himself that if his guys were in any serious trouble, surely Fio wouldn't have waited until the end of the conversation to tell him so.

He tried the phone again. Still dead, and he couldn't wait any longer. If he had any hope of getting back to New Orleans tonight, he had to leave now.

The borrowed jalopy wasn't the fastest thing on wheels, and Rourke was in a lather of impatience by the time he got back out to the airfield, where big gusts of wind were rocking the SPAD, whistling through her bracing wires and pulling at the ropes that tethered her to the ground. It was full dusk now, only a film of gray light still clinging to the sky. Rourke looked to the west, where trumpet-shaped clouds with blackened bottoms obscured the horizon.

"Weather comin'," the old barnstormer said as he watched Rourke go through the preflight check.

"I got to get back," Rourke said.

"You in the war?"

"Lafayette Corps."

"Flyin' and killin' and watchin' your friends get killed off one by one in their turn . . . Guess it gives some men a death wish."

Rourke smiled to himself at the old-timer's faddish psychology.

He got aloft without any trouble, but it wasn't long before he was overtaken by rain and wind, and he had to fight with the stick to keep her steady. He was flying low, navigating by following the lights of the few small settlements nestled among the bayous and waterways of the wetlands and the bay indentations along the coast.

He was just starting to think he'd gotten past the worst of it, when the front of a squall appeared like the sheer face of a cliff in front of him. He had but a few seconds to adjust the controls before he plunged into a maelstrom.

It was as if a damp, black blanket had been flung over his head. The air dropped out from under him as he hit a downdraft, and then rain slammed into his face, icy and biting. He had to ride the elevator hard as the SPAD was buffeted by the wind. The plane pitched, yawed, and rolled under the violent gusts, as the squall did its best to tear the stick out of his hands. He was going to have to try to get above it.

The rain froze on his goggles as he climbed, and the SPAD shuddered under the battering of the wind. Fearing carburetor icing, he kept his eye on the altimeter, his ear tuned to the sound of the engine, and even as he thought it he began to hear the rough, uneven pulse that indicated loss of power. His eyes flickered over to the airspeed indicator, and he saw that it wasn't registering. He rapped it hard with his knuckle, but it still read zero.

He knew that he had been plunging around for too long in the dense blackness, that he'd probably lost his equilibrium. He had no physical feeling anymore of what was up or down, right or left, and without the airspeed indicator to tell him, he hadn't realized that he'd been flying slower and slower, too slow for his sharp rate of climb, approaching the speed at which the plane would no longer be able to remain aloft until—

He stalled, and the SPAD shuddered and whipped into a high-speed, spiraling dive, plunging through the darkness.

* * *

Katie Rourke sat in her daddy's chair and sneaked a peek through the top drawer in his desk, looking for some chewing gum. The last time she'd been here in the squad room, he'd had some Juicy Fruit, but this time she didn't find any.

She found some rubber bands instead. She took one, stretched it out between two fingers, aimed for the nose of a man hanging on the Rogues' Gallery, and fired. She missed.

"You must be Miss Katie Rourke."

After the scare they'd just had with the bad man getting in the house, the stranger's voice rasping in her ear made Katie jump.

She twisted around in the chair and looked way up at a man with a bald head so smooth and shiny it looked made out of wax and a mustache stiff as a bottle brush. She decided she didn't like him.

She looked around the squad room to see if anybody else was taking any notice of the man, but the place was empty. All the policemen were out looking for the bad man, except for Captain Malone. He was in his office with Miss Remy and Mrs. O'Reilly. The blinds to his window were up, and Katie could see the three of them in there, talking and drinking coffee. Mrs. O'Reilly's heart had been having something called "palpitations" because of the bad man, but she seemed fine now.

Katie looked back up at the man with the waxy head and gave him the smile she used on the nuns. "How do you know I'm Katie Rourke? I could be just about any-old-body."

The man laughed as he reached over her and plucked a photograph in a silver frame from off her daddy's desk. "I recognized you from your picture."

Katie plucked it right back away from him and put it back where it belonged. She didn't like him touching her daddy's things. "That was taken before I bobbed my hair," she said.

The man laughed again and said, "So I see . . . Say, honey, is your daddy around? I need to talk with him."

"Why?"

The man's smile was full of teeth. "I've been helping with a case he's working on."

Katie didn't know what to think now. She still didn't like the man, but Daddy was always telling her that it wasn't charitable to take against someone for no good reason except that you felt like it, and so she decided to be nice.

She stretched her mouth out into a pretend smile. "Daddy went flying off in his airplane, but he's coming back soon. Miss Remy and Mrs. O'Reilly and I are going to wait for him here, because . . . just because."

She'd been about to tell him the exciting story of the bad man getting into the house, but then she changed her mind. She wasn't going to be *that* nice. "Are you helping my daddy look for the runaway girl?" she said instead. " 'Cause if you are, he thinks he might've found her."

"Hey, that's great." The man took a step away from the desk, then swung back around again. He was wearing a black duster, and it slapped against his legs like the flap of a magpie's wing. "This runaway girl, honey—what's her name?"

"Mercedes."

"Mercedes? Why, that's a pretty name, isn't it? Do you know where your daddy went flying?"

"No. I don't think he ever said," she lied.

"Are you sure? Think hard now."

She pretended to think hard and then lied again, "He just never said."

The door to Captain Malone's office opened just then, and the man's waxy head jerked in that direction. Then he turned back and leaned into Katie, so close she could see the ends of his mustache quiver as he talked. "When your daddy comes back, be sure to tell him I was here lookin' for him, y' hear?"

Then he swung around and left her, walking fast. Miss Remy came up, and together they watched him leave the squad room through the short, swinging gate and disappear down the hall, his black duster flapping.

"Look what Captain Malone found in his desk," Miss Remy said, and Katie saw that she was holding a pack of Juicy Fruit in her hand. "Who was that man, honey?"

"He said he was helping Daddy find the runaway girl," Katie said, "but I know he was lying. Because he would've known her name then, wouldn't he have? Only he didn't."

"Sweet Jesus," Miss Remy said, using one of Daddy's favorite naughty words. She made a funny little half step forward, toward the swinging door, and then back, as if she wasn't sure which way she wanted to go. "I do believe that the man the whole of the Crescent City police department is out looking for has just walked right into this squad room, and then walked right back out again."

Gillian Daly hadn't given up.

Three times she'd drifted away into the white nothingness, but she kept crawling back, and she'd pulled and twisted against the chain, strained and reached, and still the tips of her fingers fell just inches short from the wrench, and so she wept and screamed her silent screams, and listened all the while for the scrape of the bay doors and the footsteps on the oiled gravel floor, while she strained and stretched some more, and came up short.

It was never going to happen, she was never going to reach the wrench without pulling the radiator from the wall. So she tried doing that, yanking on the chain until the links cut so deeply into her wrists that blood smeared in patches on the oily floor.

She lay back, shaking from exhaustion, the pain in her arms so bad it felt like somebody was trying to twist them right off. Her chest bucked for air; tears and sweat blurred her eyes.

I hate you, she screamed behind the gag at the man who was coming to kill her, screamed at God and fate and herself, and she gave one last mighty heave against the chain even though the radiator was never coming loose, never.

One end of it popped out of the wall with such force that it swung around and hit her on the head, knocking her almost senseless. Pain blazed in white lightning flashes across her eyes, blanking out everything but the need to get at the wrench before he came back. She could feel him, like a hot breath on her neck, she could feel him coming.

One clawed leg of the radiator was still bolted to the wall, but the other leg had busted free, and she was able to work loose one loop of the chain, giving her more slack. Enough slack that she could reach easily for the wrench with her right hand now.

Her fingers closed around it—

"Hey, Gilly girl."

Chapter Thirty

Gillian Daly hadn't heard the scrape of the door and the crunch of gravel. He was suddenly just there, looming up in front of her, bending over her, coming to kill her.

She swung the wrench at his head.

He saw the blow coming and reared back, so that it missed, but the terror-fueled power of her swing popped the other end of the radiator loose from the wall.

He laughed, and his laughter snapped the few threads of sanity left inside of her, made her more furious than scared, it made her want to beat him to a pulp. She swung the wrench at his legs, but he dodged it easily and kicked out at her with his heavy brogan, connecting with her forearm and her arm broke, because she heard it before she felt it. A sharp crack, like the snap of a wishbone.

The wrench clattered to the floor and she scrambled after it, but he was on her, throwing her onto her back and pressing down on her with the full weight of his big body.

"That wasn't being a good girl, Gilly," he said, his breath blowing harsh on her face. "Not a good girl at all."

She bucked against him, tried to kick, but he was too heavy. She tried to beat at him with the chain, but he punched her hard in the face and then wrapped the loose end of the chain once more around the radiator. The radiator wasn't bolted to the wall anymore, but it still acted as a weight, effectively pinning her arms back in place above her head.

He pushed up onto his knees, straddling her, and she looked up into his face. Tears of pain and terror blurred her eyes, but she could tell that he was smiling and his smile was the most horrible thing she'd ever seen in her young life, because it made him look kind. His smile made him look like he would never hurt her.

"Don't cry, Gilly. Don't cry, baby," he said, and his voice was so low and gentle. Like her own daddy's voice when she was a little girl and she'd wake up crying from a nightmare, and he would stroke the hair out of her face and kiss her wet cheek, and croon to her in a lullaby singsong.

"I'm going to treat you really good, baby, you'll see. So good, so good, so good . . ."

The SPAD dove in a wild, tight spin. Rourke watched the sinking altimeter and revolving compass, trying desperately and blindly to stabilize the controls. Burning pain from the rushing air pressed against his ears, and the blood left his hands and feet. Darkness began to creep around the edge of his vision.

Suddenly the nose of the plane punched through the clouds, and Rourke saw a few scattered lights and the tidal path along the coastline, only the world had been turned upside down and the black water was rushing at him with dizzying speed.

He had only seconds to live, but it was all he needed, because with the sight of the lights and the water, his equilibrium had returned. He shoved the throttle forward and snapped the plane out of its spin with a jerk that jarred his teeth. The propeller bit the air fifty feet from the water, so close it sent up a salt spray into his face, and Daman Rourke laughed because he'd beaten death once again and that victory was always so sweet, so sweet.

The storm still raged around him, sharp and crooked bolts of lightning doing a dance above his head like marionettes jerking on a string, but he saw the denser lights of New Orleans now, and he laughed again and thought, *Home free.*

Half an hour later Rourke was driving his Indian Chief motorcycle down the wet and dangerously slippery blacktop of the St. Bernard Highway as if he'd been shot out of the gates of hell. That brush with his own mortality had blown through his head like a snort of cocaine, cleaning it out.

He knew where Bloom was keeping the girl.

He cut the motorcycle's engine when he was three blocks away and cruised to a silent stop alongside the macaroni factory. He studied the hot car farm across the street, the one that had been shut down in a much publicized police raid only two weeks ago. The chicken wire fence rattled and the Victory Gasoline sign creaked loudly in the stiff wind. Trash twirled and danced around the pumps.

He approached the place on silent feet. Shadows cloaked the garage, a gray clapboard building leprosied with rust. He saw no signs of life, but there was a brand-new padlock on the gate in the fence, and fresh graffiti had been chalked on the garage's bay doors, warning the hobos to stay away.

He was about to be prudent for a change, about to jog the two blocks down to the call box, get the precinct house on the line and have them send in the cavalry, when he heard a little cry, like the mew of a weak kitten.

He ran softly along the perimeter of the fence until he found a small gap that he could work into a larger one. He crawled through, snagging his leather jacket on the wire.

The bay doors were partly open, and Rourke approached them carefully with his gun drawn and held in front of him in a two-handed grip. The gap in the doors was wide enough for him to slip through silently.

He stopped as soon as he was inside, letting his eyes adjust to the deeper darkness within the building.

He smelled her before he saw her: urine, blood, and semen. Still, it would have taken a while for him to find her, stuffed as she was deep in a corner, if she hadn't started whimpering again.

He made himself take his time going to her, stopping every couple of feet to sweep the dark and shrouded spaces with his gun. He could see all of the garage now, though, and Bloom wasn't here.

The girl's naked flesh was pale as death where it wasn't battered bloody. One of her arms was bent at an unnatural angle and her wrists were wrapped up in a thick chain that was tangled up with a broken radiator.

Rourke crouched down beside her, resting his gun hand on his bent knee, and reached with his other hand to touch her shoulder, saying, "Gilly . . ."

She arched up, wild with fear, screaming and flailing at him with her legs. She kicked the gun hard out of his hand, and it slid across the floor and fell down the open shaft of what had once been an hydraulic automobile lift.

He wrapped her up in his arms, making soft shushing noises, calling her by name and she slowly quieted. He kept holding her, most of her in his lap now, while he leaned over, working to untangle the chain from the radiator. She stared up at him, and the look on her face, in her eyes, wasn't quite human anymore . . .

Eyes that suddenly bulged wide with terror.

Rourke caught the flash of something black flaring like a bat's wing and he twisted around, instinctively flinging up his arm as a wrench slammed into the side of his head.

"I knew," said Otis Bloom, "that you would find my Mercedes for me, Detective."

Rourke blinked the sweat and blood out of his eyes and strained to focus. Then his vision blurred and darkened again, as nausea rose burning in his nose and throat. An oily rag that reeked of gasoline was stuffed in his mouth.

A match hissed and then the dark around them was banished by a flood of yellow light. "Someone has cut off the electricity, I'm afraid," Bloom said as he set a hurricane lantern down on a workbench. "Now I do hope you will tell me where she is without too much unpleasantness."

Rourke had turned his head toward the lantern, and the movement almost sent him slipping back into unconsciousness. He groaned, sagging against the ropes that held him.

He was tied down to a tall-legged chair, with a chimney sweep's weighted rope wrapped around his chest and left arm, and another around his legs. His right arm was stretched out straight, across the flat top of a workbench, and tied down with another rope wrapped around his forearm to the bench's vise block.

His flying jacket had been taken off and his shirtsleeves rolled up, and his arm was tied down in such a way that his wrist and hand turned were upward. And even though he knew what this meant, his mind screamed, *Oh, God, no . . .*

Otis Bloom leaned into him, his face only inches away from Rourke's, and his stiff mustache lifted in a smile. "Regrettably, I don't have the time to tease it out of you slowly. So I'll do the one wrist without any more to-do. That should give you quite an incentive, I think, to take seriously all of my melodramatic threats and promises, and then you'll tell me what you know and we'll be done here."

Bloom straightened and went to the other end of the workbench, behind Rourke's back, and Rourke lifted his head, fighting down another bout of nausea. His gaze searched the deep shadows behind the hydraulic lift for what Bloom had done with the girl. She was still there, discarded by her rapist in the corner like a pile of trash. She looked dead, but then she stirred a little, and Rourke quickly looked away so that he wouldn't draw attention to her.

For Bloom was back again with a small carpetbag that he set on the bench near Rourke's pinioned and exposed wrist. "You are wrong about me, you know," he was saying. "You believe I'm afflicted with a mental illness, but there is a perfectly rational explanation for all of this."

He unsnapped the clasp and spread open the bag. "You see, when Mercedes ran away from me, I thought surely her best friend knew where she had gone. I picked up Nina Duboche just to have a little chat with her, but quite to my chagrin, as you can well imagine, I went a little too far and I had a dead girl on my hands . . ."

Bloom looked up, but his gaze was turned inward, as if he were reliving the rapes, the strangling, and Rourke thought, *You enjoyed it, though, didn't you, you sick bastard.*

"I had killed her very dead, Detective, but that was easily enough dealt with. My Mercedes likes to talk in bed, so I knew the girl had been fucking that nigger chimney sweep. I simply framed the boy for her murder and that was that. But as for getting my Mercedes back . . . well, I was at an impasse."

He reached in the carpetbag and took out a mallet, whose grip was about a foot long, and it had a steel-capped head. He hefted the mallet in his hand, looked over at Rourke, and smiled.

"So you can imagine my delight and surprise when one night I learn from my sweet and accommodating wife how it was that stupid, interfering priest had helped my girl to run away. I did so want to kill him for that, but what I wanted most from him was a simple answer to a simple question."

Bloom was tossing the mallet from hand to hand, taunting Rourke with it. In the soft glow of the lantern light, his eyes seemed to be gleaming with an unholy delight.

"Now I did amuse myself, I admit it—and in a rather ingenious way if I do say so myself. The saintly father's palms started bleeding at Mass one day, did you know? I was there, serving him at the altar, and I saw it with my own eyes. It might have been a true miracle, what was going on there, but I rather doubt it. I told him he should've taken the time to look it up in a book and see how a crucifixion is properly done. And then I showed him."

He caught the mallet on the last toss with a flourish and set it with slow deliberation on the bench next to Rourke's wrist. Rourke felt his throat swallow convulsively. He didn't want to be scared of what was coming, but he was.

Bloom, feeling his fear, leaned close and looked deep into Rourke's eyes, feeding off it.

Then he sighed and straightened. "Where was I? Oh yes . . . Unfortunately, not only did the saintly Father Pat turn out to be much more stubborn than one could ever imagine, but I was interrupted by that whimpering boy. And so—another impasse."

He reached in the carpetbag and took out the nails, and Rourke's guts clenched hard around his fear.

"Another impasse, that is, until I thought of you, Detective," Bloom was saying. "You see, I am quite the admirer of yours. Indeed I've made rather a project out of studying you. You have one of those minds that can leap across chasms, but you're addicted to risk. And you won't ever quit or back down before a threat, because you see that as a weakness and you're terrified of being weak."

Bloom had set the nails down next to the mallet and now he'd turned and was leaning against the bench with his elbows braced behind him and his legs crossed at the ankles, as if they were just two guys shooting the breeze.

"And as I studied you," he went on, "it occurred to me that perhaps you would succeed where I had not. That all I needed to do was start murdering more Fantastics, and you would dig and dig and dig until you found out why, and the why would lead you to my Mercedes."

He took Rourke's chin in his hand and turned his face up. "So you see, we have made these sins together, Detective Daman Rourke."

He held Rourke's chin a moment longer, and then let it go and turned back to the bench. "I do believe we are ready now," he said. "May I suggest you look away. It's going to be bad enough for you without you having to watch it."

Rourke didn't want to watch, but he'd be damned before he let the son of a bitch know it. Still, his fingers twitched when Bloom pressed the point of the nail into his flesh, then sprang straight in a horror of anticipation as Bloom brought the mallet down on the head of the nail.

It must have been making some noise—the steel head of the mallet striking the nail as Bloom drove it through his wrist and into the bench top with four solid blows. But Rourke didn't hear it through the screams in his head.

Sweat ran down his face like tears. His breath came in harsh tearing gasps. His mind kept saying, *no, no, no,* even as he was looking at the black head of the nail protruding from the flesh of his wrist and the rivulets of blood trickling onto the grease-marred wood.

Bloom set the mallet down and looked at his handiwork with pride, then bent down and cupped Rourke's chin, turning his face toward the lantern light. Bloom's own face was dreamy, his eyes gentle and far away. "That was bad, wasn't it?" he said. "Yes, I can see that it was."

He took the gag out of Rourke's mouth and used it to wipe the sweat and tears of pain out of Rourke's eyes, his touch obscenely gentle. "I'm not going to insult your intelligence by making promises I can't keep," he said. "You know I'm going to have to kill you in the end, there simply is no way around it. But there's no need to make a crucible of your death, Detective. Tell me where she is, and I'll murder you gently."

Rourke moved his dry lips, letting out the barest sound, forcing Bloom to lean in close. "Fuck you," he said, shooting out as much spit as he could with the words.

Bloom reared up and pulled his arm back, as if he would slap Rourke across the face with the flat of his hand, but then he let it fall and he laughed. "The very words Father Pat said, and you wouldn't think a priest would know such language, let alone make use of it. But then people are often not themselves when they are in extremity."

The pain, which had been ebbing some, returned now with a ferocity that almost made Rourke faint. Blood was spreading out from his nailed wrist. Too much blood.

"Shall we go then to the threat of a nail to the other wrist?" Bloom said. "Or do I make you a few promises first?"

Those times in the past months when they had talked, Bloom seemed to have to work at pulling words out of himself, but now he just went on and on. He was talking as he went back to the carpetbag—after more nails, Rourke supposed, and he wanted to laugh because Bloom was going to be at another impasse soon. He hadn't been so careful this time. Rourke thought he must have nicked an artery with the nail, and at the rate that the blood was coming out of the hole in Rourke's wrist, Rourke would probably bleed to death long before Bloom would ever let him get a word in edgewise.

Bloom came back to him, but with a brandy flask, not another nail. He grabbed Rourke roughly by the chin, opening his jaw and pouring a hefty dose of it down Rourke's throat, and it went down so fast Rourke almost strangled on it. "I want you *aware,* Detective," Bloom said. "And listening to my promises."

Rourke's laugh was more like a hacking cough, but it was real. "What're you trying to do, Bloom—talk me to death?"

Bloom snatched up the mallet and slammed it down on the nail in Rourke's wrist, and Rourke's scream echoed off the open rafters.

Bloom's face was dark with blood-rage, his eyes wide. "You find this amusing, do you? Well, we shall see who laughs last . . . I've been watching your woman, Detective. Following her in my taxi, spying on her every move. Perhaps she's noticed. Don't you think she's been looking a little scared lately?"

The pain was like an electrical fire in Rourke's wrist, snapping and crackling, but his slowly leaking blood had gone cold. He knew now that he could endure any pain through to the end, but he wasn't going to be able to bear dying with the image in his mind of Remy lying on a riverbank, naked and violated and with a rope wrapped around her neck.

"Every cop in the city is out looking for you," he said, the words rasping in his raw throat.

"And quite efficiently, too, considering that only a couple of hours ago I walked right into your squad room, had a little conversation with your daughter, and walked back out again . . . She's a tough little nut, by the way. Your Katie. I'm not going to mind fucking her either."

Rage, pure and blinding, surged through Rourke with such force that he would have exploded out of the chair if he hadn't been tied down. Every sinew and muscle in his body surged upward with that fury . . . and he felt a give in the flesh of his wrist as it pulled against the nail.

He sagged back against the chair, his heart tripping over every other beat. He had a way out now, a way out . . . To get loose, he didn't have to pull the nail out of his wrist. He could pull his wrist off the nail.

Bloom was smiling as he leaned into him, his voice low and soft like a lover's, caught up in their pas de deux of pain and pride. "So do think about that, Detective. I could take them both, your Remy and your little girl. Anytime. Anywhere."

He straightened and stepped back, and Rourke lifted his head. He forced his eyes to open wide against a wave of enveloping darkness and he saw a naked and bloodied girl rise up out of the dark with the wrench lifted high above her head by the arm that wasn't broken.

Bloom felt, or heard her, and he whirled just as the girl let fly with the wrench, and it struck him with a solid *thunk* on the side of his head. For a moment, Bloom seemed to be half suspended in the air, as if he were being held there by strings, and then he collapsed onto the floor.

She looked down at him a moment, then, moving like a wraith, her battered face strangely serene, she turned away and came to Rourke where he was tied to the chair. He wasn't sure she was even in this world anymore, but then she threw the wrench on the floor, knelt before the chair, and began to pick one-handed at the knots in the ropes.

Rourke didn't know that he was blacking in and out now, until he revived long enough to realize that the ropes were off him and she was staring down at his wrist nailed to the workbench, crying silent tears, and saying over and over. "How do I get it out? How do I get it out?"

Unconsciousness pulled at Rourke again, and his whole body felt drained of blood, but through the blackening edges of his vision, he could see Bloom stirring on the floor.

"Gilly . . . run," he tried to shout, but it came out as a croaking whisper. "Run now."

The girl jerked around to look at Bloom just as he reared up like some creature coming out of a grave. She tried to run, but he was on her. He tossed her to the floor and she landed in a heap, as if she were made of sticks and strings. He loomed over her and wrapped his hands around her throat.

Rourke gathered his feet beneath him, thrusting up off the chair, and his wrist came off the nail with a sucking, bloody pop.

Bloom lurched up off the girl and spun around, lashing out with his heavy brogan, catching Rourke in the belly and sending him crashing back into the workbench.

Bloom laughed and bent over, snatching up the chimney sweep's rope. He wrapped each end of it around his two hands and snapped it taut. "You and I, Detective," he said, breathing heavily, "have some unfinished business."

The pain in Rourke's wrist was like a white-hot flame in front of his eyes so that he could barely see. His legs slid out from underneath him and he slowly sagged to the floor, and the wrench was where he'd hoped it would be, where the girl had dropped it, and he wrapped the fingers of his good hand around the hard metal handle.

He heard Bloom's laughter and the snap of the rope. He saw the flare of the black duster as Bloom came at him.

Rourke surged to his feet and he smashed the wrench in Bloom's face, right between the eyes.

Rourke was waiting for Bloom's eyes to open.

He had wrapped the chimney sweep's rope around the man's neck and wedged the wrench in the loop like you would do to make a tourniquet, and now he was waiting for Bloom's eyes to open before he tightened it.

Rourke was lying on top of him, close as lovers. And when his eyelashes stirred and lifted, Rourke put his lips up to the man's ear. "You're gonna die, Bloom," he said and he smiled.

Bloom flailed beneath him, but weakly. He was too far gone.

Gilly, who had been kneeling next to them, started to scramble away. Rourke was afraid she was going for help, so he grabbed her leg with his free hand and pain shot through him from the gaping, bleeding hole in his wrist.

"Not yet," he said.

She could have broken away from him, but she didn't. Instead she came closer, so that she, too, could look into Bloom's eyes. "Is he dead?" she said.

"Getting there," Rourke said, and he began to tighten the rope.

"Good."

Chapter Thirty-one

Rourke drifted out of a black swell to the feel of strong arms lifting him, and a voice rough and thick with feeling. "Aw, man, Day. What have you gone and done to yourself?"

Then a moment, an eternity later, he was in a white place, everything was white, even the air, and Paulie was there, making the sign of the cross on his forehead with holy oil.

I am dying, he thought, and he laughed because it seemed too much that he would die now after just having lived through all of that.

When he opened his eyes again, he was in a bed in a hospital room and he knew he wasn't going to die after all.

Remy was sitting on the edge of the bed and she leaned over and laid her head on his chest. "You must never do that to me again, Day."

"I won't," he said. "I'll try not to."

He must have fallen asleep for a while, because he heard Remy say, "Okay, honey, he's awake now." And then his Katie was leaning over the bed and planting a big wet one on his cheek, and he laughed and said, "Hey, baby."

She laughed back and kissed him again, and this time the front of her school uniform jumper crackled.

"What you got there?" he said. "A present for me?"

She pulled a piece of white construction paper out from beneath the flap in her jumper and gave it to him. "I drew you a picture of our cat," she said.

"That's real pretty, honey. But since when do we have a cat?"

"He adopted us," Remy said.

"And his name is Cinnamon, Daddy. 'Cause that's his color."

Rourke held the picture up with his good hand, pretending to look at it so that they wouldn't see the tears in his eyes.

He wasn't supposed to have many visitors, but they kept coming.

Paulie first, his black cassock cinched tight around his waist as if he were fortifying himself with it. The color high in his round Irish face.

"I gave you the last rites," he said.

"I know."

"When I asked you if you were sorry for your sins, you laughed in my face."

Rourke laughed now, too. "Hey, come on. I was out of my head."

Paulie made a little *hunh* sound, but then he did his version of a smile, crinkling his eyes, twisting one corner of his mouth.

"I'm going to take your advice," he said.

"Oh, God . . ."

"You said some things are worth the sacrifices you've got to make to have them. So I've decided to go on a spiritual retreat, to see if I can find my way back to being a priest."

As Rourke listened while Paulie told him about the retreat, he watched his brother's face, and although he wasn't sure why it would be so, there was something in Paulie that reminded him of Mercedes Bloom.

It's in the eyes, he thought. The marble eyes.

* * *

Sean Daly came by and told him about Gilly.

"She was in really bad shape when they brought her in, but she's gonna make it. What that son of a bitch did to her . . ."

"You were right about her," Rourke said. "About her being a tough little fighter."

"Yeah."

Daly's face got hard-looking, but Rourke knew he was only stiffening up against the intensity of what he was feeling. "There aren't any words," he said. "Hell, there aren't any deeds that would repay you for what you did. You saved my Gilly, my baby . . ."

Rourke felt his face stiffen up against this own feelings. "She saved me. She could have crawled out of that place while Bloom was . . . occupied with me. Instead she took him on. She did you proud, Mr. Daly."

"Sean. Call me Sean." He swallowed, and his face was like a rock. "I just want you to know . . . You ever have it in mind that you want to be chief someday, just say the word and I'll use up every bit of juice I got to make it happen."

Fio sneaked in some booze and they drank it while they rehashed what had happened, laughing as Rourke told him about how Bloom just wouldn't shut up.

"He was one crazy fucker, I'm telling you," Fio said.

Fio, it turned out, had been cruising the streets, looking for Bloom's cab when he had remembered about the hot car farm and had gotten the same hunch that Rourke had had. He'd come shrieking up to the place in a squad car, siren blaring, just as a naked Gilly had run out into Chartres Street, screaming that a man was inside the garage bleeding to death.

Fio didn't mention anything, though, about how he had found Bloom's corpse with the makeshift garrote around his neck, and Rourke didn't mention that he'd come to for a moment when Fio had been carrying him out of the garage.

Rourke thought that he was coming to care for his partner a lot, but he didn't know how to tell him that, so he said instead, "Did you ever get a new hat?"

On Rourke's first day back on the job, Garrison Hughes of *The Movies* brought by the photographs that he had taken of all the harlequins at the Saenger Theatre's masquerade ball. Even though he hadn't needed the snapshots after all, Rourke gave him the hundred bucks and a story, because a deal was a deal and he liked Hughes.

Rourke was ninety percent convinced that Otis Bloom had been Romeo. The Ghoul, who was a fount of arcane knowledge, had taken a look at the puncture wound in Remy's arm, listened to her description of the weapon, and declared that in his opinion it was a bleeding knife. They hadn't found any bleeding knives in Bloom's house, but they had found a book on medicinal bleeding. And there was what he'd said in the garage, Romeo's words, talking about Remy looking scared and about how he could take her anytime, anywhere. And the bedroom that Otis Bloom had shared with his daughter—it had been papered with movie posters and photographs of Remy Lelourie.

Except, except, except . . . If Bloom had been counting on Rourke to find his Mercedes for him, then why would he have shot at him from a hotel roof and blown up his car?

So Rourke was only ninety percent sure that Bloom was Romeo, and he thought that the other ten percent that was doubt would be keeping him scared for a long time to come.

He looked through the photographs because he'd paid for them, but they didn't contain any startling revelations. The harlequins were all with Bright Lights Studios, except for a Charity Hospital doctor and the nurse who was his mistress.

Rourke tossed the photographs into the box with the rest of the case file on the crucifixion killing and marked it closed. He was about to tape it up, when he opened it again and took out Father Pat's notebook.

Who are you?

He wondered how much closer he was to knowing the truth behind that question than he had been on the night he had walked into that abandoned macaroni factory and seen Father Pat hanging from a crossbeam with the nails through his wrists. Who had he been, this priest who was no priest? This woman who was not a woman?

In some ways Father Pat had been an extraordinary individual. Compassionate, brave beyond measure, profound. And yet now and forever after, when Rourke thought of the priest it would be with a melancholia of disappointment.

For Father Pat, along with the rest of New Orleans, had watched Titus Dupre get condemned to the electric chair for a murder he hadn't done. The rest of New Orleans, though, could be forgiven some for their ignorance, but the priest could not. He . . . she . . . must have had strong suspicions that the real killer was Otis Bloom, and yet he . . . she . . . had kept silent. Because to speak would have exposed everything, and for Father Pat, preserving the real purpose of the Catholic Ladies Social had been more important than a colored boy's life.

And so in a way it all came back to the one question that Rourke had most wanted answered: What had been in the heart of the person who had been born Patrice LaPage that had led her to become a priest? Had she been a murderer looking for absolution? Or a saint looking for sanctuary?

Some mysteries, he supposed, were destined to remain forever mysterious. Especially those that lived in the human heart.

That Saturday the *Cutlass* crew did their final shoot, and Rourke decided at the last moment that he would go watch it.

It wasn't the last scene in the movie—they didn't film in sequence. It was, in fact, a scene from early in the story, before the heroine has turned pirate, when she still has her innocence, although she is about to lose it. In the scene she is at her debutante ball, when her brother arrives to tell her that the boy she has loved the whole of her life has been lost at sea.

The scarred cameraman, Jeremy Doyle, had told Rourke all this while he went about his business of loading film and checking light readings with his meters.

To Rourke the set had the look of controlled chaos. The director threw his script into the air and shouted that the lighting was all wrong. "I want at least two more inkies set up. We're going to do a close-up of her face."

Max Leeland, the studio boss, who had been standing off to the side and scowling, said, "The critics don't like close-ups."

"Fuck the critics, and fuck their mothers, too," Peter Kohl said, but he sounded cheerful.

The studio boss looked over at Jeremy Doyle, who shrugged and said, "The camera loves her from any angle."

They brought in more incandescent lamps.

The studio boss said, "I don't like what she's got on. Where're the tits?" But everybody ignored him.

Remy stood on her mark in the middle of what Rourke was taking on faith would look like a ballroom on the screen. She looked bored. Then someone turned on a bank of lights and it must have been a cue, because Rourke saw her start to come alive from within like a blossom unfolding.

The director walked by the cameraman and said under his breath, "Jere . . . Come in tight on her face, then fade out."

And then someone said, "They're ready on set . . . And roll 'em. Action."

Doyle cranked the camera as a young man, dressed in knee britches and a flowing blue shirt and wearing a sword, walked into the ballroom and up to the girl standing alone and lonely in the middle of it. He paused in place for the moment when the title card would tell the audience the terrible news of the shipwreck, and then he gestured wildly, enacting the tragedy for the girl and the cameras.

The girl stood in utter stillness, taking the blow, and all life drained out her face, leaving only desolation. And then in an instant, it seemed, she was a girl no longer, but a woman whose heart had passed through hell and come out of it again as nothing but ash.

"Cut," Kohl said softly.

For a moment there was stunned silence and then the people on the set all began to applaud.

That evening they took a walk after supper, and he watched her face passing in and out of the sunlight and shadows. The banquette still had a glow from the day's sun, and the river breeze smelled of bananas and her hair.

"You're looking at me, Day," she said, "as if you don't know me."

And he said, "What I saw on the set today . . . I know you can't stop being Remy Lelourie without something in your soul dying."

She linked her arm through his and leaned into him so that her head rested on his shoulder. "I have been thinking of how I can make the contract be so that I only make one or two films a year."

They walked the rest of the way in silence, arms around each other's waist, hips bumping from time to time, Rourke feeling light-headed with happiness.

They walked by a drugstore that had a sign in its window advertising its fountain's ice cream cones, and he thought of the girl who had found a ring in her chocolate scoop, and he almost proposed to Remy Lelourie right then and there, but then he thought, No, later, later . . . Don't get greedy.

Christmas came and it got so cold the water froze in the pipes and Fio bitched that when it got cold in New Orleans, the cold went so deep into you that it ate at your bones.

A present turned up under the tree for Mrs. O'Reilly from Katie, and Rourke shuddered to think what was in it. But when Mrs. O—showing the courage of a real trouper—opened it on Christmas morning it turned out to be a pair of red mittens.

"Your present," Remy said, "is outside."

She took him by the hand and led him out through the courtyard, down the carriageway, and onto Conti Street.

It was yellow. It was even the same model and year. And it was in better condition because it had never been shot at.

Two weeks later he drove her to Union Station in the Stutz Bearcat roadster that she had given him.

They stood on the platform getting jostled apart by the crowd while the train belched clouds of steam over their heads.

"You'll fly out in a few weeks?" she said.

"With bells on."

"You'll like California."

"No, I won't," he said. He was only partly kidding. He was a New Orleans boy down to the bone, but he supposed he could bear the place for the couple of weeks a year he went out there to be with Remy while she was making her movies.

He got on the train with her, went into her private Pullman cabin, shut the door, and kissed her long and deep. And they said all the things that lovers say when the parting is hard but not bitter, and the reunion already promises to be sweet.

He got off at the conductor's warning, and then stood on the platform, watching her face in the window as the train pulled out of the station.

Chapter Thirty-Two

It was a private car, but he knew she wouldn't care.

He pushed open the door and lounged against the jamb, bracing himself against the rocking of the train. "Do you mind if I join you?" he said.

She turned from the window, and he watched the emotions cross her face like the passing of the seasons, and then she laughed, threading the hair back off her face with her fingers. God, he loved it when she did that thing with her hair.

"I didn't know you were in New Orleans," she said.

Romeo smiled.

AUTHOR'S NOTE

I must confess to having taken a few minor liberties with history during the telling of this story. I've delayed the grand opening of the Saenger Theatre by some six months in order that Remy Lelourie could be the guest of honor. And if Remy had really existed, her vampire movie would have been the first of its kind to play in American theaters. (The 1922 German *Nosferatu* did not get its U.S. release until 1929.) The St. Francis of Assisi Academy for Girls, the town of Paris, Louisiana, and Our Lady of the Holy Rosary Church on Coliseum Square are wholly figments of my imagination. And finally, while the electric chair was first used in New York in 1890, Louisiana never gave the "humanity" of electrocution in the chair a test run prior to its adoption in 1940, when it replaced hanging as the state's official form of execution.